T0314782

THE ELF

by

Barry E Woodham

THE ELF

MEMOIRS
Cirencester

MEMOIRS
PUBLISHING

Published by Memoirs
25 Market Place, Cirencester, Gloucestershire, GL7 2NX
info@memoirsbooks.co.uk www.memoirspublishing.com

Copyright ©Barry E. Woodham, August 2012
www.facebook.com/scifiauthorbarry
Twitter: @sci_fiauthor
http://sci-fiauthor.blogspot.co.uk
Email: barry.e.woodham@btinternet.com

First published in England, August 2012
Book cover design Ray Lipscombe

Hard copy ISBN 978-1-909020-94-8
eBook for Kindle ISBN 978-1-909020-96-2
eBook for all other readers ISBN 978-1-909020-95-5

All rights reserved.

No part of this publication may be reproduced, stored in a retrieval system, or
transmitted in any form or by any means, electronic, mechanical, photocopying,
recording or otherwise without the prior written permission of Memoirs Publishing.

Although the author and publisher have made every effort to ensure that the
information in this book was correct when going to press, we do not assume and hereby
disclaim any liability to any party for any loss, damage, or disruption caused by errors or
omissions, whether such errors or omissions result from negligence, accident, or any
other cause. The views expressed in this book are purely the author's.

This book is a work of fiction. Names, characters and places are products of the author's
imagination. Any resemblance to actual people is entirely coincidental.

Printed in England

DEDICATION

Once again I dedicate this book to my loving and patient wife, Janet, who even now listens to the strange ideas that I still bounce off her practical mind. I also dedicate this book to Ady Bunce, who read this book chapter by chapter and kept me on the way

EPIGRAPH

Were elves ever on this world? If they were, what influence
did they leave behind?

List of Characters

Elves

Peterkin	The 'Hand' of the High King
Ameela	The 'Wife' - Waldwick's daughter
Mia	Daughter to Peterkin and Ameela
Waldwick	High King
Aurora	Queen
Dawn	Elder Sister and mother to Peterkin.
Freyr	High King of the Light Elves on the home-world of Alfheimr.
Auberon	The elder King. "Elf ruler on Earth."
Elweard	The late king. Killed by Waldwick.
Eduardo & Calando	Waldwick's guards.
Abaddon	Leader of the Dark Elves.
Inna	Female companion to Abaddon.
Moloch	First of the Dokka'lfar and ruler of Hell.
Olivia	Mother of Moloch.

Humans

Sam Pitt	Leader. Ex-Lieutenant-major, Marines.
John Smith	Engineer, Scientist.
Hoatzin	Mexican. Ex-Marine.-Works Rodeos
David & Steven Johansson	Twins. Ex-Army
Henry Spencer	Ex - Army
Ivan Koshensky	Born in Russia. Brought to America as a child. - Buyer for Acme Engineering Elfin Enterprises

Colonel Halim Djurayev, his sons

Teginbek, Ulugh, Yusuf.

Their wives - Fatma, Shara, Nila.

Dwarves

Mellitus	Hammer-hand Leader
Hildegard	Storm-bringer - She is the leader of the Stormgalt, guarding the gorge - right hand side
Althalos	Hammer-thief Leader of Skaldargate left hand side
Spellbinder	Reality shifting ship of the Ljo'sa'lfar.
Dream-shifter	Insane reality shifting ship of the Dokka'lfar.

Gnomes

Ranzmut
Boddywinkle

Raptors

Prime	Leader of the clans of Velociraptors

Foreword

The war between the Light and Dark Elves took place long ago. The time has come to re-ignite that war and bring it to a conclusion.

Preface

Thousands of years in our past elves fled to our world, fleeing the pursuit of the Dark Elves. They stayed here until we began to use iron in large quantities. Keeping to the unwritten law that Elves do not harm Elves, they moved on, taking Neanderthal man with them when the Dokka'lfar opened a rift into our world. The Ljo'sa'lfar are pacifists and have managed to evade the Dark Elves who would indulge in their cannibalistic tendencies once they have the Light Elves in their power.

Now after thousands of years have gone by the Dokka'lfar have found the Ljo'sa'lfar again, on another parallel Earth. They have been trying to pierce the poisoned brier, grown by the Ljo'sa'lfar for two centuries, inside the great gorge, entrance to the lands of the dinosaurs. At the center of this giant crater are the Ljo'sa'lfar who live inside a castle and small towns spreading down the mountainside.

After getting the High King's daughter pregnant, the punishment meted out to an elf called Peterkin sets in motion a chain of events that propels him into the annuls of history. He becomes the legend foretold by a dwarf dream-seer long ago after Abaddon the Dark Lord and his forces killed and ate a thousand dwarves before the brier closed.

In his escape from the dungeons, Peterkin learns how to open a rift between our world and his, so that he can recruit mercenaries to help him rescue his princess from a tower set inside the land of the dinosaurs. An eventual confrontation with Abaddon will become immanent.

Thanks are given to those of my loyal band of readers who e-mailed me to say that they enjoyed my stories.

You can keep in touch with Barry E Woodham on Twitter @sci_fiauthor, Facebook at www.facebook.com/ scifiauthorbarry or at the Barry E Woodham blog, http:// sci-fiauthor.blogspot.co.uk

There are more books on their way e-mail barry.e.woodham@btinternet.com for more information.

CHAPTER ONE

The High King's daughter had been taken from me and imprisoned in a tower that was guarded by a dragon and other creatures impressed into 'royal' service. Fixed around her neck was a small band of iron to fog her mind and prevent her from flying away.

After his elite guards had tightly strapped me, face down to a wooden bench, he had sliced my wings from my back himself. After which he applied the goblin wrought, red-hot irons to my back. Iron is a poison to my kind and applied to an open wound it seared them shut, sealing the toxin into the stumps. The High King then had me taken deep below the torture rooms, still alive, but weak and frail. There he had me cast into the concealed dungeons below the castle, chained to a heavy ball of stone by a golden chain.

Here I stayed in the semi-darkness of the underworld of punishment, losing track of time, ruled by the bogymen loyal to 'Him'. They fed me and allowed me to wander the endless tunnels and chambers that lay within their realm.

Bogymen and their females had huge eyes that were adapted to the darkness. They spoke in whispers and kept to the slimy walls, avoiding open places. Their long bony fingers ended in clawed tips and they were completely bald. They were scuttling creatures the colour of darkness that served the High King's whims. He fed them on the kitchen scraps and leftovers from the banqueting hall. What they did not eat they passed to me and it was never enough.

At odd times they would lay their disgusting hands upon me to haul me into King Waldwick's presence for him to gloat over my rage and helplessness, as I dragged the stone ball around with me. These few times were the only moments that I saw daylight and fresh food, deliberately left on the dining table where I could see it, but not touch.

I hated the touch of the bogymen. The slime came off their bodies and stuck to me. When I dried out later, I had to peel the stuff off my skin, as by now my clothes had almost disintegrated. The depths of the castle were cold and what straw I could find, I wrapped around my shivering body. The anklet chaffed around my ankle and I packed it with straw to lessen the amount of skin that rubbed off. My ankle grew sore and thin as time went on under the unyielding High King's punishment.

I was the High King's Lord Protector and given the task of keeping his daughter safe from the attentions of other unwelcome elves. Thrown together for many hours we had developed a fragile relationship that crumbled the day she fell from her riding beast and I picked her up in the snow. Our wings were bound under the furs we wore because of the cold and were of little use in that situation. She kissed me and I lost my mind!

The many years of restraint melted away at that moment. She was tall for an elfish woman and slender like her mother. Her eyes were an unusual blue instead of the usual green or brown. I had grown used to her lower pitched voice and loved the way that she chuckled when I made her laugh. I had seen her grow from being a child through adolescence and into a young elf. When her antennae began to sprout from her forehead after childhood, I caught the odd unguarded thought from her mind. I knew that she wanted my touch upon her fingers. I also knew that what she felt was forbidden. I once saw her eyes widen as her mind reached out to mine and found that I wanted her as much as she wanted me. From that day I had struggled with my emotions and tried to be colder in my dealings with her. I buried those feelings deep inside as one hint of what I really felt would bring the High King's wrath upon us both.

Her hands locked around my neck and she pulled me closer to her until our antennae touched and wound around each other. She bit gently on my bottom lip and any attempt of restraint disappeared.

The furs soon came away in that snow covered hollow and she gave her virginity to me, swearing that we would flee far from the King Waldwick's reach. Ameela and I made for the boundaries of his lands clinging onto a young winged dragon that I 'called' to me. It was a bitter cold winter and I dared not urge the beast to fly too high lest we froze to death upon its cold scaly back. We kept to the valleys and took too much time zigzagging through, instead of trying to fly over the mountains.

When we had not returned by sunset the High King had used his scrying mirror to find his daughter. He found the two of us wrapped in the same furs, aloft on the back of a dragonet flying straight for the border. His mind reached out in fury and forced the beast to return to the castle.

My control of the dragonet was no match for his and the beast dropped onto the landing platform, built into the veranda of the castle. We fell before his feet and in his hand he held the infamous staff of power. He carried the goblin wrought staff tipped with an iron meteorite that had been in his possession for many years. It linked him with an 'Earth Power' that ate into his soul every time he used it. Only goblins could work the unholy metal and in the end

3

it killed them.

A cold light glowed from the wrought iron ball and entered my body, paralysing my muscles, leaving me folded into a foetal position unable to help Ameela. I saw him drag her from the furs, naked to the cold, snow filled wind by her pale, lemon coloured hair. The light of madness was in his eyes as he shook her by his unyielding grip. The colours of her wings dulled at the touch of the staff and they hung useless down her beautiful back.

He screamed at me, "All my plans are to come to nothing! You! I trusted you to prevent this from happening. You I made my Lord Protector, my most trustworthy elf. You were my 'Hand', my expression of power! Now the alliance will never take place between my realm and the Dark Lord's. His army roams the countryside just outside my borders as we speak! Your life is inside my daughter even now, as we stand here. She carries your child!"

From that day, not one word did Waldwick give me about his daughter or my child, when I was dragged before him, only that they still lived in the tower that he had incarcerated them in and that I would never see them again. I believed him to be mad, his mind poisoned by too much proximity to pure iron. He carried the goblin wrought staff everywhere he went and every time he used it, my back ached where he had branded me and poisoned my wing-stubs.

Without my wings, I concentrated my powers of magic into other realms and sought a release from the High King's punishment. I 'called' rats from the darkness, killed them and drank their blood, chewing on the stringy flesh, always hungry, my stomach never full. I lived on, month after month existing on the meagre rations that the Bogymen fed me. Most of all was the terrible feeling of guilt that I had betrayed my King and through my actions, lost the one that I loved. I knew that what we felt was forbidden! Even so, my heart sang with the knowledge that Ameela had loved me as she grew up into womanhood. When the depression hit, I cried and sobbed, clutching my golden chains to my shivering body. I screamed at the unresponsive bogymen and they shunned me. In the darkness I talked to the walls and even the rats before I ate them. I soon found out that spiders tasted bitter, but the scuttling cockroaches could be crunched between my teeth to add extra vitamins! Everything had to be eaten raw as there was nothing to burn down here and no fire to set light to it if I could find anything.

I lived!

I explored my prison, dragging the stone ball with me wherever I went. Eventually my ankle grew thin enough for me to wriggle free, using rat's blood as grease. I became more mobile without the weight of the stone ball and explored the underworld below the castle, feeling my way in the darkness, searching for some way out.

I discovered the power of the Rifts.

Deep down, below the dungeons, shrouded in shadows, I found a place of eldritch power that could be manipulated to my will. It was an arch built by a warlock in his chambers and long forgotten. There was a slit of a window that looked down over the gorge that was below the castle. By the feeble light I was just able to make out the difference in the brickwork. There were symbols imprinted into the fabric of the arch. The lettering was old. Waldwick had built this castle on top of the ruins of another from another age, long before. The arch blended into the stonework at the back of the cell. I found it by running my hands across the brickwork, hunting for some secret opening to the outside world. I felt the stone warm to my touch and my mind felt something open slightly. It needed something to be given. I returned again and again to that set of rooms and studied the forgotten archway and the ancient language, set in stone.

There came a day that I realised what the archaic symbols stood for, as the essence of the arch entered my mind. The arch was alive in its own way and was slowly beginning to activate from its long sleep of dormancy. Whatever lived inside the arch required a strong mind to open to it. I concentrated all of my undivided mental power into making contact with the seat of its power. As I did this I felt my mind begin to alter and strengthen, as new pathways seemed to branch out. The ability to call the rats to me increased with my newfound ability. I fed on rats until my stomach filled and my body grew stronger. Sometimes when the kitchen scraps were emptied through the hole in the ceiling I got there first and beat the bogymen off until I ate my fill. They began to be afraid of me and made no attempt to try and take the food away that I carried off to the warlock's chamber.

Lent against the arch I called a rat to me and killed it against the stones that made its shape before I ate it. Something in my mind became more aware of the entity locked within. I called more rats from out of the gloom and killed them by crushing their bodies next to the symbols carved into the stonework.

After some time I began to understand the key that operated it and learnt how to apply the force of power to ease the Rift to open. It needed a life to energise the stones properly, much larger than a rat's.

I caught one of the bogymen sent to care for me and forced it to the arch wrapped in the chains that had bound me to the stone. I broke its neck against the stones and twisted the forces that were held in check. The life force of the creature opened the Rift to my direction. I could 'see' through it!

Over the weeks that followed I let my mind soar up and away from the damp, cold dungeons of King Waldwick's castle searching for a hiding place. Far away on the very outskirts of the High King's realm, away from the main trade routes I found what I was looking for. In between two farming communities stretching up the snow-capped mountains was a darkened forest with pathways leading into it. At the end of one of these paths was an old hunting villa that was still in good order, as if it was waiting for someone like me to find it! Long ago it had been built there by the very warlock that had lived in these chambers at the roots of the castle. There was an empty place in the great hall that once housed the arch.

It would do!

I made a bridge from the dungeon cell to the abandoned villa with my mind. Holding that bridge, I took the Arch and its spirit, placed it within the wall by the great fireplace in the main hall. Using the last of the bogyman's life force, stored within, to take me with it, I was free. I was far away from the High King's realm and I had the means of opening the 'Rifts' to wherever I needed to go. I soon found that gnomes inhabited the villa. They had looked after the villa ever since the Warlock had disappeared, for many, many years, waiting patiently for someone to arrive to claim it again. Generation after generation had passed the responsibility to the next family of gnomes.

I made it my home and the gnomes ministered to my needs, leading me back into health. They grew vegetables in the fertile soil in the villa's grounds and administered the villa, cooking and cleaning. For the first time in a long time I ate cooked foods. Nobody questioned my arrival even though some of them must have seen the arch appear in its old place and me step out of solid stone. Word spread and the local gnomes in the thriving community were glad to work for a wingless elf that had given their lives a purpose again.

The villa was sited by the side of an ice melt stream that gave me all the fresh water I needed. The pool it filled was alive with trout. An orchard grew by the side of the gardens and I soon appreciated the fresh fruit that was picked by the gnomes and shared with me. As they cared for me, I also cared for them.

When they were hungry I 'called' animals from out of the forest to be killed for their needs with my heightened ability. In return I took gemstones that they mined from the caves higher up the mountain. They never asked why I was wingless and kept me secret from inquiring eyes. Their women were skilled in the arts of healing, but the hot irons applied to the stumps of my wings would never let them recover. At least they healed without the constant pain that I suffered in Waldwick's dungeon.

I mourned for his daughter, put into eternal imprisonment for daring to love me and not the one that the High King had chosen. Most of all, I mourned for the child that she had carried that I had never seen. Somewhere in the High King's realm she still lived in some impregnable tower. I would get them back somehow and the Arch would be the key.

What I needed to do was to understand the workings of the Warlock's Arch and the Rifts that it could open. It was obvious to me that the previous owner of the Arch had discovered a better place to live and had abandoned the Arch to the darkness of the bogymen. It took some time of studying how to conduct a Rift and more important; - how to keep it open! There were other ways to manipulate the Arch without using life force, but it always came down to power of the mind. The more I worked with the Arch the more I found that it had keyed itself to my mind.

There was a presence that inhabited the arch that lived or existed beyond the Rifts. Its mind was alien to mine, but it got some kind of pleasure in being used. There was a cold logical edge to its way of thinking that had no emotions and it could not understand the reasoning behind my actions. It accepted my plans and agreed to help me put them forward without understanding my motives.

I was saddened that my first use of the Arch had used up the life of one of the castle bogymen, but the main thing was that I had got out. Waldwick had scoured every inch of his dungeons without finding a trace of me. Apart from one dead bogyman there was no clue. He had seers searching the length and breadth of his kingdom without any sign of me. Every crystal ball that could be used was turned towards my mind. They could not read my presence as I lived surrounded by gnomes. Gnomes have 'foggy' minds and cannot be read by elves. I however could eavesdrop on the goings on at the High King's court. Troops had been sent out at every direction looking for me and as they reported failure Waldwick's temper became worse and worse. He spent hours in front of his scrying mirror

9

searching for me, but I was not even in his world, let alone his kingdom.

Time went by and I searched the Rifts for another parallel world that would aid my campaign. One of them drew me back to study it and I made my decision.

Once again I opened the 'Rift' between my realm and the human world. It always opens under an arch of ancient stone in the desert outside a small town. Maybe it had been used before, long, long ago. It's a short walk to the outskirts of the town and what you call a Shopping Mall. The goods that are on sale are amazing. I soon got plenty to eat by 'suggesting' that people buy me food and drink. You have no mental resistance!

I look like a smaller version of what the people call Mexican, except for the pointed ears. You don't seem to notice them or my antennae sprouting from my forehead. In your realm it is very easy for me to only allow you to see what I want you to see. Your society thrives on violence and that supports my purpose well.

I am constantly amazed by the variety of weapons that your world has for offer. The greed that you suffer from makes you easy to manipulate. In my world, gemstones are common and are easy to obtain. Here in your world you would kill to possess stones that our young use in games similar to your marbles. When I discovered the 'Rift' and first ventured into this alternative reality I kept very quiet and set myself to learn your language.

Several times I wandered into dangerous places and had to kill some of the slow moving humans with my bare hands. I carried an obsidian blade with me after that and found that cutting a few throats got me the respect that I deserved. The higher gravity made me develop more of a muscular build to survive in this realm. When I returned to my world the effects stayed with me of the time I spent among the humans. I grew very strong.

The one thing that I had to avoid was the metal that was in abundance here. Iron is poisonous to my kind in its pure state. Steel makes me unable to control minds and too much of it around me makes me sweat. I avoid cars; as to be inside a steel box too long would eventually kill me. I have managed to travel on the back of a wooden flat bed lorry without too much trouble. I can still control minds through the glass window at the back of the cab and used this method to get around the human world when I needed to.

It did not take me long to understand money and the gold chain and gemstones that I brought over soon changed hands. I became wealthy and learned how to live in a hotel room. The Internet became my playground! What I needed were weapons that were constructed from a minimum of iron based metals. It did not take me long to find a craftsman willing to make a rifle constructed from hickory and reinforced plastic with a stainless steel barrel. The bullets I required to be cast from pure iron. These were packed into wooden containers that could be inserted into the rifle as a magazine. I also had lead bullets by the boxful ready to take back with me to my world. Money made sure that no questions were asked. Crossbows with iron tipped bolts were easy to buy and I stored these away in the desert close to the rift. I tried using the gnomes, but although they were quite willing, the heavier gravity made it difficult for their smaller bodies to carry much. It was time to collect humans to my cause.

What I needed now were dependable mercenaries that would follow me back and obey my commands. I also needed to be able to trust them!

I placed an advertisement in the national paper asking for volunteers to accompany me on an expedition to search for a missing person in a foreign land. I stated that it would be dangerous, but profitable if successful.

They came!

I took weeks winnowing the applicants and in the end I changed hotels to stem the never-ending stream of hopefuls. I took only single people with a multitude of skills. On the desert sands I watched them fight each other and bleed for the prize money that I allocated. Not every loser was discarded. I paid them all well and they kept their silence. I made it quite plain that I might need more and those who did not make it this time might be offered a place in the future as long as they kept my business secret.

I picked six big men with plenty of strength and stamina. In my world the gravity was less and these humans would have an advantage against any elf. What I needed to do now was to show them what I really looked like and take them into my confidence.

I asked the six to meet up at my hotel room that evening. They all towered over my slight figure and I motioned them to sit down. I stood for a while and just looked at them as they sat waiting for me to talk. The man I had picked as leader of the group was a tall, black American called Sam Pitts. He was skilled with the bow and knife. All of them could shoot any rifle with pinpoint accuracy and also with a pistol. John Smith was dark haired, bearded and an explosives expert. David and Steven were twin brothers and had a telepathic link that enabled them to fight hand to hand as if they were of one mind. They were excellent swordsmen and could manage any medieval weapons. Their ancestors had come from where the Vikings had ventured forth upon the high seas. They were blond haired and taller than the others. Spencer was as black as coal and was bald. He could move through the night as though he could see in the dark. He was a stalker and tracker, able to follow a trail where others would give up as baffled. The last of the group was Mexican by birth, but much larger than his fellow people. Hoatzin's skill lay in riding and roping. He was a veteran of the rodeo ring and had proved able to ride anything that breathed.

When they were all seated I began.

"You have never asked my name or asked me what I want you to do," I said to them. "I have seen you all fight and display your skills on the sands of the desert outside of the town."

Sam Pitts stood up and answered, "Mister, when you are ready to tell us what you want us to know, we will listen. Until then, its your business."

"Thank you Sam. I have called you all together as this is the time that I will tell you what all this is about. Someone very dear to me was taken. What in this world you would call my wife was imprisoned along with my child. I am going to get them back!"

There was a general shuffling amongst the group and Hoatzin spoke up and said, "I think that we would all agree that what you want us to do, is recover your woman and child. It's got to be dangerous or we would not be here. I will go anywhere you want us to go"

"In my world to know the secret name of a person is to have power over them. I am known as Peterkin amongst my people. I am about to tell you about my world. It is not here! You have children's tales of the world of Faery in many of your cultures. Some of them are uncannily true! I came from such a world separated from yours by a Rift in space-time. This is what I really look like!"

Six human beings gazed for the first time upon an elf.

13

Peterkin stood no more than five feet six inches and was slightly built, but rippling with muscle. He was swarthy like a Mexican, but that was only a resemblance. He had pointed ears and two antennae sprouting from his forehead. His eyes were slitted like a cats' and he had six fingers on each hand. His hair was blond and hung around his shoulders with the ends bound and waxed.

Sam Pitts sat down heavily and remarked, "Well he aint a human being that's for sure, but he pays well and he needs our help. I'm in."

A chorus echoed the big man's statement. "I'm in!"

"Yeah me too!"

"And me!"

"I'm in, all the way!" yelled Spencer.

Peterkin looked at his choices to rejoin him in the world of Faery and was overcome with emotion. These humans meant what they said. He could read their minds as clearly as though they were all shouting at once. He knew that he would never need to coerce them by any form of mind control. Once a human became loyal, they stayed loyal. The other thing he was aware of was that although he was paying them a fortune to assist him, they were not coming for the money!

"Gentlemen! Thank you. Thank you. Now I must enter your minds and leave information there for you to think about. After I have intruded into your surface thoughts and given you the ability to talk my language, you must all get fitted with an iron collar. Get it made comfortable and riveted shut. It will prevent my people controlling you and entering your minds. Without it you would have no protection from any of the many sentient life forms that live on my world. Besides the rescue of my family there are other problems to overcome. My soul mate was to be given by High King to the Dark Lord as a binding agreement

14

between them. She was to be an assurance that the hoards would not over-run our lands. In this world some of your gifted painters have shown visions of their world. You call it Hell! We will have to pit our wits against the Dark Lord's legions at some time in the future.

I have accumulated supplies that you cannot get in my world. I need you to fetch them from where I stored them and get a wooden flat bed lorry. Where we are going will be very dangerous and some of you will not return. There is much that you need to know about my world. Most of it is in your mind, put there by me. Think about it over and over again before we leave your world. We must head out into the desert and take our supplies through the Rift that I set up. After that you will need to learn how to live on my world before we do anything else."

The group stood up as one and one by one they shook Peterkin's hand. Each was clear in their mind about what they had to fetch and load onto the lorry and each of them were sure that they would follow the elf into the jaws of Hell itself. On Peterkin's world, Hell was a real place!

CHAPTER TWO

In my absence the gnomes had been busy. On the side of the villa they had erected from my instructions, a large open construction similar to a human carport. Over the top of it they had laid vegetation so that it looked like part of the forest. At the back of it where it was fixed to the hillside, the gnomes had brought in dwarves to burrow deep into the rocks and use their mining knowledge to create storage chambers. It was here that I intended to store the items and artefacts brought over from the human world. This deep under the granite strata of the mountain that stretched upwards above the hillside, anything could be hidden from the High King's scrying mirror.

The moment that my group arrived at my 'home' I introduced them to the gnomes who looked after the villa. My group of human mercenaries were the tallest bipeds that the gnomes had ever seen. Spencer's coal black skin frightened them at first, as the Dark Lord's people were either deepest black or fiery red. When he produced a packet of mints and shared them round, it did not take long for them to accept him. The others soon dug into their pockets for sweets and found themselves climbed over by the gnomes' few children.

These 'giants' fascinated them and word soon spread that the 'Master' was home with strange guests! I contacted the entity that controlled the arch and positioned the Rift in space-time, just in front of the opening of the 'carport' so that the modified flatbed lorry drove through the hole in space-time into the carport. A ghostly arch five times larger than the stones set in the villa hung in view and shimmered for a while until the lorry passed completely through it. I had learnt how to enlarge the arch and direct it to the

16

position that I desired, but to do this successfully I needed to 'know' the exact place that I needed it to be. I had three places that registered in my mind so far, the human world's Rift exit in the desert, here at the villa and the dungeons of the High King. The next place that I needed was wherever Waldwick had imprisoned his daughter or as close to the place that I could get to. To find that out I needed to insert my mind into someone in the High King's court.

I knew just who to ask!

Leaving my group to acclimatise to the new surroundings I sought the peace and quiet of my bedroom. I sat cross-legged on the floor and reached out with my mind to the one person that I could trust.

I found her.

"Hullo Mother!"

"Peterkin!"

"Shush, Mother dear. I am alive and well. Guard your mind! I can feel your joy. Tell me one thing. Where is she?"

"The Tower of Absolom in the Plains of Scion. She has a daughter and Waldwick, curse him, is considering giving her to the Dark Lord in appeasement. Every year that goes by, the hoards from Hell increase the pressure on the outer boundaries. Someone comes! Goodbye my son and love to you."

With that my connection to my mother abruptly snapped and I sat with the tears steaming down my cheeks. She had a strong mind, but she was no match for the High King's powers. I had been careful not to show her where I was. If he felt for one instant that she was harbouring my secret location, he would mind-strip her until he had every scrap of knowledge she possessed. It was enough danger that she now knew that I lived and that fact she wrapped in the strongest of mind barriers she could. She piled on the grief of losing her eldest son, layer upon layer until anyone who ventured into this area would come away shaken to the core. Inside it all was the new bright knowledge that I still lived. Mother was good at keeping secrets even from her sister, Waldwick's wife and mother of my forbidden love.

I left my bedroom with the knowledge of where Ameela was and that was sufficient. How to get to her would be the challenge. I made my way to where the fortified lorry was hidden away and marvelled at what my group had managed to get done.

We had the vehicle modified by an outfit that John Smith knew that did what was asked and asked no questions. Every steel part that could be substituted by aluminium, brass, copper or hard wood had been changed. Four-wheel drive had been added to the propulsion system at John's suggestion once he learned of the type of terrine that the vehicle would be travelling across, thinking of stone roads and muddy conditions. Now that we would be venturing across the Plains of Scion, extra fuel tanks had been added to the back, made from copper sheets to carry L.P.G. the lorry engine ran on steam power, fired from the gas tanks. A large water tank was also added.

What iron or steel had to be used, was coated in lead sheets to dampen the effect of the deadly poison to the kind of life that thrived my side of the rift. John had soon understood the problems and applied his engineering mind to solving them. He has contacts amongst the engineering world that were very useful and closed mouthed. Money buys silence in the human world! I did find out however that stainless steel had a far less effect on my nervous system and a lot of re-fitting was hastily done. Again plenty of money speeded things up.

The back of the lorry was surrounded by thick bronze plates for us to hide behind and defend from, similar to a castle's battlements. There was a sturdy roof covered in stainless steel chain-link fencing. Sam Pitts had managed to 'acquire' a machine gun and had mounted it just behind the cab, sighting over the top. Twin, swivelled, high intensity lights were welded to the corners of the cab on stands below the level of the machine gun's sweep. My group had worked on this vehicle for weeks refining the defences, calling in favours done in the past to obtain items not generally on sale.

I allowed my group to acclimatise themselves to the slightly different conditions on my side of the Rift. There is far more oxygen in the air and the gravity is lower in my home. The effect this has on the creatures in my realm is to make some of them bigger than in the human world. In particular, our insects are three or four sizes larger than what the humans were used to. The villa is home to many varieties that do us the service of keeping the area clean. It is a miniature eco-system in its own right. The house spiders are the size of a dinner plate and wander the kitchen floors hunting for our type of cockroach that clears away any dropped food. The gnomes call them by whistling to them, when they feel that the clean-up squad has increased too much! They are treated as working pets.

This took some while before my humans were able to get over their instinctive fear of the spiders and touch them without being bitten. I had explained that their bite was not poisonous, but they were sensitive to fear and responded to emotion. As long as they kept their iron collars around their necks the creatures would not be able to sense their apprehension.

Dwarves began to arrive at the villa as word circulated through the communities that I was back. They were resistant to the effects of iron and had insisted that they speak with me. All of them wanted to meet the humans and see for themselves the reality of the Rift. They were good blacksmiths and climbed all over the modified lorry enjoying a conducted tour by John Smith, judging the work done. The gnomes had been waist high to my group, but the dwarves were almost shoulder high to them and stocky. They all had beards plaited and bound in leather straps. It took a while for John to realise that some of them were female and that their beards were bound in a silky material!

Dwarves and elves had always had a good relationship with each other, but this had gone sour since the arrival of the Dark Lord and his army. Only once, they had broken through the fast growing brier that the elves had planted on the outer regions of the High King's realm. The dwarves had stood firm and had lost more than a thousand of their fighting strength by fighting beyond the brier. Those that had done this knew that they would fight and die on that side while the brier grew back. The High King had done nothing to rescue them and had accepted the sacrifice. Those that had stayed this side of the brier had smelt the wood scented breeze mingled with the odour of roasting dwarves. All they could do was to fall back as the brier thickened its grip on the land.

They had learned of Waldwick's sacrifice of his daughter with revulsion. They knew that she would have satisfied the Dark Lord's pleasure for a while and then she would have been handed down to the next in line. Finally she would have been killed if she had not already died from the ordeal and eaten. Nothing would stop this creature of the darkness until he was defeated. All the High King would have done was to buy a little time before the onslaught began again. Dragonet riders had seen gargoyles circling in the skies above the brier. These were a lot bigger than had been seen before and were capable of lifting two of the imps of darkness over the barrier. Many of them had been dropped our side of the brier and had built bridgeheads.

Those that had been foolish enough to try the lowlands had soon been attacked and eaten by the carnivorous dragons.

Sam Pitts called the dwarves to the back of the lorry. He opened a wooden case with a pry-bar, reached inside and lifted something out into the light. Whatever it was seemed to be a combination of wood and metal.

"Gentlemen and ladies," he said, "Let me introduce you to something we humans call a Kalashnikov, otherwise known as an AK47!"

He walked away from the hidden lorry and into the garden. Growing in the sheltered corner of two brick walls was a plant similar to a watermelon. The fruit were bright green and the size of a basketball.

Sam cradled the gun for a moment and warned the dwarves, "This will be a bit noisy, so be prepared!"

He aimed and fired a single shot at a melon and watched it jerk away from the impact. The dwarves had flinched a little at the single shot, but studied the melon intently from behind him. Sam let fly with a burst and the ball of fruit exploded into pieces. Now they really were impressed!

It did not take long for all the dwarves to become proficient with the AK 47's and the melon patch became a mess. Spencer and Hoatzin spent the rest of the afternoon teaching the dwarves all about the combat rifle. They had brought a thousand of the rugged weapons through the Rift modified to use stainless steel and brass wherever the ordinary iron based materials could be changed. Again Peterkin's money had bought compliance and silence. The elf's price for the weapons to the dwarves was a simple trade, come with him to release Ameela and they were theirs to keep, plus a small mountain of ammunition.

Mellitus Hammer-hand approached the wingless elf and held out his hand and gripped Peterkin's in a calloused grip.

"We would have come with you anyway, Elf-friend. These weapons? Can you get more of them? With such as these in our hands the defeat of the Dark Lord becomes more than possible!"

"Mellitus, dwarf-friend and ally, be assured I can do better than these few weapons. After we have Ameela safe and sound in this villa, you and I will discuss what we can do to alter the situation beyond the brier," Peterkin insisted. "For now it is enough that we are well armed and ready to begin our quest. I now know where the High King imprisoned Ameela and my child. She has been abandoned in the top of the Tower of Absolom in the centre of the Plains of Scion."

The Tower of Absolom was shaped like an upturned mushroom, sat on a fat, solid stalk. A roofed lodge had been built on the edge, overlooking the Plains of Scion. The rest of the pan shaped area at the top was devoted to gardens that grew the food for the incarcerated. Ameela had spent the last ten years or more learning how to grow her own food and prepare it. Water came from rainwater tanks fed from the roof of the lodge. Her father had allowed her a small family of gnomes to help her survive. It was they who had taught her the arts of cultivation. It was her strength and larger body that had been the one that pulled the makeshift plough. She learnt to mix the earth with the dung that they produced to ensure better crops. After her daughter had been born, she had taught the little girl to speak, but she could not teach her the mind talk that all the elves used. Her father, Waldwick, had twisted an iron collar about her neck and a goblin had hammered it shut. The hateful thing had fogged her mind and felt like an endless toothache inside her head. He had clipped her wings and fitted them with iron clips that she could not remove.

The 'tower' sprouted from the top of a low hill and was situated hundreds of miles from where the elves lived. No one would dare to try and free her even if they felt the High King's sentence unjust. The Tower of Absolom sat in the middle of the plains of Scion that was home to the many types of dragons that roamed the lowlands. Those that were meat eaters preyed on those that ate the verdant vegetation. Some of these were almost big enough to graze the gardens on the top of the tower. Their heads rubbed along the edge of the upturned mushroom shape when they suffered from an itch. Very often the toothy ones would lay in wait behind the solid base and pounce upon the slower moving long necked beasts.

Waldwick had 'pressed' the minds of some of the meat eaters so that they did not range very far from the base of the tower. Sometimes they would fling themselves at the rough stony side and cling there, hissing and slavering, unable to reach her. They could scent the two elves and the family of gnomes that eked out a meagre existence above them. Amongst the varied plants that flourished in the well-tended gardens were a number of tough vines that bore continual fruit all year round. Ameela had stripped out the old vines that were non-productive and had pulled them apart to expose the fibres. These she wove into a long, strong rope and fastened one end into a slip noose.

From time to time the dragonets would spiral down from the clouds and raid the garden of the ripe fruit. They would search for the rotting juicy plums, as they would tend to ferment. On the ground they were clumsy and were reduced to hopping or crawling on their bellies to reach the lower fruit. Here was where Ameela would fix the noose, making very sure that the other end of the rope was securely tied to a tree. The most frustrating thing was the bigger ones could be ridden, but with the iron collar around her neck, Ameela could not control them with her mind. So she trapped the younger ones by the cord and wrung their necks. They made a pleasant change to the menu and added meat to the diet. The rope was eventually long enough to reach to the ground at the bottom of the tower.

When they had finished stripping the flesh from a dragonet, Ameela would dangle the noose close to the ground with the dragonet's head fixed above the noose. Sometimes she would be lucky and catch one of the meat eater's young ones, not long from the nest. If they were young enough, they were not too gamy. If they were too big then they would choke on the rope's noose until one of their own kind, attacked and ate the unfortunate catch. This usually meant losing the end of the rope with the noose attached. Ameela accepted this philosophically and would weave another piece of rope into the length.

At sunset she would sit against the warmed stonework with her daughter on her lap and tell her of her father. She had never regretted her moment of passion with Peterkin and she loved her daughter so very much. She never learned what her father had done to him or even if he was still alive, but something deep inside her where the iron could not reach, told her that he was out there somewhere. Mia was a beautiful child with her mother's startlingly blue eyes and her father's pale blond hair. Her wings were beginning to unfurl from the stubs on her back. They were pale blond as her hair and lightly feathered and as yet to be able to lift her from the floor. Soon she would be capable of flight and that knowledge scared Ameela so much.

Hungry eyes were always fixed upon the gardens and the full-grown dragonets enjoyed a varied diet. Their long beaks, full of sharp teeth, had evolved to pull down flying prey as well as scooping up fish or smaller running creatures.

Mia would make a quick meal if she ventured too far from the safety of the overhanging roof of the lodge. She was difficult for her mother to cuddle as the close proximity to the iron collar and the clips set in her wings made her child feel ill. Always Ameela had to love her daughter at a distance and keep her at arms length. It sometimes broke her heart not to be able to hold her for too long. For that she hated her father. The fate that he had decreed for her filled her with horror and fed her hatred even more. Had she known what her father had in mind for his grandchild, she would have thrown them both off the parapet down to the beasts below.

Peterkin concentrated his will through the arch. He waved his hands over the runes set in the stone that floated in the air before him in his mind's eye. His group sat behind him without their iron collars fixed around their necks, along with a number of dwarves. The air began to shimmer and a second arch began to form in front of them. It steadied and a picture began to form inside, looking like a window into another world.

The elf started from the castle built on the edge of the gorge and pushed the portal towards the Plains of Scion. Below the castle were the cultivated steps, dug out from the mountainside and irrigated from the melt-water from the high peaks above. There were great similarities to the Inca city of Machu Picchu in the way that the steps had been dug out. A sheer drop to the gorges below kept the city safe from the teeming life of the plains. Streams filtered into a central lake fed from the irrigation systems to grow their crops.

They soon left the mountainous regions behind them and began to soar over the lower hills at the edge of the plains. Peterkin followed the river that ran out of the elf kingdom out into the flatlands, where it wandered through a swamp. Now the life that inhabited the lower regions began to make themselves shown.

Sam Pitts spoke up in amazement, "Peterkin! Creatures similar to these beasts haven't been seen in our world for a hundred million years!"

Peterkin slowed the movement of the portal so that his group could all see what they were going to have to confront.

"That looks like a type of triceratops," John Smith exclaimed. "Can you see what is hunting them? I think that we are going to have a little shopping trip in our world before we go there!"

Towards the line of low hills an odd-looking structure began to show itself. It was a natural formation rising out of the surrounding low hills. Sat upon a solid buttress that jutted out of the ground was a flat, pan shaped escarpment. The portal stopped over a flat area of ground, close to a group of tall ferns and refused to go any nearer. Peterkin could sense the metallic taste in his mouth. There was iron here under the ground.

I pulled back and scouted the area for a suitable place to take the lorry. The ground around the escarpment was dry and stony, but there were small boulders in abundance and any one could have snapped an axle if the lorry hit one.

My frustration must have connected with the minds of my group and I felt John Smith's mind inside mine.

A picture of a vee-shaped snowplough fixed to the front of the bull bars mounted on the front of our lorry showed me what to do.

I quickly passed the idea to Mellitus and he rose with the human to get the modifications underway. Try as I might I could not raise the portal any higher from the elevation of the plains. I knew that she was up there, as we could see a thin column of smoke wafted from the lodge, but I could not reach her directly. Somehow I needed to get word to Ameela that we were coming to rescue her. Again I was aware of a presence in my mind and connected with this time with the Mexican, Hoatzin.

"Fireworks my elfish friend! In particular, rockets! We attach cylinders with a message inside telling your princess that you are coming to get her and what to do. Now that we have seen the problem, we need as John said, to do a little shopping trip. Send some of us back for a few days and then bring us through the portal to the villa."

I gave him my credit card that gave him unlimited access to the millions of dollars in one of my accounts without a thought.

"Do whatever you need to do. Buy whatever you need to buy," I said, "while I and the others scout the area while you are gone."

I set the flat area that we had all agreed was easy to defend, as a starting position in my mind, so that I had the co-ordinates to orientate the portal. I next altered the focus of the arch by waving my fingers over the smaller arch in my mind. I was instantly aware of the entity that was the arch increasing its reach to memorise the fourth destination. At times I would feel that I was a mind within a mind when I used the arch and I realised that the ancient warlock was not of this world. The portal had been made somewhere else and left here. It had not been used for more years than I could sense, maybe more than a thousand.

The one thing that I was sure of was that whatever the arch was, it was increasing in its power. It was alive in some sense and becoming easier for me to manipulate. Somehow I felt that there was more it could do if I could only understand it at a higher plane.

The High King could feel the balance flutter through the staff of power. Waldwick had sunk the end of the staff into the corresponding hole in the floor in front of the throne. He held onto the shaft with a tight grip, as he sent his mind deep into the ground. The iron ball began to give off a cold light as he activated the power within. He felt the solid granite beneath the castle where the roots of the city were buried. From here he sped through the strata towards the Dark Lord's army.

Beads of sweat began to flow from his body and roll down the staff until they made contact with the stone. Now on his knees, he forced through another measure of power until he was able to see the other side of the brier. The land lay in waste! Nothing much still lived on this side. The legions of Hell had stripped the land bare of flesh and leaf. The strong ate the weak and still they pressed against the hedge. Miles thick the genetically, growth enhanced plant spread around his kingdom. Elves had altered the gene structure of this formidable hook spiked brier to make it grow fast. Cutting it just promoted growth. Burning it was difficult, as the sap bubbled out and extinguished the flames. The leaves were poisonous and also carpeted in spines that stung, while the roots went deep into the soil and rocks. When the fruit was fully ripe it spat seeds that would take hold in living flesh.

The Dark Lord was directing the demons to dig a tunnel through the softer earth underneath the root system. Waldwick had seen this attempt before and once more concentrated his mind to loosening the roof. Blood ran from his fingers at the strength of his grip upon the staff and sweat trickled down his chest as the strain increased. His heartbeat increased and the blood thundered in his ears as he pushed with his mind. A fault began to rupture along the roof and tons of earth and stones gave way, burying the legions of hell where they stood. The High King withdrew his mind and sagged upon the floor. He let go of the staff of power and the light of madness winked out of his eyes. He extended his wings to the utmost and then folded the bat-like extensions back into their resting condition. The colours were dull and the tiny feathers had lost their shine. It would take weeks before he regained his full health from the exertion of using the staff.

Waldwick rolled over onto his back and was aware of his queen knelt beside him. She had a tray on the floor with goblets of wine ready to drink and sweet cakes to give him energy.

"They still tunnel?" she asked.

"Yes," Waldwick replied weakly. "They still tunnel. I buried hundreds of them this time, but there are hundreds of thousands of them still pressed against the barrier."

"Drink some wine, my King and rest while you regain energy. Eat as many of these honey cakes as you can," Aurora said and wiped the sweat from his forehead before it trickled into his eyes. She extended her wings so that they could fold them around Waldwick, shutting out the world. The bone-structure of the wings was very similar to their hands, but the fingers were long and the knuckles were double-jointed so that they could fold forwards. The queen held her husband tightly with both arms and wings as he shook.

"They must be beaten, dear wife or we will all die. My geneticists have improved on the virus since Ameela made herself unsuitable. She has a daughter. Once she is old enough to interest that spawn of evil I will sacrifice her to save us all," the High King replied and began to sob.

CHAPTER THREE

Sam Pitts went through the Rift back into his own world and immediately felt the heat, as the desert sun baked the back of his neck. Hoatzin stumbled as he came through the rift and found Sam's strong hand on his arm, keeping him upright.

"Thanks Sam," he said as he got his balance. "Gets a little tricky going from there to here! I feel so much heavier "

"Yeah! Takes a little getting used to, I must say. I still can't get over those dinosaurs still being alive over there."

"I think that it's another world," Hoatzin replied. "When we go through that hole in space, we travel to another world orbiting another star."

"What! Where did you get that idea from?" Sam exclaimed.

"Talking to John. He knows a lot of stuff. Did you know that he studied something called astrophysics? Served in the marines, engineering corp. That's where he got all that explosives knowledge and a lot else besides. Served in Iraq, came home and packed the army in. Said he didn't join to kill women and children."

"Well! So what did you get up to until you joined this strange outfit?"

"Me? Did my stint in the army, like most. Five years, ending in special ops. Now I follow the rodeos around riding anything that can buck. Did a little sharp shooting with a travelling circus. Make a buck here and there when I need to," Hoatzin replied and wiped the sweat off his face. "What about you? Where are you from, in the scale of things?"

Sam laughed and pulled the tarpaulin off the 4x4 and got into the hidden Range Rover. He waited until Hoatzin had belted up and turned the ignition key. The engine coughed its way into life and Sam put it in gear and bounced the car down the track to the road below.

"I'm ex army. I got the rank of lieutenant major before I was discharged. They called my trick an expeditionary force. That meant that my men and I went in first and found where the enemy was dug in. You can lose a lot of good people in situations like that. Sometimes the brass asks too much! One day I said no and they cashiered me. I will not spend peoples lives because some braided fool feels that a hill needs taking, just to see what's on the other side!"

Hoatzin gave a grunt of agreement and said, "I know where to get the rockets. It will take me a few days to get there and back from the Chinese quarter, Los-Angeles. I take it that you know where to get the armour piercing rifles and ammo? How good are they?"

"I know a man who owes me a favour, lives at the same place, can get military surplus and asks no questions," Sam replied. "As to how good they are? They can put a half-inch diameter armour piercing round up to 2,000 yards with accuracy. I know someone who has access to a number of Berretta .5 – calibre M82A1, the latest in military sniper type rifles. Also he has some incendiary and explosive rounds that Peterkin's credit card will buy with no problem. They will penetrate several inches of steel with ease. I like these rifles! All you have to do is to sight through the rangefinder and where the bright red spot goes, there goes the bullet! I have no fear that we can put those big meat eaters into the happy land with some of those. The AK 47's in the hands of the dwarves will do the rest!"

Sam put the 4x4 into a higher gear and picked the speed up as they hit the main road, pointing the car in the general direction of Los-Angeles.

A week later a heavily laden truck made its way up the track that lead to the rock formation housing the Rift. Sam had traded in the 4x4 for a flatbed lorry that looked as though it had seen plenty of use. He kept the vehicle within the speed limits so as not to draw attention from some speed cop with a blank book of tickets. Hoatzin had managed to get a large sack of rockets from his Chinese friends. He had described what they were to accomplish and Ho-lank had found some suitable glass canisters that could be sealed with wax. These were fixed to the sticks at the base of the rockets. A trial in the desert had proved that they would do the job, money changed hands and Ho-lank promptly forgot the transaction.

Sam had the Berretta rifles cased up in unmarked wooden crates, placed inside lead lined sheaths. This would go some way to prevent the iron content affecting Peterkin too much, although the Elf had grown used to a certain amount of iron in his close proximity. The trail took a sharp bend to the left and Sam drove the flatbed onto the space that the group had cleared as a parking space. He dropped the side and the two men dragged the crates from the back of the truck towards the shimmer that had appeared in the air in front of the stone lintel.

David and Steven stepped out of the empty air and stumbled as the difference in gravity made them clumsy. The two blond men strode over to Sam and Hoatzin and shook their hands.

"It's good to see you again, Sam and Hoatzin," David said. "Peterkin has been fretting ever since you dropped through the Rift."

"What do you mean? Did he think we had run off with the money?" Sam angrily answered and clenched his fists.

"No! It's not that. He says that the High King is contemplating seizing Ameela's daughter and giving her to the Dark Lord. He wants to get on his way to the Tower of Absolom as soon as he can. I've never seen him in such a state," Steven replied. "Let's get these cases through the Rift and onto the Land Carrier. He's kept the Rift open for two continual days waiting for you to get here. Ah! Here are Spencer and John to help with dwarves to hump and shift. Let's get the stuff through!"

The other side of the Rift had been opened by the side of the Land Carrier, so they did not have far to carry the heavy crates. The dwarves had been busy since Sam and Hoatzin had left and had fortified the flatbed with a double row of sharp spines along the side. Anything that tried to climb aboard would impale itself on these. The bottom set pointed out, horizontally and the second set pointed up at forty-five degrees. There was a sniper platform mounted on the back of the vehicle that was well shielded. A cage surrounded the machine gun at the front so that the 'gunner' could not be snatched from his position. Sam was well satisfied with the improvements.

He felt a presence in his mind.

"Well done Sam! I see that you have everything that we need," I said to my team leader. "Thank you Sam. I see that Steven has told you the disquieting news. We must press on very soon. I can allow you to sleep this night in safety, but come dawn tomorrow I must open a portal close to the Tower of Absolom. We must get to Ameela before the High King decides to pay her a visit to take my daughter. Keep your iron collars safe and at hand. If our visits were to clash, you would do his bidding without a struggle."

I felt a wave of reassurance wash over me. The dark brown human had decided to give me his allegiance and that extended to giving his life if necessary! What strength of character these humans were capable of. Once they returned, those who still lived would be very rich men.

Yet it was not that, that brought them here, it was the love of adventure! I felt that they were crazy people, but I was proud to be with them.

Dawn broke over the mountain that shielded the Villa with storm clouds shedding curtains of rain, washing the snow from the peaks. I insisted that everyone ate a substantial breakfast. As a safeguard to the rescue party, some of the gnomes had insisted that they come with us. Even though the humans wore iron collars to prevent their minds from being taken over by the High King, there were enough dwarves on board the land carrier to make a mental beacon that would send a wave of activity through the ether. The foggy minds of the gnomes would blanket the expedition from any prying minds and give the illusion that the land carrier was a large dinosaur. They were tough little people and soon learnt how to use an AK 47 and reload them.

I stood behind the cab and beside the machinegun nest. John Smith adjusted the gas, opened the flames and brought the boiler to the boil. Sam Pitts climbed into the machinegun nest above me and released the safety catches. Dwarves, gnomes and humans were all armed and ready. The bitter taste of nearby iron filled my mouth, but not enough to decrease my abilities.

I fixed the place on the Plains of Scion firmly in my mind that I had picked days before and stretched out my hands to the miniature arch in my mind. My fingers played upon the stones and depressed the sequence that activated the portal. The air shimmered in front of the land carrier and John let the engine into gear as the steam began to whistle from the pressure vents. We began to move into the back of the tunnel that the dwarves had mined out. As soon as the vehicle pushed through the semi-transparent arch we could feel the air change to hot and humid.

The ground beneath us was hard and stony. To our left was a long stand of ferns, marking the edge of a swamp. The right hand side opened up to bushes and low vegetation. In front of us on the skyline, was our objective, the Tower of Absolom. From where I had managed to fix the portal to the base of the Tower was going to take us several days to get there.

The terrain had been well scouted by sending my mind through the portal carrying Sam and Hoatzin with me. They were skilled fighters and looked at the landscape with a different eye than mine. All I wanted was the quickest way forward to get to Ameela. Although I had been born here on this world, the realm of the elves did not extend into the plains of Scion and I had never been here before. I had only seen this place through the memories carried in other minds. Beyond the plains grew the poisoned brier, miles thick that encircled the whole of Waldwick's kingdom. It followed the contours of the outer wall of the great crater that had been the shaper of this land eons ago. We lived on the central mountains high above the plains.

Only the flying dragons and dragonets ventured into our realm. We overpowered their tiny minds and used them as we wished to fly long distances. The elves had bred them for generations, increasing their size and docility. We used them for hunting the plains for different kinds of meat, eating their eggs and young to keep the numbers down.

John bled excess steam through the vents and sounded off a loud piecing whistle. Across the plains heads came up and turned towards the intruder looking for any threat. When nothing else happened they turned away and got on with the busy need to eat. I never realised that there were so many different kinds and that some of them were so large. There were a herd of long necked creatures with even longer tails. They were big enough to have driven the land cruiser through their chests without touching the ribs. By their sides were horned beasts with bony frills protecting their necks. Some walked on two legs cropping the tops of the trees and breaking them down for their young and others to feed on.

Sam reached down to pick up one of the rifles that he had insisted on returning to the human world to acquire. He selected a clip of ammunition and fed it into the rifle.

"I need to know that they will be effective, Peterkin," Sam declared and sighted down the barrel.

He had picked out one of the big ones.

There was a sharp crack and a grunt from Sam as we watched. One of the long-necked creatures shook as the round penetrated its side and exploded. It continued to walk forwards reaching for ferns, when it began to stumble. Hooting in distress the creature began to fall upon its side. The head rose up and the tail thrashed up and down as the beast began to drown in its own blood. The herd moved on.

As if by magic a big meat eater appeared from the shade of a tree and made a wary approach to the still moving long-neck. It bent its head down to the belly of the dying creature and smelt the blood oozing from the wound. It opened its mouth and razor sharp teeth bit deeply into the long neck's belly. Intestines burst from the rapidly widening bite. The meat eater climbed on top of the shoulders and bit into the neck. More meat eaters appeared from every direction and dived into the feast. Now they began to squabble amongst themselves, as the corpse became a little crowded. Frenzied fights broke out between newcomers and half-fed meat eaters.

Sam selected another big long-necked beast and fired a round into its lungs. He picked off another one and watched it drop to its side.

"While they're eating those they won't be hunting us," he said and put the rifle down on the pegs provided.

John increased speed and the land cruiser began to leave the banquet far behind them.

Sunset brought silence to the plains and hoards of biting flies. The dwarves did a quick excursion within sight of the land cruiser to gather dry wood and build a fire. Each band of dwarves took a human with them armed with a Berretta with tracer fire and explosive heads. The extra height gave them an advantage as lookouts. Once the fire took hold the dwarves added leaves and soon an aromatic smoke filled the air. This also had the effect of keeping unwelcome hunters away from the vicinity. All unintelligent creatures fear fire. One species of dinosaur however, had profited from the extra millions of years of evolution.

When the asteroid had hit the Earth sixty-five million years ago it had wiped out sufficient of the dinosaurs to render them extinct except for birds. On this world the asteroid had come apart and part had hit and part had missed, hitting the moon instead. The velociraptors had enlarged their brain size and had increased their feathery covering. They had also developed a more dextrous hand with an apposing thumb. Language was another hurdle that they put behind them. They hunted the plains in tight groups using their senses to the utmost. Better hearing helped survival along with an increased sense of smell. All these winning attributes were passed on generation upon generation. The result stood as high as a man with semi-winged arms, feathered tails, crowns and ruffs. Their feet had an enlarged big toe, endowed with a scimitar shaped claw that was razor sharp and could disembowel with a slash. This was carried pointing upwards so that it did not touch the ground when running.

The ten survivors of the clutch had 'gathered in' another remnant of another family of raptors they had met on the plains. Instead of killing the young ones and eating them, the prime mother had insisted that they be included into the clan. Her two dominant male suitors had viewed the young females with interest, but a warning hiss from the matriarch soon put any amorous ideas away.

'Prime' was gravid and soon would require a safe place to lay her eggs. These would require guarding from predators until they hatched. This would mean that some of her children would have to stay behind whilst the others hunted. It would be a time of great danger for her family. One thing that could make the difference was the use of fire. Fire was difficult to find and required a great deal of time spent keeping it alight. Usually it was after a lightening strike that the group would find an area rich in glowing embers. These would be harvested and swept together with fresh dead wood until a branch was ignited and could be carried back to the nesting site. No matter how well the fire was tended, eventually a storm of rain would put it out. The clan would try to carry an embers bag, fashioned from the dried stomach of a meat animal, as long as they could. It was difficult to locate dry wood when the rains came and invariably the embers would extinguish before they could be blown back to life.

The faint aroma of smoke in the air brought the matriarch's head round and with it the two leading males. A hiss of enquiry passed between them. A few chirrups from one of the males to the younger members of the clan got their attention. They all sniffed the air and identified the scent. The clutch had used fire before, but not the new young ones gathered in. They would have to be taught the use of fire, just as her clutch mother had instructed 'Prime', when she was a chick. She trilled instructions to the group and tools were put into bags and hung over shoulders. Spears were placed at the ready into the hands of the two leading males. Their fresh kill had been butchered into portable pieces and tied to the backs of the younger members of the clan. The matriarch picked up her stone tipped spear and hung the loop of her axe around her neck. A number of trills put the organised group into motion and the group began to follow the scent of fire.

John Smith and Sam Pitts had drawn the first watch and were sat together inside the cage built behind the land cruiser's cab. With them were half a dozen dwarves who would climb out and refresh the fire from time to time. The increased oxygen content of the air and reduced gravity had worked is evolutionary magic on the insects, causing the biting ones able to do a great deal of painful action. Mosquitoes the size of hornets came out of the darkness, looking for warm blood. Sam had done enough army time in tropical areas of his own world to understand the need for repellent and had bought the most powerful he could get; - good ex-army issue! Without the smoky fire, even that would not have kept the night feeders at bay.

The clouds pulled away leaving a big enough hole to allow the full moon to shine down and illuminate the darkened scrub, surrounding the land cruiser. John stared up at the full moon and studied it intently.

"I think that I am beginning to understand this place a little more," he said. "Do you know much about the very beginnings of our world, Sam?"

"Not much," the group leader replied. "Just that our world cooled down from a ball of fire and eventually life evolved on it."

"There's a bit more to it than that. The new thinking has

it that two small planetoids collided and separated into the Earth and Moon. How they cooled down and became as they are is how we got here. I think that in this universe things happened a little bit differently," explained John. "When the two worlds collided, more of this world became the moon and less of it became this world. It was enough that there is a gravity difference and the tectonic plates formed differently. The continents would be different and also that would perhaps explain why life evolved similar to our world, but with marked differences. This world is a parallel Earth, not another planet as I first thought."

"What do you mean, John?" asked Sam, staring up at the moon with fascination.

"Here the dinosaurs did not die out. I think that Peterkin is an evolved dinosaur! On this world man's ancestors became dwarves and gnomes. There are other intelligent beings here as well. What they evolved from I just can't guess. His people are winged and feathered. What we have all seen is a wingless elf, that has had his wings brutally cut from his back. Also on this world there is very little free iron on the surface. It works like a poison to the elves, but quite a lot of the other intelligent species are not quite so sensitive. The dwarves for instance have soon managed to use the AK47's without too much trouble. The gnomes don't like the iron content of the weapons, but they can manage them if pushed. It seems to affect the mental powers of the elves more than anything."

"Wow! You have been thinking a great deal about this," Sam answered, casting his eyes into the silver moonlighted brush and deep shadows. "I tell you what my friend, its time we went to sleep and someone else took over the watch!" He turned and shook the hammocks next to him and said, "Up and keep your eyes peeled, twins. Its your time to keep watch!"

David and Steven took their place inside the machinegun nest and took the watch, while the others slept.

Miles downwind of the land cruiser the matriarch's clan began to close the distance.

As the first rays of the morning sun shone into the inside of the land cruiser, I awoke to find that the smell of spit-roasting meat filled the air. Also I could smell the aroma of freshly made dwarven bread, as they rose on hot stones placed on the edge of the fire. Gnomes were tending the fire and gathering dry wood to bank the fire up, when I heard a scream of terror from inside the brush. A gnome came running out of the undergrowth and didn't stop until he was safely inside the fortifications of the land cruiser.

I entered his mind and penetrated the fog, as his fear rose uppermost in his mind. I saw what he had seen and marvelled.

"Do nothing!" I shouted to my group. "Whatever you do, do not offer any violence to these people. Retreat to the land cruiser. Do not fire your weapons. Let them come to us. I will deal with them."

I scrambled out of the fortified, steam driven lorry with Sam Pitts by my side. He had an AK47 cradled in his hands. I looked behind me and could see that a forest of gun barrels pointing into the brush.

Without so much as the warning of a snapped twig, I found myself staring up at an amazing sight. What took my eye was the quantity of tool bags, spears and implements hanging from the shoulders of what the humans had referred to as dinosaurs.

They were feathered along their arms with broad sturdy feathers of brown that would enable them to run and balance. They had rigid tails that were equally feathered and flared out. Around their necks were soft ruffs of vary-coloured fine feathers that grew up the long neck to a beautiful crest that all of these creatures held erect. Their eyes were a golden hue with a piercing black centre and their ears were pointed like my own. While their feet were heavily clawed and carried a disembowelling talon, their arms ended in three fingered hands with opposing thumbs.

Curiosity filled their minds and spilled into mine. They had never seen the like of my group and yet there was an acceptance of status. They could see that we used tools as they did. Some of them pulled back into the tree line, watching us intently. The tallest trilled an instruction to a smaller member of the troupe and the creature walked slowly forwards. It had a package tied around its shoulders. The leader produced a sharp edged piece of obsidian from the bag she carried around her neck and shoulders. She cut the bindings and the package dropped to the ground by her feet. Slowly she picked it up and offered it to me and pointed at the fire.

I could feel the question in my mind as she looked at the fire.

"Trade?"

Blood was dripping from the package. It was fresh meat!

"Take the meat, Sam and offer her a burning branch from the cooking fire," I whispered. "Do it slow without any threat."

Sam pushed the AK47 strap over his shoulder and walked slowly to the fire. He selected a large burning branch and offered it to the leader, who trilled and chirruped at one of the others. One of the group with a bright blue ruff around his neck reached forwards and took it from him. To our amazement the creature began to build a fire of his own on the edge of the clearing. Once he got it going others came out of the brush and unwrapped fresh meat and began cooking it over the smoke on pieces of sharpened greenwood stakes. One by one the dwarves climbed out of the land cruiser, picking up the meat and followed suit with our fire.

Soon breakfast was being consumed by all the sentient creatures gathered around the two fires. One of the dwarves offered a piece of their freshly baked bread to one of our new friends. The creature sniffed it and broke a small piece off and chewed it and swallowed. It stiffened and let out a number of trills calling the leader over to its side. She also sniffed the piece of bread and tried a piece. Next she placed a piece of meat on top of another piece and ate this. Her reaction was immediate.

She pointed at the bread that was being eaten and then pointed at the dwarves. Some of her group moved to her side to see what was done to make this new thing. One of the dwarves opened a flour sack and mixed the dough with water and made a number of flattened rolls. She laid the rolls on top of the flat stones heated by the fire and cooked them in front of her audience. One of the watchers pulled a flint knife from out of his tool bag and gave it to the dwarf in exchange.

I was eager to get the land cruiser moving, but I did not want to upset our new friends. They had climbed in and out of the flat bed lorry with unbridled curiosity, fascinated by all the fabricated items on board. Time was slipping away and I made a decision to try to communicate to the leader of this group of intelligent dinosaurs.

I walked up to the matriarch who was stood looking at the machine-gun, mounted at the back of the cab and got her attention by holding her claw tipped hands in mine. Her feathered head swung round and the intelligent eyes looked into mine. I pointed to the Tower of Absolom that jutted out of the flatness of the plains. She stared at me and I could see her thinking. I tapped the land cruiser and pointed to the tower again and reached out to her less than primitive mind.

"We go there!" I projected and showed a picture of the land cruiser with our entire group on board, travelling across the plains.

A feeling of dread came back.

"Bad place!"

I repeated my message again, insistent that we would have to go there.

The feathered head dipped down to my level and her eyes stared into mine. She gently took my head in her sharp pointed hands and in my mind a new picture formed. The land cruiser was travelling the plains carrying some of her group with the rest walking by its side and scouting in advance! Inside the body of the land cruiser was a nest containing her eggs.

Her mind reached out to mine.

"Prime will come too, with her clan! Learn new things! Help protect your clan," she stated.

How could I refuse!

CHAPTER FOUR

John increased the gas fire into the boiler and rapidly developed a good head of steam. Once he had the gauge showing full, he let in the clutch and the four-wheel drive began to exert traction on the stony ground. Apart from the occasional hiss from a relief valve, the vehicle was almost completely silent. The velociraptors stood along the sides of the land cruiser with the dwarves and gnomes, hanging onto the outward facing spikes and watched the world begin to travel by them. Sam Pitts sat himself in the swivel seat of the machinegun nest and from that higher point studied the landscape to come through his binoculars, while John Smith drove.

The land cruiser bounced and twisted as we made our way towards the Tower of Absolom. Already the v-shaped snowplough was doing its job and forcing the smaller boulders from out of the path of our vehicle. The large heavily treaded tyres did the rest. We kept away from the swamp at our left and swung out to the right across the plains that were at a higher level and predominantly dry. These were the home to the massive herds of triceratops, hadrosaurs and iguanodon. Among them walked groups of stegosaurus and the massive giant of all the dinosaurs, diplodocus in herds of their own. In amongst them were myriad species of smaller types and hidden from sight were the meat eaters that preyed upon them.

Spencer picked a Berretta from off the carrying pegs and loaded the rifle with explosive bullets and said, "I think it might be a good idea if we fed the meat eaters again!"

David and Steven picked off a rifle apiece and checked them over. Mellitus also decided to try his luck with something more accurate than an AK 47.

Sam called out from the 'high seat' at the back of the cab, "Make sure that you spread your shots. John will stop the vehicle for a few moments. Choose those animals on the edge of the herds or groups as far away as possible. The meat eaters will be eying those of their prey that are on the edges. Also we want to draw them out of hiding. If they fill their bellies they won't be interested in us!"

The dwarf propped the rifle on the edge of the land cruiser's side and sighted down the telescopic sight. Mellitus waited for John to stop the vehicle before he took his shot. He picked a triceratops that had wandered a little distance from his group and squeezed the trigger. The rifle recoiled into his shoulder pushing him back a little, but he saw his animal fall.

Mellitus kissed his rifle and said, " These weapons of yours, my human friends fill me with dread that I should ever have to protect my people from them. Having said that, I would be only too pleased to take one to the edge of the brier and slaughter the minions of the Dark Lord!"

The other humans dropped a number of dinosaurs into the ferns at long range and picked off some nearer targets. While the meat eaters gorged themselves on the suddenly abundant carrion, at a safe distance, close by, several smaller hadrosaurs had fallen to the armour piercing bullets. As the herd panicked and stampeded away, the velociraptors were quick to take advantage and began butchering the animals with the dwarves for company. They sliced off the easiest pieces and quickly made their way back to the land cruiser. The scent of blood soon brought scavengers and smaller hunters to the scene.

John let the cruiser into gear and rapidly put some distance between the closer kills and themselves, as the sun rose higher in the skies. Now the occupants of the land cruiser were grateful for the shade that the roof provided.

The next wonder that the velociraptors enjoyed was to be able to drink from the bottles of water stored at the front of the lorry.

It was the dwarves that felt the full brunt of the mid-day heat and they soon opened the water stores. They were immediately aware of being scrutinised by the raptors as they drank. Mellitus showed them how to remove the tops from the bottles and handed them around.

Prime held the bottle up to the light and stared into the clear water. She undid the cap and drank gratefully from it and carefully replaced the cap, resealing it. She gestured to the bottle and pointed to her carrying pouch.

Mellitus nodded and handed another bottle to the male by her side.

He also shook the bottle and carefully unscrewed the cap, drank and passed the drink around to the others. When the bottle was empty it was returned to the dwarf and the velociraptors showed their feathers erect as a sign of pleasure. Mellitus refilled the bottle from the water tank and handed it back. Prime put it inside her leading male's carrying sack and trilled a number of instructions to the group.

Four of the raptors began to clear a space in the back of the lorry in one corner and began to build a nest from ferns and branches that they stripped from the trees as the land cruiser passed underneath. After a while Prime trilled an insistent series of notes that got a response from the two leading males. They took up a defensive stance on each side of the nest leaving the corner clear. Into this space wriggled the velociraptor and turned to face out from the corner. She began to shudder and strain. Each time she squatted into the tightly woven ferns, a light blue egg the size of a human fist dropped into the nest. Prime's eyes were tightly closed as she concentrated on the serious business of birth. Eventually she rose from the nest and studied the eggs. Reaching forwards, she examined each egg and placed them back in the nest discarding several as she did so. These she packed away inside her carrying bag. Finally she was satisfied the odd number of eggs were settled in their correct place.

As she walked away, her prime male settled himself over the eggs and sat tight. The second male kept by his side ready to take his place when he needed to feed. The two of them would keep watch over the nest until the hatching took place. Prime would leave them to it until that day came round. She made her way to Mellitus and handed over one of the spare eggs to him.

The dwarf took the egg from the velociraptir and had no idea what was expected of him. Prime took out the other discarded egg and cracked it, swallowing the contents. She stared at Mellitus and raised her feathers over her crest, dropping her head level with his. A series of trills filled the air with an ascending note of inquiry. The other velociraptors swivelled their heads around to all stare at the puzzled dwarf.

I inserted my mind gently into Mellitus and told him what to do.

"Prime has given you a great honour. She has presented you with her unborn child. You must eat it in front of her! She has selected those of her eggs that she deems worthy of life and discarded those that must be culled."

Mellitus cracked open the egg with the edge of his knife, slid it down his throat and swallowed it, still warm. Fortunately it stayed down. Prime uttered some more trills of a more friendly fashion and grasped the dwarf by his shoulders. She then flicked her tongue out and lightly brushed it over his face. Once she had finished doing this she hopped to the side of the land cruiser and stared out over the moving landscape.

The Plains of Scion stretched on into the far distance right on to where the mountains rose out of the flatness. Beyond the edge of the crater walls lay more of the lands until the open seas. What lay beyond those storm tossed watery reaches we had no idea. It was difficult alone scratching out an existence on the high mountainous realms of the Elf Kingdom above where the land-based dragons lived and thrived. No Elf had explored beyond the crater's rim, as the risk was too great. Crossing the plains on foot was suicide. Flying there by the power of our own wings was just too much. We used the flying dragons to travel to the edge of the kingdom, as their minds could be easily controlled. They were bred for our use by goblin dragon-masters, generation after generation.

The lands beyond the mountain range now lay in the possession of the being we called the Dark Lord. Somehow this creature and many more of his kind had appeared a century or so in our past. They had come from outside the 'Kingdom of the High King' and had been stopped the other side of the Great Gorge that was the only way into the crater from outside.

It was the dwarves that kept them at bay until Waldwick's geneticists had perfected the poison brier. The tips of the mountains extended so high into the skies that it was not possible to breathe and were caked with ice. The Great Gorge was miles across and fed by many rivers that surged towards the sea. Outside of this boundary, the Dark Lord's creatures had stripped the lands of flesh and green-stuff. Once inside the barriers they would do the same to our lands and once everything had gone, move on or stay and enslave us all. We had no way of knowing what the being that led them had planned. He had been with his legions from the very beginning of the invasion. It would seem that his kind was as long lived as ourselves. He too was winged like an elf, but much bigger. His colouration was as black as night and he was covered in red stripes with the underneath of his wings bright red. Unlike elves, he carried a tail with an arrow shaped barb at the end. His weapons were made of hardened bone, shaped into axes, spears and swords. His advantage was the sheer number of his minions. We were better armed but vastly outnumbered.

I now believed that the Dark Lord had opened a Rift from their world into mine. If this was so, it gave me plenty to think about. He must have similar mental abilities as I possessed to be able to do this. Their world must be a barren and empty place, for them to come here in such numbers.

As the sun moved relentlessly across the sky I could see that the Tower of Absolom was getting closer. Underneath the ground I could feel the stink of iron increase, as we got nearer to the base. I guessed that sometime tomorrow we should be at the bottom of the pedestal. The ferns had thinned out and were growing in clumps, following an underground water line. We had left the more dangerous swamp long behind us and were climbing a slight rise. On the higher ground wild fruit trees grew and formed woods with other types of trees. Among the branches lived tree-dwelling creatures that never ventured onto the plains below. Birds as well as flying dragonets filled the air around the trees in great numbers.

Sam called out from his place in the machine-gun nest, "John, stop on the top of this small hill. We'll make our night stop here. David and Steven ride shotgun over the wood hunting party. I've a good all round view from up here and this area seems to be relatively quiet. Hoatzin, dig out some fireworks so that we can direct a barrage up and over the top of the Tower. Peterkin you need to communicate what we are going to do when nightfall comes. The velociraptors have managed to accustom themselves to the bangs of our guns, but fireworks could be a bit much for them to take."

"Good idea, Sam," I replied and cast my mind out to reach the raptors that had disappeared onto the plains in the fading light.

They had fanned out away from our direction of travel towards a group of duck-billed hadrosaurs that they had spotted, as they travelled in the land-cruiser. They were feeding on a clump of ferns, bending the tops down so that the younger ones could chew on the upper leaves. Three of the raptors made their way around the group, so that they were the other side of them. Prime gave off a high-pitched trill and the three allowed themselves to be seen. The lead male hadrosaur put himself to the front of the group while the young ones shuffled behind him, flanked by the cows. The three began to dance closer to the adults that kept turning sideways, so that they could bring their tails into play. The leader snorted a challenge and spinning round he swept his tail through the area that the nimble raptors had just been stood. On his hind legs, he stood three times taller then the raptors and outweighed them by a factor of ten.

Behind him the young hadrosaurs panicked and broke away from the protective flanks of the cows and lumbered straight into a volley of spears. Prime had positioned her people well and they were able to pick off two young ones not much larger than themselves. The male charged the three velociraptors in front of him, intending to crush them under his feet. One of them was a little slow and was caught by a flat duck-billed head that flicked the raptor into the air. He landed on his back, knocking the wind from out of his lungs. As the lead male surged towards him to stomp the raptor into the earth, a chug, chug ran out, as David put an explosive round into its body through his back, followed by another into his spine. The hadrosaur dropped onto its chest, just in front of the raptor that frantically rolled out of the way. The berretta had stopped five tons of enraged dinosaur with two shots that had totally disabled it, as it died.

Prime had watched the actions of the human with increasing feelings of gratitude. She trilled a sequence of ascending and descending notes detailing her group to dismember the young hadrosaurs as quickly as possible. As they worked, blood began to drip into the dry earth and fill the air with its scent. Soon clouds of flies circled the kills making it difficult to see. Soon the big eaters would come, signalled by the aroma of death. They should not be here when they did so. Already a smell of wood-smoke also filled the air to her sensitive nostrils. There was enough fresh meat for all of her extended group. Through the actions of the humans and the dwarves, she was including them into a sense of family. The young raptors that she had found on the plains had soon integrated into her group and had become part of her family. She pondered the new situation and began to think new thoughts. The newcomers had weapons that she could not understand, but she could appreciate what protection that they could provide.

The one that could speak in her mind was different from the others. He seemed to be the group-leader although the Sam-Pitts creature also made decisions for the group. Similarly the dwarf that she had given her spare egg to eat was also a leader of his people. As for the much smaller humanoids that did most of the wood gathering and chores, they seemed as if they had no leader or needed one! She found all of this new thoughts fascinating and challenging. Where they were heading for was extremely dangerous. It was the home of a large family of 'Eaters' that were permanently hungry. Why these beasts could not leave the area and hunt on the plains she could not understand. She could not know that it was Waldwick's pressing of their minds that would not let them stray too far from the base of the Tower of Absolom.

Prime cleared her mind and trilled the instructions to leave the young, dead hadrosaurs and rapidly get back to the relative safety of the dead thing that moved with the meat that they had cut away. It was far enough to be a reasonable distance away from the kills. What ever smelt the blood and feasted during the night would not be interested in the strange thing that the group travelled inside. Besides which the fire would keep the meat eaters away while they slept.

Once again a good fire was lit and well stocked with dried ferns to produce plenty of smoke to keep away the night feeding blood-sucking flies. What meat was left uneaten the gnomes smoked and cured for the next day. Again the dwarves made flat cakes of bread by cooking them on long handled pans instead of flat stones as none were at hand. Darkness fell and Hoatzin dragged out the sealed box of fireworks made by his Chinese friends. I had already written the same letter over and over again and sealed it inside the glass tubes, fixed to the rocket's stick. All I had to do was to try and explain to the raptors what we were about to do! Sam lit up the wide-angled searchlight to illuminate the area where the Mexican would do his work.

Hoatzin had already set up his rocket launcher while it was still light someway from the land cruiser. It was a simple rack of pipes that could be leant in one direction. He was ready and waiting for my signal.

I approached the velociraptors and sought out their matriarch known as Prime. Most of her group were sleeping, having been well fed by roast meat while others kept watch. She had a far more complicated mind than I had imagined.

I made contact with her almost elfish mentality and was surprised at the clarity of thought that resided there, "Prime. I would speak with you."

Her head swivelled round and her eyes fixed me with an un-blinking stare. All her head and neck feathers were erect.

"Speak and I will listen," she replied.

"In a few moments my friend Hoatzin will send fire into the sky. I do not want you to be alarmed."

"This day I have seen the meat animals fall at a great distance when you point those strange shaped sticks at them. You are the masters of death and know the secret of fire! I have travelled great distances inside a strange beast that is not alive. It is a place of safety and a good place to keep my eggs. I have met your kind and these others that travel with you. They are not prey! I feel a sense of family although they are not of my kind. You have shared your food with us, as we have shared ours. It has been a good day," the raptor answered.

I was amazed at her perceptions and replied, "You are most welcome. We honour your presence amongst us. Never the less, warn your people that we will send fire into the sky and it will be very bright! There will also be a great noise like thunder."

I could feel the waves of curiosity from her mind.

"Why do you do this?"

I put it as simply as I could, "I seek to rescue my female and young from the top of the tower. I am sending her a message to tell her that I am here."

She trilled rapidly to the others, who thrilled back. Those that were sleeping arose and joined the group.

I called out to Hoatzin, "Light the fireworks!"

The Chinese firework makers had listened carefully to Hoatzin's explanation of just what we needed to achieve. They had calculated the amount of thrust necessary to accomplish getting the rockets to the top of the escarpment and beyond. Once up there it was necessary to produce a large enough bang to attract Ameela's attention.

The Mexican lit the fuses and retreated back to the land cruiser. He had seen Chinese fireworks explode before. Suddenly a shower of sparks lit up the bushes around the site and the rockets took off. Up, up and further into the dark night sky they went, leaving a trail of silver sparks behind them. The illumination was so great that they could see the rockets light up the edge of the Tower of Absolom as they coasted over the edge. Then there was a series of bright explosions of silver sparks coupled with the booming sounds as the heads of the rockets blew apart.

Ameela woke at the sound of the rockets as they passed the lip of the escarpment and went to the small window of the lodge. Her eyes opened wide as the shower of sparks lit up the sky and she ran outside. High above her the rocket heads exploded with a bang large enough to shake the windows in their sockets. By her side Mia shook with terror and grasped her mother by her arm.

"What is that," she cried.

"Whatever it is, it does not come from your grandfather! Light an oil lamp and bring it out here. There are things dropping from the skies," her mother shouted and thrust her daughter inside.

She was aware of the gnomes all around her listening to the empty air with their minds.

One turned to her and said, "Lady Ameela, there are gnomes down on the plains. We can feel their presence."

Her daughter appeared with a fresh lamp, lit from one of the ones inside. Ameela snatched it from her and held it aloft as high as she dared. There in amongst the beans was a long stick joined to a cylinder that was smouldering. At the bottom was a glass bottle bound to the cane. As she looked around she could see more of them dropped into her bean-field. With trembling hands she smashed the neck of the bottle and fished out the paper inside. Her heart hammered in her chest as she read the note inside.

"Ameela, My dear love, I have come to rescue you. I am on my way to you and will be underneath the lip of the tower tomorrow. Look for the smoke. Do not be afraid. I will explain more when we meet. When I am ready I will light a fire. You must fly down to me and I will get us away to a place of safety."
Peterkin.

Ameela shook with anticipation and fear. Draped over her shoulders was a strong golden chain that was attached to clips sank through the bending joint of her wings. They were made of iron and riveted over on the other side so that they could not be torn out, without breaking her bones.

Her father had shackled her wings together with enough chain to prevent her from flapping them. All she could do was to glide down. Once off the Tower of Absolom there was no way back! The iron collar stapled around her neck prevented her from sending her mind to his. If she sent her daughter first one of the ever-present flying dragons would snatch her out of the air as she made her way down. Ameela began to sob. Against all odds Peterkin had crossed the plains of Scion to get to her and he could not have any idea of her plight. There must be a way down to him. She sat in the light of the oil-lamp and racked her brains.

Nothing had disturbed our slumbers during the night and except for the odd scream of agony as some creature lost its fight for life in the darkness. The fire was kept bright and well fed by the members of the watch. The smell of the burning wood smoke was enough to worry most of the nightlife and keep them away. Dawn brought heavy mist that swirled and eddied around the land cruiser. I agreed that we would not start to move until the rising sun had burnt the mists away.

The velociraptors that had stayed inside the back of the land cruiser had made a nest of ferns and mud in one corner. It was here that Prime had laid her eggs, covering the ferns over the tops of the progeny to be. One of the high-ranking males had lowered himself over the tightly placed group and spread his feathers over the eggs to keep the body heat constant. The raptor was jammed against two walls of the corner and facing into the back of the lorry. He watched the goings on of the gnomes, humans and dwarves with interest.

Breakfast was under way and toasted meat and dwarf bread passed around with stored fruit. I cast my mind around the area to try and seek out any of the large meat eaters that might live in the vicinity. Between us and the Tower of Absolom the way seemed clear. We would not be going right up to the base of the pedestal, but I hoped just as far as we needed to be seen. I wondered if Ameela had seen our signal and then laughed, as I thought about it again. The explosions of the rockets had echoed over the plains. Up there at the top of the inverted mushroom it must have been deafening! She must have found one of my messages. I had to go on trust that she did and would be ready to fly down to me. Little did I know of Waldwick's cruelty to his daughter and his insurance that would keep her where he left her.

CHAPTER FIVE

Ameela waited impatiently for dawn to break over the edge of the escarpment. She had a polished piece of metal in her hand and lay as close to the edge of the parapet that she dared. Her daughter lay by the side of her, keeping a watch on the skies in case any of the larger flying dragons were aloft and hunting. They had thrown over them a blanket covered in leafy branches to act as camouflage. Ameela had instructed her daughter over and over again what she must do, but first she had to find the smoke of Peterkin's signal fire. Mia had tried so very hard to penetrate the heavy blanket of hidden iron that stifled the telepathic gifts that the elves possessed. She had no collar around her neck, but lacked experience in using her talent. Once she got close enough to Peterkin, she would be able to make contact with him and tell him her mother's situation.

The plains below were shrouded in early morning mists and any wood-smoke was still too hard to see. Ameela strained her eyes looking for any sign that the mists were beginning to disperse. Gradually she became aware of the reflections in the great swamp as sunlight dappled off the water. Once it started, the mists began to quickly disperse and she could make out the tops of the tall fern trees poking out from the sea of grey. Suddenly it cleared and she could see the ground far below.

It took a while before she was aware that there was an odd trail being scraped across the plains. The one thing that she knew, was any straight lines leading across that wilderness had to be unnatural. She followed the track towards the Tower of Absolom and saw smoke curling up from something strange. There were definitely people down there, but what kind she could not see at this distance. It

58

was too far from the tower to risk Mia flying there yet. She would have to wait until they got a lot closer to where her father had imprisoned her.

She began to catch the rising sun and flash the mirror towards the rescue party. After a while she could see that the volume of smoke suddenly increased. They had been seen!

It was Sam Pitts that had noticed the flashing light from the top of the escarpment.

"Peterkin! We've been seen. The fireworks have done the trick," he shouted from his position at the machinegun nest. "Someone is flashing the rising sun at us!"

I turned and stared up at the tower and my heart leaped, as the reflected light showed that someone had read my messages. I reached out with my mind, but was just rewarded with a throbbing headache. The ground was saturated with iron in all directions and made it impossible for me to use my talent over any distance. The fact that I was sat in a nest of gnomes did not help the matter. Their 'foggy' minds just added an extra blanket of security from Waldwick's mental probing.

I broadcast a wide band instruction to my group in simple terms.

"Break camp! We have been seen. Keep a strong lookout for the big meat-eaters. As we get closer to the tower, we will enter their impressed territory."

As the miles trundled by, the going got rougher and the land cruiser had to backtrack a few times as some of the larger boulders would not move. I noticed up in the skies the flying dragons that John Smith had told me were called peterosaurs, were making use of the morning thermals. In amongst them were the very large ones that we used for transport. To my amazement John even knew what they were as well. He called them quetzalcoatlus and also told me that they were the biggest flying reptiles that had ever lived, but on my world they had grown and evolved to become much bigger. They were masters of the air, but had easily dominated brains. The ones that had been bred by the dragon masters at the castle were docile and used to being ridden by elves. These however were wild and would look upon us as an easily captured meal.

The sun was now directly overhead and the heat was beginning to have its effect upon the dwarves. They steadily used the water stores to quench their thirst. We would soon be reaching the shadow thrown by the escarpment high above us. I judged that we should be close enough for an elf to be able to fly down to the safety of the land cruiser, so I gave the order to stop and light a new fire.

In the inky darkness of the shadows at the base of the escarpment that held the upturned mushroom, movement began and heads lifted with nostrils flared. The scent of sweaty dwarves, humans and gnomes spread in the air, as a breeze began to blow towards the cooler darkness. The herds of plant eaters had learnt quite quickly that the area under the upturned mushroom shaped rock was a place to avoid. When the high King had left his daughter in exile, he had 'pressed' the simple minds of several families of meat eaters to stay under the shadow of the Tower of Absolom. So as the shadow waxed and waned the hunters spread out over the plains killing anything that came into range within the darkness. Only when it rained could they hunt further a field during times of bright sunlight they were forced to hunt within the shadow.

The family of Giganotosaurus held this area of shadow by virtue of hunting as a pack. Indeed the pack had turned a week ago onto the aged mother of the clan. She has sustained an injury to her left hind leg from the horn of a triceratops and this time it had not healed. The scent of blood and rotting flesh had been too much for her offspring and they had torn her to pieces. She had damaged one of her sons enough that he too became part of the feast once the mother had been digested several days later. Now once more their almost permanent state of hunger had returned. They began to follow the scent. Mingled with this new smell was a familiar reek of velociraptor. This could be competition and would be dealt with. Their mother would have been more careful, as she had competed with these creatures before and come off second best.

I had instructed the gnomes to bring as much wood as they could find and load up the land cruiser before we had struck camp this morning. This close to the escarpment there was little more than scraggy bushes to collect. The ferns we had loaded on to make smoke would soon burn out so I asked them to forage for as much as they could find. The dwarves lit the fire and soon a trail of smoke began to make its way up into the sky towards the area that had flashed to us. All we had to do was to wait and hope that Ameela and her daughter would soon take their chance and fly down.

Sam kept his eyes fixed into the shadows, looking for any movement. He reached for his night glasses and sucked in his breath and reached for the Berretta. It would not be enough.

"Stand ready," he shouted to the others. "There's a lot of something big and hungry coming our way out of the shadows."

Mellitus dropped over the side of the land cruiser with a group of his people. Each dwarf made sure that their AK 47's were loaded and safeties off. They fanned out and called out to the foraging gnomes to make their way back to the land cruiser.

My eyes were towards the sky when there was a scream

of pain from a gnome, some distance from the land cruiser. Forty foot of starving dinosaur was suddenly between the gnomes and the 'safety' of the steam lorry. At their backs was a group of meat eaters fanning out to pick off any of the gnomes that ran the other way.

I saw a terrible sight as the group of big meat eaters shook the earth with the weight of their strides. They were so fast! Standing on their hind legs the beasts were agile and the long tails hanging straight out balanced them perfectly. They had an advantage of height, as stood erect, they were three times the height of any human and could look down at us. They had teeth the length of my arm!

Several of my faithful gnomes had been snatched from out of the scrub and were being crunched in half by the creatures. They were then tossed to the back of the mouth, swallowed and the great heads dipped down for more. The dwarves opened up with the AK 47's and poured round after round into the charging beasts. Unless they hit something vital the killers just got angrier. Seeing this some of the dwarves opened up at the hind legs smashing through the knee joints to bring them down.

Sam fired an explosive round through the back of the Giganotosaurus that had taken up the position between the land cruiser and the dwarves. At this close range it passed straight through the soft tissues. The round exploded at its feet and the creature spun round to face the land cruiser. The eyes of the eater took in all the food morsels inside the lorry at below its head height and it charged, gushing blood down its front, from the exit hole. Hoatzin put an explosive round through its open mouth and blew the back of its head off. The monster crumpled onto its knees and the head hit the ground with a bone-crunching thud.

The other killers had been brought to a stop, by being almost cut into two by emptying magazine after magazine into the beasts. Above me the chattering sound of Sam Pitt's machine gun opened up. Tracer fire told him where the bullets were going! Each Giganotosaurus shook with the heavy impact of the shells. Even then some of them refused to die quickly and still strained their necks to bite at the dwarves and gnomes that were struggling to get away. These, the dwarves dodged behind and fired into the backs of the heads. The velociraptors understood the action of the rifles, kept out of the way and used the obsidian ends of the spears to cut through the main artery in the meat eater's necks. Those the dwarves missed bled to death very quickly. I saw one of our velociraptors run up the back of a killer and with a backwards jab, put both of its eyes out. Prime and her clan were faster than these giant beasts and had crossed their path before.

In the middle of the carnage Spencer shouted to me, "Watch the sky. There's something making its way down to us. I don't know what it is. Could it be your family?"

I looked up and saw a young elf spiralling down and doing a poor job of avoiding the lift of the thermals. Dropping down to intercept her was one of the big dragons. Its long beak, full of ripping teeth was wide open and the creature was heading straight towards her.

I entered his mind and begged him, "Kill it Spencer. Please don't let her die!"

The black man coolly raised the rifle and inserted a tracer round and sighted through the tube mounted along the barrel. He squeezed the trigger and I watched as the bullet left a trail behind it. Spencer had aimed correctly and I saw the fiery trail enter the dragon's chest stop it in mid-flight and send it bursting into flames. This made the other two in pursuit veer off in alarm and flap away. The elf had tucked itself into a ball and dropped like a stone. The wings opened and broke the speed of descent.

Spencer gasped, as the elf broke her descent, no more than six feet above us. The iridescent feathers shone in the mid-day sun as she caught the air and hovered for a moment, wings at maximum extension, with her arms clasped to each other. She was so beautiful my heart missed a beat at the vision. Spencer and Hoatzin were making some strange signs over their chests as they stared at her wide-eyed in disbelief.

"Daddy?"

At last I heard the mind of my daughter, but where was Ameela?

"Mia! Where is your mother? Why has she not dropped down with you? Show me the problem," I asked her and reached out with my hands to help her into the back of the lorry.

She tucked her wings onto her back and dropped into my arms and she showed me what a picture of what her grandfather had done to her mother.

I screamed out to John, "Turn the land cruiser. Make your way back along the trail as fast as you can make this thing go and keep going until I tell you to stop!"

John increased the fire under the steamer and turned the steering wheel hard right. The dwarves and gnomes made a run for it towards the land cruiser and climbed onto the open back. The velociraptors left the big meat eaters to continue to die, keeping a sharp lookout for any more of their kind. The smell of blood and the clouds of flies were drawing into the area every carrion eater and killer that was 'mind pressed' by the High King. Prime's clan were used to dodging these creatures and made better guards than we could ever be. They lived here after all!

We were pulling out of the shadow when I spotted Ameela high in the sky. With wings outstretched she was trying to glide away from the Tower of Absolom and kill her speed by avoiding the thermals that constantly gave her lift. Again the flying dragons that John called Quetzalcoatlus had noticed her restricted flying. I saw her bank, as a dragon began to drop towards her and she folded her wings. She curled into a ball and dropped like a stone. There was too much iron in the ground for me to even try to influence the pursuing dragon with my mind.

Spencer and Hoatzin were both aiming at the hungry dragons using tracer fire, as it had stopped them before. One of them jerked in the air and flew into its neighbour making it veer to the side with its body a ball of flame. Ameela saw this and opened her wings again to put a brake upon her speed. The chain that Waldwick had fastened across her back, made it impossible for her to flap her wings. All she could do was to glide and that was almost tearing the securing pins of the chain through her muscles. Once again the dragons had her in their sights and more of them dropped from the sky above the upturned mushroom from where they had climbed the thermals. Now all of my human friends that had these incredible rifles, turned their attention to the skies. As we were well out of the shadows cast by the escarpment, John stopped the vehicle for a few moments so that they could take aim with better results. There was a volley of sounds from the sharpshooters and six more of the dragons dropped untidily from the sky.

Ameela tucked herself into a ball again and dropped towards where the land cruiser was headed. At my instruction John opened up the steam valves and the lorry sped forwards once more. It was obvious to me that she would land some distance in front of us and I had no idea what could be hiding in the undergrowth hungry and opportunist.

I sent my mind out to Prime who was running along the side of the lorry, "Defend my mate if you can. She will drop out of the air in front of us. She will not know that you are friend and she will be scared of you."

"We will keep her safe," do not fear, the raptor replied.

Ameela could see the strange box shaped thing below her was full of dwarves, gnomes and some kind of giant wingless elves, as it travelled along. Her keen ears had heard the crack, crack from below and the dragons had dropped from the skies above her. She had also seen huddled in one corner of the box two strange kinds of dragon travelling with them. Outside of the moving box were many more of them, now running in front to intercept her landing. She could not see Peterkin! Once again she opened her wings to kill her speed and gritted her teeth against the pain as the chain dragged on the riveted pins. She comforted herself with the fact that it would soon be over and she would be free of the unending pain and the collar around her neck. The ground was coming up too fast!

A clump of large fern trees stood out from the plains, not far from the track that the strange travelling box had made. She angled her wings to direct her towards them. Ameela opened her arms to reach for some purchase, as she directed herself toward the soft tops. A cloud of birds erupted from the top of the fern trees as she barrelled into the resistant boughs. She bounced off a bright green mass and spun in the air, folding her wings so as not to break them. She felt the ferns in her hands and grabbed on tightly. One hand made contact with a strong branch, but the other one snapped off some green shoots and she swung out. Ameela screamed as she was catapulted away from the tree and spread her wings again to get some lift. She was about twenty feet in the air when she slowed her descent and managed a small amount of lift before she smacked into a mass of ferns growing in a large clump. From this softer landing she managed to roll with the impact and dropped onto the hard ground beneath.

As she lay gasping for breath a moist, foul mouthful of air enveloped her face and drool began to drip into her eyes. She wiped the slime away and stared directly into the beak of a triceratops that was munching ferns above her head. Ameela began to wriggle away from the incurious beast while sat on her bottom. A strong three-fingered hand grasped her arm and lifted her to her feet. She folded her wings and turned to her helper and gasped in amazement. What had helped her to her feet was another of the dragons that lived on the plains. These were the creatures that were travelling with the moving box! They carried weapons and bags of tools. Their feathers were much longer than the ones on her wings. They carried them around their necks in a ruff and over their bodies. The light of intelligence shone from their eyes and she found them beautiful to look upon.

The creature put a finger to its lips, shook its head and pulled her away from the area. Beyond the beast that had dripped slime over her was a herd of horned beasts twice as high as she could stand. The rest of the feathered creatures formed a box around her to keep her safe. To Ameela's rising sense of disquiet they were very bloodstained, but seemed friendly enough. She limped alongside them as quickly as she could and suddenly they reached something that she could not understand. There in front of her was a great box covered in metal spines with glass in the front. White steam was escaping from underneath it and it rolled along on wheels! Inside the box were the people that she had glimpsed from the air, as she had dropped towards them. It had stopped moving and some of the occupants were getting out to meet her.

I had seen my love stop in amazement and showed some fear as we wheezed to a temporary stop. My elf princess had lost her girlish looks and a leaner, more muscled person stood tall and defiant. The treated skins of dragonets had been fashioned into a tunic and daggers hung on leather straps around her waist. Every last aspect of civilization had gone. The High King's daughter had become a killer and it showed!

She was shackled as my daughter had shown me with a gold chain across her back and round her neck was a band of iron. I had been prepared for this and jumped out of the lorry carrying a set of bolt-cutters.

"Ameela," I cried. "I have found you at last. It has taken so long! So very long!"

We touched and even with the hated collar of iron around her slender neck our minds fused. I just held her tightly, unable to even think past the moment and felt the bolt-cutters taken from my hands by Sam Pitts. There was a metallic snapping sound and her mind was free! Two more shattering sounds and the iron rivets that had held the chain for so many years across her back, dropped out of their bloody sockets. Ameela spread her wings and curled them around me. We wept tears of joy and pain. Our minds sang of the triumph of our togetherness and our love.

Ameela suddenly staggered and her anguish washed through my mind as she cried, "Where are your wings?"

I answered, "Your father cut them from me, before he committed me to the deepest dungeons under the castle."

I felt the heat of her anger as her mind sucked at my pain when she realised what he had done by using hot iron on the wing-stubs. Suddenly Mia joined us and she entered our tight bond. I told them what Waldwick had planned to do with our daughter and their blood ran cold.

A killing rage swept through Ameela, as she understood Waldwick's plans and she said, "I want him dead! How could he do such a thing?"

"There is much we have to do before that confrontation can take place," I replied and gentled her mind.

Ameela opened her wings and stared at the group that had rescued her and asked me, "What are we to do now? Where can we go?"

"I have a place of safety and first we must get back to it," I replied and was aware that my human friends were at my side.

Sam had his hand upon my shoulder, shaking it to get my attention.

"Peterkin, wake up! We must get going. We are too exposed out here. Get your family into the back of the land cruiser and some sort of safety!"

I was numb with emotion and just nodded. We climbed into the relative protection and security of the steam lorry and John Smith let the vehicle into gear and we got under way. Mile by mile we steamed back along the trail that we had made and as we left the iron deposits behind us we elves felt so much better. The constant nagging headache began to lift and for Ameela bereft of her iron collar as well, a mental balsam washed over her.

From time to time Ameela and Mia took to the air and exercised their flying muscles. This far away from the tower the flying dragons were easier to see and they remained high up seeking carrion from the herds upon the plains. Whenever they took to the air my human friends watched the skies and for the most part watched them fly. I could survey the terrain to be travelled by looking though their eyes. Another day would take us to the place that the gate was anchored to and we could slip away from this dangerous place. That night Ameela and I made physical love inside the relative safety of the land cruiser on a pile of bedding. I was amused by the embarrassment that this caused amongst my human friends. The concept of total privacy in a telepathic society is not something that is really possible! Our joy in our reunion was such that a certain amount of 'mental leakage' took place and Sam and the others donned the iron collars so that they ceased to pick this up.

Once morning had dawned John fired up the boiler and began to build up a head of steam. Breakfast was quickly got under way and what was left of the smoked meat devoured by the group. The dwarves had shown the raptors how to operate the crossbows that we had taken with us and they soon became quite adept at loading the bows and firing the trigger mechanism. The only trouble with this arrangement was once they were broken or the last bolt used up, they would be useless.

Mellitus decided that he would teach prime and her group how to make a longbow and arrows from the raw materials around the direction of travel. The dwarves allowed the velociraptors to escort them into the bush, so that they could search for the springy wood and the shafts. With the raptors own obsidian knives they trimmed and crafted the weapons. Mellitus bound the compound bows with sinews taken from the prey they brought down. He watched as the dinosaurs built their own bows from scratch. The dwarf showed them how to straighten the shafts of arrows and fletch the ends with their own feathers. The other skill he taught them was how to make fire with a bow drill. Now they would be totally independent with regards to fire and never need to carry it around with them any more.

By the afternoon these skills were firmly impressed into the raptors and it was fast approaching the time for us to leave the primitive world of the Plains of Scion. Up ahead was the imprint of the portal, fixed in position by my mind. All that the arch needed was the trigger of my mind to open it and we could all go home to the lodge.

It was time to say goodbye to our new friends and return to the unfinished business that I had left behind.

CHAPTER SIX

By late afternoon the land cruiser had reached the shimmering presence of the portal and pulled to a stop. There were a few provisions to do before we crossed over to the lodge. The velociraptors had started to build a new base for the nest that was located in the back of the lorry. This would have to be lifted out and carefully placed onto the new setting. They were able to consider the safety of the situation and its defensibility. Amongst all of the leaving preparations Prime came to me and presented herself.

Her mind was clear, questioning and within mine, "You have your mate and you will return to your world? You will not return here? What will you do next?"

"I have much still to do, that may mean that I will still need your help should you chose to give it? Far from here there is an invader to your lands that is without mercy. He seeks to dominate the life on this plane of existence. The Dark Lord is as much your enemy as mine. Should he and his kind break through into these lands, all of the creatures that live here would perish. To be blunt about it, you would eventually starve to death. The High King fears him and was to use my mate as an instrument in his downfall and lacking her, my daughter. I have to find another way to defeat him or we will all die," I replied to her telepathic question.

Ameela also entered our rapture and added, "You have served my mate well and have helped to save my daughter and myself from being food for the 'eaters.' I would, that you and your clan are more then just friend to us. I feel that you are family. We are bonded together, your people and mine."

Prime expanded her feathers with pride and bent her

head down to meet mine. Her three fingered hands cupped my face and again her tongue flicked across my eyes and cheeks. At the back of my mind was the knowledge that if she needed to, she could quite easily tear my head off. Prime caught that stray thought and quickly assured me that nothing was further from her mind! She turned and embraced Ameela, running her tongue over her face and once again entered my mind.

"You have given my people so much. I must meet with others of my kind and grant them the gift of fire! With this and the bows and arrows that we shall also teach them the art of 'making' I can assure you that when you need us, a multitude will be yours to command!"

"We must go," I insisted and climbed aboard the land cruiser, leaving the 'raptors' behind.

I reached out with my mind and felt for the Arch. It was clear to me and was eager to be used. I set the co-ordinates within the structure of the portal and opened the way to the other reality at the lodge. Suddenly the tunnel under the hill opened up in front of us and John let the vehicle inch slowly forwards and through the gap in space-time. Once we were under the 'carport' roof, I closed the portal behind us.

It was only then that I was aware of my Ameela's mind frozen in terror soundlessly screaming with fear. My daughter, Mia was also paralysed with terror. I had not explained in any depth to them about my manipulation of the Arch and I had expected surprise, but not this!

"My love! What is the matter? We are safe now and beyond the High King's reach," I reached out to their minds. "What has frightened you so much? I repeat we are safe!"

"There is a shadow in your mind Peterkin! A dark shadow! I cannot reach it. I cannot touch it, but it is there. What scares me the most is that it is part of you now,"

Ameela whimpered.

Mia shuddered and added, "I too can feel it. Whatever it is, it is not part of being an Elf!"

I was staggered by this revelation and watched in confusion, as the Land Carriers' occupants climbed out and made their way into the Lodge. After all of our adventures and the horrors that we had faced together, this was the last thing that I had expected. My humans had just accepted that the opening of the Rift was just something that I could do and that it was an elfish ability. Ameela and Mia were elves and had never been subjected to the powers of the Arch before. To them it was an unnatural thing. I searched within myself for the shadow that Ameela had insisted that she could see. Something was there! Try as I might I could not sense evil intent from this co-occupant of my mind. I decided that it must be the link that I had forged to the entity that controlled the rift contained in the portal!

I put the problem to one side, as there was so much to do, now that I had my Ameela and my daughter Mia safe. Already the land cruiser was being unloaded and the guns stacked inside the dwarf-built tunnel along with any unused explosives. Mellitus Hammer-hand and his group were by now expounding the attributes of the AK 47's and the Berretta armour-piercing rifles to the dwarves left behind. There would be some sagas built upon their exploits down on the Plains of Scion! The beer would be drank this night by both human and dwarf in great quantities! The gnomes were a more sober bunch and would enjoy without excess, most of all they were fussing around Ameela and Mia, basking in the pleasure of serving winged elves again.

It had not gone unnoticed by my perceptions the frantic gestures by Hoatzin and Spencer when they had first seen my daughter as she momentarily hovered over the lorry at the Tower of Absolom. Since then they had both stared

74

at my wife and daughter from time to time with a fearful wonder? I also caught a glimpse of the other humans surreptitiously glancing at them from time to time with the occasional look of crumbling disbelief. I set myself the task of unravelling this question later on in the day, but now I needed to talk with someone very dear to me.

I found a quiet place in the great hall, sat down and composed my will to send my mind far from the edge of the crater wall.

First I gently inserted my mind into hers and saw what she saw, heard what she heard. I was in luck, as she was alone in her chambers.

"Mother," I whispered, "your eldest son has returned from the Tower of Absolom. I have been successful! Ameela and Mia are with me in my gnome shielded hideaway."

"Oh my son! My son! You have slipped them away before his very nose. This very morning he set out with a wing of his elite guards mounted on the largest dragons, to bring back Ameela and Mia to the castle. His geneticists have perfected a virus that will spread throughout the Dark Lord's people. All it needs is one of us to be a living carrier to incubate it and that was Mia's purpose. It will take him several days to get to the tower and find out that they are gone. You have four days at the most to take the castle before he returns. There is a large body of the people that have become resentful of his rule and are fearful of his increasing madness! All you have to do is to break through from the dungeons from where you escaped and force yourself to take command. I have seen through your memories that you have a contingent of well-armed dwarves and your human companions. Against your weapons of human ingenuity the elfish crossbows will soon lay down,"

"Mother!"

"Well?"

"I have only just arrived from one expedition and you want me to advance to another!"

"You do it now or you will lose your chance at a near bloodless revolt! I have thought about all that you have endured. I have read all of your memories. It is the only way! See your people and speak to them. You have four days, my son. Four days!"

I sat stunned, in the softness of my armchair staring sightlessly at the gardens bathed in sunshine through the window. I could hear the sounds of the household as they prepared a great meal for the returning 'heroes' and the voices of the dwarves and humans as they told their stories, but nothing registered. My thoughts had been concentrated on releasing my family from the fate that Waldwick had planned for them. After that had been taken care of I had thought to rest a while and plan.

My dear mother had schemed and planned the next stage of the enterprise while she had waited for me to succeed. She was so confidant of my success that her plans had been refined over and over again! In a matter of seconds she had skimmed my memories and fitted my achievements into her plan. She was centuries old and just as clever as her sister Aurora. Mother was a past master at the manipulation of people and her queen, but she could do nothing about my punishment at Waldwick's hands. Her revenge for that act was about to bear fruit! My mother, Dawn, was the eldest of the two elves by nearly a century and was already partnered to my father, Peter, who was a distant cousin to the High King. Peter was a legitimate heir to the throne, but had never desired it. He had died in a 'hunting accident' when I was a youngling. My mother had always had a sneaking suspicion about his death, but could never prove anything. The only certainty that she did know was Waldwick's ruthlessness and his will to succeed at anything that he desired.

During the next few days she would be active amongst the elves that were ripe for rebellion and prepare the way. There was no going back now, I realised. Right now I needed to convince my group that the adventure was not ended. The first person I needed to talk to was the indomitable Sam Pitts.

I tensed my mind's powers and reached out for the leader of my group. He was sat back at the main table enjoying a dwarf-brewed beer when I slipped into his mind. The mental fog generated by the gnomes kept anyone from thrusting their mind into my group from outside. It was a shield that even Waldwick could not breach and before he tried, he would need to know that we were here at the lodge!

"Sam! Could you leave the group and join me in the great hall and bring Mellitus Hammer-hand with you?"

He stood up and said to the others, "I'll be back in a few moments." As he passed the leader of the dwarves he whispered in his ear and Mellitus followed him.

I sat in my chair by the roaring fire and watched the two of them approach. Mellitus came up to the big American's chest, but was as broad as the ex-army human. I could see that the two men had forged a tight friendship. They sat in the two other chairs by the fire and waited for me to speak.

"My dear friends," I said, " events have overtaken us. I have spoken with my mother at the castle. We have not yet completely finished the task I laid before you. I thought that we would have more time before I needed to ask you for your help again. Waldwick has taken a wing of dragons to the Tower of Absolom. He will of course find it empty! We have four days before he returns, to take the castle from below or not at all. Without him to reinforce his mental commands I think that we can overthrow the guards left at the castle without too much bloodshed. Open your minds and I will show and tell you all that my mother has told me."

My two trusted companions sat quiet as my mind filled in all the gaps. I then had my turn at astonishment, as the big human's mind also filled in the gaps in my knowledge of his last 'shopping list' from the military supplies.

"Peterkin, when you slip knowledge into my mind a certain amount of 'seepage' occurs," Sam replied and opened his mind to my inspection. "When you planned the assault on the tower and what you knew of the High King was fed into my mind, a great deal of other information slipped in! It was not hard to realise that someday we would need to take control of the castle from Waldwick's grasp. You would need us again. Hoatzin and I brought a lot of other military equipment back besides the rifles. We have stun grenades and tear gas as well as a few other things like tasers that are out of your experience, including pepper spray. We have the means to take the castle without killing a single elf as long as you leave it up to the humans. Mellitus will take a contingent of AK 47 armed dwarves as backup. Once the elves have seen them in action I feel that this will accomplish what you need to show. Against crossbows, a Kalashnikov in the able hands of dwarves will soon show a military advantage that will be more than obvious! All we need, is to get back into the dungeons below and use the Semtex and C4 that John has in a safe place to blow the walls and ceilings down."

Mellitus laughed and clapped me on the shoulders and said, "These friends of yours are amazing. We will sleep on it and plan the assault tomorrow morning. The Hammer-hand and his people will be there to be counted! A fearsome sight they will make I assure you! "

"Before you go, Sam, there is something that I noticed

several times concerning Ameela and Mia. Hoatzin and Spencer stare at them and sometimes they tap their chests and make signs with their hands. I have also seen the other members of your group look intently at them," I said. "Is there something the matter?"

Sam sighed and scratched his head as he considered my question and replied, "Peterkin there are some odd things about my world and society that you are unaware of. There are many different religions practised by many of my people concerning a supernatural being that created the universe. Some of us do not profess to have any attraction to any of these, but there are some that depict creatures very like yourselves as holy figures. They call them angels and they are winged. The paintings of them that are centuries old do show them to look a lot like Ameela and Mia. You have no wings, so the others of the group never thought of it until they first saw Mia and then Ameela. Thinking about it, I cannot but wonder if your people have been on my world before? I have also seen paintings of the Dark Lord and his legions or something very like them."

"I am beginning to wonder that myself," I answered and waved them away to their meal and joined them.

The gnomes had been busy baking pies, roasting meats and cooking a variety of different foodstuffs. The great wooden table groaned under the weight of so much food. A barrel of beer had been mounted on a trestle at one end of the table and mugs of foaming dark brew were being passed along the table from both directions. My wife and daughter were shamelessly tucking into the feast and trying things that Ameela had not seen in ten years, while incarcerated at the Tower of Absolom. It had been some time since I had eaten gnome-baked food so I put my worries behind me and joined in, but kept the beer to just the one mug full! I needed to be able to think clearly and make decisions, come the morning.

Later that night Ameela and I lay exhausted by our lovemaking in the soft sheets and down filled mattress. Ameela rolled me over onto my chest and examined the healed wounds on my back where Waldwick had sliced away my wings. The gnomes had managed to heal the 'iron-sores' that her father had scored into my flesh. Only the two stubs remained that lay parallel with my arms. The muscles that opened my wings had atrophied because of lack of use. Ameela probed her fingers along the edges of the wounds, searching for something other than just healed flesh. Given time an elf can regenerate a missing limb, but hot irons had been driven into the roots of my wings. It depended whether the healing practised by the gnome women had driven out all of the poison. I heard a small grunt from Ameela as her fingertips touched something different.

Her mind slipped into mine, "Something grows! You may fly again, my love, in time. Now tell me about tomorrow! Agh! There it is, the shadow in your mind. Peterkin you share your mind with something else! Share it with me! I know that it aided your escape from the darkest dungeons under the castle. I was shocked before when we went through the portal. I have got used to the idea now. Open your mind to me and let me meet this 'thing'!"

I rolled over onto my back and linked my fingers into hers drawing her naked body close to mine. Ameela spread her wings over the two of us making a private place within them. I activated the arch and ran my fingers over the runes within my mind. We opened the portal together and saw through it the plains of Scion. High above the plains, a wing of dragons were flapping their way towards the empty Tower of Absolom. We drew back, lest Waldwick's powerful mind eavesdrop the building hatred of his daughter.

We withdrew from our world and I opened the portal to Earth and showed Ameela the world of the humans. After a while of looking at the teeming cities and the massed armies, Ameela said, "This place scares me more than the plains of Scion! Take me home, Peterkin. Take me home."

I worked my fingers over the runes and closed the arch.

"It is a fearful place my love, but that is where I found the men who risked their lives to find you and rescue you from the tower. It will be their adapted weapons that will enable us to overthrow the Dark Lord. They will help me tomorrow to enter the castle from below and secure it, before your father comes back enraged from the Tower of Absolom. Sam Pitts has shown me how we can take the castle without too much bloodshed using their weapons to do so."

Ameela considered my plans and asked, "Are you sure that you can trust these human beings, Peterkin?"

"I have learnt that, once their word has been given in friendship, these mentally isolated beings are steadfast. I have trusted them with my life and to walk the Plains of Scion to rescue you and Mia. Yes my love, I do trust them. They have a sense of honour and it is enough! Now let us sleep as I have much to do in the morning."

The morning broke to thunderclaps and lightning as a wild storm engulfed the lodge. The cold rain hissed down onto the roofs and filled the melt-water stream to capacity so that in places it overflowed into the lodge gardens. Whilst I had slept beyond the rising of a watery sun, Sam had roused the others of the team and had pulled out of the dwarf-built stores a stock of strange looking weapons. John Smith had filled a rucksack with explosives and things he called detonators. Each human had a large haversack, well stuffed with items that I was not able to recognise.

They were all sat around the breakfast table explaining to the dwarves what the sacks contained. I was amazed at the eagerness of my group to be briefed and to get started.

I took my place at the head of the table with Ameela and Mia sat at each side. The table was well stocked with fresh bread, butter, boiled eggs, what looked like grilled bacon and fruit. Jugs of milk were scattered around with jars of honey. There were many different types of Earth animals living on this world that must have been transported here so long ago, it had been forgotten by my people. My mind went back to Sam Pitts' explanation of the ancient paintings and their resemblance to my people. It made me wonder if the portal had once been much used by my ancestors. We ate sparingly of the gnomes' feast, as we all knew that fighting on a full stomach was as bad as fighting empty.

I hammered the butt of a carving knife against a pewter plate to get everyone's attention.

"First I need to know what these 'non-lethal' anti-personal weapons will do without harming my people," I said. "To do that I will have to enter each of my human friend's minds and scan for that knowledge. Once I have done that I will be able to plan the assault."

Seeing that each man nodded, I set forth a quick examination of each mind. It shocked me to see just how much death these human beings had witnessed. It also showed me how much I could rely on each man. Elf had not raised a hand against elf-kind since records had been kept. The High King's treatment of me was a symbol of his madness. What he had commanded grown and nurtured in the secret laboratories in the west wing of the castle was an abomination. To my humans it was just an end to the means. All of the humans were familiar with the stun grenades, tasers, tear-gas, pepper spray etc., but it was John Smith that was the explosives expert. His rucksack was full of semtex, C4 and the necessary detonators to ignite the explosives.

I opened my mind to the group around the table and gave them the layout of the dungeons as I remembered them. My memories of what lay above them was sketchy to say the least, as I had never had cause to venture into that realm. I concentrated my thoughts around the area that had the hole in the ceiling where the table scraps were thrown down to the waiting bogymen. John Smith studied my memories of this area and estimated the floor to ceiling height and calculated the amount of ladders we would need to get to the floor above. The hole was far too small to enable us to get through. This would need enlarging and John would blow it open. After the noise of the alterations to the floor above had echoed around the castle, I was sure that Waldwick's guards would gather themselves to that area quite quickly. This was a stumbling block to my plan and filled me with anxiety.

Sam's mind came up with the answer and he said, "We lay timed charges in different places, so that the floor will collapse some way away from where we are going to invade. John will preset the charges so that all we have to do is to place them wherever we can. They will go off first, leading the castle guards away from the area that we will enter from. Some will stay behind at these places and throw concussion grenades into the rooms above while the main force will make our way upward. I want Mellitus and his men to use the AK 47's as a frightening weapon only. John has replaced the magazines with 'rubber bullets' to prevent any accidental deaths. Spray the walls, but do not injure any of the elves unless you really have to. Once Peterkin takes control of the throne room I'm sure that all resistance will evaporate. Keep the element of surprise going in our favour. The tasers will drop anyone who fails to stop their aggression and the tear gas and pepper spray will totally incapacitate any shreds of defence."

I stood at the head of the table and thanked them all and added something else to the plan.

"There is one other thing gentlemen," I broadcast on the mental web, "You must all wear these iron collars at all times. Should any of you forget to wear them, any elf that noticed you, could control your thoughts with ease. My human friends, remember how long I lived in your world and how easily I suggested that I be fed and looked after! As we are finished here, I recommend that you buckle them around your necks now. If you have any questions, now is the time to ask them before the iron band closes you off!"

I watched as my group strapped on their iron collars and one by one their thoughts became their own. Mellitus and his group of dwarves did the same. My blood ran cold at the thought of just one of them falling under the mental command of one of the guard and firing his AK 47 into my group. I had learnt all of my military training from my association with the humans in my mercenary group. Even so the majority of the planning of this exercise was down to Sam Pitts and John Smith. Each of them was wearing Kevlar vests that would deflect a crossbow bolt and helmets carrying gas masks and lights. We were armed and ready. All I had to do was to open the portal in the main hall and we could go. I made ready to turn towards the great hall and found myself face to face with Ameela.

"Where you go, I go," she stated, clutching a spare helmet.

Without my noticing it she had donned a Kevlar vest and bullied a taser from one of the dwarves. She had her obsidian blade that she had used on top of the Tower of Absolom pushed into a sheath, along with a 9mm. automatic pistol strapped to her thigh. A bandolier of teargas grenades hung over one shoulder, leaving her wings free. I was about to protest when I glimpsed the determination in her eyes and turned round to see my ten year-old daughter similarly dressed!

The sight of these two furies almost paralysed me with astonishment, as I just stared at the killers that Waldwick had made from his daughter and my child.

"It's time to go," I said and lead the way to the portal.

CHAPTER SEVEN

We stood in the great hall before the 'Great Arch' and I reached out with my mind to connect with the being that was the portal. In my mind I tapped the runes around the miniature gateway that was now fixed in my mind, to give the sequence that would open into the dungeon where I had spent so many years. The brickwork inside the arch became translucent and the darkness of my old prison lay beyond.

Sam did not hesitate and waved his group through as I stepped into the chill, dampness of Waldwick's dungeons. They turned on their helmet lights and dragged through the equipment that was going to be needed. John Smith switched on the portable generator and more lights shone into the home of the bogymen than had ever been, since the castle had been built. Cries of fear came from the inky darkness that sat in the corridors branching out from the Warlock's quarters. Scuttling sounds receded into the distance as the poor creatures that lived down here retreated from the lights.

I pointed to the archway at the entrance to the cell and said, "Through there, Sam and up the stone staircase to the next level. Keep going for two more levels and we will eventually come to the place where the High King used to throw his slops for me to fight the bogymen for my share. I never did find the way that those disgusting creatures used, to drag me into his presence. I do know my way into the castle from above that hole and that's the way we will travel."

Mellitus and his men took the stairs two at a time, making sure that the way ahead was clear. The humans took their time, making sure that the extending ladders were handed on to each floor. At last we found our way to the 'feeding room' and Hoatzin unfolded the ladder and pressed it to the entrance to the floor above. Whatever food had been thrown down to the floor that we stood upon had long been scooped up by the bogymen and their females. The flagstones had been licked clean. Above us was a hole that was too small for any of us to crawl through, fixed with bars of bronze. Even these had been licked clean by the starving creatures of the darkness.

John climbed the ladder and inspected the hole above him. He used a hooked stick to gauge the thickness of the slabs above him and examined the roof supports that buttressed across the ceiling.

After a short while he climbed down the ladder and spoke to us.

"Gentlemen we are going to make quite a bit of noise. I shall have to bring down some of the supports around the hole. The rubble will drop right where we are standing so when that happens we need to be somewhere else. When this lot goes I think that the other charges should be set off to bring down some of the walls and supporting ceilings down some way from here. Mellitus I want you to use your mining skills and assess the structure on this level. We want to make lots of noise and bring down enough of the ceilings to make confusion spread amongst the guards above us. I will preset the explosives to go off after ten minutes. That should leave you enough time to be out of the way and also be close enough to scramble through the holes onto the floor above. Use the radio link in the helmets to warn me that you are ready. When I hear the bangs, I will set the explosives here and the main force will make its way upward.

Mellitus took the haversack of explosives with glee

and suppressed excitement. He had gone over the setting of the explosives with John and was quite confidant of what he needed to do. He gestured to the other ladder and two dwarves picked it up and they made their way into the darkness with helmet lights shining. The leader of the dwarves had seen the power of the Semtex once it was unleashed and although the amounts that were going to be used were quite small, it was quite effective. The last thing that Peterkin wanted was to bring the castle collapsing down around their collective ears. So there was enough explosive to prise the floor slabs up and out of the way and of course make lots of noise.

John had placed his charges around the hole in the ceiling and had the wires looped together, down the walls and around the corridor into the next chamber. He had used C4 so that the noise would be minimal, but effective. I looked at my group of humans and dwarves with satisfaction. I knew that they were ready and willing. My mouth was dry with excitement, as we all strained to here the sounds of Mellitus and his engineers.

In the space of time that we had before the attack began, I took the chance to link to my mother. I quietly slipped into her mind and found her waiting impatiently in the throne room.

"Look through my eyes and see all that I see," she said.

With that she turned round and gave me a panoramic view. After centuries of living a quiet pastoral life, farming the terraces around the castle and the surrounding hills, the 'palace guards' had never fought against anyone. Since the arrival of the Dark Lord and his legions they had made some effort to train in warfare, but with little idea of how to fight as a group. Against Sam Pitts' hand picked men and the well-armed dwarves; they would stand no chance at all. I knew that it would be like attacking children and I did not want any of them to be killed. After all they were my own kind and I knew most of them quite well. They were armed with crossbows and bronze swords that had never been used in real combat.

With Waldwick away and out of sight, most of the guards had not even bothered to carry the heavy crossbows into the throne room. The majority were still being stored in the antechamber next to the throne room, until the High King returned.

My mother walked through the throne room and stared round the castle giving me an appraisal of the situation. She made her way towards the main stairs and down them into the great hall beneath. It was here that the mid-day and evening meals were set out on great wooden tables. In the far corner was the hole in the floor that any leftover food was shovelled down to the waiting, hungry creatures below.

I returned my mind to my own body and called out to my group of humans, "Remove your collars for one small moment and I will show you the situation as my mother has shown me."

The six of them stood silent as they absorbed the information and snapped the iron collars shut when I had finished.

Mellitus turned on his helmet radio and spoke to John.

"Fire in the hole," he exclaimed with glee, pressed timer buttons and ran for it down the adjoining corridors.

After some time John raised his hand and brought it down to set the charges.

There was an echoing series of shuddering bangs from far off along the corridors and a dull crump from the slop-hole, the other side of the wall. This was followed by the sound of three large slabs falling through and crashing onto the flagstones below.

Sam gave a shout, "Ladders up and let's get through. You all know what we have to do! Lets get the job done!"

I had to forcibly restrain Ameela and Mia from climbing up the ladder into the banqueting hall above.

"Let them go first. They are trained in warfare and we are not. Trust Sam to lead our forces to do the minimum of damage. All the humans know what is at stake and what needs doing," I said. "Wait for the signal and keep your helmet on. Do not remove it until I say so!"

Above us I could here the loud bang of concussion grenades and teargas mists began to drift down the enlarged hole.

Sam's voice spoke in my ear from the radio-linked helmet.

"Come on up. This level is clear," he said.

We climbed up the ladder and into the mists that were billowing round the hall. Whatever resistance the palace guards could offer had soon crumbled on this level and they were retching and gagging on the floor. I pointed up the main stairway to the throne room above where several guards had positioned themselves with crossbows. Hoatzin aimed and fired his Taser at one of the armed guards. The crossbow bolt hit his Kevlar armour and bounced off as the shock caused the guard's fingers to spasm.

David and Steven were up the stairs in an instant, bowling teargas grenades into the confused massed ranks of the guards as they sought to retrieve the stored crossbows. To add to the horror of the situation, my group of humans were a good head taller than any of the elves and with the gas masks and helmets they looked as if they had stepped out of their worst nightmares! When they saw Spencer's coal black skin they fled in terror, believing that the Dark Lord's army was inside the castle. Then Ameela spread her wings and rose briefly above the chaos in the high ceiling of the throne room. She fired her taser at the commander of the guards and took him down. Mia swooped down from besides her mother and dropped his second-in-command to the floor with a well-aimed taser bolt. Both elves folded their wings and descended to the flag-stoned floor. They both removed the metal spikes and reeled in the filaments and stood next to their unconscious captives with their obsidian knives ready to slit their throats if necessary.

"I think you have done enough, son," my mother telepathically insisted. "I will let those who have secretly supported me that the throne is now in other hands! As for the rest? Well we will soon see how quickly they change allegiance! Now I must confront my sister."

With that Dawn dropped her robes to the floor and dressed in her leather flying gear she spread her wings and leapt over the parapet, to swoop through the window of her sister's apartments. Aurora was stood, transfixed in fear by the sounds of the explosions and the sounds of the AK 47's. She was facing the door, when my mother hurtled through the open window. She smacked feet first, into the back of her sister right between the wings that were folded under her gown, hard enough to knock the breath out of her. In her free hand she held an iron-meshed collar that she wrapped around Aurora's slender neck. Dawn quickly snapped the catch shut and pulled the pin out.

My mother then slit the back of the gown with her obsidian knife, so that the main ligaments of her sister's wings were exposed. With a quick slice she cut through them before the queen could get her breath back. Aurora was now flightless until her ligaments knitted together and that would take months. All she could do was bleed and scrabble about the blood-soaked floor.

"I have waited a long time to do that, sister dearest," Dawn, hissed into her ear. "I have not forgotten that you did nothing, when my son was taken and tortured. Now Peterkin is back with your daughter and her child. Waldwick's reign of madness is ended and you will not give him any warning. The collar stays on; just as the 'High King' trapped Ameela in her own head these long years. Now we will make our way to the throne room to meet him."

Aurora began to scream and my mother slapped her head down upon the cold flagstone floor to shut her up. She then wrapped her free hand around her hair and began to drag her out of her rooms and into my presence.

I walked over to the throne and climbed the steps, to the seat that was only sat on by elvish kings. From this elevated position I could see that the mists of teargas had dissipated. Dwarves had lined the walls, all armed with tasers or AK 47's and dressed in Kevlar armour, carrying grenades. All of them wore the human's helmet and gas mask that hid their faces. They had used the AK 47's with deadly effect; by spraying the guards at kneecap level with rubber bullets. This had severely bruised the legs of the 'soldiers' and brought them down into crumpled heaps. The noise of the guns and the confusion of the teargas, coupled with concussion grenades, had done the rest. In the matter of no more than fifteen minutes, my small force had paralysed the High King's guards and taken over. They looked a fearsome sight to my elvish kin and all wore an iron collar to prevent my people influencing their minds. Scattered amongst them were the giant presence of my human friends. Sam Pitts and his men stood tall and menacing. I had been amongst them for so long I had forgotten that I only came up to their shoulders. Dressed as they were, they looked totally alien to my elvish kin and the helmets made them look even taller. It was Spencer that terrified them the most as he was as black as one of the Dark Lord's people. At my nod all helmets were removed and at least the elves could see that my forces were a mixture of dwarves and Sam Pitts group and not some alien beings.

I could feel the presence of my mother approaching through the crowd, long before I caught sight of her. Her anger and triumph resonated inside my mind along with the terror and pain of her younger sister. The crowds parted to allow her to move towards my position and I could see that she was dragging a bloody figure by the hair.

I heard Ameela hiss in fury as she realised who my mother was dragging over the flagstones; it was her mother Aurora. The High King's Queen wailed in fear and pain and had bled copiously from her back. I could see that my mother had sliced through the ligaments of her wings and they hung useless from her back. At her neck she had an obsidian blade ready to slit her throat at a moments notice. Dawn had overpowered her sister at the first sounds of my entrance back into the palace. She had wrapped around her neck an iron meshed collar and snapped it shut. There would be no warning to Waldwick's mind through her telepathic reach. The high vaults of the throne room echoed to the sounds of the High Queen's cries of terror.

There was a brief crack of outstretched wings from my side and Ameela swooped to the side of her aunt and lifted her mother's face to receive a resounding slap from her well-muscled arm and hand. The blow tore her from my mother's grasp leaving a handful of hair behind and laid her in a disorganised heap at her daughter's feet.

"Ten years you left me to rot on the Tower of Absolom. Ten long years to birth my daughter alone and fend for ourselves. Ten years of mental silence, wearing an iron collar just as you do now. I could not mesh minds properly with my daughter or hug her, without she recoiled from me because of that collar! You allowed my father to plan on using me to infect the legions of the Dark Lord and then when I became pregnant, my daughter was to be the carrier instead," she screamed. "What kind of mother are you?"

"A frightened one," Aurora answered. "The strain of constantly trying to hold the Dark Lord at bay turned his mind! Using the staff increased the power of his mind, but it sent him into maddened fits. He became ruthless and able to think the unthinkable! Once he conceived that way of destroying the creatures that constantly pound upon the borders, he could think of no other. I could not stop him. There is not one elf in the kingdom who could."

"There is now! Peterkin is back in the kingdom. He wields a power far beyond anything that Waldwick could dream of. My mate and nephew to the royal line will stop them," Ameela declared.

I removed my helmet and walked off the dais to take control of the situation.

"Hello aunt. Things have changed, as you can see. When the High King lands on the Tower of Absolom he will find it empty of elves. I am content to wait for him here. I who was his 'Hand' will be his hand of retribution," I said to the shivering wreck whose hair was still held tightly by my mother.

I gathered my mental strength and broadcast my thoughts to each and every elf in the palace and surroundings.

"I would have your support. Elves do not kill elves! What the High King has set in motion is evil. How long do you think that it would be, until he began to pick those of you outside of his family? I promise that I will not make you do anything that you would not voluntarily do. I will defeat Waldwick when he returns and I will send him to the Dark Lord infected with the virus that he meant for his granddaughter. I have other weapons and allies. You see them here. They are called human beings and they have weapons that we can use from a different world. I have been to that world. All I ask is that you keep a mental silence. Do not answer his mind. Shield yourselves and do not let him into your thoughts. If necessary wear an iron collar if you fear that you are not strong enough to keep him out of your minds."

Over the top of my thoughts came that of my mother, "Support my son or you may be looking at your own death. Not from him, but the High King's madness."

Many of my people had experienced Waldwick's madness and lived in fear of his anger and his shortened temper. Many of them had shuddered at his treatment of me and the isolation that he had imposed on his own daughter. Fear of the High King had kept them silent and obedient. As my aunt had said, use of the staff had increased his mental powers, but it had sent him into fits of madness.

At that moment Waldwick had spiralled down from a cloudy sky on the back of his dragon. The Quetzalcoatlus carried the weight of the High King with ease. Generations of selective breeding had made the flying reptiles much bigger than its wild cousins. Waldwick became the beast, blending his mind with the flyer, buckled onto its back by a leather harness. He looked through the creature's enhanced eyes for any signs of his daughter on the top of the Tower of Absolom. It was mid-day and there was no movement in the fields. He has kept his mind tuned to his granddaughter's from time to time to ensure that they both survived. He brushed aside the foggy minds of the gnomes and mentally swept the area under the dragon.

Nothing!

Waldwick brought the beast across the fields and made it drop onto the ground. "The land was still being cultivated so they must be hiding here somewhere," he thought and increased the power of his mind to seek them out.

All he could feel was the knitted fog of gnome minds dispersed around the escarpment. A feeling of unease began to fill his mind as the others of the 'wing' landed amongst the beans and still there was no sign of his daughter.

His guards searched the lodge without a sign of his family to be found. Waldwick walked to the edge and looked below at the ground. To his amazement a scene of carnage was spread out over the stony area at the bottom of the escarpment. Hundreds of bones lay littering the region and the dismembered corpses of the 'eaters' that he had pressed long ago were scattered around. Sleeping by the side of the dead killers were more of their own kind that were in a cannibalistic stupor induced by the quantities of meat that they had ingested.

"What has happened here," he wondered, "as the 'eaters' do not usually feed upon each other?"

"Sire!"

Waldwick turned to see one of his guards running through the crops towards him, holding a glass bottle, tied to a stick.

"There is writing inside the bottle Sire," the guard gasped as he reached the king. "There are many of them all saying the same thing," and he gave the High King Peterkin's message.

Waldwick's mind filled with maddened rage as he read the note. Peterkin had stolen Ameela away with his daughter from this impregnable stronghold.

"How could he have possibly done this? Where could they have gone? He had seen no sigh of them on the plains of Scion as they flew above. Had they been underneath, his mind would have picked up any activity."

Waldwick sank to his knees and beat the ground in

impotent fury.

The guard, who had given his king the message, trembled in fear and backed away from him, while the others of the 'wing' watched with trepidation.

"Sire! What do you want us to do? Command and it shall be done," he begged.

The High King pulled himself to his feet using the staff of power as a crutch.

He concentrated his mind into the power of the staff. The goblin wrought ball of iron and crystal mounted at the top of the ironwood wand was a mental amplifier. It had travelled amongst the stars until it fell to this Earth and was found by a goblin artisan. He had recognised the potential in the crystals locked and fused into the nickel iron of the meteorite that has been captured by this world's gravitational force. Goblins have little telepathic ability, but in the hands of an elf, it worked as an amplifier. What the artisan did, was to fray the end of an ironwood staff, so that filaments fused with the crystalline circuits and fed the Earth power from the tip inserted into the ground to the ball on the top. It required a special type of mind to draw on the power of the Earth itself. Waldwick had that type of mind. His mental powers were the strongest in the elfin kingdom, but association with the power of the staff was losing him his reason. His mind recoiled from the effort of trying to connect with the castle. Mental silence was all that he could feel. Not one mind was open to him!

Since the coming of the Dark Lord and his legions he had pushed his abilities to the limit. It was not enough to defeat him, but just enough to hold the status quo. The pressure and the creeping addiction to the staff had allowed him to think the un-thinkable. Elves have an affinity for living things. They are incredibly clever genetic engineers and amongst Waldwick's people there lived such a genius. It was he who had genetically engineered the poisoned brier that kept the army of the Dark Lord at bay. The dwarves had held the breach until the brier had filled the gap between the mountains. They had managed to capture some of the dark elves and had brought them to the elfin scientist to study. He found that they were another type of elf. The dark ones were mainly flightless and they were susceptible to certain infections that the elves were almost immune. Ten thousand years or more, Waldwick's people had escaped from the same world that was dominated by the 'dark elves' and settled here bringing the gate with them. The home world was now a ruined hulk of a planet nearly devoid of life.

Abaddon, the Dark Lord, had overseen the manufacture of a new gate carried in a reality shifting ship known as the Dream-shifter. He had followed the mind signatures of his elvish kin through the multi-verse to this world. Here the ship had fixed itself and would not move again, but the gate remained open. Through that gate came the hoards of starving dark elves, constantly increasing their numbers without any thought for the dwindling resources. Fortunately for the elves that already had settled here, the Dream-shifter had fixed to this reality outside of the great crater that was home to both dinosaurs and elves. The great gorge was the only way in and Waldwick's geneticists had sealed it with the poisoned brier. Abaddon's legions had tried throwing themselves against the brier to make a carpet of dead flesh for them to climb over. The brier grew too fast. Tunnelling underneath was of little use as the tunnels kept collapsing. Unknown to the Dark Lord, it was

Waldwick's psychic powers that kept collapsing them, but it was getting harder for him to bury the digging throng.

Waldwick opened his mind to his guards and told them, "Mount up and fly home! It will take us two days at least to return. I do not know what we will find there, as there are no thoughts that I can read. The castle remains silent. Only the outskirts of the castle grounds and the farms can I read and they know nothing about the silence."

The High King began to wonder and doubt.

"It must be Peterkin," he thought. "What has he done and how did he achieve it? What can one elf do on his own?"

CHAPTER EIGHT

It was later that day that I felt the probing mind of Waldwick search for answers from the silent castle. In the end I had insisted that every elf inside the castle walls wore an iron collar for the next few days. It was Sam Pitts who had brought a case full of iron mesh collars through the rift. It had been his mind that had dreamed up the duplicity of making sure that the castle remained mentally silent. I had listened to him and the others of my human band who had studied warfare on their own world. Indeed it was a fact that human beings were far more adapt at warfare than elves. They lived in a world that had evolved through thousands of years of conflict. The 'arts of war' had been brought to bloody perfection time and again.

Elves develop telepathy from puberty onwards. We have never developed the art of lying to one another. The best we could do was to shield our innermost thoughts from one another to attain privacy. We live in constant mental contact with each other. The years that I spent down in the depths of Waldwick's dungeons I spent in mental silence. There was something built into the floors of the bottom living area that inhibited mental communication. When I discovered the arch, I found that I could only project my mind through the walls horizontally. That was when I found the Warlock's lodge and returned the arch to the great hall inside it. I took refuge inside the walls of the foggy minds of the gnomes and remained outside of the High King's mental reach.

That morning Sam and I had made our way to the laboratories where the High king's geneticists laboured over the development of the virus that would hold the Dark

Lord's legions in check. John Smith studied the glass retorts and the safety protocols that were in place. He became wildly excited by the entropy sinks that gave us the chilled conditions to preserve the viruses developed by the elvish scientists.

John pulled Sam by the arm to the frost covered retorts and said, "They have no electricity! Somehow they are linking these retorts to bleed entropy into space and in doing so achieve the temperature of liquid nitrogen. They have knowledge of science and physics in areas that we have never explored. Our world could benefit in so many ways if some of this could be taken back."

Sam stared at his friend thoughtfully and answered, "Only if we make sure that our race cannot come here. It has to be a one-way traffic, John. Think of the exploitation factor. Human beings can never come here in great numbers my friend. By all means take the knowledge back with you, but not the means to get here. We have enough to do in our universe without expanding into this one."

I saw John's face register a great disappointment, but agreement with his friend was uppermost on his features.

"I understand and I do agree with you, Sam. I would like to stay down here with these elves and learn more about what they have achieved. By extending the iron collar around both of our necks we can remain outside of Waldwick's mental powers while we share it and share our minds. 'Shard of light' has agreed to do this with me and explain as much as she can while I in return tell her of human science."

"Do stay here as long as you need to, friend John," I said and turned to go back to the higher levels.

Sam and I walked along the linking parapet from the science halls towards the main hall. Having once had wings I was used to heights, but Sam found it a test to walk along the bridge, as it had very little in the way of sidewalls. We usually constructed bridges from tower to tower for ascetic values, to enhance the symmetry of the castle form. Add the fact that the castle was thousands of years old and the brickwork showed that fact, I could understand why my human friend was nervous!

Whilst we were examining the laboratories, Hoatzin had found the dragon pens and stared through the cage bars at the Quetzalcoatlus with a speculative eye. His elf guide was a trainer of these huge and genetically enhanced beasts. The wingspan had to be fifty feet at least and the head was at least ten, from nose to the peak at the back of the head. The eyes were as big as his fist and the head terminated into a huge, sharp edged, toothless beak. Around the long stiffened neck was buckled a leather harness that anchored back to the pterodactyloid's back legs. A saddle with stirrups, sat securely at the joint of neck to body. A harness had been strapped around the creature's beak and head and the reins tucked into a buckle on the saddle. Hoatzin knew that he had to ride this creature or die trying!

The elf beside him had a bucket full of chunks of rotting meat and she took off the lid. As the smell of the contents reached the nostrils of the Quetzalcoatlus the beast swung round the long beak and uttered a harsh cry. The Mexican had learnt to speak enough of the elfin language from allowing Peterkin to impart the ability into his mind.

"Can I feed him?" asked Hoatzin.

"Human called Hoatzin, I do not need to read your

mind to know that you want to ride him! That is what the bucket of food is for. Gain his confidence by thrusting chunks of this stinking meat into his beak. We feed them that way and he is used to it. Let him gain your scent before you offer him any and wait until he opens his beak."

Hoatzin entered the pen carrying the bucket and stood before a creature of nightmare. The pterosaur towered above him. He had folded his wings and was crouched on all fours with his weight taken at the front end by walking on his knuckles. The head dropped down to his level and the cruel beak rubbed along his neck and shoulder. There was an indrawn hiss from the slitted nostrils as the beast breathed in the unfamiliar scent of human being. The Quetzalcoatlus gave a snort and expelled a breath that could have rendered any other human unconscious! He nuzzled the bucket and opened his beak wide enough that Hoatzin could have climbed inside. The Mexican emptied the bucket into the gaping maw and watched as the creature tilted his head back to swallow the contents.

"Climb up the harness and secure yourself onto the saddle. Do not forget to strap yourself in place. You have no wings! It's a long way down, human," the flyer warned. "Guide him with pressure on the reins and your knees. He will be used to my mind controlling him, but he will respond to how your body blends with his."

Hoatzin seized the harness around the pterosaur's head and swung himself over the great neck so that he could mount the saddle. Once sat in the 'bucket seat' he quickly strapped himself securely in place and found his elfin instructor sat behind him. She wrapped her arms around his body and he was surprised to find how warm she was.

"Dig your heels into his neck and think, 'up' and lean

which way you want him to fly," she said.

The pterosaur turned from the confines of the pen and stepped off the edge of the parapet with wings extended. He caught the morning thermal and began to rise effortlessly into the warming air and above the castle. Hoatzin gasped in amazement, as he was able to see for the first time all of the castle and the terraces built around it.

The view from here was as if he were aloft over a giant sized Machu Picchu, but not built by the Incas. From the castle grounds and buildings the mountain continued up into the sky well above the snow line. He realised by what he was looking at, that the elves had been here a very long time. Hoatzin leant to the left and the pterosaur banked into the same direction and took them over the fields and settlements further down the mountainside. Smaller towns and villages had been scooped out of the sheer sides of the cliffs. The mountain had been collapsed into shelves over and over again. Each shelf of the civilization was terraced and drained into the next one down. Here the elves grew their crops, well away from those that would want to feast upon them. The most alien thing about them was that true to a winged species, there were no connecting roads winding up and down the mountainside. Self-sufficiency was built into each projecting level. Here and there were construction sites where the mountain was being tunnelled into and weakened so that a new scoop would be taken into the heart of the mountain. Hoatzin guessed that it would be here that the mining skills of the dwarves would come into their own.

He leaned to the right and straightened the flight path to travel onwards towards the Plains of Scion and the realm of the dinosaurs. Mile after mile of deep valleys and sheer cliffs gradually gave way to flatter areas where the dinosaurs could penetrate and the tree line gave way to the giant ferns. The distance seemed endless and try as he might he could not see the mountains that encircled the central castle mountain. Wherever Peterkin's lodge was from here was anybodies guess. The wind whistled through his hair and penetrated all the chinks in his clothes. At this height it was colder than he was dressed for and with reluctance he urged the Quetzalcoatlus to bank round and make his way back to the holding pens.

The warmth at his back moved up his body so that the flyer could shout in his ear, "You have done well. He trusts you and will do your bidding. Feed him when you get back. I have business in the lower town below the castle. I will leave you when we are closer to the pens," the elf continued.

After a while he felt a tap on the shoulder and the warmth at his back was gone. The elf soared up into the air above the pterosaur, banked to the right, gave him a wave and dropped down to the township below.

Hoatzin leant forwards and the flyer dropped gently towards the pens, gliding into a landing stall. There was a gentle lurch forwards as the creature dropped to his fists, wrapping the wings parallel to his body. The Quetzalcoatlus lowered his neck to allow his human passenger to slide off onto the ground and waited expectantly for his rider to reward him.

The Mexican laughed at the attentive beast, reached for another bucket of rotting meat and bones. The great beak opened and Hoatzin emptied the contents into the grateful bill. He opened and closed the gate of the pen behind him and just stared at the monster that he had just taken him into the air.

"If nothing else," he thought, "it had been worth coming here just to do that."

With those thoughts uppermost in his mind he returned to the castle to find his friends.

Spencer was stripped off to his toes and washing the grime from the dungeon away from the areas of his body that had resisted his quick wash, before bedding down for the night. The room that he had been allocated had a breathtaking view of the terraced gardens around the castle. He watched fascinated, as rows of elves dropped from the high windows of the building, spread their wings to catch the morning thermals and soared up, to glide out over the fields below. To his eyes they were a beautiful people. It had been a shock to Hoatzin and himself when they had first seen Peterkin's daughter hovering momentarily above the land-cruiser at the Tower of Absolom. She had looked so like the pictures of angels that they had seen in the churches that both of them had frequented as children. It took a while for them to get used to the idea that they were just different.

The morning sun picked out the tiny feathers that covered the out-stretched wings and they shimmered, giving a sparkling effect. In effect the elves had become six limbed beings, as the upper arms and wings had separated from each other. When they flew with wings extended, they clasped their arms together so that only the muscles controlling the wings were active. With a closer look at the elves it soon became clear that they were a totally alien life form from the human beings. They were a humanoid species, but had evolved on a totally alien world where there were similarities to Earth life, but a totally different DNA sequence. The six fingered hands and feet set them apart from any Earth formed life. The two antennae that sprouted from their foreheads and the cat's eyes that could stare un-blinkingly into direct sunlight also made a difference. In the dusk they would expand until the entire coloured iris was taken up by the pupil. This gave the elves' faces a striking effect in poor light, as their eyes would seem to glow with the reflected light gathered in by them. With their pointed ears that sprouted tufts from the tips, they slightly resembled humanoid cats.

He was suddenly aware that he had company. There in front of him, hovering on a thermal, was a female elf staring at him. She tilted to the side and sailed into the room over his head, dropping effortlessly to the floor. Spencer stood transfixed as she walked nimbly towards him. She was un-earthly beautiful and came just up to his shoulders, with the morning sun reflecting from her reddish blond hair. There was an aura of suppressed power about her that was a little intimidating.

The voice was husky and deeper than he expected, as she said, "You are very similar to an elf. More similar than you realise! You look too much like our enemy, for us just to trust you on sight. There are things that I need to know about you that can only be understood by contact with you intimately! I will have the truth from you this very morning!"

She ran her hand down his naked stomach and grasped his rapidly expanding organ. With her other hand she released the ribbons that held her flying leathers together and let them drop to the floor. Spencer could feel the elevated heat from her body as she pressed herself against him and his response was swift. He ran his hands down under her wings and squeezed her buttocks. She gave a little gasp and wriggled upwards directing him into her responsive and very receptive organ with his willing help. Then she wrapped her legs around him, fixing him into full sexual union. He dropped carefully onto the bed and slowly made love to his willing partner, each stroke inwards pushing the elfin body deeper into climax.

"Not quite yet!" she whispered into his coal black ear.

Spencer concentrated all of his mind on delaying the climax as long as he could and as he felt her spasm, let go, over and over again.

Elfin wings had curled around them holding them together, locked into sexual harmony. There was no escape yet.

He felt his partner squeeze him rhythmically until he began to stiffen once more. This time she wrapped her antennae around his forehead and even with the iron collar that each of them wore, Spencer began to feel what she felt, as she also felt his pleasures. Their minds became joined and all of his memories became hers to see and experience. Also he understood a little of her life and registered just who she was!

Upon climaxing again together, he managed to roll off and lay exhausted in mind and body besides Peterkin's mother. She sat up besides him and stretched her arms wide to flex her muscles in contentment. The long reddish hair fell in waves around her shoulders and she began to plait it into two long braids.

"It has been a long time since I was pleasured in such a fashion," Dawn remarked without a trace of embarrassment. "I have learnt a great deal about you, Henry Spencer. I have also learnt that my son was wise in recruiting human beings such as you. He was right in what he said when he told me of your commitment and your sense of honour. Peterkin always was a good judge of character!"

"How will he feel about what we have just done? Will he be angry with me?" asked Spencer with a worried face.

Dawn laughed until her breasts bobbed up and down and she had to hold them still.

"I am an elf! I do as I please, as long as what I do does no harm; it is of no business of anyone else's! Long before your ancestors were being gathered into groups to be sold into slavery, I was living here at this castle. I have seen deep into your mind Henry Spencer. You carry scars of resentment that go as deep as I have seen. There is prejudice against your type of human because of the colour of your skin! Some of the light skinned humans have treated you without respect because of the fact that your skin is black. I understand your anger at the fact that these people once held you as slaves. This is not an elvish idea and the concept disgusts me to the roots of my being. Surely as this was hundreds of years ago that this happened, still yet the feeling lives on!"

"Only the ignorant still feel that I am a lower cast creature. Even after such a long time prejudice still lives on in the minds of some! I have many good 'white' friends that do not feel this way," Spencer replied and began to dress.

A six fingered hand reached round to his face and brought his face to hers. Dawn kissed him long and slow, allowing him to feel the heat of her body close to his before he had buttoned up his shirt. She then ducked away from his embrace and quickly dressed herself in her flying leathers.

"When this business is finished I shall visit you again. I shall not wait another half-hundred years before I taste such fruits of lovemaking again!"

With that remark hanging in the air she launched herself from the window and out into the rising thermals produced by the approaching mid-day sun.

It was a strange feeling to have your mind completely to yourself. I had always been used to the continual mental 'chatter' when I lived amongst my own kind. The years in the dungeons had been unspeakably lonely, cut off from any contact. My people were feeling the strain and conditions inside the castle were very tense. I had used the High King's scrying mirror to hunt for his return and soon found him. The dragons were tired, as he had pushed them hard. I could see by the laboured beat of their wings that the beasts would have preferred to glide. Waldwick would have none of this and blended his mind with the dragon, urging him onwards. Once again I had the company of Sam Pitts and John Smith as he marvelled at the surface of the 'mirror' that was showing a scene many miles away from where we were.

John was more than curious about the scrying mirror and examined the device from every angle. There were no wires to be seen leading away from it, just tilted mirrors on its opposite sides to catch the sunlight. When he touched the mirror it just became a reflective surface and nothing else. It needed a mind of some power to activate it and guide its 'seeking' abilities. I knew better than to get too close, or Waldwick would sense me and I intended to keep him guessing as long as possible.

Sam stared at the image in the mirror and asked me,

"How long do you think it will take him to get back here?"

"He will have to stop soon as the dragons do not fly well at night," I answered. "They will have to sleep somewhere safe at the top of a tree and start at dawn tomorrow. I think that we can expect them late morning."

"Then we shall be ready for them, my elfin friend. As before we do not want to injure his escort unless we have no alternative. You are sure that you want him alive?"

"I do," I answered my command leader, "Oh yes, I defiantly want him alive. He will carry the virus in the same way he had planned to use Ameela and later Mia!"

We walked out onto the terrace that was the landing place for the High King's flying dragon. From here we could see for miles across the rugged countryside that rolled away from the castle mount.

Sam placed his hands upon my shoulders and turned me to face him.

"We will do what we must then, my strange friend. You will stand in full view on this landing parapet, so that you can be easily seen. Have Ameela and Mia in full sight also, to entice him to close on you. Show no sign of being armed or dangerous in any way. Stay calm, as if you are expecting him to negotiate with you. Without any mental contact he will be unable to influence you or anyone else. This will take him outside of his 'comfort zone' and lead him into making wrong assumptions. He will think you weak, as you show no sign of strength or weapons. My men will be stationed all around you, but out of sight."

I looked up at this tall, dark brown, human with great respect and asked, "What do you have planned?"

"I think that he will be so amazed that you are waiting unarmed in front of him that he will try to take you out with the Quetzalcoatlus. A well-placed bullet will stop that dead! When he tumbles off in confusion he will be at your mercy," Sam replied and laughed. "Slip an iron collar around his neck and his mental powers will do him no good whatsoever. His staff of power will not be capable of being wielded, if his mind is cut off. Be assured, should there be any sign of him getting the upper hand, he dies, quickly! I am very mindful that this encounter is just the beginning of the saga, not the end."

"I only asked that you help me free my wife. You have done more than I could ever ask of you, friend Sam Pitts," I said and clasped his hand.

Sam shook his head in disbelief and smiled at me.

"Peterkin my friend, we are here to the end. We are a species that have been honed by war. We are fighters and natural born killers, but we do have honour. You have need of us and what we can do. All of us have the same idea about being here. This is more real to us than the life we left behind us. We could go back at any time. Why would we do that with a job part finished? Your enemy would destroy this world and consume it. We really can't let that happen without a fight. Let's get this part over and done with and then we must plan the next stage."

I bowed my head in acceptance and felt overcome by emotion. These six human beings that I had picked were exceptional men, or were they? I had to ask myself the question that came uppermost in my mind; were other humans the same? In my time walking amongst the human beings I had not thought so at the time. Could I find more if I needed? Maybe I had been unusually lucky in the type of men who had applied to my advertisement. I decided then and there that if the situation occurred again I would leave it in the hands of this man, Sam Pitts, to make the choice. He was a better judge of his fellows than I.

I loosened my iron collar for an instant and that was when I felt Waldwick's probing mind reaching out to the castle. I blocked him out. The use of the portal and everything connected with it had strengthened my mind far beyond the old boundaries that Peterkin the 'Hand of the King' had managed to attain. I listened to his disquiet, as he urged the tired dragon to keep flying towards the silent castle. Soon he would have to direct it to roost in a high tree and rest. Tomorrow all the beasts would be hungry and more difficult to control on the last leg of their journey. The anxiety in the minds of the 'wing' that flew with him was frantically being blocked by each and every elf, as the beasts grew tired. All of the guard were terrified of their king. In all of the tens of thousands of years of elvish history no such emotion had ever been born by an elf. These elves would not fear to change their allegiance to me once Waldwick was defeated.

With that thought uppermost in my mind, I withdrew to consider the situation that would develop tomorrow.

CHAPTER NINE

That night, Ameela and I were visited by my mother. She looked radiant and glowed with a sense of well-being that I had not seen in decades. Ameela had developed that same sense since I had rescued her from the Tower of Absolom. I knew from where it came.

"Mother! What have you been up to? I do not need to read your mind to know that you have been up to something," I said and fixed her with an unwavering stare.

She hummed happily to herself for a moment and smiled at me.

"Peterkin! I have been making sure that these human beings are all that you say they are, that's all. I picked the one who looks so like our adversary. They are indeed a complicated people, my son, but those you picked to aid you are honourable. I do not feel that I need to examine the others. Henry Spencer has elfin qualities. I have mourned your father long enough and I shall meet with him again," replied Dawn candidly.

"Just remember, mother dear, their life spans are so pitifully short measured against ours," I sadly reminded her. "I have learnt to trust these men with my life in situations that would freeze your blood. They are brave beyond the scope of any elf. All of these men have served in their armies as soldiers and have seen their friends die or be wounded. They are battle tested in conditions beyond your imagination."

"Peterkin, I have been inside Henry Spencer's mind and have experienced his past life. I know what kind of man he is. He was a sniper in his army, who was capable of cold bloodily killing people that he did not even know! An elf could not do this act. The High King's guard are not capable of fighting against the dark legions, should they break through the poisoned brier. We need these people far more than the other elves realise. They need to be taught how to fight. Generations of peaceful lives have softened our people. What you have done by bringing them here will tip the balance in our favour. I said that they are complicated people, my son. They are able to balance being possible killers with compassion, love and a nobility of the soul that gives me a sense of humility. I cannot begin to imagine what it must be like to endure this mental silence engendered by the iron collars all of the time. Their minds are shut in, yet they manage to rise above the isolation," Dawn stated and rose up and walked to the open door.

"Mother, tomorrow we must deal with Waldwick. Make sure that you are out of the way of the action when it begins. You may make your entrance once I have an iron collar around his neck! Until then I want to be sure that you and all of the castle-dwelling elves remain collared. It must be driving him mad that the castle is mentally silent."

"I to must hide away, unless he senses me with Mia and drives my mind into darkness," Ameela said and knotted her fists in fury. "There will be a reckoning between us once he is collared. I will come with you, Dawn and wait our time together. Now I will say goodnight. Peterkin and I will need our sleep and I for one will sleep without difficulty knowing that Waldwick uneasily sleeps at the top of a tree."

Many miles away from the castle Waldwick sat hunched against the wind and rain, securely tied to the spindly ferns that bushed out from the highest point. The straps of the dragon's harness were knotted around his wrist. He had 'pressed' its tiny mind to stay near him, but when asleep the mind could wander and so could the dragon. Each elf of his 'wing' was also tethered to their flying beast and Waldwick had pressed their minds as well. As a precaution the High King had dominated the personalities of his guards, so that he could bring them into the gestalt mind that would be controlled by him in the morning.

Still the castle remained silent and not one mind shone in the dark as a beacon for him to plumb for information. He had examined the minds of those who worked the farming levels outside of the castle and had learnt nothing. Whatever had happened inside the castle grounds had not filtered down to the lower ranked elves. Even when he had used the staff of power, he had been unable to find one mind that could give him any answers.

He now regretted not killing Peterkin when he had the chance. Imprisonment seemed a fit punishment at the time when he had found out that his most trusted 'Hand' had got his daughter pregnant! It also gave him the satisfaction of watching him suffer as the years had gone by. Waldwick had never discovered how Peterkin had escaped and it was a complete mystery how he had crossed the Plains of Scion to rescue Ameela from the top of the escarpment. Again and again his mind returned to the question of how could a wingless elf manage to do so much?

Peterkin had never known that it was the High King himself that had engineered the 'hunting accident' that had took his father, Peter's life. A crossbow bolt had ended any possible rivalry for the throne from Waldwick's cousin. Even Aurora's elder sister, Dawn could not be sure that he had killed her husband, although she had her doubts. Her mind was no match for his, so she remained in ignorance and after a century had passed since then, all avenues of investigation had been closed.

He remembered how the 'Old King' had died and had taken all the memories that had been passed down to him from the elder king before him. He had not realised just how much had been forgotten of their origins until he had wrested power from the King. Upon Elweard's untimely death the custodian of the library had hidden the master crystal and had disappeared from the elfin world. Nothing remained of the knowledge of the 'Old Ways' and much of the ancient knowledge had vanished with him. Waldwick had used the staff of power to unsettle the minds of the dragons during a ride over the Plains of Scion. King Elweard's dragon had dropped abruptly out of the sky and tipped him from the weakened harness. He had no time to open his own wings before another wild dragon had picked him out of the air as he was dragged upside down by his foot.

It had been easy for Waldwick to take control and play upon the sympathies of the other elves. Elweard had no heirs to hand over to except Waldwick and Peterkin's father who were loosely related to Auberon, the elder King. The High King's surreptitious use of the staff of power and his augmented mental powers had 'changed' the minds of those who might have apposed him. The addiction to the use of the staff had made him far more ruthless than he had been to begin with. Now the need to be in power was a siren song that throbbed in the deepest reaches of his soul. The iron circuits in the globe at the end of the ironwood wand were tuned to his mind and the crystal amplifier inside those circuits allowed Waldwick to send his telekinetic strength against the legions from Hell. The cost was his diminishing sanity.

Morning dawned with a steady wind blowing from the east. It brought cold rain that penetrated the clothing and chilled the bones. I had the satisfaction of knowing that the dragon riders would be colder than we were and anxious to get home and dry. Crossbows lose a lot of their power when the strings get wet. Everyone of my group wore a Kevlar vest and had oiled and checked their rifles. Sam Pitts had organised the offensive defence very carefully. The dwarves had once again been supplied with AK 47's with magazines loaded with rubber bullets. They were all up higher than the level of the landing parapet and settled into the open windows. Again the idea was not to take the life of any of the elves flying 'wing' by Waldwick's side. I had guessed that a spray of hard-hitting rubber bullets would unsettle the dragons and make them sheer off leaving Waldwick alone. I had no doubt that Spencer would bring down the High King's mount, forcing him to vacate the dragon and fly on his own. He would then be much more vulnerable to my other plans.

We took our breakfast on the terrace, under cover, overlooking the fields below. Spencer spent his time watching the skies with a high-powered telescope while he ate sparingly. I could see my mother watching him and smiled to myself. They were a good match! Steven and David had positioned themselves a level down at the windows of the banqueting hall just in case it was necessary to intervene at the windows at both ends of the long room. Sam and Hoatzin would hide in the tapestries hung at the windows as soon as the 'wing' was sighted. I would stand alone to give him the feeling that I was alone, defenceless and just waiting for him.

Some miles away Waldwick had taken control of the minds of his 'loyal guard' and with them, the minds of the dragons. He could see through all of the dragon's acute vision much better than elvish eyes. From here the castle looked deserted. Even with six dragons independently collecting information for him the answer was the same.

Except for the landing terrace the rest of the castle seemed empty. Not a single mind shone out from the generally teeming building. As they got nearer Waldwick could see that a single elf stood waiting for him to arrive. A mounting rage began to rise in him and was reflected in the reactions of the dragons under his control. The single elf must be Peterkin! Claws spread open the flight of dragons began to swoop towards the single figure, beaks at the ready.

A little earlier, at the castle, the steady drizzle had eased off and a watery sun began to shine down on the parapet. Slowly the puddles began to dry out and the stage was set. On every level of the castle, elves waited for the signal that they could remove the iron collars that shut them off from the usual hubbub of mental communication. Not one dared to release the catches until Waldwick had been captured and collared himself.

After about four hours of watching the skies, Spencer gave a shout, "I see them. There are six dragons with riders bearing to the west of us. They must be several miles out. All I can see at the moment is that they are being ridden slowly, as they are gliding more than they are flapping their wings."

He lay full length along the parapet with a piece of tapestry pulled over his body and cradled the berretta, ready for use. Gradually I could make out the 'wing' as the tired dragons headed for home and the pens. At the lead was Waldwick dressed in bright red flying leathers. I could see that he was holding the staff of power in both hands. He was a mixture of elf and dragon, his mind blended with the beast.

Spencer sighted through the small telescopic mount on the armour-piercing rifle and lined up the crosshairs onto the chest of the Quetzalcoatlus. He had filed off the point of the bullet and cut a cross over the flattened head. The last thing that he wanted was for the bullet to pass right through the beast. He needed to stop it in front of the parapet and have it drop dead to the roots of the castle walls. Spencer was well aware that a ricochet could quite easily hit the rider if it was deflected from a bone. The dum-dum slug would expand in the beast's chest and disrupt its internal organs in less than a second. Death would claim the pterodactyl immediately. The high King would have only moments to disengage himself from the riding leathers and open his wings to escape.

Below him David and Steven had also been primed about their targets should the need arise to kill the Quetzalcoatlus ridden by the five other elves. They too had loaded their berretta rifles with dum-dum bullets as the usual rounds would go right through the pterodactyls and possibly through the elves under Waldwick's control.

My mouth became dry as I watched the approach of the High King and the 'wing' of elves and dragons. Scrutinising the synchronistic advance I became immediately aware that Waldwick was using his mind to control his guard and the other dragons like puppets.

I spoke into the radio link that Sam Pitts had instructed me to use, "Take out all the dragons if necessary. Waldwick has them under his control! Mellitus, spray the incoming wing as they come into range, but leave the King's mount untouched. It may break his control. If not, David and Steven, I want you to take out the nearest beasts to the castle. If they drop in front of the others, the remainder may shear away. If they don't and Waldwick still has control, take them out, but try not to harm the elfin guards. Let them get away from the scene. I am going to make myself obvious and that should make him careless!"

With that message carried to the members of my group,

I stood forwards on the parapet alone and watched the royal dragon set its eyes on my undefended form along with all the others. I waved to Waldwick as he plunged towards me, the dragon's great beak opened to tear me apart. The other dragons were following on and no doubt to make sure that what Waldwick missed; - they would eat!

As the High King flew into range a hail of rubber bullets peppered the backs of the dragons and stung them sufficiently that some wrested themselves from Waldwick's control in panic. It was not enough! Steven and David fired together and tore two of the dragons from the sky. Their riders tumbled off and opened their wings to glide away from the area, free of Waldwick's control. The high King's mind was losing all control as the deaths of the dragons abruptly terminated their consciousness. The others sheered away with the High King's control broken.

They were now close enough for me to recognise the members of the 'wing' who had been under Waldwick's control. I could 'see' the High King's eyes looking at me from the enraged dragon's face as it dived towards me. Twenty feet away from the parapet a large bloody hole appeared in its chest and the wings stopped beating and then underneath him his own dragon stopped thinking. The other dragons came under fire again from above as the dwarves let loose with showers of rubber bullets. Waldwick's control of the three others faltered as his beast dropped from under him and he tumbled through the air towards me, his wings frantically opening. His grip around the staff of power remained, but not for long.

Hoatzin stepped forwards from behind the curtains to the edge of the terrace and the long pliable length of a dragon-hide whip cracked through the air wrapping itself around the staff just below the ball. The Mexican pulled away and the whip wrenched the staff of power from the mad king's hands. The extra pull from Hoatzin caused Waldwick to crunch into the flagstones in front of me. I leapt upon the back of the High King right between his outstretched wings and curled the iron collar around his neck. I snapped the catch shut and tossed the key over the edge of the parapet. The next thing I did was to cut through the main ligaments that powered his wings and watched them go limp as he bled over the flagstones.

In the abrupt silence of his mind, Waldwick began to scream out loud and froth at the mouth, as he fought to release the collar's hold upon his mind. I seized his leather helmet and cracked his head against the hard stone floor, beating him unconscious. I reached round to my iron collar and slipped it loose. My mind reached out to the other non-collared elves still trying to gain control of their flying beasts and the ones that had toppled off.

"Hold! It is Peterkin, come back to the castle. Waldwick is in my power and you need fear him no more. Take the dragons back to their pens and spread the news. The High King is no more. Sanity will now come back to the elvish kingdom. I have him in chains and collared in iron so that his mental influence is finished! The staff of power is mine and I am in no great rush to unlock its powers."

Ameela and Mia approached the unconscious body of Waldwick and Ameela unsheathed an obsidian knife. The point of the knife had already sliced through the strap of his leather helmet and it slipped off to lie in the pool of blood. She knelt in his blood and clasped her fingers in his hair and lifted his head.

"He must pay for all that he has done to us. When he wakes I want him to look into my eyes and know that I am free. Then I shall take his sight from him! The last thing that he will see will be his daughter who he would have given to Abaddon, the Dark Lord," she screamed.

I reached across, disentangled her hand from the mad king's hair, gently took the knife away and said, "Would you be no better than him? I shall send him to Abaddon, infected with the diseases that he planned to impregnate Mia, to live or die at his hands."

I put the obsidian knife back in the sheath that Ameela wore around her waist. My people had regrouped around me and I held the king's head up by the long hair and pulled him into a sitting position, holding my partner close to me with my other arm. My daughter Mia flung her arms around her mother and held to her tightly.

I gave the command, "Sam Pitts, chain him with the special chains we brought with us."

The human smiled and produced a set of wrought iron restraint handcuffs complete with waistband and leg irons that had been bought from a blacksmith who asked no questions. He worked for a Texas sheriff from time to time and was an old friend of Sam's. Once the cuffs were operated, a hidden catch engaged that could not be undone. They had no keys.

I began to be aware of a gathering crowd and an increasing mental chatter as word had been passed on and the iron collars came off. The dwarves had unobtrusively become an honour guard. Dressed in their Kevlar armour and with their beards bushed out from where they had tucked them inside, they looked a formidable group. The unfamiliar weapons drew the eyes of the elves, but my group of humans were the ones that stopped them from looking anywhere else.

I had forgotten that I had lived amongst these people for so long that I had ceased to notice how different they were from one another. Elves all look very similar to human eyes and apart from differing hair colours our skin tones and appearance were of a Spanish nature. I was tall for an elf and still only came up to the human's shoulders. The dwarves came up to their chests!

Hoatzin still held the Staff of power, insulated from its touch by heavy leather gloves. He at least looked like a giant elf, but the others just looked big and very different.

The one that drew the stares the most was Spencer. He resembled the dark elves with his coal black skin, but he was the size of Abaddon and could have been taken for a Dark Lord.

Sam Pitts was a chocolate colour, bald and exuded authority. He had leader stamped all over him and held the chains that the deposed king was tethered to. I owed him a great deal and I knew that in the future I would need his organisational skills even more.

David and Steven were alike as two peas and were white-skinned with blond hair. David had a scar on one cheek where a knife had sliced him on a 'black ops' mission. During my time spent on Earth I had seen pictures of Vikings in history books and had they grown their hair as long, they could have passed as such as they!

John Smith was also pale skinned and not so well built as the others. He was my thinker and engineer as well as a fighter. John was a man of science and had spent a great deal of time at military college where he had learnt far more than he was taught! I was constantly amazed at the knowledge that lay behind his forehead.

These people were my group and my friends. I had opened my mind to them and they to me. We knew each other. Each of them carried a small part of my personality that enabled them to speak the elfin tongue and also the dwarfish dialect. I in turn carried some of them deep inside me. They were not telepaths, although the twins David and Steven had a rapport between themselves that was very close to what an elf took for granted. Through mixing with elves a slow transformation was taking place in the nature of their brains. Certain dormant areas were linking up and forming new neurological pathways. This was definitely happening with the twins as time went by. I could sense this continual change, taking place amongst my new friends.

The fact that my human friends could not shut out the minds of my elfin brethren meant that they could hold no secrets from them. As all elves shared minds; they shared their minds with the humans in response. This rapidly meant that the trust that I had in them was reciprocated on a massive scale. This all happened in moments as the collars came off. I could see that the effect on my friends was overwhelming.

I broadcast on a wide band to all of those minds attempting to reach the humans, "Hold! Retract your efforts to make contact with these humans. They are not equipped to deal with so much. Be gentle with them, as they have no defence. They cannot shield themselves from your most innermost thoughts. They are not natural telepaths! Look at what you have done to our saviours!"

By this time my friends were on their collective knees holding their heads between their hands. I quickly replaced the iron collars around their necks and watched anxiously as the strain of the encounter left their faces.

Sam Pitts still had a secure grip on the chains joining him to the deposed king. He stood shakily upright and wiped the sweat that had poured from his brow.

"I think in future we will keep the collars on, my elfin friend. Your people's friendship is more than we are used to," Sam gasped and looked around at the other members of his group, as they to got to their feet.

"Do not fear my dear friends. There are those amongst us that can train you to control the amount of thoughts that can enter your minds. Your brains are changing and it is elvish in origin so it behoves us to solve the problem."

I could see the deposed king returning to consciousness as he began to squirm inside his bonds. His eyes opened wide and he stared uncomprehendingly at his captor and then at the other 'giants' before his maddened gaze fixed on me. The iron bounds had cut his telepathic powers from the rest of us and he was imprisoned in the silence of the single mind. He had lost a tooth when I beat his head upon the flagstones and spat a bloody gobbet onto the floor.

"Peterkin! You! I should have had you killed," he growled. "You have my kingdom at your disposal and the threat of the Dark Lord to solve. Good luck with it. Will you have the ruthlessness to deal with it? Eh, Peterkin, son of Peter, will you?"

"Oh yes, High King I will deal with it. The first thing I shall do is to send you to him loaded with all those nasty diseases that you planned to give to your daughter and then to Mia. Sam, put this thing into the safe place we made for him."

Sam Pitts waved to Hoatzin and John Smith. The two of them pulled a cage of bronze bars into view and dropped it into place next to the High King's throne. Sam pushed him inside and locked the door, securing the chain to the bars.

"This is where you will stay in full sight until we are ready to use you. Any elf can come and see you. Indeed any elf can bring you food and drink if they wish. I shall not stop them, but if no-one does, then you will just have to make do on what your gaolers bring."

With those words ringing in his ears I put my arms around my wife and daughter and walked away from the throne room.

126

CHAPTER TEN

Several months had gone by and Waldwick's addiction to the staff of Power was slowly being cured, although the withdrawal symptoms were dreadful to experience. He was left in the cage for all to see and to be sure that his power had been well and truly broken. I allowed Aurora to visit him, as long as her two allocated guards accompanied her and the chain from her ankle was fastened securely to one of them.

She fed him and took away his wastes. Now that he was in my power I found that the need for revenge had ebbed away from my mind. It was enough that the iron collar isolated his mind from elfdom. The wrought iron shackles allowed him to walk around his cage and use his hands to groom himself, but they were a heavy load to carry. Waldwick's wings hung at an odd angle due to the severance of his flying ligaments. The wounds had soon healed, but it would be a long time until they would be capable of flight. He would be dead long before then by the 'improved' viruses that he would be carrying into the Dark Lord's presence.

I had set John Smith the task of trying to understand the principals of the Staff of Power. The reason that I did this was that the shadow in my mind recognised the artefact as being similar to something that it had lost. I treated it with caution and I still would not touch it with my naked skin. My band of humans and dwarves had set about exploring the ancient foundations of the castle. With a generator supplying electric lights they had found a wealth of storerooms and chambers deep beneath our feet. What I had supposed the Warlock's rooms were a puzzle to the dwarves. As they were used to mining in the bowls of the earth they had a feel for spaces and three-dimensional areas. Mellitus was sure that the spaces among the position of the Arch were not in the right proportion. Either there were thicker walls than they seemed or something was being hidden from them as they searched.

At the beginning it had been necessary to feed life force into the Arch to activate it. Now that it was fully awake the portal drew power from the sunlight and stored it. For a time I kept the Arch permanently open to the Lodge, so that my group could move back and forth, ferrying useful items from my old home to the castle.

Soon after the fall of Waldwick, John Smith had asked to go back to the human world of the parallel Earth. There were things that he needed from his old civilization that would require lots of money to buy and alter so that my people would not be damaged by the components. He well knew what the effect of refined iron did to the elfin population and needed to lessen the iron content of what he needed. Mostly it was the use of aluminium and harder alloys of this material that would require money to modify. I gave him my 'gold' card and the pin number to activate it.

Three weeks later he reappeared with something he called solar cells that collected and stored the sun's energy as electricity. Now the whole of the deeper reaches of the castle were illuminated. He established a workshop down there where he could experiment and modify the equipment that he brought over. Soon he had something built that he called penetration radar and began to map the unknown reaches of the castle foundations. He also brought over a number of 'laptops' that he incorporated into the systems that he was building. These were all powered from the strange mirror shaped plates that he kept pointing at the sun from morning till dusk. He had directed the elves in my 'guard' to position them onto the outside of the walls of the castle and fix them securely with the battery operated drills and tools that he had brought back. Much of the steel parts he had modified to bronze at some expense so that the effect on the elvish bodies were minimal. Never the less the elves had to limit the amount of time that they spent using the tools and used thick leather gloves when operating the battery driven drills. Dwarves had a much greater tolerance to iron, but unfortunately they could not fly!

Mellitus Hammer-hand and his people had soon put right the damage to the floors done in the fake attacks during our move on the throne room. He had also built a substantial stairway from the banquet room down into the lower levels. New windows were added to let in the light and to feed cables through to John's equipment.

I made sure that the bogymen and their females were regularly fed and left a part of the depths of the castle only dimly lit. I had made it my duty to look after them and they soon showed me the 'secret' way that they had used to drag me into Waldwick's presence. Under the dimmed lights it was easily seen that these poor creatures were goblins that had been denied the light of day for so long that they had mutated into these odd looking creatures. I saw to it that they had ample water and material to wash themselves and they soon preferred to be clean rather than covered with slime. They had long forgiven me the taking of a life to activate the Arch, which enabled me to escape from Waldwick's spite.

John Smith had managed to scrape off a portion of the ironwood staff and took it back to the human world to be carbon dated. It had taken some time, but he now had the results in a 'printout' and he was in a state of excitement when he returned.

I was down below the castle floors, examining the room where I discovered the Arch when the human translated through the portal. The portal was left open from the Lodge where I had left the rift still active from there to the parallel world of the humans. My mental connection to the Arch was such that I was instantly aware of his coming.

The inside of the portal went translucent and John stepped through holding a new laptop. His face was red with excitement and he was out of breath. Wherever he had come from, it had been at a fast rate of travelling.

"Peterkin! What good luck that I should find you here," he said and sat down on a heavily carved chair.

"You seem excited, friend John. What have you found out about the staff of power that should make you so excited?"

"We have a method of searching through the radiation of carbon atoms to give the date of ancient items," he replied and opened the laptop.

He switched it on and I was soon staring uncomprehendingly at figures and graphs outlined on the screen of this small powerful computer.

"John Smith, I am no wiser looking at all the pretty colours and reading the runes, so tell me what you have found," I asked.

"Peterkin, the Staff of Power is very old! It is more than ten thousand years old. What you have been told about it is not true. The meteorite did not fall on this world; it fell on yours! Your race brought it with you when you came here."

I stared at the human who had thrown every bit of his knowledge at the puzzle and followed the thought to its logical end. The scraps of history that had been passed down through the generations told of the elves escaping from a ravaged world. When Waldwick had seized power the custodian had hid the library's master crystal. It was a time of great upheaval within the elfin kingdom. The original king, Auberon had passed his memories down to Elweard as a reference before he had died. Waldwick had wrested power without these memories to draw upon.

My mother had lived under Elweard's reign and had told me stories of our past as her mother had told her. The ship's name had been Spellbinder and it had carried the entire elfin race away from their birthplace. Auberon had hidden it and wiped the hiding place from all of the minds of the elves who had settled here. Mother said that he had decided that this world would be our new home, so after several missions back and forth to the human world to stock up with animals and seeds, he hid the ship.

What I did not know at that time was that the Spellbinder had been stationed on Earth over thirty thousand years ago. Human beings were on the increase and spreading across the lands of Europe at the time. Auberon increased the outer perimeter of the ship's influence and the rate of time inversion, so that a thousand years passed by outside the bubble of the Spellbinder's influence to a century inside. He had taken the last of the dwarves with him before the humans out-competed them from existence. The humans of the present day called them Neanderthals and they had become extinct on their world. Finally the time came, when for several centuries the increasing use of iron, drove Auberon to look for a new secure home world.

I suddenly began to comprehend why the floors above did not allow thoughts to penetrate down here and why it was sealed up. The Arch was part of the ship and that was why the dwarves felt that the dimensions were wrong. I was sat in the control room of the Spellbinder and somehow the Staff of Power was used to guide the ship. Quickly I gently inserted my analysis into John's mind.

His eyes widened as he reasoned out the next step. He leapt to his feet and fell on his knees.

"Look for a buried hole in the floor," he said. "Something that has been filled up with dirt over the thousands of years!

This area is the only part of the castle that the penetration radar will not map. I believe that something has been hidden here!"

We both got down on the floor and followed the edges of the flagstones towards the vicinity of the Arch. John gave a grunt of satisfaction and proceeded to dig with the point of his penknife. Soon there was a hole the same size as the bottom of the staff at the junction of four flagstones, directly in front of the Arch.

"I'll get the staff," said John and disappeared from the room towards his workshop.

I continued to clean out ten thousand years of accumulated dirt from the hole with John's penknife using a pair of leather gloves to minimise the sting of the proximity of iron.

John came running back to the chamber and handed me the staff.

I took the Staff of Power from him and thrust it into the hole. There was an audible peal of bell-like clarity that rang out through every room in the warlock's chambers. The walls began to glow with a silvery light and we could see quite clearly.

"I think that you should take off your gloves, Peterkin and grasp the staff. I have a feeling that you are genetically tuned to this device. Was not the original king one of your ancestors? In fact, wasn't he your great grandfather? Waldwick was not related and that's why I think he went mad after using the mechanism," insisted John.

Something in my mind flooded forwards and I felt the shadow's support to do this. I trusted that strange silhouette in my mind of a greater whole. It had lent its support at opening the rift to Earth and had been there step by step as I painstakingly learnt how to manipulate the Arch. I knew that it was a part of me, no matter how afraid Ameela had been that first time she had found its presence in my thoughts. There had always been a sense of waiting about the shadow that had made its home under my thoughts. I sensed that the waiting had come to an end!

I took off the heavy leather gloves and stretched out my hands to grasp the staff. Before I touched it, I could feel a vibration building up between my very soul and an alien presence. As I grasped the staff, the floor opened beneath me and a command chair rose from its ancient hiding place, for me to sit upon. Around me in a semicircle other chairs emerged from the flagstones. John sat on the one next to me as his legs gave way in shock.

The shadow in my mind turned to light. An intelligence that was built to serve elves expanded into my consciousness. I became aware of the ship all around me that lay buried inside the very stones of the chambers. The Spellbinder existed trans-dimensionally within the atomic structure of this world. It was similar to a giant soap bubble co-existing inside the fabric of the castle walls.

"Where is Auberon?" asked the mind within mine.

"Long dead, Spellbinder," I answered. "Ten thousand years have passed since you were hidden here."

"You are of his line. You may command me. What manner of creature is this that sits beside you? It is not an elf!"

I grasped John's hand and gradually let his mind open within mine and connected him to Spellbinder.

"He is a human being and a friend. There are five more of these beings within the castle. Without them we could never have over-thrown the false king," I explained to the mind that guided the ship.

"Welcome, John Smith," Spellbinder replied. "Your mind is full of questions. Some of them I can answer and some I cannot. I too have much to catch up with since I was

133

deactivated so long ago. Peterkin I am aware that your use of the trans-dimensional gate has been such that you have left two wormholes open. This is a strain in the fabric of reality! You must close them down before a permanent kink is forged."

I rapidly did this by running my mental fingers over the runes set in my mind and closed them.

Spellbinder re-entered my mind and said, "There is another wormhole being held open! A constant flow of life from another universe is holding it ajar. There is an injured mind similar to mine that is involved. I feel that it is insane! It will not answer me!"

"Abaddon has maintained a portal between our old world and this one for centuries. There is a constant migration from Aifheimr to here. We the Ljo'sa'lfar have penned them out of our kingdom with the poisoned brier for two hundred years. How much longer we can keep them out I just do not know. Spellbinder, my first order is not to answer the other ships' mind. Do not contact it at any price! We have a conflict with the Dokka'lfar (dark elves) that cannot be resolved as long as they continue to reproduce without control. They would destroy this world with their rapacious ways."

"It was a sad day that after Deedlit finished constructing me and gave me to Auberon, he chose death of his body rather than let the secrets of my assembly fall into Abaddon's hands. His mind and a copy of Freyr, last High King of the Ljo'sa'lfar, who fought to keep the dark elves out of our kingdom, are woven into my sphere of consciousness along with other elvish minds. All of their memories are yours to read and understand. You are descended from kings, Peterkin. If you were not then you would be in the same state as Waldwick! I have severed all connection with Dream-shifter and it is locked into eternal madness. The portal remains open however. Abaddon keeps it open by feeding the lives of the dark elves into its vortex. Whoever built the Dream-shifter did not have all the knowledge of Deedlit's crafts. He must have found just enough information to build something similar to me, but not enough to perfect it! Destroy the ship and the portal goes with it," Spellbinder declared.

It was too much to completely comprehend and I rested in the command chair for some moments before I gave my next order.

"Spellbinder, take the ship out of the castle walls and restrict the size to this control room and whatever else is necessary to maintain yourself," I ordered.

The edges of reality shivered and a soapbubble translated beween the stonework and ourselves. We slowly moved through the wall and floated outside the vertical walls of the castle. The flagstones remained beneath our feet and the walls of the vessel stayed of a stoney composition about knee high. The rest of the bubble was transparent, except for the Arch. This remained solid stone except for the centre that seemed to be made of solid fog! I visulised the parapet outside of the throne room and the fog dispersed to become that place. As it did so the bubble was there! It settled with its nose projecting over the stonework and anchored itself to the castle wall. John and I walked through the Arch and looked back at the Spellbinder. All we could see was the stone arch and a distortion behind it. I had to remind myself that it was there. This ship had once transported the entire Ljo'sa'lfar nation of light elves and the ancesters of the dwarves to this world with all of its livestock and plants.

As I stood there trying to come to terms with all that had happened, my mother's mind slipped into mine.

"Peterkin! What have you awakened? Your mind has

altered! Somehow there is more of you."

I gave a shaky laugh and replied, "Mother I am related from kings! I have the mind of a king! Indeed I seem to have more minds than I can count! Mother dear I have found the Spellbinder and activated it. There it is on the edge of the parapet."

My mother appeared with Spencer at her side. I noticed that he looked tired and she was radiant. Ameela and my human friends had also joined the group that was increasing by the moment. They were all staring at the impossible ship that lay like a giant soap bubble fixed to the ramparts.

"What the hell is that, Peterkin," Sam Pitts asked.

"It's the ship my ancestors came to this world in, my human friend. And yes, it was a whole lot bigger then! In fact it would seem that I could make it become whatever size that I require.

We all heard the bubbling scream from the cage behind us as Waldwick caught sight of the trans-dimensional ship. A 'coldness' in my mind recognised him and the mind of Elweard made contact with me.

"Assassin! This elf caused the mortal body of mine to die at the jaws of a wild dragon," the clear voice of the ancient king rang clearly in my mind. "Mind-ream him and discover all you need to know about his treachery."

I swung away from the Spellbinder and strode across the intervening space towards the caged ex-king. My leather boots made a slapping sound that echoed around the throne room. He was pressed against the farthest bars of the cage and his face was white with fear. Even through the iron collar his mind had caught the edge of the multi-mind that was Spellbinder. I opened the cage door and hauled him to me by the chain that was fixed to his manacles. His grip upon the bars broken he scrabbled on the barred floor of the cage without impeding his journey to my hands.

With the power of kings I pressed my hands to the sides of his head and extracted all of his sins. Everything that he did not want others to know streamed into my mind. I did not need to dig very far as the mental resistance crumbled.

When Waldwick cut through the harness of the King's mount, I was there. Elweard's expression of horror when he fell from his seat, caught up by one foot and unable to cut himself free, as he dangled in front of Waldwick, was printed deep in his memory. The attacking dragon that swept him away before the guards had time to stop it with crossbow bolts had been 'pressed' into service by the assassin.

Next, I saw my father die in front of Waldwick, as he altered the mind of a guard to see my father as a dragonet during a hunt. The crossbow bolt took him through the head before he had time to see it coming. A second bolt entered the chest of the dragon he was mounted on and the two of them dropped down to the Plains of Scion. Predators made short work of the bodies and there was nothing to bring home and bury. Minds had been altered to tell a different story when the hunting party got back to the castle.

Other shameful actions were shown to me as I threw him back into the cage and I slammed the door. This was a dark elf living amongst us and ruling us for his own ends. I felt my mother's touch upon my shoulders and her rage, as she had 'heard' all of Waldwick's terrible crimes against elfdom.

"Dokka'lfar!" she screamed. "You robbed me of my mate. Peter had the blood of kings running through his veins. His son will make a far better king than you. He will solve the problem of the dark elves. Abaddon will welcome you as one of his own. The Ljo'sa'lfar will give you to him as a parting gift. I will bide my time and wait for your own scientists to infect you with the hell spawn that you would have given to your grandaughter. Then I shall be there when you are dropped the other side of the poisoned brier! Now that my son has activated the Spellbinder we shall all live to see the end of the dark elves on this world. Peterkin has made good friends amongst the humans. We have the resources of their people to call upon and they are more skilled in the ways of death that you can imagine!"

She spat through the bars and into his face before he cringed into the back of the cage again.

By the shocked faces around me it would seem that my mother was not the only one to receive the overflow of my mental broadcast. The group who were with me at the throne room now knew Waldwick's sins. By night time it would have travelled around the whole community. Soon every elf would have passed on the knowledge throughout the kingdom. It was written in our very souls that elf did not raise their hand against elf! Something had corrupted Waldwick's soul to make him act the way he had. There was no way that I could tell whether it was born in him or placed there. Our ancestry goes back a long time and a mixing of the blood is not impossible.

There was one thing that that had become apparent to me since I had joined my mind with the Spellbinder and that there were subtle differences between my mind and the other elves. None of the other elves could 'hear' the voices in my mind of the long dead kings. Unlike the others of my kind, I could kill another elf. I would send Waldwick to his death at Abaddon's creatures without a trace of remorse.

A voice whispered into my mind, "It is a kingly ability, passed down from king to king. It is in the genes, my grandson. You will learn to live with it as did we all. We are here when you have need of us," Auberon reminded me. "Only then!"

I shuddered and walked away from the cage. My mother caught the stray thoughts that eddied from my mind and threw her arms around me.

"My beloved son. Whatever you are, you are still Peterkin, as well as king. I am your mother, flesh of your flesh. When I carried you I was aware of the others that you carried deep beneath the surface of your thoughts. They would not talk to me, only to reassure me that you were special."

I kissed her brow and set her down.

"Gentlemen," I said to my group, "there is much that I must think about. Things have changed far beyond the boundaries of my experience. We now have an edge that needs to be used in the best of my newfound abilities. Before we sit together and plan the next step I need some rest."

"Sire! Sire!"

I turned and saw an elderly gnome walking with some difficulty with the aid of a stick. He was carrying a leather pouch hung over one shoulder. I could not read him, as his mind was the foggiest that I had ever met.

"My name is Boddywinkle. Ranzmut, Boddywinkle my liege and I have something that has been in my keeping for centuries. The custodian gave it to me before he left the castle, knowing the Waldwick would never think of a lowly gnome as a hiding place. Here Sire is the master crystal of the elvish library. It is rightfully yours."

With that small speech ringing in my ears he placed the leather pouch into my hands.

I opened the bag and an amber crystal lay in the palm of my hand the size of a hen's egg. This was the key to the great crystal library that had been brought from the home world, Aifheimr. It contained all of the elfish knowledge that had been discovered and the records of my race.

In one day I had restored Spellbinder to life and awareness, found out that I was of royal lineage, with the minds of long dead kings tucked away in my subconscious. Now I also had the library restored to my kingdom's brightest minds.

I stood straight and tall and took a deep breath.

"Ranzmut, I thank you with all of my heart. If there is anything that you need, then all you need do is to ask for it and it will be yours. John Smith, I think that you might like to care for this packet of information and unravel it with the aid of the scientists in the laboratories below. I for one must go and rest my mind before it explodes!"

As the sun went down that night, my ancestors and I entered a restful state of sleep filled with other peoples' dreams.

CHAPTER ELEVEN

Waldwick's old rooms caught the morning sun as it rose over the mountains, filling the walls with pink and then rapidly gold. The tapestries hung around the walls soon gave up their pictures from the darkness. Now that I had the mind of Spellbinder at my disposal along with those of the kings who had gone before me, I understood them at last. Before, they had remained a puzzle to me, as there was little on them that related to this world. My mother's stories had filled in some of the blanks, but without a clear knowledge of history, most of the figures depicted were strangers to my mind.

One large tapestry hung at the head of the bed, lit by the morning sun. It depicted a hill surrounded by a living sea of beast-like elves the like of which I had never seen. The lone figure facing the hoards of the Dokka'lfar holding a star aloft in his hands was Freyr, High King of my people. He was bathed in silver light from the star, whilst behind him the Ljo'sa'lfar were streaming into a giant transparent bubble at the top of the hill.

The dark elves were bowing down and turning away from the light in terror. At the back and urging them on was a larger black figure that could only be Abaddon. He was drenched in darkness and from that curtain wriggled more of the dark elves. The impression that the tapestry gave me was that there was an endless number of the hoard behind him. They were thin, starved and so very ugly.

I looked upon the tapestry with new understanding. Whilst Ameela still slept I communicated with my inner voices and I reached for Freyr.

"Tell me what was done here, High King?"

The voice in my mind spoke, "I stood in the path of the multitude of the Dokka'lfar and fed my life energy into the 'Star of Light' until my people had escaped through the multiverse. When the last of them had gone and the Spellbinder with them, I let the light wink out and died."

The horror of the situation welled over into my mind and I understood just what the term, High King really meant. Freyr had given his life to save his people. The 'Star of Light' had driven the dark elves away and protected my people. It had burned itself out, taking the life energy of the High King with it. The weapon was a single use device, requiring self-sacrifice to power it. Would I have the courage to lay down my life as Freyr had? I was his descendant and had 'the blood of kings' running through my veins, but was I the 'stuff' of kings?

Ameela had woken.

"Do not doubt that for one moment, my love," a silvery voice spoke in my mind. "I know of no other elf that has opened up a rift to another world, carried out a rescue across the Plains of Scion and awoken the Spellbinder! You and you alone have done these things, bringing allies into our world from a place so dangerous that the place still scares me even now!"

I turned to Ameela and bowed my head to her wisdom and replied, "I never sought the position of High King. All I wanted was to save you and make you and Mia safe."

"Peterkin! My love and protector; that is what makes you so special to me and to your people. What scares me so is that you would do what Freyr did if it was necessary. I could not bear to lose you that way. I would be there next to you if it came to that. Do not think that you would go alone!"

"Ameela! Do not cry so! Stop this sadness. What will be will be, but I have friends that will help us. Freyr had nobody but himself at that terrible time. The humans think differently to us. I shall use that edge without remorse and rid this world of the scourge of the Dokka'lfar forever. Now I must dress and walk amongst my people. It is time to form a council of war consisting of all representatives from the two worlds. We need humans, dwarves, gnomes and goblins to sit down with one another and plan. Do not forget we have other allies living on the Plains of Scion. I will need to speak with Prime and her people. She knows that the threat is against her people as well as my own."

"You are the High King, Peterkin, without any doubt," Ameela replied and hugged my naked body to her, wiping the tears from her eyes with my hair. She curled her wings around me and placed her hands upon the scars on my back, willing the new life to take hold in the cauterised stumps. For a moment I could feel an itch within the scars respond to her will and then, nothing. It would take a long time for my wings to regenerate if at all and I knew better than to hope for too much.

By mid-morning I had the eight of the banqueting hall tables arranged to form an octagon with a hole in the centre. Benches and chairs were arranged around the conference table so that any who felt that they had anything to offer could sit. My human friends had reduced the density of the iron collars around their necks, so that they could send and receive, but without having to cope with the volume of mental chatter that would have rendered them mad. Day by day their telepathic abilities grew a little stronger, but they were a long way off being to walk amongst elves without some kind of shielding.

I stood at the table, faced my council and said, "Members of the elfin kingdom, I bid you welcome to the war council. The problem of the Dokka'lfar has been with us for over two hundred years. Waldwick has done his best to keep them from flooding into the kingdom by using the Staff of Power. It was never his to use and he has paid the ultimate price in madness. His plan to use his daughter and then his granddaughter to spread sickness amongst them still has some merit as a plan. I shall use him as the carrier. By now you know his past crimes, so it is fit that he be chosen to do this. John Smith, I would like your opinions about this."

As I sat down, John stood a little uncomfortable and replied, "There is one problem with that idea. Once he is carrying the viruses, he will be as infectious to the elves, as he will be to the Dokka'lfar. I will need to go back to the human world and get an isolation suit. This would encase him in an airtight plastic suit fitted with breathing filters. The virus could then be introduced into the suit through a one-way system and then he could be carried by the Spellbinder to the other side of the brier. Once the suit is breached, the virus will do its work amongst Abaddon's dark elves."

"I will arrange a trip back to Earth for you John and if there is anything else that we may need, I am sure that Sam Pitts will have some ideas about what to purchase." I could see that Mellitus wanted to speak and said, "Hammer-hand, you have the floor," and sat down again.

Mellitus swept the room with an embarrassed glance before he spoke.

"We have a unique gathering here, my friends. The dwarves and the gnomes have both fought alongside humans with High King Peterkin, here and on the Plains of Scion. All of us are in debt to the Ljo'sa'lfar. Without your help many thousands of years ago, we would all be extinct had we stayed upon the human's world. We owe a blood debt to the elves and the time has come to pay it! Now we are armed as never before. The dwarves are

144

not sensitive to iron as are our elvish brethren. There are many weapons that the humans use that can be used by my people. If the Spellbinder can pass them through the rift, then dwarves and goblins will be able to learn how to use them. I propose, that we find out if more can be brought through onto this world. They could be set down just this side of the poisoned brier for us to practise and gain the knowledge of how they work. We would need them anyway to control the dragons that live there!"

As Mellitus sat down the aged gnome, Ranzmut Boddywinkle climbed shakily to stand upon the bench, supported by a younger gnome.

"I have kept the custodian's master crystal for all the years of Waldwick's miss-rule, waiting for the rightful High King to appear. In the records of the elfin sciences are many things that have been forgotten by the elves, born after Waldwick's rule. I propose that teams of elves and gnomes comb those records for anything that can be turned against the Dark Lord. I also propose that groups of gnomes accompany elves and dwarves to the area that the human weapons are taken, if it is possible. With my people situated around the perimeter of those learning how to use the human's weapons, Abaddon will be unable to read their minds. He will not know that we are there! We may be small, but we have that useful ability. Call upon it at your will, High King and it is yours to use as you think fit."

Waldwick's commander of his guard stood next. Eduardo was tall for an elf. He had served Waldwick as his second 'Hand' and was one of the guards that had held me down, when the High King had sliced off my wings. Calando his brother sat beside him shifting about in his seat with embarrassment. It was he who had applied the red-hot irons to my back to seal the wing stubs and poison them. I knew that both of them had been just instruments of Waldwick's hatred for me. His mind had dominated them, but the memory of what they had been forced to do was always in their minds.

"My liege, I propose that we establish a spying post as close to the brier as we can, protected by the gnomes ability to create a mental fog around us. We can take the new improved crossbows that you brought from the human world. The bolts are tipped with pure iron and once in the flesh of any Dokka'lfar they will ensure that they die! If we take a flight of dragons with us, we can each take a gnome aloft to make sure that although we may be seen, we cannot be controlled and our minds remain our own! If we are well gloved, maybe we can stand the proximity of iron in the AK 47's that our dwarfish friends can wield, sufficient to be able to use them as well."

"All of you have given thought to all aspects of the problem. Well done all of you," I said as stood and looked with pride upon my 'War Cabinet.' "Eduardo and Calando you have raised a moot point. It is time we found out more about the elves tolerance to iron. The fact, that all of you were able to wear an iron collar to stop Waldwick from communicating with your minds, shows that there may be more tolerance than you think. The thing to do is to find out! Report back to me this afternoon. The rest of you will assemble here tomorrow morning with supplies and ready to travel on board the Spellbinder. Any questions, seek me out. I'm off for lunch. John and Sam come with me and tell me what we need from the human world."

At lunch I sat with all six of my human friends along with my family. Bowls of stewed dragonet with vegetables and bread rolls soon put paid to our hunger. As we finished our meal with fruit, freshly picked from the castle gardens, I opened the discussion with my human friends.

"Are there any other things that we should need to do?"
I asked.

Sam Pitts bit into a juicy apple, chewed, swallowed, wiped his chin and said, "Yes there is one thing that we the human part of this conflict need. We need to know our enemy. We need to know what sort of adversary they are capable of becoming. What I propose is that we capture some of these Dokka'lfar and study them. The other thing that you need to be certain of is whether your people are capable of killing them. I remember something that you stated a while ago. Elves do not raise their hands against elves. The fact that these are dark elves may make no difference! All of us need to know that once armed with our weapons, your people will be capable of using them."

I sat confused as I brought those statements to my mind. I knew that I could kill, as I had done so on the human world in self-defence. It was a salient point that Sam had brought up.

It was Ameela that ventured an answer.

"I spent ten long years fighting for my life and the life of Mia on top of the Tower of Absolom. My soul has been hardened by those experiences so do not be shocked at what I propose. Sam is right in what he says. In our recorded history the elves have been pacifists and never raised violence against there own kind. We do not know what manner of elf these dark one are. As Sam says, we will have to capture some of these Dokka'lfar and keep them for study. We also need to know how to kill them and whether the Ljo'sa'lfar can learn the art of inflicting death. I propose that we build a stockade that has an arena built into it. Here inside that arena will be our training and fighting ground. This is where we find out how hard it is, to kill a dark elf!"

"A brilliant idea, High Queen," said Sam Pitts. "We need

to start work on this as soon as possible. The fact is, if any of them escape they will not live long in the prehistoric jungle and plains outside of the stockade. We also need Prime and her people. They could camp outside or inside whatever they felt easier with. Peterkin you need to meet with her again and ramp up the relationship."

"A good point, Sam and everything else that has been discussed this morning and this lunchtime," I replied.

John Smith raised his hand and I nodded.

"When Sam and I go 'shopping' I think that two isolation suits should be purchased. Before we drop Waldwick over the poisoned brier, we need to know how effective the viruses are that his scientists developed in the laboratories beneath our feet. We also need to know how long do the viruses remain active and how fast do they work. Do they die with the infected elf or linger on after death? I spent some time at a biological research unit during my time with the U.S. Army, so I do have some knowledge of this kind of warfare!"

I wondered to myself as I sat there, just what other tricks and training my six mercenaries had brought with them. These human beings had been born into another society that could consider acts of violence beyond anything that an elf could envisage. I shuddered inside, as I considered the consequences of bringing these people through the Rift. They would become the greatest weapon that the elves had ever envisioned. All of them were now rich men far beyond what they had ever thought to be and yet each and every one of them was determined to stay and fight for my people. In fact I was quite sure that all of them wanted to stay here after they had solved my problems. Whilst Spencer had proved that they were sexually compatible with elves, no progeny would result from that union and what little I had learned about humans was that they desired family.

This would be a problem for another time and there was much to be done before then.

Eduardo and Calando, both carrying Kalashnikov AK 47's, visited me that afternoon with a feral grin upon both of their faces. They were both wearing light leather gloves and flying leathers.

"High King," Eduardo said, "as you can see, we have persuaded Mellitus to allow the two of us to keep a rifle each. We can use them! As long as we use gloves to make no skin contact with the iron parts of this killing device, there is no problem! The important fact, is that my brother and I can keep in telepathic contact even allowing the close proximity of the iron. The rifles do not inhibit sending and receiving the same as an iron collar."

"I am not surprised, as these AK 47's were modified on Earth to have as much of the steel parts replaced with wood and bronze. Never-the-less it was necessary for you to find out what they would do. Mellitus would not let you try an unmodified rifle, just in case of accidents. Be careful when reloading with fresh clips of ammunition, as some of the bullets are pure iron. These were to make sure that we kill Dokka'lfar more easily when we meet them. The dwarves have used them as you know with many different types of ammunition. They are only one of the many weapons that are common on the human's world," I reminded them. "Make sure that the safety catches are on at all times, as you are not used to these killing devices."

They both nodded and stood waiting for my next instruction.

"Tomorrow we will travel inside the Spellbinder to the edge of the brier. Do not think that the new weapons will stop dead all of the beasts that live on the Plains of Scion. Remember that we need to build a stockade that is secret

149

from Abaddon's attentions. Make sure that you take all that you need to make a secure camp. The humans will be in charge and you will obey any of them as if they were myself. I must travel on through the Rift to the human world to take Sam Pitts and John Smith to where they can procure the many things that we will need in the near future. We will also be taking Waldwick as well. You two I charge with the task of keeping him safe and well. No matter what, do not remove his collar that is locked around his neck. Remember what he forced you to do to me!"

"Sire that memory sours my mind and fills me with grief. Neither of us will ever forget what he made us do to you. We would not allow that to happen again. It is a great trust that you empower us with, High King and I implore you to look into our minds and see that we are loyal to you."

I looked into their minds and could only see that these two brothers were totally mine in body and soul. Not forced to be as they were to Waldwick, but through deeper feelings of a loyalty freely given, not taken. In turn I was responsible for them with the entire elfin kingdom and those responsibilities weighed heavily upon my shoulders.

"I will see you in the morning, my friends. Adventure beckons us all and I do not know how many of us will live to tell our descendants of what we did. All that I do know is that we defeat Abaddon or lose all that we have achieved on this world," I said and sat down, waving them away.

Ameela and Mia joined me as I sat in the seat staring out over the elfin lands that stretched to the horizon. The room that I occupied was a corner situation that caught the rising and setting sun through the high windows. In the afternoon sun I could see elves working in the fields that were cut out of the side of the mountain as descending terraces. I could see orchards and grasslands brought from Earth long ago. Cattle, sheep and pigs foraged for food with fowls of all kinds pecking amongst them. The high parts of the mountains had been seeded with life taken from the world of the humans when we came here.

Very little of elfin life had been carried across from our world of Alfheim during the crossing. My new memories told of a great exodus that had just vacated the old world in time to stop being food for the Dokka'lfar. The dark elves were cannibals that ate their own kind and viewed my people the Ljo'sa'lfar or light elves as no more than an easy meal. My home world had once been fair and abundant until some mutation amongst us had brought the dark ones into being. To begin with they were just an oddity within our people until they began to breed and breed. As elves lived extraordinary long lives measured against humans it took some while before we realised just what was happening. We controlled our rate of reproduction so that our numbers were never a strain upon our world's eco-system.

If the Dokka'lfar broke through the poisoned brier into the Plains of Scion they would kill and eat every living thing until they reached our carefully nurtured lands. They numbered in the millions against our thousands. Ameela being so young had let her egg go in the moment of passion and had become pregnant at her very first lovemaking. Mia was one of the few children that we allowed to come into this world and I loved her dearly. The three of us sat watching the sun go down, hand in hand, thinking about the morning to come.

That morning every elf that had been 'pressed' into the palace guard had made their way to where the Spellbinder was fixed to the parapet outside the throne room. They numbered but a few hundred grim determined souls. My small group of dwarves had marshalled them into groups, dividing them into riders with dragons and foot patrols. Sam Pitts had organised the available weapons amongst the groups. Crates of ammunition and other equipment were stored ready to be loaded. The dragons wore blindfolds so that they would not panic. Waldwick's cage had been dragged onboard by the humans and had been set down. Eduardo and Calando sat close enough to keep him safe from being harmed by other angry elves.

I opened Spellbinder with my mind and watched as the reality shifter extended its volume to accommodate our requirements. As the members of my group of newly armed 'men' marched aboard I became aware of a rising tumult behind me. A large contingent of elfin females began to make themselves known, as they strode unflinchingly towards the Spellbinder.

"High King! We are going too! We can use a crossbow, as well as any of our men," called out an elfin lady that I did not know. "You will need all the willing hands that are available. So, do not think that we are going to be left behind while our mates fight and maybe die without us being there!"

I gestured to the still expanding soap bubble of the Spellbinder's mass and said, "Ladies, come aboard and welcome. We are going to the most dangerous place that I know of, the Plains of Scion! There we must build a beachhead and hold it against the beasts that dwell there. Our geneticists will sow a circle of the brier around you. It will take a little time to get started, but once it has taken root, you will be safe behind it. I shall have to leave you there to settle into the place. You can call it Haven, as it will protect you from the beasts, but watch the skies! Now once the gnomes are aboard we will go."

A dark cloud seemed to obscure the window and I looked upon a sight that took me by surprise. Hovering upon the morning thermals were hundreds of elves from the towns below the castle and the farms that stretched away from our home. They were drifting towards the parapet to join the throng that were boarding the Spellbinder. They brought axes, farming tools and weapons with eager hands to use them. A single collective thought echoed in my mind.

"We are your people. We will go where the High King goes and if we must die to keep what is ours, then we will give our lives gladly for that one idea."

The song of my people sang in my mind and spirit, for a moment filling my eyes with tears. More and more of them came from the lower towns as I watched, flapping their wings strongly to catch those elusive early morning thermals. Each of them was determined to do the bidding of the High King no matter what it cost them.

I watched until every soul was safely aboard and took my seat behind the Staff of Power. Taking off my gloves, I held the Staff with my right hand and became the Spellbinder! The two of us became one entity and each king laid his essence into mine. I became many and I became one! The mind of Spellbinder and High King altered reality and weightless as a soap bubble we soared aloft, speeding over the Plains of Scion towards the brier and the Great Gorge.

CHAPTER TWELVE

My view from the Spellbinder was incredible. I saw not from my eyes, but the full range of the senses that the ancient 'machine' was capable of. We had climbed to a height of five miles and the lands of the elfin kingdom spread beneath us. From here I could view the high mountain that the castle was built upon. The icecap at the top clung to every nook and cranny with the lower reaches melting into thousands of streams. These joined up to become rivers that tumbled down the gorges and spread out through a network of valleys onto the Plains of Scion.

Some of the rivers emptied into a great lake system that interconnected throughout the great basin. One large river over a mile across found its way to the great gorge. This was a thirty-mile wide split in the land that cut through the crater rim. Two hundred million years ago an asteroid had hit the Earth full tilt and had destroyed the land that it had hit. It had thrown up a circular mountain wall over a mile high a thousand miles across. In the centre a great volcano had burst from the ground and had built a cone several miles high. Over the millions of years this had crumbled down and weathered into the mountains and valleys that surrounded the castle. Tectonic plate movement had pushed the surrounding mountains even higher at the edges opposite the great gorge and had tipped the gorge area downwards. New icecaps fed more rivers that fed both sides of the mountains.

A hundred million years ago in the long past this ridge had sunk, allowing the waters to empty through the gap and on to the sea. The great gorge remained dry and passable for several million years as the river occupied the centre. Many dinosaurs had made their way inside the old crater and onto the Plains of Scion. Over time the river had spread out into a great swamp and delta filling the gorge, thus trapping all life inside the mountains and the crater walls. Here isolated from the remnants of Pangea and other evolutionary forces, life had remained locked inside a theatre.

The super continent had broken apart long ago and seas had filled in the gaps ending the great drought. Only the minor continent had remained untouched by Pangea's drought due to the immense mountain ranges that cupped the inside, where the elf's kingdom lay. On this parallel Earth the asteroid that had ploughed into the bay of Mexico had hit this world a glancing blow on the other side of this world, sixty-five million years ago. The lands cupped inside the mountain ranges did not suffer the ravages of the firestorm. Also the arrangement of the tectonic plates had been different on this slightly smaller world. John Smith had explained all of this to me from the books that he had brought over to my world.

Inside Spellbinder, the walls had become slightly translucent having the appearance of solid fog. From outside, the ship had the look of a bend in the light warping the clouds on the other side of it. Only from the control room could the visitors look out. Sat around me were my human friends, my family and Mellitus Hammer-hand. Stood by my side was the ancient gnome, Ranzmut. The Spellbinder was carrying more than a hundred gnomes and the mental fog that they produced made the ship mentally invisible too. I sat in the control seat with the Staff of Power between my knees, clasping it like a giant gear lever and directing the Spellbinder to my will.

As I sat, eyes tightly closed, but seeing through the ship's senses I was aware of every mind on board. The strength of these minds helped to power the Spellbinder and enabled it to twist reality to our needs. Life force was part and parcel of the very essence that made the Spellbinder a reality in its own right. I had partially awoken it, by feeding the tiny souls of the rats that I broke against the Arch. When I killed one of the mutated goblins against the runes, it was just sufficient for me to activate the arch and take it to the Lodge. Now that it was fully awake, the death of any living creature was now unnecessary to keep it fuelled. It drew its power from the sun and the proximity of elves.

I reached out to the humans that had pledged their lives in my service and included them in the sensory loading that the Spellbinder was furnishing me. Ameela, my mother and Mellitus also blended into the mixture and gazed in wonder at the unfolding scenes underneath us. We were approaching the encircling mountain range and the great gorge. A bright sun shone upon the ice-covered peaks reflecting the white inhospitable high reaches. Here the air was too thin to breath and made a natural barrier to the Dokka'lfar, keeping them out of the kingdom.

As we began to drop into the edge of the gorge the full extent of the brier began to be seen. The elfin genetic engineers had set a limit to the extent into the Plains of Scion or the brier would have taken over every inch of the crater. The leaves were of a dull waxy green and the stalks that brandished them were of hard wood carrying thorns the size of swords. The leaves were covered in stinging needles that easily detached and hung heavy with poisonous sap. Each plant vied with its neighbour for its share of the sun. The result of this was an impenetrable mat of thorns, stinging leaves and dripping, sticky sap and as the brier flowered, the scent induced vomiting to those unlucky enough to be close by. The seedpods exploded when ripe, scattering the sharp edged seeds like shrapnel. It had kept the Dokka'lfar at bay for more than two centuries.

The dwarves had sacrificed themselves in front of the freshly growing brier and kept Abaddon at bay until the brier had presented the impenetrable barrier that it was today. More than a thousand dwarves had died in that fierce fighting. It had not been forgotten that High King Waldwick had abandoned them to the cannibalistic dark elves. A new generation of dwarves had pledged allegiance to the new High King. Peterkin had brought arms from the human world and was willing to risk his own life in ensuring the safety of all who lived in the elfin kingdom.

Mellitus Hammer-hand had made it very plain that this High King was of the 'old blood' and would not abandon anyone. He was anxious to make contact with the dwarves who had settled this side of the brier to keep the Dokka'lfar from flying over the brier. His first priority was to show these suspicious dwarves the new weapons that Peterkin had brought from the human world. There was a group on each side of the great gorge living and mining the mountains with no contact with each other except by the difficult route along the edge of the brier. They had been there since the conflict had begun and watched the difficult overland route, picking off every dark elf that tried to climb across the high reaches where the brier would not grow. The air was too thin for most of the dark elves to make it, but every so often a new breed would try the ice and snow and the dwarves would make sure that they did not.

Beneath us, the river that eventually emptied into the sea filled the gorge from side to side and with it the poisoned brier. Both sides of the river had been covered with the brier and it had kept on growing until both sides had been carried downstream and touched. The tangled mass of the brier had soon intertwined and the plant began to grow and fill up the vee shaped gap. Here and there the bottom of the gorge would rise to almost the level of the river and in these places the brier would put down roots and anchor itself securely in the swamp. Since its full growth the Dokka'lfar had not managed to cross it. Waldwick had pulled down the tunnels over and over again that the dark elves had dug. The brier stretched for a full thirty miles, filling the gorge and growing up the sides right to the snow level. It also extended along the sides of the lower reaches of the mountains for many miles. The amount of water sucked up from the swamp to keep the brier alive had caused much of the swamp to dry out in its area.

I could see smoke rising from a township built into the side of the hills that rose each side of the gorge. In front of the palisade was a deep ditch lined with sharpened wooden stakes at the bottom. This was at least fifty foot across and looked as though it was well maintained. The bottom was littered with dinosaur bones that lay around the impaling sites. The carrion attracted the predators that died on the stakes thus attracting more predators into the area. Over the length of time that the dwarves had decided to live here, the count had gone down, as the larger meat eaters learnt to ignore the smell of easy meat and stay away. Every so often one of the larger vegetarian dinosaurs would stumble over the edge and die. When that happened the dwarves would quickly butcher the animal before competition arrived. Behind the palisades the dwarves had terraced the hills and adopted the same style that the elves had used at the castle. Here the farms were built on the edge of each terrace where the irrigation systems drained down to the next terrace. The town behind the fortified walls supported observation towers that looked out over the Plains of Scion.

I looked for a flat area fairly close to the fortified town and close to one of the rivers that flowed into the swampy delta. The Spellbinder's senses also told me what the condition of the ground was under the surface. For safety we would need a hard stony ground without any soft areas that anything could bury into and bide its time before attacking. I found just what we needed and set the Spellbinder down.

I extended the boundaries of the Spellbinder and pushed all life forms away on the outside by hardening the 'walls' and increasing the refractive index. The outside of the bubble became a reflective surface constantly rippling from silver to multicoloured strands. It was so unnatural that the dinosaurs took one look at it and moved further away.

My genetic scientists began to sow the seeds of the brier into a large compound. They constrained the growth so that it grew as a stockade. A tunnel formed, leading in and out, with a sound sensitive door at both ends. This faced towards the mountains of the gorge. During the day the brier constantly grew along the seeded lines that the geneticists had laid down. The dwarves soon cut a channel to the river so that fresh water began to fill a pool that they had excavated inside the brier's domain. Once the stinging plants took hold and were shoulder high I released control of the bubble and brought the boundaries back to the area of the control room, leaving all of my forces outside. Now came the stacking of the stores and supplies we had brought through.

Now the next stage of the project needed to be implemented. It would now be necessary to activate the Arch and drop my human friends back to their world to buy the other items we would require. I would take Sam Pitts and John Smith with me and leave them there for one month before returning to my world. During their absence the other four humans would manage the elves, dwarves and gnomes into a force capable of using the weapons brought into this world. Those elves that were most resistant to the effects of iron would be allowed to use the modified AK 47's and learn how to use them. The dwarves would all find out how they could do the most damage with them. Those who had an aptitude would use the armour piercing Berettas and also learn how to alternate the bullets to suit the needs of the day. Our journey to the human world would also need vast amounts of ammunition to be ferried back here.

Sam had warned me that he had just about bought all that he could in the USA and the quantity of bullets and rifles that we needed would make an indelicate mark. We might need to go to one of the border countries on the edge of the old Soviet Union with gold to buy the quantities that my small army wanted. Now that I had the Spellbinder at my disposal this was not a problem. Human greed was such, that on the edges of civilisation, gold could make most things come true!

Some time ago I had ransacked the jewels that were scattered throughout the castle workshops and stores. Once word had had passed around that the High King required as many of these useless items as could be found, a large wooden bucket began to fill. This was placed on the High King's throne in full view of the people that arrived to fill it. I had instructed some of the gnomes to help bring the people to the throne room in my absence if they did not know the way. Within a few weeks the pile of cut and uncut diamonds, rubies and sapphires had reached halfway to the top. A pile of gold also sat upon the throne once it became known that the human world valued this as well. A dwarf artisan spirited this away and returned with the gold cast into ingots the size of small bricks. They were just small enough to be carried in twos and soon began to form a cube that was larger than the bucket.

All of this 'wealth' I had entrusted to Sam Pitts and John

Smith to ferry it back to the human world. This would be turned into money and filtered into various bank accounts. I now owned a research, development and engineering firm that I had saved from liquidation, complete with staff. I had made Sam Pitts and John Smith directors of this firm, whilst I was the unseen managing director.

A team of scientists were exploring the elfin science of genetics and the entropy traps. Weapons engineers altered the design of the rifles to use the minimum of iron and steel. The most useful part of owning the firm was being able to ship items from all over the world to the warehouse on the edge of the desert. Sam had this warehouse built to a secure design and surrounded by razor wire. It was permanently guarded by men that Sam had hand picked and well paid so that secrecy was paramount. There was one road in and out to the warehouse with empty desert on both sides. When I needed to pick up weapons and ammunition all I had to do was to take the Spellbinder inside the warehouse and get the lorry-loads of goods delivered straight into the craft. The guards never got to see inside what was to all purposes an empty warehouse and their minds never registered the fact. Sam Pitts made sure of that.

I had named the firm Acme Engineering; - Elfin Enterprises after watching a cartoon on human television. It had become a multi-million dollar enterprise by exploiting elfin science. This paid easily for any weapons sales that my arms dealer required. The rest of the blatantly illegal operations were paid for by the 'riches' ferried across from my world. Sam Pitts had personally picked the managers of the various departments and had ensured that their salaries reflected their ability to do their professions without question. They were content to run the firm as instructed in the knowledge that they would continue to do so and become wealthy people as long as they did not break their oath of secrecy.

Sam's mental abilities had increased in the time that he had worked for me and all my human friends had become good telepaths. If there were any problems of inquisitiveness, Sam had learnt to tweak the minds of his managers to make sure that they did not think too much about 'why', but concentrated on 'do'! The consequence of that ability meant that all of us could remain in the elfin world for lengths of time without anyone wondering where we had gone. John Smith was now head of research at both worlds and shuttled backwards and forwards across the Rift. It was this human who discovered how to clone another Arch from the Spellbinder and set it inside the managing director's office. Once this was done, a number of Arches were set up in my world connecting to each other from the nexus at the old dungeon at the castle. Now that the Spellbinder was fully awake and functioning it was not necessary to shut down the Arches completely. They could remain in standby mode and be activated by my human friends, now that they had developed telepathic powers. Here in John's secret laboratories from the human world, his elfish scientific staff pursued many research projects blending human and elvish science.

I activated the Arch and the three of us stepped through into the managing director's office. A change of clothes was waiting in the wardrobe and the two humans soon altered their appearance after a wash and shave. I to was glad of the opportunity to wash and shower the accumulated grime away from my body. The castle plumbing was not in the same class as human washrooms!

Once I was neatly dressed and presentable for this world I decided that I should make myself known to my workforce. My two human friends would introduce me to the managers and then go off on their own to pursue the items that I would need back on my world. Once again on this world I would make sure that they would only see what I needed them to see. The pointed ears, antennae and six fingered hands would not be seen and I would adopt my guise of Spanish descent.

First I stepped up to the window and stared out at the view. The small firm had been ideally located on the edge of an industrial estate right on the perimeter of the city. I had a view of rolling hills and clumps of trees from where I stood. My office was at the top of a five-story building and was sealed off from the floors below by a set of combination locked oaken doors. Outside of the doors was a lift that only came to this floor when keyed in with the activation key that we all kept on a chain around our necks. In the basement was located the car park where our cars were kept.

There were no more than fifty people employed here and they were the best that money could buy. Some of them had worked for the previous owner of the firm and were kept on for their business contacts or their skills. The senior buyer was the man I had come to see. His name was Ivan Koshensky of Eastern European descent. He had been recommended by Sam Pitts and had proved invaluable in locating difficult to obtain items. The last batch of AK 47's had been 'found' by him and modified here. Ivan had made sure that all the paperwork was in order and there were no problems importing them into the country.

Sam knocked at his door and walked straight in with me by his side.

"Ivan! Its good to see you again, old friend," he said. "Let me introduce you to Mr. Kin, the owner of this firm and the money behind it!"

Ivan Koshensky immediately stood up and walked

round from behind his desk and offered his hand.

"It is indeed a pleasure to meet you after all this time. What do you want from me? If you have come in person then it must be something that may be difficult to find," he said.

I took his hand in mine and in that few seconds I was able to read his character. He was good at his job and he knew it! He was also completely dedicated to his employer and would keep his mouth shut about any of the more clandestine operations at Acme Engineering. He was a man that I could trust. I made a decision there and then.

"Mr. Koshensky," I answered, "I have indeed come to see you in person. I do have a problem and I have come to see you in person to talk to you."

I turned to Sam Pitts and John Smith and spoke to them with my mind. "I am going to take him back for a short visit while you get busy sorting out our business. I feel that I can trust this man and for what I am going to need in the future it will be best that he knows what it is for!"

My two trusted associates turned and left me with the bemused human.

As the door closed the ex-Russian asked, "What do you want?"

"I need to be able to trust you with something that will defy your senses," I replied. Come with me in the lift to the top floor and I will show you something that I feel that you must know. It will also answer many of the questions that you must have thought during your time with this firm."

I opened the door and waited in the lift while he followed me in. I pressed my key into the lock and the lift began to rise. The doors opened. I activated the combination on the polished wooden doors and walked into my office. The Arch dominated the room as it shimmered in and out of reality.

"This is a door into another world. You need to see it to be able to do what I ask of you. I can assure you that you will not be harmed if you come with me," I said and dropped my mental thrall so that he could see me as I really was.

"God in Heaven! What are you?"

"I'm what you would call an elf from your folklore, Mr. Koshensky and I am quite serious about wanting your help. I will open a doorway to where I live and show you an alternative Earth," I replied and opened the Arch.

From where he stood he could see quite clearly the castle rooms where the Arch was situated. The old dungeon was now well lit and this was the level that was occupied by John's laboratories. I stepped through and beckoned to the human.

Slowly he walked through the Arch and felt the change in gravity immediately.

"I'm not dreaming am I? This is real," he said quietly and placed his hand against the cold, stone wall.

"Ivan Koshensky you are the seventh human being to see my world. I am certain of the trust that I can put in your hands; otherwise you would not be here. I need you to believe in the things that I am about to show you. When I am certain that you do, you and I have much to discuss."

I led him upstairs towards the throne room, allowing him to see the banqueting hall with its octagonal table. The views through the high windows over the elfin lands were at its best, as the full midday sun shone down on the terraces and the smaller townships. Some of my people were aloft catching the warm thermals, doing various errands. This stopped the ex-Russian in his tracks and he walked unsteadily to the window to gaze upon the Ljo'sa'lfar soaring away from the castle.

I led him still upwards to the throne room where we

had an all round view of elfdom. He stopped abruptly by the throne and stared down at the pile of gold and bucket of gemstones that occupied the seat. At that moment a dwarf appeared pushing a small cart loaded with small ingots of gold and a large bag of jewels and precious stones followed by two gnomes. He nodded to me and began to stack the precious cargo on the throne, while the gnomes began to sort the jewels into different bags.

"Well met, High King," he said. "This delivery just arrived at the gathering point and has been ferried up by your elves. I have melted down the gold into bricks as you can see. The news is that more will be arriving soon from the western approaches. Who is this?"

"Abbathor, gold-smelter of great skill, it is good to see you again. Thanks as always for your help and ability. This human is my weapons gatherer in his world. He is of great use to our cause. I would appreciate it greatly if you would take his hand in yours and shake it and show him your rifle."

Ivan had not understood a word of this, but reacted as I thought he would as the dwarf walked over to him and shook his hand. Abbathor undid his smock and to Ivan's surprise brandished an AK 47 that he had strapped to his back. The human stepped back and his face changed expression as his mind began to piece together the transactions that he had arranged. He studied the dwarf intently and could plainly see that he was not of human descent and quite different from the gnomes.

"Where am I Mr. Kin? I think that I am ready now! Tell me and also tell me why you needed me to come here," Ivan asked.

CHAPTER THIRTEEN

"Mr. Koshensky I will do as you ask. There is so much that I need to tell you, that it would take hours. I will tell you a little and then if you are willing, I will impart all the information that you need to know directly into your mind," I stated and called one of the palace staff from outside the throne room with my mind.

I asked her to obtain some refreshments and bring it to us on a tray and remain with us. She made her way to the kitchens to find a bottle of wine and some biscuits and cheese.

My new recruit stared out of the window entranced with the view as I settled down to give him the bare facts. As he sat gazing at the view a wing of elves mounted on what the humans called Quetzalcoatlus or pterodactyls climbed into the sky using the evening thermals.

"All that you can see from here is the elfin kingdom. It is located on a parallel Earth that is separated from your world by a rift in space-time. I have learnt how to control the rifts, so that a small band of humans can travel back and forth with me. We are under a great threat from a deviation of our own kind. My people are called the Ljo'sa'lfar (Light Elves) and the others who would destroy us are known as the Dokka'lfar (dark elves). We have kept them at bay for more than two centuries, but the time has come when we must do what has always been unthinkable to us. Elves do not kill and injure other elves, yet I must do this, or all on this world will die here and I mean every living thing. The Dokka'lfar place no restraint upon their breeding and will eat every living thing that is made of flesh. Many of them have the mentality of animals and are directed by the Dark Lord, Abaddon. They destroyed our home world and they will destroy this one. When every breathing creature is gone they will move on to the next world if Abaddon can make the rifts obey him again. At the moment and for some time, his ship the Dream-shifter, can only keep the portal open between our old home world and this one. I have become the High King and the responsibility of keeping my people safe has come to me. It would also seem that your world is also under my protection. Judging by some of your paintings it would seem that the Dokka'lfar has been to your world before, hunting us. Once they have exhausted this world they will return to yours and feast on you.

Elves are gifted with extensive powers of the mind. Your people call it telepathy or mind reading. Mostly on your world you tend to view it with scepticism and disbelief, but the only way that I can make everything plain to you is to enter your mind and fill your mind with knowledge! I would only do this with your permission, as not to do so would be a violation of all elvish principals."

The human continued to stare out of the window as his mind tried to put everything together. He swung round on the bench as 'Light in the Sky', known as 'Sky-Light.' entered the throne room with a carved wooden tray of refreshments. She opened the bottle of wine and poured the vintage into cut glass goblets, cut the cheese into cubes and spread butter on the biscuits.

He stared at 'Sky-Light' as she quietly did my silent bidding. Her hair was of a light, chestnut colour and bound in tiny pigtails that had been pulled into a bun on the top of her head. Her eyes were green and slitted just like a cat's, but with long lashes that swept over her cheeks. The wings were folded behind her and were tucked into a strap that that buckled under her breasts. She was dressed in a blue silky material that fell from her shoulders to her knees and was contained by the broad, leather belt. Her pointed ears were pierced at the lobes and hung from each gold wire was an intricately carved, hollow ball of dragon bone. Around each antenna was a carved jade ring that was placed against her forehead and around her neck dangled a single dragon's tooth, mounted on a golden chain. The human seemed to forget to breathe, as he stared at her open mouthed.

With great effort Ivan Koshensky drew his gaze away and back to mine. He reached for a goblet and drank the vintage, red fruity wine to the bottom of the glass. 'Sky-Light' poured him another and placed it in his hand. The human sipped the wine, savouring each and every drop, deep in thought.

The human sighed and stared straight into my eyes before replying, "I worked at the firm that you bought out of liquidation for many years before you came. Since then I have been instrumental in procuring many items under the instruction of Mr. Pitts or Mr. Smith that have caused me to wonder what was being done with them. Today I have seen a dwarf with an AK 47 and things that I cannot name. The sort of salary that I have been paid has ensured that while my mind has questions, I have always remained silent. You have shown me some of the obvious wealth that you have access to. I feel that if you did not trust me, I would not be here. From what you have told me it would seem that to do my job for you it would be necessary for me to fully understand what is at stake. So, yes Mr Kin I agree that you enter my mind and fill in the blank spaces."

With his agreement, I slipped into his mind and showed him the events that had led to the Ljo'sa'lfar leaving our home world of Alfheim. I showed him the spread of the Dokka'lfar and the phenomenal rate of the increase of their numbers that produced cannibalistic behaviour to stay alive. He shuddered as the facts of the situation began to accumulate in his new memories. I allowed him to 'remember' the journey across the Plains of Scion and the help that we were given by Prime and her clan. Next I showed him the downfall of Waldwick and the subsequent empowerment of my taking over as the High King, who alone amongst the elves could make those decisions that others could not. My problem in teaching the elves to kill their own kind, warped and twisted though they were was uppermost in my mind and I showed this to Ivan Koshensky. Also I explained to him our lack of perception of the use of weapons against a foe. He could now understand my need of Sam Pitts and the other military trained humans.

I withdrew from the human's consciousness and waited for him to assimilate the heavy load that I had left in his mind. After a while I became concerned for this new human's well-being.

"How are you, Ivan Koshensky?" I asked and reached out and held his hand.

"I shall never be the same again," he replied and gripped my hand fiercely. "What you have shown me leaves me without words. Now I can understand the need for the things that I have bought under the company's banner. I often wondered about the Elfin Enterprises part of the name! Never in a million years would I have thought of the truth behind it. You have my undying loyalty and my silence. My kind must never learn of this place or your method of travelling between the realities or parallel worlds. It has to be kept a secret."

"Don't worry about that part of the bargain my new friend. You would find that even if you wanted to, it would not be possible for you to tell anyone." I reassured him. "Even under drugs or coercion everything that we have shared here would just disappear from your mind. You may talk all you might want to, with the other six humans, but you will find that you cannot speak about this to anyone else and neither can they. I am sorry that I have had to do this, but I hope that you do understand?"

"I am relieved, High King, not angry with you. I have spent enough time rubbing shoulders with those who would exploit this world until it had nothing of value left on it, to know that they would rape it!"

"Thanks for that attitude. You must call me Peterkin in the future, my new friend. Now I think it would be sensible if I introduced you to the other human beings working for me. We need to go downstairs again and use the portal to relocate to the Spellbinder at the Great Gorge. I have other things to do there and you can get home from that point."

With my permission, 'Sky-light' entered his mind and showed the human her name and for a brief moment he saw a starry night sky illuminated by an iridescent rainbow of colours that hung in the darkness in a halo of light.

We finished up the wine, biscuits and cheese, leaving 'Sky-Light' to tidy away. Ivan followed me down the stairs and back to the old dungeons where the cloned Arch was situated. I opened the portal and we both walked through into the world around the gorge. Instantly the heat and humidity made itself felt and we both broke out in a sweat. Down at the swamp level the dinosaur world's lower altitude made a temperature jump of more than twenty degrees. Ivan's face ran with sweat and his balding head became quickly shiny. As he quickly took off his suit jacket his shirt became soaked.

"Good grief, Peterkin, where the Hell are we now," he gasped and undid his tie.

"The Great Gorge," I replied and connected to the Spellbinder. "Water for my new friend, please."

A glass of water appeared from the stonework by the side of the control chair and I handed it to the sweating human. Ivan took it gratefully and drank the cold drink down in one go. I sent a mental summons to the other four of my human friends and Mellitus.

It was not very long before Hoatzin appeared, followed by Spencer who was talking with Mellitus. David and Steven came into the control room each carrying a berretta rifle.

"Gentlemen I would like to introduce a new member of the group. This is Ivan Koshensky who is the man who finds and buys the equipment that we need. He holds the title of Senior Buyer at the firm we bought out, some time ago. I have briefed him and brought his knowledge up to date. Whatever you need to carry out this operation; this is the man to ask," I told them. "Make sure that you give him a list of all you need and he will get it for you."

The humans all shook hands with the newcomer and exchanged names, as is their custom. I could see that Ivan was a different type of human from the others. His abilities were channelled in a different direction. He was not a fighter, as these humans were.

After a couple of hours I called the meeting to a close and gave Ivan a quick tour of the new compound. I showed him the pens where the quetzalcoatlus were kept and the elfin masters who flew them. He made several suggestions about camping equipment that he could quickly procure. From a hill in the corner of the camp I was able to show him some of the 'dragons' that roamed the Plains of Scion. The herds were not easy to miss and already some of them had found out the hard way that the glossy leaves of the brier were not to be eaten. By now my new recruit was beginning to look somewhat travel stained as several hours in the heat and humidity had taken their toll.

"I think that I should take you home my friend. Do you have a change of clothes at the office? It would hardly do to have any of your staff see you in this state," I said and led the way back to the Spellbinder.

Ivan looked at his watch and laughed.

"As it is early evening at the firm, I hardly expect to see anyone, except the security guard. In answer to your question, Peterkin, I do keep a few shirts and a spare jacket handy. My wife and daughters are used to me keeping odd hours, so as long as I phone them when we get back to say I shall be a little late, all will be well."

We stood in front of the Arch and I ran my hands over the runic symbols and gave the Spellbinder a mental twitch. The space inside the portal became misty and then the view of the office became clear. We stepped through and immediately felt the chill of the air-conditioning. The office lighting had come on and the lamps outside were illuminating the road outside. I opened a drawer and took out a lift-key on a chain.

"This is yours, Ivan. When you need to get hold of me you will need to come up here and enter this office. You must always come alone. The Arch will know if you are not and will take appropriate action. To activate it and find me, you must place your hands upon these two runes and think my name. If our enterprise goes well, my gratitude will be extensive. Much of our success will depend on your efforts on our behalf, so believe me when I say that you are an asset to my group."

Ivan chuckled and said, "Thank you Peterkin for your remarks. Just don't ask me to fight. I can buy the weapons that you need, but I shall not be firing any of them."

I smiled at the human and shook his hand.

"That's all I ask, my new friend. Do your best to achieve

the items on the lists that my group gave you. If it means going somewhere else on your home world to collect them, rather than getting them into this country, then the Spellbinder can do this. All we need is a quiet place to take my vessel and we can load them inside and take them back. We will not be seen!"

I reached inside my jacket pocket and pulled out a ruby the size of his small fingernail.

"Have this set in a gold ring for your wife to wear. Charge it to the firm and give it to her from me as a token, to make up for the times that you may be away from home. You must warn her that you may have to travel the other side of the Atlantic on some of your business trips. Tell her that you are more than just Senior Buyer at the firm, that you have been promoted, but you cannot tell her about your business. Hint to her if you like that it is a matter of National Security and that I work for the government!"

Ivan stared at the deep red stone that had been cut by a gnome craftsman with awe. He held it to the light and watched the facets reflect upon the wall. It was stunning!

"Thank you again, High King! I am lost for words. Be assured that I will do all that you ask and I will contact you when I have more information," Ivan replied and sat heavily into a chair. "My wife, Susan will be the soul of discretion once I put this on her finger. This stone would take half a year's salary to buy at Tiffany's."

I tapped the sequence through the Arch and activated the portal. The Spellbinder's control room lay on the other side, but before I stepped through I paused as a thought entered my mind.

"Spellbinder!"

"Yes High King."

"I want you to fabricate a recall bracelet, that will allow the wearer to return to this room instantly if necessary," I instructed the ancient machine.

The air shimmered by the apex of the Arch and a green, flexible, stony bracelet dropped into my hand. I turned and placed it over the human's left wrist, next to his watch, where it shrank to fit him.

"In an emergency and only then, press this bracelet on the round button and you will be instantly be transported here. Get in touch with me as we arranged and we will sort things out," I instructed.

Ivan Koshensky stared at the bracelet clinging to his wrist and gasped, "What the hell is this Peterkin?"

"Elfin science, my new friend. It occurred to me that what my other human friends have asked for might take you to some dangerous places. I do not want to put your life in peril so I have given you an insurance of a kind. Now I must leave you and return to my world."

The air in the Arch shimmered for a few moments as I walked through and once more found myself back inside the Spellbinder at the Great Gorge.

Inside the Managing Director's office a sweat-stained human being sat in a comfortable chair, staring out at the night. He held a ruby in his hand and his sanity by a thread. Ivan Koshensky sat and thought about all he had just experienced. It was some time before moved from the chair.

Slowly he stood, walked to the lift and inserted his new key. The doors opened and he dropped down to the next level, where he went to his office on the deserted floor. He had a strip wash at the basin of his private toilet and changed his clothes to more casual wear. Next he re-entered the lift, dropped to the underground car park and opened his car door. Ivan got in, just sat for a moment and stared again at the ruby and the bracelet before starting the engine. Once out of the building he stopped the car and phoned home to say he was on his way.

Peterkin also sat quietly in the command chair and thought about the next stage of the plan. Outside, the compound was all in darkness and fires had been lit and tended by the dwarves. Elves had patrolled the airways to make sure that none of the many aerial dinosaurs made their way into the compound for a quick and easy meal. The poisoned brier kept the rest at bay. In the middle of the compound a circular ring of the genetically engineered brier had been grown to shoulder height. This was to be the cage that would contain the selected Dokka'lfar in captivity for the elfish scientists to study and for the others to learn to kill. A bronze door had been fitted to one side that was connected to a solar cell and remained electrified. Waldwick's cage was positioned in the centre of this ring where he could watch the proceedings. A large smoky bonfire had been lit so that the night blood-sucking insects would avoid the immediate area.

A voice behind him brought his thoughts to and end.

"Will the High King not go to his bed? I have waited patiently for your return," Ameela whispered in his ear and a pair of arms encircled his shoulders.

I kissed the backs of her hands and stood. In the pale lights of Spellbinder's control room my queen was a vision of light and shadow. Ameela's beauty stunned my heart and I surrendered myself to her. We made our way to the sleeping quarters that Spellbinder had provided for our use and we fell asleep in each other's arms.

The morning sun had been climbing in the sky for several hours when there was a commotion inside the compound.

Eduardo, who I had commissioned as one of Waldwick's guards, came to my sleeping quarters and called out, "High

176

King, we have company. A group of dwarves have arrived at the brier."

I awoke and rolled out of the bed onto my knees and stood wondering what I should wear to meet these isolated dwarves. Pulling on a pair of clean human briefs I followed them with a pair of kaki shorts. I hauled a comfortable camouflaged pattern tee shirt over my head and fitted on a Kevlar vest, just to be sure. It had been a long time since elves had been in this area and I knew that the dwarves would not have forgotten Waldwick's abandoning their ancestors to their grisly fate. I slipped a pair of leather sandals onto my feet and made my way out of the Spellbinder.

"Let them inside Eduardo," I ordered and made my way to the opening in the compound. "For goodness sake you know as well as I do what dangers are prowling round, waiting to eat us!"

The elves began to trill a high-pitched sound that the brier was sensitive to, at the doors and the tunnel opened as the branches pulled away. Immediately a large group of dwarves came running inside, carrying crossbows and spears. Mellitus and his group surged forwards and mingled with the newcomers, hugging and slapping each other on the back. I stood with the morning sun behind me and waited for the introductions to slow down.

Mellitus brought forward a female dwarf who was dressed in leathers from head to toe. She had a hood over her face and drew it back to allow the morning sun to highlight her silver hair. Her beard had been braided in tiny individual rats tails that ended in golden tags. Her hair was drawn back into a ponytail and her piercing brown eyes stared straight at me with astonishment and awe.

"You are the new High King?" She asked.

"I do have that honour. I am called Peterkin and I have deposed Waldwick. He is the one that sits inside that cage, guarded by elves," I stated and bowed to the matriarch. "Who have I the honour of speaking to?"

"I am Hildegard Storm-bringer. Leader of the Stormgalt and you are the one foretold by a dream-seer long ago. In her dream she saw the new High King of the elves and he was wingless as are you. This dream came to her the night the Dokka'lfar feasted on roast dwarf and Waldwick turned his face away and left them. We have waited through the long centuries and held the secret ways through the brier free of the dark ones. The dream was passed down from crone to girl until my grandmother told me to watch for you and you would come. I was to be the one who would meet you at daybreak and I would know you by the shadow that you cast.

The morning sun has your name upon it and it shows upon the ground. You are the Great High King that that she named as Peterkin the 'Long-shadow'. You are the one foretold that will rid this land of the curse of the Dokka'lfar."

I saw the rest of the dwarves that had come with her, fall to their knees as she said this.

Amongst the dwarves I could hear the call as each verified "Long-shadow. The Long-shadow has come," to each other.

I turned to my friend and said, "Mellitus! Will you please persuade these good people that I am just an elf that is trying to protect all of those who are part of my kingdom!"

Mellitus laughed and replied, "Sire let me assure you that you are not just an elf. You are the rightful High King and you have not walked away from your responsibilities. These are your people as much as any in the elfin kingdom and you do not think of them in any other way!"

I walked forwards and held out my hand to the dwarf leader and kissed her knuckles, pressing her callused hands to my face.

I drew her to my side and said, "Hildegard Storm-bringer,

you and I have much to talk about. Please tell your people that they have the freedom of the camp. My only restriction is that you do not exact any revenge on Waldwick for his abandonment of your forces long ago. I am putting him to good use, be assured of that and I need him alive. Mellitus will show you all the new weapons that we have brought with us. There will be many more in the future. I intend to enter the world held by the Dokka'lfar and remove them and I would take allies with me."

"Great High King, where you go, go the dwarves of the Stormgalt, armed and ready," she replied and turned to stare at Spencer as he walked towards us. "You have a dark one amongst your force?"

Several of the dwarves began to unsheathe their weapons as my tall black human came closer. At the same moment David and Steven appeared and stood with him to meet the new dwarves.

"These are not Dokka'lfar my new friends, they are called humans and they are not giants either! They too are here to fight the dark ones. There is also one other, but I suspect that he is aloft, riding one of our dragons. Two more are away from here at the moment, but they will soon be here. You will see many things that here that you have not seen before. I ask you to stay with Mellitus who will explain to you all you need to know," I reassured the new recruits and turned to Hildegard. "Come with me and meet an ancient entity called Spell-binder. It will be the means of our entering the lands beyond the poisoned brier and I will tell you what we plan."

CHAPTER FOURTEEN

In the security of the Spellbinder I sat Hildegard down and began to outline my plans for the future. I made the necessary mind bridge to the entity that controlled the vessel and manipulated the rifts. Although it had been generations since the dwarves had been in the company of elves, she was able to take to the mental communication quite readily.

The noise of the AK 47s being demonstrated carried into my craft and the dwarf leader heard the rat-a-tat-tat sound of rapid fire.

She stood up and said, "These are the weapons that you brought back from the human world. I would like to see them demonstrated. It was seen long ago by the far-seer that the 'Long-shadow' would bring many weapons with him that would defy comprehension. She also said that it would not be necessary to understand them, to use them."

I laughed and replied, "Indeed Hildegard I can assure you that they are easy to use, but how they work is not necessary to know! I have used them many times and the result is the same. You point the weapon at the target; squeeze the trigger much like a crossbow and death erupts from the muzzle. The humans are very good at killing their own kind with weapons such as these. These beings that I have selected and brought over from a parallel world, would all fight and if necessary die to save this world. They have honour and commitment. I recruited them to accompany my on a quest to rescue my wife and daughter from the intentions of Waldwick. This they did and they could have all gone home after this was done, as rich men. Instead they elected to stay and depose Waldwick and cleanse this world of the Dokka'lfar. I trust them and I know them, for I have been inside their minds. On the Plains of Scion, they fought beside me and risked their lives over and over again, not just for me, but for the others who came with me."

Outside in the noonday sun the humans had made a target range that would allow the bullets to tunnel into the brier and not ricochet into any bystanders. Mellitus had taken over the demonstration of the Kalashnikoff rifles and was showing the new dwarves how to load a fresh clip of bullets. I noticed that another box of ammunition had been opened and empty clips had been scattered around it.

I cast my mind around the compound searching for David and Steven and found them watching the dwarves learning how to operate the semi-automatic rifles. A quick mental query reassured me that there were plenty of boxes of AK 47 magazines left and a good store of them kept back at the castle. My group of humans had been busy on my authority and had been backwards and forwards, ferrying weapons and ammunition from the stores at the lodge, directly here at the gorge. The Spellbinder had kept the portals open under their instruction and closed them off when they had finished.

Hildegard watched her people as they gained experience with the semi-automatic rifles.

She turned and said, "We should contact our neighbours at the left-hand side of the gorge and tell them of the developments. They should know that the High King is here and will annihilate the Dokka'lfar with new weapons and allies. Once I have told them whom you are and what you are sworn to do, I know that they will want to be involved as much as we do! This day had been long in coming, my king. At long last we will strike back at the dwarf eaters. We will have our vengeance!"

"Come then, Hildegard Storm-bringer, leader of the Stormgalt we shall go and meet your opposite leader on the other side of the Great Gorge," I replied to her and led the way back into the Spellbinder.

I gathered in Mellitus, Steven and a group of gnomes to make sure that we were not overheard by any of Abaddon's mental adepts. Included in this introductory party were my queen, daughter and my indomitable mother.

"Spellbinder, take us to the other side and seek out the other dwarves' town that keeps the Dokka'lfar from entering the Plains of Scion.

We floated upwards and levelled off at a hundred feet. Beneath us the poisoned brier spread, impenetrable across the river delta. The late afternoon sun beat down onto the glossy deep green leaves and we watched the other side of the gorge approach. The dwarf garrison town was built into the mountains similarly to the Stormgalt and was terraced in levels right down to the Plains of Scion. There was a deep dry moat in front of the stockade studded with sharpened stakes that were littered with bones. The two towns could have been a mirror image of the other. There was a large open area in front of the road that led into the town that contained the livestock. The tops of the stockade were guarded by many dwarves, armed with crossbows and sheltering from the heat of the sun, under roofed awnings.

"Make us visible," I commanded the vessel and Spellbinder turned the outside walls silver.

Now the guards could see a large grey ball reflecting the bright sun advancing towards the open area. A hail of cross-bolts spattered against the impenetrable sides as we settled to the ground. One dwarf flung himself at the Spellbinder and beat it with his axe. The impact was enough to tear it from his numb grip and leave him stood wringing his hands in pain. Several of the others prodded the vessel with their spears and walked round it in puzzlement.

"Now make the walls transparent so that they can see us, Spellbinder," I said and watched as the dwarves stood back in amazement.

They soon realised that there were others of their kind aboard and stared in disbelief at the rest of us. I held my hand up in the sign of friendship and gestured that we would like to come out, if they would drop their weapons. The dwarves did so and I allowed the Spellbinder to dissolve one wall.

Hildegard stepped through the arch and said, "I am Hildegard Storm-bringer, leader of the Stormgalt. Send for whoever your leader is, for I bring great news. The 'Long-shadow' is here! The legend of the wingless elf, the Great High King has come true. This is Peterkin, true and rightful king of the elfin kingdom and the saviour of our world! He has Waldwick caged at his camp before the Stormgalt. These giants that are with him are from another world and bring weapons the like of which you have never seen! I tell you the days of the Dokka'lfar are numbered."

In the distance a cloud of dust revealed three dwarves each mounted on a beast that ran on its hind legs. Its smaller front legs were tucked under its chest while it ran and an outstretched tail hung out behind for balance. It had a long neck ending in a blunt head with eyes at the side. The dinosaur carried a saddle and a harness around its head that connected to reigns that were held by its rider.

The lead dwarf hauled the beast to a standstill and dropped it to the ground. He dismounted and stared at the group stood just outside of the arch.

Removing his hood from his face the stocky dwarf walked up to Hildegard and asked, "Who the hell are you?"

The leader of the Stormgalt laughed and clapped him on the shoulders and repeated her statement to him. The colour drained from his face for a moment, before the redness of embarrassment took its place.

"I am Althalos Hammer-thief, leader of the Skaldargate, keeper of the secret ways over the mountains. I make you welcome, High King and apologise for the oversight that led to my men attacking you!"

I took him by the arm, shook his hand and said, "I am Peterkin, High King of the elvish kingdom, protector of all my people. Would you like to step into my vessel, known as Spellbinder and I will tell you everything that you need to know?"

We sat inside the coolness of my strange vessel while I explained the events that had lead to me becoming the leader of my people. With Althalos's consent I entered his mind and gave him a set of false memories so that he could understand my plans for the future. Mellitus and Hildegard joined us as soon as I had finished imparting the mental images.

The leader of the garrison town called Skaldargate sat very quiet and thought deeply about all that I had planted in his mind. He reached out and took the AK 47 from Mellitus and examined it carefully. The safety catch was securely fastened so that accidents did not happen. Althalos kept his fingers well away from the trigger, but turned the rifle over and over.

"This weapon has been manufactured by machines! It has not been crafted by a smith. I have never seen anything like it in my life. Even our crossbows are individually built and fashioned to suit the owner. May I try this weapon outside?"

I nodded and said, "By all means do so, but be very careful where you aim it. Draw on the memories that I gave you for guidance."

Mellitus led the way and pointed to the stockade wall,

where an old shield had been fastened as a porthole cover.

"Try a burst at that shield, Hammer-thief. Just make sure that you keep a tight grip on the rifle and keep it pointed at the stockade wall!"

Althalos pointed the rifle at the shield and sighted down the barrel after disengaging the safety catch. He gently squeezed the trigger and watched in awe as the shield disintegrated under a three second burst. The dwarf concentrated his mind and altered the weapon to a single shot. He chose a different target by the stockade wall, comprising of an empty jar sat on a table. It took several shots before he got the range and shattered the jar. The AK 47 ran out of bullets as the clip emptied and Althalos gave it back to Mellitus.

"I can see that this is a formidable weapon, my friend, but one must be mindful that all too soon it will run out of these things called bullets," the leader of the Skaldargate remarked.

"This is why we carry haversacks full of clips," Mellitus grinned. "I tell you what, friend Althalos these rifles will kill many Dokka'lfar. What we must be careful of is wasting too much ammunition in the heat of the moment and remembering that they are close range weapons. The humans have long-range rifles that have different types of bullets. Some of them can drill straight through the armoured hide of the really big dragons and explode inside them. They die really easy when these rifles are used, but they do need a more careful aim!"

"There is a lot to take in, Mellitus Hammer-hand, but my heart is with you and this new High King. I would avenge the deaths of the valiant thousand and I feel that I must be part of everything that Peterkin has planned."

"Hammer-hand and Hammer-thief welded together will make a powerful alliance," grinned Mellitus as he took the other leader's hand in his. "Welcome to the new elfin kingdom. Wait until you see the other allies that the High King as taken by his side. Examine those memories that tell of the journey across the Plains of Scion and the Raptors that joined the rescue party!"

Like ripples on a smooth surfaced pond, the exploits and knowledge handed down to Prime and her clan had spread amongst the 'People of the Plains.' The instant command of fire and the far-reaching range of the bow had gained the clan enormous status. The ideas that had sprung from the association with the elves, dwarves and gnomes had spread throughout the many isolated clans as they met each other on converging hunting trips. When the bonfire had been lit inside the compound the smoke had been quickly noticed and the news of the encampment had spread. Runners had been sent to notify each clan to find Prime and seek advice.

Prime was examining the bindings around the shaft and arrowhead of a newly fletched arrow when she heard the trill of awareness from an outlying lookout. As one being, the clan turned to face the possible threat. Another trill of recognition echoed over the ferns from the same sentry and the clan relaxed. A tired female raptor limped into view carrying her bag of tools, a quiver of arrows and an unstrung bow in one hand. She caught sight of Prime who was standing tall with feathers erect on her crest and approached her.

"I am 'Fast Runner' of the clan of the standing stones. I bring news that you have asked for. There is a tended fire at the great split in the mountains to the setting sun side of the river. Around that fire is the plant that stings and will not burn. The winged ones that you have told of are there. There are many different creatures that walk as we do inside the safety of the encampment," she gasped.

Prime considered the tired raptor and reached out to the dust-stained face. She held her gently by the ears and ran her tongue lightly over her eyes. One of her males offered the news-carrier water from a filled skin and a large piece of sun-dried meat.

The matriarch gave a long whistle and the tribe gathered around her.

"That which was foretold when we met the one who talks to minds, has come to pass. We will break camp and follow this one back to her clan. I will gather others of the lands of the Tannin as we make our way to where the elf known as Peterkin has gone. The time of killing will be with us soon," she said as she replaced her arrow in its quiver.

On the human's world Sam Pitts and John Smith had returned to the premises of Acme Engineering to use the arch, located in my office. John had managed to 'acquire' three isolation suits and associated equipment. Sam had called over some well-owed favours and had brought a crate of intense magnesium flares into the top office via the lift, from the underground car park.

My new recruit had made contact with an ex-communist regime colonel in Uzbekistan at Tashkent. He was in charge of several warehouses on a military base of still boxed AK 47's and thousands of rounds of ammunition. As colonel Halim Djurayev had received very little in pay since the dissolution of the U.S.S.R. he was more than amenable to being paid in small gold ingots. A gift of one of these at the beginning of the negotiation had concentrated the colonel's mind on the future possibilities.

Once Ivan Koshensky had explained to the colonel what he had come to negotiate for, Halim had weighed the possibilities. Acme Engineering's chief buyer then offered even more than money could buy. What he presented to the colonel was the agreed removal of his family and himself to the USA if he got the lorries to the waiting aircraft.

Halim would issue orders to load the lorries and drive them ten kilometres away from the base on the outskirts of Tashkent. Here on a lonely road to Ishan-Guzar he would meet the lorries and they would follow his car to the place that Ivan had designated. His three sons would be the drivers. Once they had travelled far enough from the sight of the guards they would pick up their families and hide them in the cab with them. Nothing was to be taken with them and no suitcases were to be packed. The wives and children were to walk out of their barrack's homes that late afternoon and make their way along the lonely approach road. Once they had been secreted safely inside the cabs, their husbands would then follow the colonel's car out into the far countryside and follow his instructions.

Ivan Koshensky had managed to buy a full set of false papers that would pass scrutiny. Once they had managed to learn to speak English positions would be found at Acme Engineering for the sons while the colonel would sink gladly into retirement. Homes had been bought for the three families in a neighbourhood where they would blend in without problem. All that the ex-Russian needed was to get in contact with Peterkin and get him to take the Spellbinder to a very isolated part of Uzbekistan where the lorries would be waiting.

The ex-Russian sat on the grim hotel bed and considered the situation. Somehow he needed to get in touch with his new boss and tell him of the arrangements that he had set in motion. There was no doubt in his mind that I would not honour them.

He knew that he was being watched. Downstairs in the foyer sat the same man reading a newspaper that he had seen walking behind him on the last visit he had made to colonel Halim at a quiet café not far from the hotel. All arrangements were in place and the time and the date was set. Outside the main entrance he had observed a black van had been parked close by at a no waiting area. As he peeped through a gap in the curtains at the van, two men got out and stood outside in the rain. Another two opened the van doors at the back and got out to hold them open. One of them answered his phone and glanced up at the hotel window, put his hand in his pocket and pulled out a set of handcuffs. He walked quickly over to the illuminated entrance and disappeared from view.

Ivan grabbed his case that was already packed and reminded himself about the strange world he had briefly visited and Peterkin's promise. He had one last quick look around the room just to make sure that he had left nothing behind him and pressed the button on the stone bracelet around his wrist. There was a plopping sound of imploding air, at the same time as the door was kicked in and two Uzbekistani police agents burst into the room. Seeing that the room was empty, they ripped the bedding off and stared uncomprehendingly at the empty space under the bed. Next they wrenched opened the wardrobe doors, only to find that their quarry had vanished. There was nowhere else in the room for him to hide. All they knew about the visitor was that he was an American, of Russian extraction and he had come to see colonel Halim Djurayev about tracing old family members that might have left the area.

When they questioned the colonel, he had told them that the American had a great-grandmother of the same name, Djurayev and wondered if they were related! Halim had looked into his own family tree to find out if this was true and could find no corresponding records. This was the reason that they had met several times and the reason why the American had been allowed onto the military base. Although they begrudgingly accepted the colonel's explanation, they were concerned that Mr Koshensky had seen things that they preferred that he should not have seen, so they organised his pickup to question him.

While a frantic search of the hotel and the adjacent streets was taking place, a disorientated Ivan Koshensky had found himself propelled through the strange arch that was part of my office wall. It felt as though he had travelled through a long tunnel that was both endlessly long, but took no time at all. Here it was daytime and the clock on the wall showed that it was mid-day. The hotel in Uzbekistan had been shrouded in night. He dropped his case onto the floor and sat himself in the big leather swivel chair. What he had just experienced was beyond any science that humanity had mastered. It reconfirmed that he was dealing with an alien life form that was master of powers beyond his conception. He shuddered for a moment as the full implications struck his thoughts. In his mind was a false set of memories that enabled him to 'remember' all the events that had happened to the elf he knew as Peterkin.

By just sitting and thinking he was able to access these memories as if he had been there himself. The other six humans had been with the elf from almost the beginning of the adventure. He had won their loyalties by leading them through the most awful dangers. Ivan knew that at any time this alien being could have just altered their minds so that they would have done his bidding without question. Instead his group had continually expanded to include all kinds of the sentient life forms that occupied his world. Wherever Peterkin went, he pulled people to him like a magnet picking up iron filings! Ivan knew that had the state police taken him in for questioning, they would have made him disappear without trace, if they thought he had been a spy.

"It all comes down to trust," he thought.

Ivan rose from the chair, approached the arch, placing his hands onto the two runic symbols set to one side and thought my name.

Amplified by Spellbinder my name echoed in my mind as Ivan Koshensky placed his hands upon the runes.

"Peterkin!"

I awoke from my sleep and made my way to the control room where the arch waited for my command. Ameela rose instantly and walked by my side to see what had awakened me.

I reached out to the Spellbinder and gave the command, "Open the portal and transport the human here."

The face of the arch shimmered and my new friend walked through. He stopped abruptly when he saw the two of us and averted his eyes.

"High King! I am sorry to take you from your sleep, but I have returned from a very urgent matter that will need your attention," he said.

Ameela laughed and swept her wings around herself, covering her nakedness.

"I am sorry friend Ivan! You are embarrassed! This will never do," she exclaimed, walked forwards, kissed him on his forehead and disappeared back into the bedroom.

Within a few moments she reappeared wearing a loose robe and carrying one for me. Ivan sat down on one of the auxiliary chairs and looked around the control room.

"May I scan your mind? It will be much quicker and more explicit if I do that, than listen to you tell me," I asked.

Ivan nodded and I gently slipped into his memories.

The human world opened up in all its complexities. My new recruit had been very busy since our last meeting. Using the wealth that I had accumulated and John Smith had invested, Ivan Koshensky had flown into Eastern Europe and made his way across the Old Russian states until he had arrived in Uzbekistan.

Here in these far-flung outposts of the collapsed super state, he had found what he was looking for. There were large armies of disgruntled soldiers who had received little in payment since the collapse of communism. Many warehouses were still packed with weapons and guarded by senior commanders with no future except penury.

Colonel Halim Djurayev was just such a man. He had risen through the ranks during the peak of the Russian expansion only to find himself isolated on a military base on the outskirts of Tashkent. Now entering his early fifties he found himself staring down on a rapidly diminishing future for him and his family. Increasing hardship was all that his three sons could look forward to within the decaying army. All his sons had made it to military command and held rank, but rank without good pay bred dissent. When Ivan had laid a small gold ingot of dwarfish smelting on his desk and pushed it towards the colonel, Halim had come to a quick decision when the ex-Russian laid two more by its side.

When Ivan made the increased offer of escape to the west with new papers for his entire family the Uzbekistani broke out in a sweat. All feelings of loyalty to his country vanished as the American showed him the houses that had already been built to house him and his family.

"You made him an offer that he couldn't refuse," I chuckled. "Well done, friend Ivan. Have you seen inside these warehouses?"

"Yes, very briefly and that is why the special police raided the hotel. They are bound to question Colonel Halim about me. He is high enough up in the chain of command that they will have to believe what he says. When he is sure that they have lost interest in him, as routine takes over and things go back to the humdrum normal, he will phone my office and say, 'Halim is ready'. I will then contact you again and you will take this incredible ship to a lonely deserted airfield where he thinks a plane will be waiting. I will then phone his office and say that Yusif is here. The lorries will have been stacked with everything that I have asked for and if there is any space, it will be filled with whatever can be pushed into that hole! Halim and his three sons will drive those loaded lorries and we will intercept them on the airfield."

I sat stunned by the planning and deviousness that Ivan had worked out. He had thought every little detail through and I filled in the plan with all the extra features that lay in the ex-Russian's mind.

"Thank you Ivan Koshensky. Once we have those weapons here we can go to that phase of the plan after I have engineered the next stage," I replied and stood up to shake him by the hand. "Now I must get you home, as tomorrow I must take the Spellbinder over the poisoned brier."

CHAPTER FIFTEEN

The sky was grey, with heavy rain-swollen clouds when morning dawned. It was deceptively quiet inside the compound as my group assembled and began to drag into the Spellbinder the cages that the dwarves had been fashioning. Althalos Hammer-thief had sent his men into the mountains to gather bamboo, sufficient to restrain any of the Dokka'lfar once we had captured some of them. A great deal of the Skaldargate had been fashioned from this versatile giant grass that grew in profusion in the higher reaches of the township.

Hundreds of lengths had been cut of a thickness just greater than a dwarf could span within thumb and forefinger. These had been stored inside the Spellbinder and ferried across the delta to the compound. Althalos and Hildegard had established a strong relationship soon after meeting each other and were as both determined to travel beyond the brier.

This was to be a scouting expedition and to see if we could take a number of the dark elves quietly prisoner. I also wanted to see for myself just what had been the impact of two centuries or more of occupation by the Dokka'lfar. John Smith had bought from the human world's Internet, six 'X-Calibre Gauged' CO_2 rifles that were virtually silent in operation. The darts were filled with enough sedative formula to stop a maddened gorilla. They came in boxes of a hundred so I felt that there was plenty of scope in the usage of these non-lethal weapons. As insurance we also packed all of the tasers and armed the dwarves with these. Mellitus was overjoyed to be reacquainted with these devices and checked that they all carried a maximum charge.

I sat myself in the command chair and reached forward

for the control staff. Once my hands had made contact with the actuation globe at the end of the staff, I became the Spellbinder. I detached the reality of the vessel from the anchor points set into the Earth and willed the vessel towards the brier. Lifting the ship fifty feet above the glossy leaves of the genetically mutated plant was just enough to prevent the seedpods from exploding and peppering the underside of the vessel. Although the viciously sharp edged seeds would do us no harm, I did not want a show of exploding seedpods following the wake of the ship. The plants could sense the approach of the Dokka'lfar and reacted to their presence by spitting the seeds outwards in a lethal shower. As the brier wasn't fussy about what they grew in, the seeds would rapidly sink their roots into living flesh and use the dying elf as fertiliser before settling into the ground.

The gorge was thirty miles across and from edge to edge the brier thrived in an unbroken line. Elfin genetic scientists had determined the spread by seeding both edges of the brier with a restrictor set in the inherited makeup of the brier. The Great Gorge was twenty miles long where the fault in the earth had split the crater walls and the mighty river had done the rest on its way to the sea. The other side of the mountains stretched towards the sea in a series of rolling plains. Prevailing winds tended to keep these lands dry and desert-like except for a narrow strip that followed the delta. It was not the fertile green land that lay inside the crater's mountainous walls. The tops were covered in ice and snow and were high enough to make breathing impossible, so the only way in was through the gorge. Any other ways to the outside were through the few fiercely guarded passes that the dwarves kept constantly patrolled.

The Dokka'lfar had soon learnt not to try entering single file through these narrow passages with sheer sides.

"What had they been doing for more than two centuries?" I asked myself as we sped along.

Abaddon lay on his oiling couch and nursed the feeling of accomplishment. A number of female elves adorned his chamber rushing to be first to indulge his every whim. Two of them were rubbing an aromatic oil into his muscles to loosen the tension that he suffered from. The oil was made from boiling down one of his many female children and combining the grease with herbs brought through from Alfheimr the home world, using the arch of the insane Dream-shifter. Moloch himself had sent the potted herbs as an accolade to Abaddon's coming achievement. After more than two centuries the Dark Lord was close to breaking the deadlock with the Ljo'sa'lfar barrier. Soon a great sacrifice of dark elves would open the arch further so that millions of the Dokka'lfar would swamp the lands beyond the poisoned brier.

He rolled over onto his back and allowed the handmaidens to oil and massage his groin and penis. It soon stood up erect and proud and he beckoned the youngest to mount him. As she sat astride him with one of the others to guide him inside her, he reached out to take the head of the nearest female and kissed her. In the rush of pleasure from his loins as the young, tight female bore up and down upon him; he lost his control and snapped the neck of the female he was kissing. She fell to the floor and lay by the side of the oiling couch in a crumpled heap. He arched his back as the spasms took over and drove himself upwards to meet his partner's ecstasy with his own.

Abaddon lay quietly on his couch as the young elf climbed off his flaccid member and waited for the others to wash and dry him. Once they had finished he sat up and looked down onto the body laid along the couch.

"Have this one removed to the kitchens and prepared for the evening meal," he ordered and stood by the window. "As for you my pretty, do have a name? Can you speak?"

"Great Lord, my name is Inna. I am the only one of my brothers and sisters that can speak."

At the sound of her voice the other handmaidens hissed and bared their teeth at the young one. Abaddon turned from the window and stared at the young female with renewed interest.

"If this one comes to any harm, another of your group may find themselves in the kitchens! Do you understand me?"

An answering hiss and a uniform cowering conveyed to the Dark Lord that they understood only too well.

"You may help to dress me, Inna, as I wish to go outside and view the progress that my busy workers have managed to do since yesterday. You may accompany me, so dress yourself." He cupped her face in his hands and said to her, "I shall keep you near me. It will be interesting to have a partner again that talks."

Those of the Dokka'lfar that were capable of speech had amongst them, those blessed with a greater intelligence. These were the architects and builders of the dark elves. The majority of the mutated race of elves were gifted with little more than the intelligence of apes and could not speak, but they could take orders. A few hundred that were as immortal as the Ljo'sa'lfar and just as intelligent, ruled millions of the dark elves who were telepathically mute. The other difference was that few of them were winged. There were a few gargoyles born amongst the legions of the dark elves, but their intelligence was of a lower order. The Dokka'lfar also came in various sizes, some of them exceeding eight feet tall, while the majority were the same size as the Ljo'sa'lfar. Abaddon was over seven foot tall and was as black as coal. Once he had reached maturity he had ceased to age and had moved ruthlessly up the ladder of opportunity over the thousands of years.

The leader of the Dark Elves was Moloch who could trace his line right back to the original mutation. He stood over eight feet tall and was as red as fire and choose to live upon the home world until Abaddon signalled that the time to swarm under the poisoned brier had come. Under his rule Alfheimr had been turned into Hades. Not one Light Elf had been left behind when Freyr had held Abaddon at bay and the entire world belonged to the Dokka'lfar, who had laid it waste. Only the strong survived here. The weak were eaten. There was never enough food to feed all of the mindless multitude. Soon, due to Abaddon's efforts, a time of plenty would dawn.

Over a hundred years ago a chance accident had focussed the attentions of the Dark Lord. A large block of stone had become loosened from the sheer sides of the gorge and had tumbled down onto the brier. The block was big enough to crush the brier underneath and prevent the mutated plant from rooting into it. Since then Abaddon had built a road upon a causeway leading from the Arch of the wrecked Dream-shifter towards the left hand side of the brier. Thousands of blocks had been carved out of the mountains and dragged by the brutish elves to form this road. Each block was hauled to the edge and tipped over onto the poisonous brier. Built over the top of the road was a constantly expanding roof to shield the workers from the exploding seedpods. The brier had managed to grow over the roof in places, but Abaddon had flat stone slabs laid over the structure before the brier could begin to grow over it. These were dragged along inside the tunnel and forced upwards onto dressed stone sides. Every half mile or so chimneys were built into the stone roof to allow air to circulate inside the tunnel. Even so it was stifling inside the construction. Sometimes the brier got in through the chimney and had to be pushed back with long poles. It had taken a hundred years and the stone tunnel was now over fifteen miles long. The many Dokka'lfar worked the quarries under the lash of the whip and endlessly split the blocks of stone away from the faces of the gorge.

Abaddon had attempted to dig underneath the poisoned brier many times only to have the tunnels collapse on top of the burrowing Dokka'lfar. There came the day when he caught a whisper of Waldwick's mind and realised that it was the High King that was collapsing the tunnels. Once he started building the causeway he had other tunnels dug in the soft earth under the roots well away from his new construction. This was where Waldwick would sense an attack was going on and defend these fake intrusions under the brier.

He would occasionally mock the High King and taunt him about the tunnels drawing him to attack them. He never gave him any idea what he was really up to and the High King offered him his daughter to make a trade. This made Abaddon's mouth water, just to think about the taking of the virgin princess. For a while he dreamed of little else over the years as he waited for the offer to materialise. He raged when Waldwick told him of Peterkin's lust for her and the result, but agreed that he would be just as satisfied with the granddaughter, when she was old enough. Abaddon had no intention of stopping the building of the causeway and laughed to himself at the mad king's offer of a truce. It had been some time since he had mentally spoken to Waldwick and he felt sure that the deranged High King had been silent for longer than usual. When he was not so busy he would search for the High King's mind and taunt him with his continued presence.

The Dark Lord was patient and he had an endless supply of slaves. Eventually the causeway would break through the other side of the brier. When it did there would be fat dwarves to roast and their crops to plunder. Beyond that point would be the vast herds of the dragons to round up and feed the multitude of the Dokka'lfar. Eventually the cultivated lands of the Ljo'sa'lfar would fall like a ripe fruit from the hands of the Pacifists.

He had all the time in the world. Just the thought of the Light Elves made Abaddon's mouth water. It had been thousands of years since he had tasted the sweet meat of an Ljo'sa'lfar, but he still remembered. He still recalled when Freyr had used the 'Star of Light' against him and the multitude had been kept at bay. The High King had used all of his life energy to make sure that the last of the Ljo'sa'lfar made it inside Deedlit's creation. Abaddon had torn the heart out of the High King as he died and ate it raw, staring at the space that the Spellbinder had vanished from.

He had tracked down enough information for one of his gifted Dark Ones to build something similar after nearly ten thousand years of trying. The Dream-shifter had taken him through the long years and shifted realities to the planet that the Light Elves had stayed on first, called by the inhabitants Earth. Auberon had altered the time shift inside the bubble of the Spellbinder to hide it, but had flown from this world because of the usage of so much iron. It had taken many hundreds of years before the beacon of the Ljo'sa'lfar's mental abilities had shone through the maze of shifted realities and pointed the way for Abaddon to follow.

During the Dark Lord's stay upon Earth, as he searched for Auberon's trail, he had ferried many of the humans to Alfheimr as food for his master, but the constant contact with iron had made them bitter. He allowed those who had not gone mad, back into their world to tell tales of Hell that would terrify humans for centuries. It amused him to use the females for sexual gratification and some of the more handsome males. Eventually the stink of iron made it a welcome day when the Dream-shifter found the reality that the Ljo'sa'lfar had moved to. At the time he had thought that the Earth was always there to return to once the Light Elves' world had been sacked.

Abaddon had guided the Dream-shifter to this world of plunder, only to have the fragile mind of the vessel break down into madness once it arrived. Now only the Arch remained active and it required a great deal of life energy to keep it open to the home world. There were an ever-increasing number of the Dokka'lfar coming through the Arch from Alfheim so that was never going to be a problem.

Fifty feet above the poisoned brier I brought the Spellbinder to an abrupt halt. Using my alter ego's senses, I could perceive beneath us what seemed to be a hollow tube inside the brier. I backtracked towards the dwarves' home and found the termination of the tunnel, still some miles short. There beneath me was a large rectangular slab of stone showing through the expanse of brier. As I watched another one appeared and was levered over the edge of the last stone. The brier retaliated by exploding the nearest seedpods and peppering the new exit. I could see a number of dark elves fall as the seeds tore into their flesh. Long poles were used to push the still living slaves over the edge of the stone and into the brier.

Immediately two sidepieces of dressed stone were pushed forwards and another slab manipulated over the top to make a roof. Here the side of the gorge was soft and the brier had been rooted into the walls of the gorge. Where the side of the gorge was hard rock, this had been used as a wall. I could see that once they had progressed beyond this point, then the gorge wall would be the anchor for the roadway Abaddon was building.

Already the brier was trying to grow over the stone slab and I could see that this had already covered many of the slabs behind. Under the bottom slab, the sap bubbled and frothed from the crushed brier. Now that I knew what to look for I could see that the brier was not as thick as it should be, in a line that lead back towards the sea, hugging the wall of the Great Gorge. I followed the direction and flew over the edge of the maze of thorns and stinging leaves.

A straight road led across the desert to a huge arch that spanned the thoroughfare, easily twenty foot across. This had to be the remains of the insane Dream-shifter, operated by Abaddon. I caused the ship to hover and opened the viewing ports through the substance of the Arch. My loyal gnomes clustered around all of those who had come forward to see the extent of the Dark Lord's empire. The last thing we needed was to be noticed by Abaddon. A mental fog surrounded the ship and kept us safe from prying minds. We could see that there was a crudely constructed castle built into the side of the mountain this side of the gorge. The causeway passed by the front of it, before disappearing into the poisoned brier. Terraces had been built by chopping the ground out and banking it up to stonewalls similar to our home castle. Water from the mountains had been used to irrigate these fields that were planted with crops. It was quite evident that these fields had been over-harvested and badly managed.

I pulled away from this area and concentrated on looking for an isolated group of Dokka'lfar. This was not going to be as straightforward as I had hoped, as there was thousands of them scattered around the causeway.

They were all hauling large blocks of stone along the road towards the poisoned brier. The morning's promise of steady rain on our side of the brier had funnelled through the gorge and was dropping onto the parched earth. It would help to hide us from prying eyes.

I followed some of them walking back towards the quarries hacked out of the mountainside. It was a broken area with large sandstone boulders scattered around. Eventually I found a place that was hidden from the busy slaves and where there were plenty of places to stage an ambush. Trees followed streams that tumbled down the mountainsides and snaked their way towards the great river delta. Groups of dark elves were being shepherded with whips by several larger types dressed in leather kilts and jackets. The others were naked and bore the marks of being beaten often. We saw one of them drop through exhaustion onto the stony ground. When the whip had no effect on him, the overseer made a sign and the others fell upon the silent creature and tore him to bits, eating him raw. The big elf with the whip, picked up the head, cracked it open like an egg and sucked out the brain. When he had finished, he chewed the rest of the flesh off the head and threw it away. Within fifteen minutes there was only a few scattered bones lying amongst the stones from the impromptu meal. These had only been discarded when all the marrow had been sucked out from the shattered skeleton.

One of the overseers cracked his whip and the tired elves got to their feet and began to make their way towards the quarry. Tucked in amongst the boulders and trees well out of sight, I opened the Arch.

Henry Spencer was first out followed by Mellitus and a group of dwarves. The humans were armed with the gas operated dart guns and the closest overseer was Spencer's first target. Hoatzin walked to his left, while David and

Steven took the right side that was open country. Two dwarves carrying tasers flanked each human.

Taking advantage of the boulder-strewn area, Spencer lent against the side of the rock, took his aim at the overseer and shot him in the back with the dart. There was a small pop and the dart hit him and stuck in his neck. The Dokka'lfar abruptly stopped and buckled to his knees. He fell forwards onto his face and lay still. Three more elves fell to their knees and the other overseer turned round to see what had happened. Hoatzin let fly with a dart and caught him in the chest, dropping him to the ground. When they saw that the overseers were helpless the other elves rushed at them to kill and devour the two of them. They caught sight of my group and stood for a moment mesmerised at the nearness of dwarves. The sight of Spencer made then ridged with fear. Mellitus and the dwarves opened up with the tasers and soon all the dark elves were stretched out upon the ground.

We had taken out the whole group without being seen. Quickly the cages were offloaded and each elf was packed into place. Longer poles were inserted through the cages and they were picked up by these carrying handles. It took very little time to shuttle them back into the Spellbinder. Within half an hour we had all of them inside and I was on my way back. I had what I had come for and the scouting expedition had given my group plenty to think about.

Once back into the compound many hands were ready to offload my live cargo. The cages were soon dragged out of the Spellbinder's cargo hold and placed inside the holding area of the encampment. My genetic scientists had modified the brier around the compound to be sexless, so that there would be no fear of being hit by sharp-edged stones from the exploding seedpods. A row of holding pens, seven feet tall and three feet thick had been grown specially to house the Dokka'lfar. The dwarves had fashioned towers made from bamboo that had a clear view inside the holding pens where the Dokka'lfar were to be kept. Over the tops of the brier they had built bridges linked to the towers that could be levered over any of the pens. Ropes and pulleys could drop a ladder down so that the dark elves could be retrieved after being darted and examined.

Water had been piped through the entire compound and diverted into the holding pens so that whatever we kept in them could relieve their thirst. We had a total of ten of the brutish dark elves and two overseers that were a good head taller than the slaves. All of them were still incapacitated either by taser or by dart, but the electrocuted ones were beginning to show signs of returning to consciousness. Mellitus and his group made sure that they were tipped into the holding pens to 'come to' away from us. The ones that were darted were solidly asleep and it gave my elfin scientists some time to examine them before they were added to the pens. The two overseers were well muscled and could be any age from maturity to a thousand years. These were the Dokka'lfar that drove the cretins by whip and fist to do their bidding. Where the Ljo'sa'lfar possessed antennae on their foreheads, the Dark Elves had turned to pointed horns protecting the soft tissue inside. One of the overseers was bright red while the other was as black as coal. Apart from that they were identical in size and general shape.

Of the ten slaves, three were female and seven were male. Some of them were emaciated while the others were relatively strong and healthy. There were no traces of any telepathic antennae on their foreheads. As these awoke they scuttled about the living cages looking for a way out. When they found the water they knelt and drank like an animal. The only reasoned thing that they did was to keep away from the stinging and thorn clad brier. Each overseer had been placed in a single enclosure to wake up and could not see the other through the brier until they stood up. As they woke they stood and stared around the small deadly pen, taking in the fact of their prison. Each of them knelt by the water and cupped their hands to drink from the stream that flowed through the pipes. I heard them shout out to each other and acknowledge the general position and relationship.

"Ipos are you there? I smell dwarves and the scent of Ljo'sa'lfar hangs heavy in the air," the red one called out.

"Where are we, Volac? What do you remember?" The black elf answered.

"I remember seeing dwarves and something almost as tall as me that was not an elf and he was as black as you," Volac replied. "I was struck by something that stung and then I slept and woke up here."

"We are imprisoned! Look above you," answered Ipos. "I can see dwarves watching us from a bridge spanning the pens. With them are Ljo'sa'lfar staring down at us as if we were animals! I'll show them animals," he shouted and leaped up to grasp the bamboo supports above him.

As he struggled to pull himself onto the bridge, Mellitus tasered him and watched him fall back unconscious. As Ipos lay in a heap of untidy arms and legs, Mellitus dropped the ladder down, rapidly descended and pulled the darts from the dark elf's chest. He kicked him in the ear before he climbed the ladder back on the bridge.

"That's one lesson learned," he shouted. "The bastards can jump even if they can't fly! Remember that when you manipulate the bridge over the pens. Keep an eye on them all night. We will need the High King's scientists to examine them in the morning. Pull the bridge away and keep watch from the towers. Just remember they are not going anywhere and they can't get out unless someone does something stupid."

In the morning the two weaker Dokka'lfar had been killed and eaten and the slave count was down to eight. Two of the males had been dismembered and bloody fights had gone on for the spoils. The two overseers were sat in the centre of their pens waiting for whatever was going to happen next. The almost mindless dark elves had not shared their grisly meal with them.

In the single cage that housed Waldwick, my predecessor sat shivering in fear, as the facts of what he had intended to do to his granddaughter became horridly clear to him. Once my human scientist and my elfin ones had tested the infection upon the captive Dokka'lfar, inside the isolation suits, a one-way trip over the brier was coming his way.

CHAPTER SIXTEEN

I gave the order to John Smith to ready an isolation suit and Mellitus to immobilise one of the overseers. The time had come to find out just how effective the virus was in infecting the Dokka'lfar and how long it would take to kill him.

My head virologist was over a thousand years old and had spent a very long time perfecting this virus. It had been centuries ago that a few dark elves had been taken when the brier had been let loose to seed and grow. They had been imprisoned and bred so that the virologist could assess the effects of the virus when he had cultured it. Several generations down the line they had been treated with the virus, which had some effect. Some had died quite quickly and some had recovered. All had died in the end and fresh subjects could not be taken once the barrier had been established. Alaric had been waiting a long time to see the result of his improved virus. It was an adaptation of a virus that the few elfin children would acquire soon after puberty and recover from the illness within a week. The Ljo'sa'lfar were immune from the majority of the ailments that accompanied the sickness. They had a few spots and a fever, combined with fits of sneezing that lasted a few days.

Mellitus and his men had dragged the unconscious overseer up the ladder and over the top of the adapted brier to the waiting cage. They laid him on the stony ground and John dressed him in the isolation suit. Then Sam Pitts made sure that he was securely bound. The one thing that we had to make sure of was that he could not tear his way out of the suit and infect any of the light elves with the mutated virus. Even Alaric could not be sure that the virus would not turn against its maker! He had prepared an anti-virus just in case, but as yet it was untested. He intended to try it on the Dokka'lfar just before point of death. The killer agent was a contact virus that could be transmitted by touch or by breathing in the living organism.

John checked the suit was in totally isolated mode. He nodded to Alaric who placed the capsule inside an access port from the entropy sink flask that carried the doses. With great care John broke open the capsule from the flexible side of the suit and got rapidly out of the bamboo cage that encapsulated the overseer who was beginning to awaken.

A circle of elves, dwarves, gnomes and humans watched the dark elf come back to life. As he realised that he was bound, he stared belligerently at his audience and got to a sitting position. Then he became conscious of the fact that he was encased in a heavy plastic envelope. His eyes widened in terror as he sat there trying to wrestle his arms out of the securely bound rope. Sam had pushed a bamboo pole through the crook of his elbows and tied his arms back to this. The Dokka'lfar began to thrash around the bamboo cell in panic, trying to bite his way through the reinforced plastic of the suit without any effect.

I had watched, as this bright red creature had eaten the brains out of a dead slave's head and so I felt no remorse towards this 'thing'. It was a male Dokka'lfar and he had no feelings of regret for what it did to others of its race who could not talk. I could feel the other minds that shared my head echo the self-same feelings within me. I needed to know that my own people could kill these things so while the imprisoned dark elf screamed his hate and fear, I had other things to do.

"Mellitus old friend, fetch the occupants of one of the pens and set them free within crossbow range."

The dwarf nodded and once again he climbed the ladder to a bridge after it had been positioned over a pen. A group of dwarves armed with tasers quickly put four of the primitive elves to sleep. These were quickly hauled out of the pens and laid onto the ground to wake up.

I turned to Eduardo and Calando who were clutching their modified AK 47's with safeties on and said, "Once they are fully awake, kill them. Do it in such a way that no one else is harmed. Have your wits about you, as when they wake, they can be very fast. I will say when to shoot. Mellitus, you and your men are backup, should my two elves find that they cannot do this thing. Tasers only, as I do not want to waste them."

The two elves switched to single shot and took off the safety switches and raise the rifles to sight down the barrels.

The dark elves began to stir and awaken. They began to sit up and get an idea of where they were. They could smell the scent of dwarves and light elves and their nostrils began to twitch. Their backs were to the brier and all they could see was a fence of stinging leaves and thorns at each side. As a group they leapt to their feet and eyed the empty ground between us. For a few moments they stood still, then as a pack they charged across the gap between us. They screamed defiance and killing lust, as they bounded into the air each time that they hit the ground, showing their teeth. Clawed hands extended they had only eyes for their prey.

"Now," I shouted as the leading male got to within twenty feet.

There was a crackle of gunfire and the two leading Dokka'lfar fell to the ground and trashed around. The other two were only about fifteen feet away when Eduardo switched to rapid fire and took the both of them out with a burst. These two died more or less instantly and Calando walked round the two bodies and hammered the skulls in of the other two with the but of his rifle.

"I thought that it would be a waste of a good bullet," he

said and grinned. "Elves can kill elves, if they are Dokka'lfar it would seem, High King! I shall have no inhibitions taking the lives of those beyond the brier. When the time comes, you will find us ready."

I became suddenly aware of my wife and mother stood beside me armed with the adapted AK 47's.

"Peterkin, I need to know," my mother said. "If you have no further use for the mindless ones, I would like to make sure that I will have no inhibitions taking their intrusive lives! I want to be sure that I can ascend away from the ritual that has been passed down from elf to elf. We do not kill our own! Over a thousand years I have obeyed that mantra and lived it and believed it. There are many more of my age that will find this thing difficult to accomplish. Let the others see that someone of my age can overcome the conditioning and lead by example. Remember that these two loyal elves of yours once had their minds 'pressed' by Waldwick, to assist him torturing you. Their minds were under his control at that time. Could it not be that your mind has also influenced them? I am sure that they would do anything for you, so this would be a greater test."

Ameela flicked the safety off her rifle and said, "I too will fly over the pens and show that I can also do this thing. After all it was to be my fate to be among these beasts and to be used by them."

I stared at these two females of my race with a mounting feeling of horror. They had been changed out of all recognition by the events that had caught them up in this coming war. I realised that like Pandora's box, the lid had been opened and terrible things had ventured out. The only thing left in the box, according to the human's story, was the spirit of hope. What had been an ability only bred into the High King's genetic line, was now surfacing in my people. The ability to kill our own race, be it Dokka'lfar, had once only been the burden of kings. Waldwick had descended into madness because of the evil of his own doing, driven by the unnatural urge for power. I had not asked for this burden, but I would not give it to anyone else to carry. Once we had taken out the menace of our dark brethren, I would wish that the spirit of hope would enter my people.

"Do it," I reluctantly answered, "but be sure that all of the elfin contingent are aloft to see this thing done. Let them all see what we have to do on a much larger scale."

I felt a ripple of minds reaching out and saw my people flex their wings and soar aloft. Once they had caught the thermals and were able to hover, I saw my wife and mother swoop down over the pens and the sound of automatic rifle fire filled the air. There were several bursts and then silence hung over the execution pens and a single scream of terror came from the last occupied pen. The other overseer had seen everything and waited his turn. I had other plans for him, so he needed not to worry at the moment. There was much information in his mind that I would be interested in dragging out. Never the less it did no harm to let him wonder about the once contemptible pacifists, who were now able to bring death from a distance.

Mellitus grasped my arm and pointed away from the gorge to where the dinosaurs held sway. A column of smoke was rising from the wilderness many miles away.

"I think that we shall have company soon, my elfin friend. There is only one type of dragon that has the use of fire. I just hope that she has not saved me another of her eggs!"

I opened my mind to a full broadcast to all of my group and sent these instructions, "We have allies arriving soon from the Plains of Scion. The leader is called Prime. These are the people that aided us in the rescue of my Ameela and Mia. They are not to be feared, no matter what happens.

They would feel that a great act of disrespect was judged against them and would take great offence. Prime promised me, that when I moved against the Dokka'lfar, she and all the tribes scattered throughout the plains that could travel to the Great Gorge would do so. They are a proud and free people. Prime has told them of the struggle to come and there is not one amongst them who is not prepared to die if necessary to defeat the scourge that has followed us to this world. Make ready a feast of welcome and sing the brier open when they come. They can understand by mind-to-mind contact and will expect that the elves will do this. Dwarves will have to do what they can with sign language and gesture."

Many miles away Prime watched for the answering thickness of smoke to her bonfire and grunted with satisfaction when she saw it. She whistled and trilled to the others of her extended family. The command to move on carried to troops of her kind scattered over the plains. With torches of smoky fire they drove a herd of hadrosaurs at a steady pace towards the Great Gorge. The scent of smoke made the great lumbering animals nervous and kept them moving. There was more than a thousand of her kind all armed with bows, crafted from the dwarfish design that Mellitus and his people had instructed them to make. In each raptor's mind was an urge to pay back a debt of gratitude and the knowledge that what they were about to do was to ensure that their hunting grounds remained theirs.

Never in the history of the folk had so many gathered together. New and novel ideas had been passed from group to group. The idea of herding their prey could never had come without the gift of fire-making, given by the dwarves along with the ability to kill prey at a distance. In the time taken since Prime's meeting with Peterkin and the present a massive social change had taken place amongst the clans. Instead of competing they had banded together into loose associations. Any sub-standard progeny were ruthlessly culled if they did not show signs of intelligence soon after hatching.

They soon found themselves with the edge of the river at their left and penned the herd between this deep obstacle and the fire torches. The column of smoke from the hidden bonfire inside the palisade showed them the way. Before long a strange sight presented itself. A wall of glossy green, far too tall to jump over obstructed further progress. Once the hadrosaurs had touched it they recoiled with snorts of pain and would not travel any further. Above the barrier were wooden towers with dwarves at the top, staring down at the amazing sight. They were waving and gesturing to Prime and her people to walk along the brier to their right. The hadrosaurs were securely penned between river, brier and fire-torches by the raptors. Prime left her people to this task and along with others of her rank they made their way along the brier to hear a high pitched ululating sound. It was the sound of my elfin people singing the door open at the side of the brier facing the dwarf's stronghold. As the pitch concentrated the brier began to pull away from itself and a tunnel appeared.

I stood waiting to see the unlikely friend that had helped me rescue my Ameela. Velociraptors are taller than elves and strong enough to tear off an arm. They were also beautiful to look at. With their feathered ruffs around their long necks, crested heads and tails covered in plumage they had a birdlike quality until you saw their hands. I recognised Prime immediately and held out my empty hands to her. She walked out of the tunnel with the other members of her group and the tunnel collapsed behind her. Prime ignored the sealing of the brier with the logical attitude that when it was time to go, the brier would open again. She reared up to her full height and stared around the compound, taking in all the strange sights and filing them away.

Prime took my hands in hers and joined her mind to mine.

"It is good to see you again, my friend. There have been many changes in your people since we last met," I said.

She swung her head down to my level and fixed me with her large golden eyes and replied, "All good for my people, High King! High King, what is that? Are you now leader of your people? There is much that has happened to you also, since I saw you disappear into a hole in the air!"

I was amazed at the sharpness and perception of this creature. Since those first faltering communications involving telepathy with Prime, she had developed her abilities just as the humans had been able to. It would seem that I was instrumental in unlocking a sealed door in the mentality of others. Unfortunately it did not work with dwarves.

Ameela and Mia dropped out of the sky and embraced the velociraptor as she stood there holding my hands. Totally unafraid, Mia wriggled round until she was seated just behind the giant's ruff of feathers. There she wrapped her arms around the raptor's neck and hugged her. Prime stood transfixed as she was smothered in elves. She was aware that the other leaders of groups were staring at her with the black centres of their great golden eyes, wide open with astonishment.

She trilled an explanation to the others that these were her special friends and she did not expect them to do this behaviour with them. Whilst this was going on a dwarf could be seen hurrying up to the velociraptor. I recognised that it was Mellitus who was carrying something in a leather bag. He clasped his hands over Prime's fingers and then he reached into the leather bag, pulled out a woven leather strap and tied it around her neck. It carried a magnifying glass mounted in a handle. He had shown her this new thing that had belonged to his father, before he had left with myself to go back to the lodge. In his quieter moments he had ground another glass lens so that he could give one to Prime when they met again.

Prime immediately showed her companions what a magnifying glass could do when it concentrated the sun's rays. She also showed how it could make things appear bigger when looked through. After much trilling and chirping, the velociraptors stared at Mellitus and myself with even greater interest.

One of the raptors spotted the untidy heap of dead Dokka'lfar and trilled a question at Prime. All the raptors swung their heads round to stare at the bodies and I heard Prime's voice inside my head.

"Are these the foe? They are small!"

I answered the leader of the clans, "Yes my friend. These are the enemy, but do not be fooled by what you see here. There are more of these the other side of the brier than all of your people many times over. Some of them are much larger than these creatures. They breed in huge numbers and outstrip all food supplies. There is a doorway similar to the one you saw us disappear through over the other side of the mountains and it leads to their barren home. Once they can get through to our side, they will come in uncountable numbers and they will eat everything that lives. We will not overcome them once they are here."

One of the raptors picked up a body and asked, "Are they good to eat?"

I heard her trill the question and heard her voice in my mind!

"Feel free to try them. We do not want them. They would eat us if they could," I answered telepathically.

The raptor wrenched off an arm and tasted the blood that pooled from the ragged end. She nodded and passed the arm around for others to taste.

"Once we are on the other side, we will not need rations," Prime assured me. "It would be no hardship to prey on these. When do we go?"

"Soon my good friend. Very soon! Before this time comes however there is something that I shall need you to do for me. I have to go away from here and fetch some more weapons from another place. When I return I shall need you to find me the meanest and largest 'eaters' that you can. Bring them here and I will 'press' their minds and take them across the brier, setting them loose amongst the Dokka'lfar to wreck havoc.

Prime looked towards the bonfire that the dwarves and gnomes had kept alight and trilled to her companions. They immediately hauled the bodies of the fallen Dokka'lfar towards the glowing embers and buried them in the coals to cook. I could see that a feeling of revulsion swept through my people, but was quickly repressed and was not passed on to our new allies. While they were there they helped themselves to the haunches of meat that had been left for them as part of the evening meal.

I felt the mind of my strange alien friend pose the question, "I have seen that the stinging plant cannot be pushed aside and that it fills the gap between the mountains, so how will we get to the other side?"

"I have a means to get there and I will show you something that will be even more strange to you than what you have seen. Come with me and I will take you into the sky above you, inside a thing that flies," I replied and walked to where the Spellbinder was anchored.

The arch was clearly visible to my velociraptor allies, but until I sat upon the command chair there was nothing else to see except a ripple in the air behind it. I led her and some of her group inside the vessel and sat in the chair.

"Stand beside me, Prime and be ready to fly as I show you what I can do," I told her.

I became the Spellbinder for a short while and took the ship across the brier and showed Prime and the others the extent of the barrier and the efforts of the Dokka'lfar to burrow through it. The initial stab of fear of the unknown soon disappeared from the velociraptors as we climbed over the brier. They saw the multitude of the ever-increasing dark elves filling the lands between the crater walls and the sea. We scouted the area around the road and also the castle defences, looking for places of ambush. After a while we returned to the compound and I set the Spellbinder down.

Prime stood silent for some time and then said, "A long time ago I offered to come with you and learn new things. I also told you that I would help protect your clan with mine. I have now seen the menace that would destroy our lands. As you said to me, they are many. In the battle to come, you will need all of my people, as well as all the ones who are here in this enclosure. We shall speak with them and tell them of all that we have seen."

"I give my thanks to you my friend. It gladdens my heart to know that you will be there when we fight against this menace. I know that we will need every willing fighter that we can muster," I replied and clasped her clawed hand in mine.

I was aware of her large golden eyes staring straight into mine, as her mind entered mine and she said, "I am not the creature that I was when we met so long ago. You have changed the way that I think. Where there was fog, you have replaced this with clarity. Those that I have been with me upon the plains have adopted my new ways of thinking. You have done much for my people in ways that you cannot imagine. New ideas have been embraced by all of the clans. We owe you a great debt. Our land needs to be protected from those who would take it and rape it. It is as simple as that!"

I heard several loud chirrups and trills from those who had elected to stay behind and tend the cooking Dokka'lfar. I turned round to see the velociraptors raking the roasted elves from the embers. Prime joined them and the group soon devoured the flesh and many of the smaller bones. The feast was offered to others of my group but tactfully refused, without giving offence.

This was the real start of the building friendship between the Ljo'sa'lfar, dwarves and gnomes with the people of the plains. Once the dwarves of Skaldargate showed the raptors how they had domesticated the breed of dinosaur that they referred to as 'runners' this prompted ideas amongst the clans of doing something similar. They had already learned how to herd the hadrosaurs, but the idea of riding the almost mindless creatures had not occurred.

I felt the presence of the Spellbinder in my mind.

"Ivan Koshensky has operated the arch in the parallel world. He needs to speak with you at this time."

This was the final set of pieces that were required to complete my plan. I opened the arch connected the two realities and watched as my new human ally stepped through the arch into the humid heat. This time Ivan had remembered to change into shorts and a loose fitting shirt. He took a little while to stare around the compound and when he saw Prime and her companions, he shook his head in disbelief.

"High King," he gasped, "What are those creatures?"

"Allies," I replied. "They are what the dinosaurs on your world might have evolved into, had they not all been wiped out, millions of years ago. The Plains of Scion are their lands and they are willing to fight and die if necessary to keep them. Come with me and I will introduce you to Prime, leader of her people."

With that I turned and walked out of the Spellbinder's control room towards the group of velociraptors. Ivan stayed very close to me, as the sharp toothed mouths opened and their tongues flicked out to taste the air. It was fortunate that Ivan had sweated so much that he had washed off the aftershave perfume from his face. I could see that he was a man of considerable courage as he stood very still as the group surrounded him. Prime extended her three fingered hand and opposable thumb to him and he clasped it in his. Ivan's hand disappeared inside the larger grasp, like a human babies inside an adult's.

Prime's question was as direct as her mind could be.

"What use is this person? He does not hunt! Why is he here?" She asked.

I smiled at her directness and answered, "He has found weapons for my people, more of the sticks that kill at a distance. You saw them used when we rescued my mate. We need many to arm all of these dwarves, gnomes and elves."

She stared down at the sweating human and asked, "Can he acquire weapons for my people?"

Because of the closeness of my mind to the two of them a link was forged between us all and Ivan answered, "Yes, I think that I can. Steel axes and sledgehammers would be easy to obtain, but the proximity of so much strong iron would not be a good idea due to your sensitivity. What I can do instead would be to buy large wooden mallets set on hickory handles" and he projected a mental image of the hammer being used by a velociraptor.

Prime thought about it for several seconds and replied, "Good! This will do well. Thank you human. High King I must be amongst my people outside of the compound. We will be there when you return with your weapons."

Ivan turned to me and said, "The time has come Peterkin to collect those weapons. I have had a phone call from colonel Halim that he ready to proceed. We should go as soon as we can and set things in motion."

I projected my mind to Sam Pitts and said, "It time to take that trip to Uzbekistan. We have a shopping trip to organise!"

CHAPTER SEVENTEEN

I called my advisory war council together inside the Spellbinder. Facing me were a mixture of elves, dwarves, goblins, gnomes and human beings. I had drawn these people together and counted them amongst my dearest friends.

I stood there for a moment and stared at this strange assembly and said, "My people, we have reached the point that requires that the gathering of weapons has to be done. I have to return to the parallel Earth and take the Spellbinder through the realities. I shall need Sam Pitts and a number of others as an escort," I said and placed my hand upon my newest human recruit's shoulder. "Ivan has arranged everything for me and all we need to do is to load up the weapons. This might get a little messy and I think that we may need plenty of back up in case of trouble. So we will go fully armed. Ivan will explain."

"On my world, I have reached an arrangement with a colonel in the Uzbekistani army. His position in the army has been downgraded over the years to a situation where he finds that he is just held responsible for the storage of excess weapons.

These weapons are exactly what we need to take the fight against the Dokka'lfar. My human friends will understand the situation. I have promised this man, that we will transport his family to America where they will be safe and he has given me his trust. He has communicated to me that the weapons that we need are loaded onto transports and are ready to go. All we have to do is to be at the place that I have specified and he will have the weapons delivered, as soon as I give him the signal. He has no knowledge of this place and the people that live in it, so I feel that this should be a mainly human expedition," Ivan told them. "I feel that the only other people that can ride on the Spellbinder has to be elves, as they can disguise themselves by projecting a mental image of someone else.

There is another problem as well. Civil unrest has erupted in a very volatile area near to the city of Tashkent. If the unrest spills over the borders of the three countries linked together beyond what is termed the Ferghana valley, that forms the border with Kyrgyzstan, Tajikistan and Uzbekistan, then our colonel may be drawn into the conflict. There are hundreds of thousands of refugees crossing the borders, causing great confusion. He wants to get away from this situation as fast as he can. The fact that he has loaded the weapons onto transports will soon bring down the authorities to find out what orders he is fulfilling and from whom. My human colleagues will understand what I mean when I say that we have to move very quickly."

Inside my mind I listened to the voices of long dead kings. These were the ancestors that had produced me and running through my genetic makeup was the ability to plan and if necessary, kill those of my own kind. I had inadvertently passed this ability to others of my people. In that strange tableau that had played itself out inside this very compound, some of my people had found out that they could slaughter their own kind, without remorse. It did not matter that the ones that they had killed were dark elves. They were elves! No matter what they had done or were capable of, their deaths had come so easily to my mother and wife that I was still shocked by the awful deed. I mentally shuddered, but put the picture out of my mind. If that killer instinct had not been roused, then what then? This was not something that an isolated High King could do alone. If I were to succeed, I needed every kind of killer that I could find.

"I will leave John Smith behind to monitor the progress of our infected Dokka'lfar and to follow up with anything else that Alaric requires," I ordered and turned towards the Spellbinder. "Those of you that are coming with me had better get a move on. Make sure that you are armed, provisioned and warmly dressed, as it is winter where we are going."

I gave them enough time to do this and quickly made my way into the command chair of the Spellbinder. Sitting for a moment, I looked around and made sure that my group had assembled with me. To my surprise Mellitus and his friends had joined me along with a good number of elves as well as my human companions.

Mellitus laid his hand upon my arm and said, "Where my King goes, then he will find me by his side. If it is the place that I will breath my last, then that will be as it is! I will not leave you."

"The leaders of the Stormgalt and Skaldargate will be also be by your side," insisted Althalos holding the hand of Hildegard who had an AK 47 clutched in the other.

I looked around the chamber and saw that Eduardo, Calando, Ameela, Mia and my mother were amongst the many elves that accompanied me. All of them were armed with Klashnikovs except the humans who had made sure that they were armed with the armour piercing Berrettas. I grasped the globe at the top of the staff of power and became one with the Spellbinder.

The reality of this world blurred, ripped open and we slipped through into the alternative Earth. We were somewhere over the African desert and travelling towards Egypt. I put the Spellbinder down and let Ivan Koshensky out to stand upon the cooling sands under a star bright sky.

He took his satellite phone out of his pocket and rang the number that connected him to colonel Halim's office.

The phone rang for a short while and Halim's voice was heard speaking in Uzbekistani and Ivan replied, "Yusif is here!"

After he had made this phone call he rang his office at the factory and left some explicit instructions concerning the large mallets that he had promised the clans of velociraptors.

Ivan walked back into the Spellbinder and stated, "It will take them a few hours to drive away from the warehouse and to the abandoned airfield. Will it take that length of time to get there?"

In my mind was the location of the airfield and built inside a valley. Tall mountains enclosed the few buildings that had survived neglect.

I slipped the Spellbinder through a twist in space and answered, "We are there now!"

The Spellbinder took on the shape and image of a large transport plane and bent the reality of this place out of phase, so that it did not appear on any radar screen. Elves and dwarves felt immediately the increased gravity pull of this parallel world. The humans had gone back and forth so many times that they were used to it and were not affected. Sam Pitts stationed his men around the airfield to get a good view of the incoming weapons as they came along the only approach road. It was a dark cloudy night and at this altitude the winter wind cut like a knife. The airfield sat at the bottom of a valley with mountain ranges stretching for miles in all directions. This had been a Russian supply strip and had been abandoned after the collapse of the Soviet Union. Most of the buildings had stood up to the ferocious winter weather and the summer heat quite well, but rust and decay were doing away with the roofs.

There were two buildings that sat one each side of the runway and Sam split his forces between the two of them. The twins, David and Steven forced the doors on the left hand building and made their way towards the offices at the top that overlooked the single road into the complex. Sam took Hoatzin and Spencer with him into the right hand building. The stairs were still in good order and they were soon making space to mount the Berettas on tables that they forced towards the walls. There was no need to knock out the glass as most of the windows had been shattered. All three of them settled down to wait and made sure that they were loaded with exploding armour-piercing shells. The bitter wind sang through the many holes in the windows.

Mellitus and his faction spread out on each side of the airstrip with a number of elves battling the extra gravity by flapping their wings and generating enough lift to get them airborne. After spending so much time in the steamy warmth of the Great Gorge both creatures were finding the cold difficult to deal with. Although they were well wrapped up to beat the cold, they could not ignore the shivering wind and it sapped their strength.

After a while I opened my mind to Sam's anxious thoughts and asked, "Can you see any sign of the lorries?"

He scanned the far reaches of the road with night scopes and replied, "Something is on its way towards us. I can see three sets of headlights following each other, coming towards us at some speed. Open the side of the Spellbinder and make ready to load the crates straight into the hold. Behind them and some way back I can see other vehicles following with dipped lights. We will take out the leading cars with the Berettas by blowing up their engines. That will mean that they will have to make it to our position on foot."

Using my mind as a bridge, Sam gave his orders to David and Steven on the other side of the airstrip.

There was a crackle of firearms from the roof of one of the buildings as Hoatzin took out the first three cars. Steven and David opened fire from the top of another building and took out the rest of the vehicles just to make sure that no attempts would be made to drive round the road block. Sam and Spencer concentrated their fire at an armoured carrier that was following the cavalcade. The armour-piercing shells ripped through the inch thick steel front and destroyed the engine behind it.

I could see the headlights at the end of the airfield as three lorries drove straight for the side of the Spellbinder. Ivan Koshensky was there to meet them and was picked out by the headlights as he waved his arms to the colonel and his sons. They screeched to a halt and the doors opened and four women and a number of children climbed out of the cabs and began to run for the safety of what they could see, as the transport plane. The elfin women quickly shepherded them aboard, blanketing out their appearance as they did so. There was so much raw iron in the construction of those lorries that it set my teeth on edge and that made it impossible to drive them straight onto the Spellbinder. The dwarves soon cut the ropes and pulled the tarpaulins off. They made a human and dwarf chain to unload the boxes into the safety of the ship.

The extra gravity made the task just that much harder for my people, but they did not complain. The colonel's sons had not noticed anything different about the people that had helped them unload the lorries as my elves kept up a constant camouflage of mental interference.

More gunfire sounded across the airfield as Sam Pitts and his men kept a covering fire keeping the Uzbekistani soldiers well back at the two-mile mark. Not wanting to kill anyone, the human group had kept firing at the vehicles and used exploding ordinance to keep the soldiers under cover. Now and again they took out a scrawny tree or a wall close by. As the soldiers had no real idea where the shots were coming from two miles away, they kept their heads down. Nobody wanted to be a hero and go back in a body bag.

After some while the lorries became empty and I entered Ivan's mind with an instruction to ask the colonel's sons to drive the lorries away from the Spellbinder. I suggested that they were in the flight path and would prevent us getting away.

I could see that Sam and his men had made it down from the roofs. They were making their way back to the ship as fast as they could. That could only mean that the soldiers were on the move. They would be in range in a few minutes and they would be intent on killing as many of us that they could. A crackle of fire erupted from out of the sky as several elves let fly with the AK 47's from fifty feet in the air. They then dropped like stones down to the Spellbinder, as the answering bursts of fire swept the area from whence they had fired. I felt several agonising spasms of pain from some of my people as they collected a stray bullet. I gave what comfort I could by mentally sharing their wounds and helping to diminish the pain.

The colonel's sons had removed themselves from the lorries and were running as fast as they could back to us, dodging the bullets that were beginning to come from out of the darkness. This was answered by automatic fire as my dwarves opened up again with their AK 47's. This was rapidly getting out of hand and I needed to do something quickly. I expanded the size of the Spellbinder so that it covered my new allies. Now the returning hail of bullets spattered on the impenetrable shield of my ship. I changed the shape into something from their mythology and just hung in the sky above them for a few moments.

A huge saucer shape twinkled with bright lights that revolved slowly around a central ball. All firing stopped!

Slowly I took the Spellbinder up into the air, above the forces on the ground and drifted away towards the African continent.

I twisted the reality around the ship and concentrated my mind on translating the Spellbinder back to the compound. The cargo that we had taken on affected every elf on board. It was like continual toothache, throbbing in the roots of the mind. The most important thing was to unload the weapons and scatter them about the compound in neat piles. Concentrated together they would affect too many of us and though we had demonstrated a certain acclimatisation to the iron content, too much of it was damaging. The strain of piloting the Spellbinder carrying so much iron had made my nose bleed and drenched my front with my own blood. Added to this was the need as High King to assist with diminishing the pain of the wounded. I felt the minds of my mother and Ameela link to mine and ease the load as they moved amongst the stricken. In the strain and confusion I lost the blanketing cover that my mind was giving out and we were seen for what we were. The individual bending of reality tends to be forgotten when you are having a bullet dug out of your body.

Ivan Koshensky stood in front of me with colonel Halim at his side.

"Peterkin! Whatever is the matter with you?" he asked.

"There was more iron in that cargo than I realised, my friend. It upsets elves. It can work like a poison," I answered and slumped into the chair. "Forgive me colonel Halim, this has been somewhat of a strain. You were not meant to see us as we really are. From the expression on your face I should think that it has come as a bit of a shock. I apologise. We desperately needed those weapons that you risked you life to get for us. You have my utmost gratitude."

"Ivan Koshensky has explained to me your problems and

your needs. My son Teginbek is a medic-surgeon and has already removed a bullet from a dwarf and sewn up a tear in a wing from one of your people. He is still removing bullets from the other wounded. His wife, Fatma is a nurse so she will have a look at your nosebleed. We want to help you in any way that we can. Ivan has explained to me all that you have done to ensure our lives in the free country of America. We could not ask more.

I hung my head in exhaustion for a few moments and took in what the colonel had just said. This man who I had never met, was willing to help my people in any way that he could. It was too much to take in through words. I needed to go into this man's mind and see if he really meant it and show him just what he and his sons were volunteering for.

"Colonel Halim, will you allow me to enter your mind? If you do I will give you the knowledge and information that will really show you what you will be involved with! Ivan will assure you that I did this with him and he is none the worse for it," I guaranteed him.

Halim gave me a measured stare and nodded.

I slipped into his mind and found a well ordered, disciplined personality that was yearning to express his abilities as a trained soldier in a just cause. His mind was very similar to Sam Pitts, except that he was a family man not single, as was my leader of the human band. This man loved his wife and sons greatly and all of the rest of his family. His one desire was to get them to a safe and stable place. This I vowed to do whenever he made it clear to me that the time had come to pay my side of the bargain. I made my decision and filled his memory with the information that I had imparted to Ivan. I also improved his ability to speak English and added basic elvish as well, so that he could understand the dwarves and my people. The

Spellbinder slipped through the last chain of realities and centred itself into the middle of the compound.

I was aware of a young human women mopping the blood from my face and removing my shirt as we landed. She had pressed a cold compress against the bridge of my nose. The relief was soothing and the throbbing began to die down.

Once down I released the staff of power and became me again, or as close to being me as I could! Ameela appeared and handed over a fresh shirt and took the soiled one from the young woman. She squeezed Fatma's arm in affectionate care and sat down facing me. The Spellbinder had now diminished to just the control room and of course the Arch. The bindings around the cargo returned to the central core of the ship and the many boxes were unshipped and rapidly scattered around the compound. As the concentration of iron diminished I began to feel much better.

After a few days my new guests began to take in the new world that awaited them. I had reassured them that this was only a temporary home until this whole business was finished. I did offer to transport them directly to their own world now, but they were having none of it. All of them were determined to stay for as long as they were needed. These humans were determined that they would become part of my plans and once again I was filled with gratitude that these people wanted to become allies! Once they had given their trust to me I became responsible for them. I was beginning to really understand what it was to be High King!

Amongst the dinosaurs that lived on the Plains of Scion, the intelligent velociraptors were the greatest shock for them to cope with. Not so the children, who had no fear of these giant birdlike creatures. To them they were part of the great adventure that had suddenly unfolded into their lives.

Some weeks later I found Prime with a boy of around ten years old sat upon her shoulders, being carried around the compound. He had one of her feathers stuck behind his left ear, held in place by a rawhide band. To my amazement he was able to chirrup and whistle to her and be understood!

More and more dwarves had moved into the area to swell my 'army' the legend of 'The Long-shadow' had spread throughout the mountains on both sides of the gorge. It was told over and over again that the High King lives! He needs us to rid the land of the Dokka'lfar and he will fight beside us.

So the stories spread that I had the ability to travel between the worlds. I had weapons that could kill at a distance and much more than that. The Arch at the castle was in constant use as the elfish farmers ferried in supplies to the grounded Spellbinder. Also more able-bodied elves added to the problems of feeding the multitude that were camped here. More goblins than I believed existed came as well and quickly showed an aptitude for mechanisms by stripping down the weapons and removing iron where possible and replacing it with alternatives. Wooden stocks replaced steel ones and the cannibalised iron was turned into spears.

The red Dokka'lfar had died slowly and painfully from the virus. We loaded him into the Spellbinder still in his isolation suit. To all purposes he was dead and the virus with him, but we would prefer to err on the safe side. We tried it on the other black elf and he got very sick, but survived long enough to develop antibodies. Alaric my chief virologist became quite excited about this and drew some of them off the Dokka'lfar before he killed him. On dissection in an isolation chamber he found to his delight that the dark elf had been rendered sterile.

This presented a new angle to the struggle. Now we

needed to infect Waldwick with the virus and let him loose behind the brier. Whether the virus killed them or rendered them sterile mattered not to us. We preferred them dead, but unable to breed would help the situation. That morning we walked over to where Waldwick's cage was securely fixed to the ground. As he caught sight of us he became frantic and threw himself against the bars of his cage. He tried to hide in the darkest corner, but to no avail.

I stood with the gas rifle at the ready, loaded a dart and said, "Waldwick it is time to pay for your sins. What you intended to do to your own daughter and when that was not to be, your granddaughter is to be done to you. You killed my father and my grand uncle in cold blood just to be High King. To be High King is a genetic thing, not chosen by the individual. It is the laying down of responsibility for your people, not the ruling of them. This may cost me my life, as it has done so before to my predecessors. It is a price that I am willing to pay if I must. You would not and would use others to achieve your desires."

Waldwick screamed, "No! No, no, no, no! Please no! Don't send me there. Have mercy upon me. I am truly sorry for all that I have done to you and your family. Please! Don't let me die in this way. Please, please spare me."

"You had not one shred of mercy for me or my daughter," Ameela shouted back. "Goodbye father! Dart him, Peterkin and send him on his way."

I took aim and shot him in the leg and his sobbing cries grew weaker as the anaesthetic began to take effect. Mellitus dragged him out of the cage and John Smith dressed him in the other isolation suit. Once he was safely inside, Alaric inserted the entropy jar and broke the seal. Whatever was frozen inside that jar would rapidly come back to life and spread within the confines of the suit. Mellitus and Althalos dragged the unconscious ex-king back into the cage and they hauled the cage back into the region of the Spellbinder. Here we would leave him until the morning securely tied so that he could not damage the suit and release the virus. As I stood there looking into the cage at the pitiful figure I felt a twinge of compassion and entered his mind.

I quickly isolated his mind from the higher functions and blocked it off. Waldwick died in his own brain and ceased to exist. The benefit to us would be that if he were to be taken into the presence of the Dark Lord, he would be unable to tell him anything about us.

Now I had another task that needed to be achieved and that would need Prime and her people.

I found her outside the compound with her clan, butchering several hadrosaurs and roasting the cuts over a huge fire of red-hot embers. Ivan had gone back and forwards through the arch in my 'office' at the engineering works. He had managed to acquire hundreds of specially crafted mallets to suit the velociraptors. The hickory shaft was two inches diameter and the head was the size of a small double bucket bound with brass. Once Prime had approved of the design, Ivan had placed an order for a thousand to be made and delivered to the firm's warehouse, where another arch made them accessible to us. I often wondered what the guards thought about at that place, when so many goods travelled into the warehouse and nothing came out! Still they were paid enough to keep silent.

Her feathered head swung round at my approach and the black spots in her golden eyes fixed me with an unblinking stare.

I heard her whistle and trill as her thoughts travelled into my mind as she asked, "Is it time? Do we move against our enemy soon? Is it time to go onto the plains and find the great eaters of flesh and bring them here?"

"When you are ready and fully satisfied with the meat that you have prepared, it will be time to go and do this for me. I shall need them here at the edge of the compound in as many days as you see on the fingers of you hands."

It was the closest that I could go in explaining the quantity of eight days. This would give me time to travel over the brier with our parcel of germ warfare and get back in plenty of time. We needed the virus to start to spread before we raised the stakes by introducing a number of Giganotosaurus into the killing fields. I intended to drop them well spaced apart so that they would instil widespread panic. With nothing to eat on that side of the brier, they would feed on the Dokka'lfar and hunt them down. I would 'press' their tiny minds into concentrating their appetite totally on the dark elves and to leave the rest of us alone. As they hunted by scent, they should be able to tell the difference between us. I comforted myself with the fact that Waldwick had managed to do this and keep the meat eaters under the shadow of the Tower of Absolom. There were other strong-minded elves amongst the force that had come with me that had enough power to accomplish this. Without an iron band around her neck Ameela was quite capable in dominating the minds of these terrible dragons.

In the morning, Waldwick's mindless infected body would be transferred to the other side of the brier, as close to the castle that I could take the Spellbinder. Here he would be released from his suit and allowed to wander. John Smith would be the one to trip the quick release mechanism, by pulling on a long cord attached to the zipping system and the isolation suit would peel off the ex-king. Once that was done we would close the hatch and speed back after staying aloft and invisible until we were sure that he had been found.

Indeed the spying post had developed into an armed

garrison well defended mentally by the presence of so many gnomes. It was fast approaching the time when I would unleash a force of warfare against the dark elves that they could never imagine. Why was it that the thought of all this killing sickened me? Never the less I had committed all of my people to this venture and without its bloody success, my world would be doomed to die under the unstoppable onslaught of the millions of Dokka'lfar trampling the land underfoot. The thought tormented me that once this was done the world that we had all known would change completely. I was the bringer of death to my people as well as to the Dokka'lfar and there was no going back, ever.

CHAPTER EIGHTEEN

Morning had dawned and Waldwick was flushed and feverish. It was time to take him across the brier. I sent my mind into his and found very little of his personality left in the husk that was to be one of my weapons. It was time to gather a small force into the Spellbinder and deliver him.

I 'called' for gnomes and my two bodyguards, Eduardo and Calando as the morning sun began to eat into the mists. Mellitus and his group were already dragging the cage into the ship. John Smith and Alaric were studying the gibbering wreck that once was the High King with some interest.

John looked at me and asked. "What have you done to him? Even to my limited telepathic ability I can feel that this body is empty. Waldwick's mind has gone. Is it the virus changing him or have you put out the lights?"

"I removed his higher functions. His state of terror and fear was more than I could stand, so I gave him a painless death. All we need is for him to be taken alive by the Dokka'lfar and the virus will do the rest! The use of the staff of power had sent him slowly mad over the years and I took pity on him," I replied and made my way to the command chair.

Once the globe on the top of the staff of power was in my hands I became the Spellbinder. I was instantly aware of the envelope of the ship and who was on board. There were sufficient gnomes generating mental fog to keep us out of Abaddon's mind. I lifted the ship and floated it down the gorge and across towards the castle that the dark elves had built. It was an ugly, functional thing with no attempt to be other than a place to sleep and eat. The intelligent ones lived here in a certain amount of ease while the speechless ones slept where they dropped. There were no doors to the castle, as only those who were installed there would enter.

The great causeway extended past the castle entrance and into the brier. Although it was early in the morning, already work parties could be easily seen, dragging quarried blocks of stone along the road and into the tunnel. With my extended senses I could see the Arch of the insane Dream-shifter delivering another thousand or so dark elves through the portal. Something had caused the control chair to crumble and the globe on the end of the staff of power was shattered. Even the base that the Arch was fixed to had started to show signs of extreme age. It was as if the dream-shifter had suffered a millennium of time passing. Whatever energies had driven the reality shifting entity had left a terrible mark upon the remnants. Where the stones of the Arch met the granite floor, a pile of skeletons of those who had fed their life force to keep it open lay scattered about. Decaying away on the top of these were the half-eaten bodies of those who had contributed recently.

I mentally shuddered and brought the Spellbinder against the buttress that extended out from the outer wall of the castle where the morning mists were thickest. Mellitus dragged the docile creature that had been Waldwick, from out of the cage and to the Arch. This I now opened just enough so that John and Alaric could manipulate the isolation suit and its occupant through the portal. Once Alaric was safely back inside, John pulled the cord attached to the seals on the suit and the plastic ruptured. The mindless thing that had been Waldwick scrambled free of the suit's embrace and stumbled forward. I lifted the ship with the suit dangling underneath us by the cord and swung away from the area, shielded by the morning mists. We dropped the suit into the edge of the brier where if it were to be found, then with luck the virus inside would still be active.

The mind-dead High King scrabbled through the

entrance of the grim-looking castle and began to cry out with pain as his naked body began to bruise and scratch on the sharp edges of the walls and floor. Feral hungry eyes fixed on this tender morsel and Dokka'lfar began to wriggle out of sheltered places in the walls. They drooled at the promise of a feast. Before he could be touched however, the crack of the lash stopped the mindless ones from tearing him apart. Their masters had seen him and recognised that he was not one of the dark elves. His flesh was covered in white skin and his hair was silver.

The overseer flexed his wrist and sent the lash curling around the throat of the brain-scrambled king and dragged the thrashing figure to his knees. He immediately noticed that the ligaments controlling his wings had been cut, making him incapable of flight. Grabbing the prisoner by the hair, he lifted him up and stared into the dull eyes of the Ljo'sa'lfar. He probed into the skull with his mind and found nothing inside. Whatever personality had organised this body was gone and only the basic functions were left. It was as if he were trying to find personality in one of the 'empty ones' that bred outside the castle.

He concentrated his thoughts and called, "Lord Abaddon!"

The Dark Lord was finishing his breakfast and enjoying the attentions of the female, Inna, when he felt the mental tug.

"What is it Mordant? Why have you disturbed my morning pleasures?" He inquired and finished eating the remainder of the smoked slices of flesh.

"Master I have something here with me that you should see. It is an Ljo'sa'lfar male and he is mindless! Also he has been cut so that he cannot fly," replied the overseer. "Do I bring him to you or shall I wait here for you to come to me?"

"I will come to you, Mordant. Keep him safe and restrained."

The overseer dragged the stumbling figure through the slaves who clutched at the bedraggled wings and plucked tiny feathers from the tips to stare at with their brutish eyes. Many grabbed him around the legs where he was caked in excrement. Mordant kicked them off and they licked their trophies from their fingers and ran hooting through the gateway amongst the others of their kind. Other overseers gathered them up and formed work gangs from the more able bodied ones. The weak were added to the groups as a later lunch and headed to the quarries.

Mordant hauled the light elf roughly up the steps to an observation point where he could keep an eye on the comings and goings on the road. He noticed that the elf kept falling over and had to be dragged to his feet over and over again. This puzzled the overseer, as the Ljo'sa'lfar was well fed and quite plump. Mordant stood over seven feet tall, well muscled and strong, so he picked up Waldwick by the upper arms and stared into his eyes, looking for some clue as to his actions. The ex-High King responded by sneezing right into his face and Mordant threw him across the flagstones against the wall.

Abaddon arrived at that moment and watched as the light-skinned elf made no attempt to escape from the courtyard. He could feel Mordant's rage, rise up, as he wiped the snot from his face.

"Leave him," he ordered.

The Dark Lord concentrated his will and sent a telepathic probe deep into the bowels of the mind-dead elf. There were no memories and no trace of any personality in this creature. Someone had erased all traces of the original person, but had left enough to keep the elf alive. The wing muscles had been sliced apart and the skin had been allowed to heal across the cuts. What was even more interesting was how did the elf get across the brier?

Abaddon drew back and stared again at the shambling, well-fed elf that was rolling around on the flagstones and making grunting noises. He knew him! They had last met over two hundred years ago when the Dark Lord had first opened the portal between this world and Aifheimr. This pathetic thing was the High King of the Ljo'sa'lfar. The 'Light Elves' had cast him out from their people. Why?

The Dark Lord suddenly noticed the number of sores that had suddenly erupted across the mindless elf's back. When the creature began to vomit, he leapt away to the stone stairs and stood for a moment very still. His mind began to understand what he had no words for. There was something radically wrong with this elf and it was something that never happened to the 'Dark Elves'. Abaddon had no words for the affliction that had taken over the body of this outcast elf and it scared him. He stared at Mordant with a suddenly perceptive eye.

Mordant stared back and began to cough. He tried to walk towards the Dark Lord and stumbled over to fall full length upon the cold flagstones. The overseer climbed to his feet by holding onto the wall. The virus began to rage through his body, as he had inhaled Waldwick's sneeze! Delivered point blank the onset of the disease was rapid.

"Abaddon, I feel strange! There is a fire in my head! I cannot see you in my mind," he cried and held his head in his hands.

The Dark Lord shouted to his loyal overseer, "Take the 'Light Elf' away and burn him. Do not let any of the slaves near him and whatever that you do, do not let them eat him. Build a fire so strong that it will consume every part of him, while I go back inside. I will join you later when you have done this."

241

"Yes master," Mordant replied and dragged the silver haired elf out of the courtyard and outside the castle walls. He laid the whip across the primitive 'Dark Elves' and made them find wood to build a blazing bonfire.

Inside the castle, Abaddon washed himself and rubbed sand over the places he was sure that he had touched the damaged 'Light Elf'. The thought that continued to torture his mind was the fact that somehow the Ljo'sa'lfar had managed to cross the brier. He had seen the great dragons that flew in the skies and reasoned that his light skinned brethren had learnt how to ride these creatures. What sort of attack would they mount if they were to use these creatures? He would make sure that all of the overseers were armed with crossbows from this moment on, just to make sure that they were protected from aerial attack. Abaddon's people numbered in the tens of thousands and he knew that the numbers of his enemy were few. Soon the tunnel would break through the brier and the Dokka'lfar would stream through in their hundreds of thousands. He would make sure that extra efforts were made in the quarries this very day.

Beyond the castle walls Mordant stumbled as he was adding wood to the fire and fighting the fire in his brain, when a block of wood buried itself into his head. His weakness had been seen. A howling mob of primitive 'Dark Elves' threw themselves upon the sick bodies of Waldwick and Mordant tearing them to pieces. They ate every piece, before disappearing into the distance.

When Abaddon walked carefully out of the castle a few hours later, the bonfire had gone out, there were only scattered bones to be seen and he realised that he had a new problem on his hands.

Back in the compound I settled the Spellbinder down

242

and for the first time in ages I felt that I could rest for a while. I had six or seven days left before Prime arrived with my cargo. How many she had managed to drive here was a matter of conjecture. I was sure that dominating the tiny brains of these predators would not be beyond the abilities of my people as they had used the flying dragons for thousands of years. I would ask my riders to go aloft and over-fly Prime and the clans after a few days had passed to see how far they had got.

The following morning I had a visitor in the shape of an elderly gnome.

"Ranzmut, Boddywinkle welcome to my humble presence. You look as if you have something to tell me," I said and offered the gnome a beaker of hot sweet tea.

The old gnome gratefully sat and sipped the beaker. Tea was something that Auberon had brought over from the human world and was grown locally to the castle. I waited patiently as the custodian of the elfin library collected his thoughts.

"Great High King," he said and bowed, "I have been researching the records, looking for something that we could use against the Dokka'lfar concerning the gnomes. We have the power to use the foggy minds that you quite often in the past found irritating in a different way."

"Speak old friend and do not bow to me! And, I am not a 'Great High King.' I am just an elf that has a terrible responsibility to his people," I replied and squeezed his wrinkly hand with respect.

"That is what makes you who you are, my king," Ranzmut firmly stated. "The dwarves believe that you are the Long-shadow. You are the wingless elf who became the Great High King and that is the end of it! Now the reason that I came to see you, all the way from the castle through the Arch that you keep active, is this. I have found a set of tuning crystals that were brought on the Spellbinder when the great exodus took place. Deedlit, who built the Spellbinder and keyed it to the High King's descendants, also worked with other crystals not used in the spellbinder. I now know that with these crystals mounted around the necks of the most adept gnomes, we can project a blanket of mental silence over the Dokka'lfar. In short, we can project a mental fog that is only on their wavelength. Once we are above the brier and on our way we can stop all but verbal communications amongst the Dark Elves."

I sat stunned, as the full implications of what this ancient gnome had told me. I studied the crystals intently and held one in my hand, only to find that it did nothing for my mental abilities at all.

Ranzmut smiled, held out his hand and said, "These are not for you High King. They are only adjusted for gnomes and Deedlit tuned them for the Dokka'lfar. Otherwise they would have been a weapon against the Ljo'sa'lfar and that would have rendered them useless to our forces."

"Now High King, I must go amongst my people and find the best of them that can project the barrier. I need twenty at least, one for each crystal to be carried over the forehead in a turban. We will travel in front of the Arch with the portal open and once we are there, you must put us somewhere high and well protected."

"My dear old friend, I hear you well. It shall be done. Now I need to pass on this information to my other allies. It is wonderful news that you bring me, wonderful news!"

I watched Ranzmut hobble painfully out of sight and couldn't help wondering just how old was he? I was sure that he had journeyed on the Spellbinder to Earth from Aifheimr, our home world, but had kept the secret of the ship to himself. It must have been a promise to Auberon that sealed his lips. I called my council together and passed on the news of Ranzmut's discovery.

Now the time had come to transform the Spellbinder into a cargo carrier. I had the ship provisioned with fresh water and plenty of food, as we knew that there would be very little foraging to be had except for the velociraptors who would feed on the Dokka'lfar. This took several days and I began to wonder about Prime and her clans. I needed to know whether she had been successful and how far away she was from the compound.

Finally with a few days to go I called Hoatzin, Spencer and a group of elves together.

"I need to find Prime and find out how many predators she has collected. Hoatzin and Spencer I want you to fly out in front of us and locate the velociraptors. As for the rest of you, I want you to double up on the flying dragons so that one of you can overcome the tiny minds of the 'eaters' and dominate them. I want to bring them to the compound docile. I will bring the Spellbinder outside of the compound so we can load them up. Once I have them on board, the ship will be able to restrain them," I ordered.

The two humans walked quickly over to where the Quetzalcoatlus were kept and selected one each. As I watched them get airborne, a small figure slipped out of the air, folded her wings and sat herself behind Spencer. It had to be my mother! Strapped around her waist was her personalised wood and bronze modified AK 47 and a bag of clips.

"Mother!"

"Dear son," the answer came ringing back, "Where he goes, I go! Go and be king! It's what you are here for!"

I had long ago decided that arguing with my mother was a waste of time and returned to the Spellbinder. This time the cargo had been iron cleansed as much as possible. The goblins had done wonders with substituting wooden stocks for the steel skeleton chassis where achievable. Colonel Halim had loaded up the three lorries with crate after crate of ammunition clips for the AK 47's. In amongst these he had added grenades and RPG-7 grenade launchers. These were self-exploding after 920 meters, 4.5 seconds after firing and were going to be used by colonel Halim's sons. These I intended for the insane dream-shifter's Arch if all went well. Also the cargo had been stored as far back as it could be stacked, leaving the central section for loading and carrying the predators.

Some miles out on the Plains of Scion, Prime and her clans were driving a family of Giganotosaurus steadily through the ferns. As with the herding of the hadrosaurs, it was the fire torches that kept the beasts moving. The smell of smoke drove them on and the velociraptors kept far enough away that they did not induce the reaction to chase. There was a slight breeze from behind the beasts that sent the smoke towards them. Prime was well aware what a change of direction would do and made sure that there were outriders on each side of the meat eaters with torches.

She scanned the skies anxiously for any sign of the elves riding the big pterodactyls. This was a really dangerous thing that she was doing at Peterkin's request. The clans had used fire many times to drive off the eaters from their meat herds, but had never tried to shepherd them! She knew that others of her kind had managed to drive a good number of the more nimble Allosaurus into small family groups. These were very quick and a lot more intelligent than the larger Giganotosaurus, but so far the fear of fire kept them moving.

The elves that rode the flying dragons were used to dominating the minds of their sometimes, unwilling carriers, so did not envisage any problems. From high up they could make out the smoking torches and the uneasily driven beats. The fear of fire made them accept that they travelled closer to each other than they normally would. It would be necessary for them to be split up a little more so that each elf that made contact with the tiny mind would zero in onto the right one.

Eduardo & Calando got the dragon riders to swoop down to Prime's side away from the group of beasts. She saw them approach and waved them down. Once down they quickly dismounted from the Quetzalcoatlus and made Prime aware of their needs.

They had driven the beasts into a clear area of the plains. Here the fern trees grew in clumps, leaving clear areas between them. The meat eaters had no fear of open spaces as once they got within sprinting distance of their prey they rarely missed a meal. This was good ambush country with excellent visibility, but the velociraptors had made sure that the herds of prey animals had been moved on. The family pod of Giganotosaurus had eaten well at the last kill and would have rested up for a few days before hunting again. The wisps of smoke carried by the breeze made them uneasy and every time they stopped the smoke increased, driving them onward. Now they were getting even more irritated with the constant motion and swung their heads from side to side trying to find a path of safety. Now mingled with the smoke was the scent of velociraptors.

The huge meat eaters had learned to give way to these smaller creatures, as conflicts with them always ended in death, no matter how many they killed. A new scent mingled with the raptors' that the beasts could not identify. Added to this was the definite smell of flying carrion eaters. The matriarch realised that the younger members of her family group were further away from her than she would like. She stopped and stared around, searching for the others and found that she was sleepy. It became too much of an effort to keep walking. Her nostrils filled with the new scent and she realised that it was not prey! Easy food was located in front of her and to the left. Her mind filled with this thought and she was aware that by her side was the 'not food' that was no danger. It climbed up her tail and onwards along her back until it sat just behind her great head. Her mind filled with pleasure that the creature was so close and she soon became used to the slight weight on her neck. The matriarch soon found herself amongst the other members of her family group and was content. That each member of her hunting pod had a small winged figure perched upon each neck seemed perfectly correct. Even the hated velociraptors became of no threat or importance and the smell of fire no longer filled her with fear.

The only thing that now dominated her mind was the need to keep moving at a faster and economic rate towards where the easy food was located. She became aware that other family hunting pods were also on the move in the same direction that her group was headed. Above them were the flying carrion eaters that also carried the other scent that now sat upon her neck. It drew comfort from this fact and that the pleasure centres of her tiny brain were flooded every time she thought about the weight upon her neck.

I sat in the command chair of the Spellbinder and I used the senses of this incredible entity. Waldwick had tried to use the staff of power without the Spellbinder as a psychic amplifier. It had eventually driven him mad. Without the genetic binding to the elfin ship, there was no shield to the mind and none of the experience of the elder kings to draw on. When I merged my mind with that of the Spellbinder,

I became something else altogether. It was no wonder Ameela had screamed when she touched the shadow of the mind that was yet to awaken. I spread myself across the Plains of Scion and gave help and power when needed. I slipped in and out of the minds of my people, reinforcing a mental conditioning here and just adding strength when a meat eater became stubborn. Once I was not quick enough and one of my men died.

Another elf quickly took his place and dominated the killer, hoisting himself onto the neck of the allosaurus. Beneath it feet were the remains of the unfortunate elf who had failed. The rider urged the beast on so that it did not imprint the scent of the 'Light Elf' into its tiny mind. A velociraptor dragged the body to one side and left it to be consumed by whatever followed the driven meat eaters. The sight and scent of the groups of predators had unsettled the vast herds of vegetarians that were moving away from the area. Occasionally panic ensued and a herd of triceratops stampeded away into another big family group of diplodocus. This started a chain effect that scattered across the plains for miles. At the compound the herd of hadrosaurs were beginning to get uneasy, as the breeze began to carry the odd wisp of predator towards them.

I lifted the Spellbinder from out of the compound and set it down several miles away from the herd on a flat area of the plains and waited. In my mind I could 'see' the positions and location of all the elves and the velociraptors. I adjusted the size of the Spellbinder to suit the 'new recruits' and coloured the outside dark brown, so that the ship could be plainly seen by the elves riding the meat eaters.

My mouth went dry with tension as I waited for the last part of the plan to come to fruition. Soon the problem of the Dokka'lfar would be addressed once and for all. I would be ready as soon as the predators were on board.

249

CHAPTER NINETEEN

By the time that a week had gone by, the virus cultured by Alaric and his team of genetic scientists had spread throughout the primitive Dokka'lfar, killing four out of every ten and leaving the remainder weak and infectious. Some recovered more quickly than others and were put back to work. Many were so crippled by the illness that Abaddon had them killed and burnt on huge bonfires. Now only fresh arrivals were killed and smoked for food, then stored in the castle kitchens.

Abaddon had caught the virus and had survived after hiding himself away in one of the castle rooms, high up in a tower. His faithful new consort Inna had tended to him and driven away anyone who would have killed him out of fear. She brought him water when he was thirsty and smoked meat when he was able to eat. Inna washed his sores and wrapped cold wet cloths around his head when he was burning up with fever. As he began to make a recovery she began to cough and sweat. He found her body by the side of his bed one morning when he regained consciousness. She was covered in sores and was stick thin except for the beginnings of her pregnancy beginning to bulge.

The Dark Lord carried her to the bonfire in the castle grounds and threw her into the flames embrace. He stood for a while and watched her burn as his heart enflamed with rage at the cunning of the Ljo'sa'lfar and the way that they had delivered the virus. He turned his pockmarked face away from the flames and cursed those that had used such a weapon against his people.

He sent his mind out to all the overseers that were capable of rational thought and received a progress report. There were so many of the 'mindless ones' still streaming in through the Dream-shifter's portal that even with the dead and infected littering the road, there were still thousands to drive into labour. Soon he was sure the tunnel would be finished and he could lead the hundreds of thousands through towards the lands of the dwarves. The only knowledge of the lands beyond the other side of the brier, were the fragmentary visions that the few gargoyles had shown him before a crossbow bolt cut them from the sky. He knew that the lands were fertile and full of meat and the knowledge of this had kept him here for over two hundred years. In all that time he had never set eyes on any of the 'Light Elves' that had settled here. Apart from the occasional mental brush with Waldwick, there had been no contact with them. Now this!

The mindless creature that had once tried to make a deal with him was now part of the digestive system of most probably a dead Dokka'lfar. Who had taken his place he wondered and what else had he planned?

Thirty miles down the edge of the gorge I was preparing the next and I hoped final stage of the Elf-war. I sat connected to the Spellbinder and added my personality to the mind that controlled the ship built by Deedlit, who was the finest elfin engineer that had ever lived. His mind was bound into the consciousness of the Spellbinder, as were the minds of previous High Kings.

What I was about to do was beyond any other High King's remit and it weighed heavy on my mind. To my new human friends what I was about to do was entirely justified and it bothered them not one jot! The dwarves had an ancient score to settle and were determined to settle it once and for all. The gnomes had a more pragmatic view and acted along with the fact that with the Dokka'lfar removed from this world then an endless peace would prevail. The goblins had no other reason to remove them other than the fact that they would be considered a delicacy by the dark ones. That was all the reason that they needed. Prime and her people knew that the numbers of the Dokka'lfar and their propensity to breed without control would make them a competitor on the plains. The logical thing to do was to remove them permanently and now was the time. Besides she had reasoned, once they were defeated the meat need not go to waste as it could be smoked, cured and stored for leaner times!

Whilst I was thinking all of this through I realised that the time had come to implement the start of the invasion. I extended my senses and was aware of the predators that were being driven towards me. I opened the side facing the open plains and made ready the holding pens. I could feel the unease of these giant beasts as they approached the wooden looking sides of the ship. I included the green of living plants into the mixture and felt a better acceptance by the driven creatures. Now the hole in the side of the Spellbinder seemed to be the entrance to a giant cave.

The first Giganotosaurus entered the Spellbinder and made her way deeper into the 'cave,' ridden and coerced by her elfin master. The rest of her family pod rapidly followed her and I shunted the walls around to contain them. Each group became contained inside the bubble of the Spellbinder while I found room for more! Prime and her clans had driven more than a hundred of various types of predators towards the compound. I found room for them all! I spread my consciousness over the tiny minds like a blanket, inducing them all to sleep, giving all the elves that had overcome them a well-needed rest. I stimulated their bloodthirsty minds with the sight of the Dokka'lfar and the scent that they would smell once I released them into the lands beyond the brier. I blocked out all feelings of prey that included the members of my multi-species, travelling with me inside the Spellbinder.

I lifted the ship and began to take the Spellbinder towards the brier and the gorge. The iron content of the weapons that had been loaded on board had been reduced as much as practical and was not such a drain on my abilities, as when I had taken them from the parallel Earth. Besides I had a shipload of elves with me to draw upon their strength. I could feel the personalities of everyone and their love for me as their High King. At the back of my mind was the driving force of my mother that gave me the will to do what was abhorrent to any sane Ljo'sa'lfar, except those of my genetic line. I had been the instrument that had 'changed' the minds of my people. It was an awesome responsibility.

Sat cross-legged in front of the Arch were the twenty most mentally adept gnomes that Ranzmut had found. I opened the portal to allow their mental fog to radiate throughout the Dokka'lfar's bridgehead when I gave the signal.

As we approached the brier an idea occurred to me and I grounded the ship in front of the thorny barricade.

I called for Alaric as I paused the ship's progress. He was by my side in moments.

"Alaric, is the brier controllable by sound as was the entrance to the compound," I asked.

"If sufficient of us sing, then High King, yes we can force the brier to give way. What do you have in mind?"

"The tunnel that the Dokka'lfar have built runs along the side of the gorge and is within a few miles of breaking through. If you could force the brier to give way we could allow the first of the meat eaters through. I suggest the young of the beasts that humans call Allosaurus would be just small enough to enter the tunnel. Select as many that you can less than eight feet tall. I wouldn't want them to jam up the tunnel! We can select the smallest of them from what Prime and her people have collected for us and send them inside. Once they are inside we can carry on and let the brier close over again and seal it shut."

Alaric stared at me in awe and said, "Great High King! I will go and collect the very best singers this very moment. Rest assured we will clear the way!"

My mother led the band of singers to the edge of the brier. There must have been more than fifty of her friends amongst the throng who could sing into the high range of sub-sonics. I was ashamed that I did not know them all by name, but I was confidant that they could do what was necessary. They started off with a common low note that they crept slowly into a higher registrar. As the pitch ascended the brier began to wither and pull back. Alaric performed as choir manager and tuned the sound by holding each mind into small groups that harmonised with each other. The brier pulled away from the wall of the gorge leaving a narrow path deep into the undergrowth that fell away as the group moved forwards. Seedpods wilted and did not explode as the song took hold. Behind them slowly walked the selected smaller Allosaurus mesmerised by their handlers.

As the brier pulled away from the side of the gorge the elves marched on, leaving behind sufficient singers to keep the brier from growing back. Using the senses of the Spellbinder I was able to see the mouth of the tunnel some way ahead. The Dokka'lfar were sliding a large block of quarried stone out of the tunnel and about to send it to crush the brier beneath it. It tipped over and dropped in front of the passageway. This coincided with the arrival of the singers and the young allosaurus being driven by their mental riders. The beasts jumped onto the stone and eyed the easy meals in front of them. With the urging of the Ljo'sa'lfar and the registering of the scent of the designated prey, twenty hungry dinosaurs scrambled into the tunnel.

The singers drew back and began to change pitch, allowing the brier to grow once more right up to the tunnel entrance. Quickly my mother and her friends turned and ran towards the Spellbinder, still singing the sub-sonic harmony, but at a lower pitch. Rising over this constant choir came the sounds of terrified screaming from inside the excavation. By the time that they were back inside and protected by the Spellbinder, the brier had grown back into its impenetrable jungle.

I lifted the craft and swept onwards towards the other side of the barrier. Now the gnomes began to concentrate their minds, amplified by Ranzmut's crystals, tuned to the same mind patterns as the intelligent Dokka'lfar. They began to knit the fog of gnomish minds into the mental frequency of the Dokka'lfar overseers. Some of the gnomes produced flutes and began to play.

Inside the Spellbinder the rest of the cargo was waking up and pointing towards the walls that I would soon dissolve. Perched on the neck of each beast was an elf directing the tiny, bloodthirsty minds of the predators. We skimmed over the last of the brier and I put the ship down near the causeway. There were thousands of the Dark Elves attempting to drag more blocks of stone towards the tunnel mouth. By the sides of the road were piles of bodies where the virus had done its work. As the first of the Giganotosaurus and their riders were seen, the ropes were dropped. More groups of allosaurus began to stride towards the overpowering scent of the prey and panic ensued. Forty-five feet from ugly head to tail and weighing over five tons, they were suddenly close to easy food. With a head that measured over six feet in length and mainly teeth, the sight of those opens mouths were enough to instil terror. The elves left the shoulders of the beasts and climbed into the sky leaving the programmed predators to wreck havoc.

The overseers tried to make contact with Abaddon and found that a mental fog surrounded them. Gnomish songs rang through their heads. Everyone was cut off from each other and nobody knew what to do or where to run. Soon the sound of screaming echoed throughout the stony lands. Prime and her clans fought behind the flesh eaters, swinging the huge mallets up and down, crunching heads. Each hammer was attached to the velociraptors by a leather strap around their wrists, so that they did not lose their preferred weapon. Those that were missed with the hammers were bitten and crunched by the velociraptors as they waded through the massed ranks of the Dokka'lfar. Then the disembowelling claws on their feet took up what was missed by the mallets.

Mellitus and the dwarves made for the castle, opening up with the Kalashnikoff automatics at anyone that got in their way. Every dwarf held in his memories the tale of the thousand that had held the hordes of Dokka'lfar back until the brier had filled the gorge. There would be no prisoners taken this day! They swore an oath that the scent of roasting dwarf would never be smelt again.

In the skies, flocks of Quetzalcoatlus ridden by elves and carrying a gnome projecting fuzzy thoughts soared upwards catching the thermals, heading towards the quarries. Hoatzin rode his dragon through the skies with a gnome sat in front carrying iron tipped crossbow bolts. The Mexican carried a saddlebag of tear gas canisters as well as two AK 47's strapped together.

Spencer, carrying his armour piercing rifle and my mother armed with an AK 47 made their way with them towards the quarries. Alongside them were a contingent of elves all armed with modified Klashnikovs carrying plenty of clips of ammunition.

Below them were the Dark Lord's quarries where the Dokka'lfar toiled. Thousands of black and red figures pulled on ropes, dragging the stones away to the road, while hundreds of them split the block of stone away from the cliff face. Overseers cracked their whips to make sure that the primitive elves did not slack. None of them looked to the skies until the sound of the AK 47's spat death into the massed crowds. To add to the confusion Hoatzin dropped tear gas canisters amongst the terrified elves. It was not long before crossbow bolts lifted into the aerial bombardment and some of the pterodactyls began to take fatal injuries. The elves made them swoop across the fleeing crowds and continued to open up with the automatic rifles seeking the overseers. Those whose beasts took a direct hit lifted away carrying the gnome passenger with them. When this happened, the gnomes opened up with crossbows tipped with iron, always seeking the overseers, while the elves circled away from the killing fields, their arms clasped around each gnome.

Spencer took careful aim at where cracks had been placed into the rock-face to release the stone slabs using explosive rounds. Large pieces of the cliff-face began to tumble away and drop onto the Dokka'lfar below. In front of him sat Peterkin's mother picking off any overseer that she could find with single shots from her adapted Kalashnikov.

Once they were certain, the aerial contingent wheeled away towards the road building and continued the steady fire. Behind them at the quarries winged predators and carrion eaters 'called' by the Ljo'sa'lfar, spiralled down to the once forbidden hunting grounds and fed. Kept away by the Dark Elves mental powers they soon 'forgot' the keep away signal that used to echo in their tiny minds. The nesting grounds located higher up in the mountains soon emptied of the leathery winged killers. Soon they were flying back to feed their young on fresh elves.

Abaddon had left the castle and made his way towards the Arch, once he had heard the dying screams in his mind from the tunnel exit. He had seen what now roamed the tunnel and fed upon the unfortunates that were trying to escape against the throng that was in the way. He had a good idea what the new High King was going to do. Then his mind had filled with gnomic music and made it impossible to contact any of his chosen people. Total chaos was now the order of the day. He had separated from the other inhabitants of the castle, reasoning that this would be a killing target of the normally pacific Light Elves.

A new sound rattled across the air as the dwarves opened up with the AK 47's. He watched from his hiding place, as hundreds of his people died under the assault of the dwarves. Each dwarf held a strange metal stick that spat something out of the end to a continuous noise. Wherever they pointed these weapons the Dark Elves fell and bled to death. Those that were still alive and wounded as the line of dwarves passed had their throats slit. Even with his mental powers diminished by the gnomic music filling his mind, he could almost taste the hatred!

Whoever the new High King was, he was not thinking in the same manner that an Ljo'sa'lfar would consider. Abaddon grudgingly gave his opponent respect and acknowledged that he was different from any of the High Kings that he remembered before the exodus from Aifheimr. In all the tens of thousand of years of history the Ljo'sa'lfar had never thrown up a killer before.

Then he saw the Spellbinder and realised how Waldwick had been delivered. This was a fully functional reality shifting ship. The very one he had pursued from world to world. Where it had gone for the last span of years he could not guess, but the new High King had managed to find it and reactivate Deedlit's invention.

To his increasing horror he watched as the side dissolved and the cargo of huge predators disgorged, all being ridden by the Light Elves spreading out over the causeway that he had nearly finished! With them were something out of a terrible nightmare. Behind them strode smaller feathered killers of the same kind of creature to the giant killers, but these carried large hammers! They were intelligent and fought with the elves. What was worse, they dined on his people as they killed. Some of them were bagging up the corpses for later collection. What kind of elf had taken control of the kingdom, he wondered? Then he saw something that dredged up from his deepest memories, of the time he was searching for the Ljo'sa'lfar. He remembered that for a long time the Light Elves had taken shelter on another alternative reality. He was using humans from that world! The Dark Lord remembered how clever they were at killing each other and what weapons that they invented in the time that he had lived there. He remembered the stink of iron that had driven him away and the explosive weapons that they had developed.

Abaddon realised that he was beaten for the moment. There was only one thing to do and that was to let the High King think that he had won. There was a chance that he would go to the remains of the Dream-shifter and try to stem the flow of the Dokka'lfar onto this world. He had to be there when that happened. The Dark Lord quickly made his way towards the active Arch hiding when he had too, but steadily getting closer to his goal.

I lifted ship again and made my way towards the Arch of the insane Dream-shifter. I had an extra special cargo still restrained in the hold. It was a complete family of tyrannosaurus that some of Prime's people had captured far to the north of our elfin castle. With them were some adult males that had separated from other families. What I had was a perfect breeding set of meat eating dinosaurs. They were rare on the plains, as Giganotosaurus had got the upper hand inside the crater. I had a place for them to go and multiply. It was a personal gift from me to Moloch. Each of them had a rider settled on the broad neck broadcasting reassuring thoughts to the predatory minds. At the same time they were encouraging the hunger that always dominated the beasts, to surface. The mouths began to drool as instincts took over. Seven tons of hungry dinosaur began to strain at the mental leash.

I dropped the Spellbinder onto the road in front of the mad Dream-shifter. The gate was open and the Dokka'lfar were streaming through in their hundreds.

"Colonel Halim, stop the flow of migrants and clear the way for the T Rex's to go through the portal," I ordered.

The Uzbekistani and his sons deployed the RPG-7 grenade launchers with stunning results. First they fired a salvo through the arch to drop inside and explode within four and a half seconds. The next round was to fall just inside the gate on the other side. The tide of Dark Elves ceased almost immediately and the ones that had came through fell to the rapid fire of the AK 47's used by my elves. With the road cleared it was time to send the T Rex's through. I opened the side of the ship and the elves rode them up to the Arch. Forty feet from head to long tapering tail and weighing more than seven tons, they shook the earth as they rushed forwards, dipping their heads to take and swallow whole any Dark Elf within reach. As each dinosaur reached the arch, its rider spread their wings and lifted away from the neck of the beast. Emblazoned in each tiny mind was the lure of unlimited feeding that spurred it on.

Soon the Arch was clear of incoming Dokka'lfar except for the sight of dead and dying elves. We had lost very few of our own group so far, but we had a problem still in front of us. The insane Dream-shifter had been soaked in life energy. It pulsed with power. In front of my horrified eyes the mad ship began to re-form. The crumbling stones of the Arch began to smooth out and the control chair began to rise from out of the piles of dead elves.

Rising from the floor from out of the dust of centuries was the staff of power! Mounted on the top, shard by shard, the globe that accepted dominance of the shipmaster began the transformation back into a working mechanism.

Quickly, fire grenades at that chair," I cried. "Destroy the Dream-shifter's seat of power, while we can."

Three rocket propelled grenades sped on their way to the chair, only to explode harmlessly in the air in front of it. I realised that the Dream-shifter was expanding its bubble of invulnerability to the confines of the control chamber. When the dust had cleared away I saw a large muscular coal black figure sat in the control chair. It could only be Abaddon!

I felt his hatred as he joined his mind to mine and said, "You win this round Ljo'sa'lfar. Thank you for repairing my ship. I will be back. Sleep uneasily in your bed, High King. What weapons you managed to discover! I wonder what I can find?"

I watched in mounting horror as the arch began to shrink to a more manageable size and the ship lift from the ground and rotate so that it faced the Spellbinder. The portal had closed into the home world sealing the T Rex's behind it. I had left something that would stop them from influencing this generation. Each elf as he had left the beast, had wrapped an iron collar around each neck and buckled it closed. There would have to be another generation of T Rex's before the Dokka'lfar could insert any mental control and only the mentally adept would be able to do that! They would have to wait for the every tyrannosaurus to die of old age before they could rest easy and I knew that they could live a good hundred years.

"Contact the Dream-shifter and merge minds," I ordered.

My mind made contact with the insane, reality shifting entity. It was the sum total of the minds that had built the Dream-shifter blended with Abaddon's. My strength resided in the High King's minds that were overlapping in my brain. I floated in icy calm with expanding consciousness. The power of kings flooded through my senses and drove through Abaddon's defences like an obsidian knife. First of all I drained the memory banks of all the locations that the Dream-shifter had been. I took away Aifheimr as the reality shifter's location peg. Dimly I could feel Abaddon screaming as I pecked away at his grip on the Dream-shifter. I filled his mind with the death that I had caused and the burden of responsibility that I had taken freely. I watched him shrivel as his mind travelled the road to insanity that the Dream-shifter had been forced to go as it was powered by death. I drew on the combined strengths of my human friends and their alien ways of thought. I overloaded his mind with the song of the gnomes and the hatred of the dwarves. Welling up was the disgust of the goblins that I funnelled into the very bottom of his mind. The 'Long-shadow' of my dwarf namesake foretold centuries ago and the simple faith that I was that wingless elf, become High King, hammered this fact into his psyche.

Abaddon bled from his ears, nose and eyes as his mind gave out. Ten thousand years of unbridled power leaked away and he fell to his knees, vomiting uncontrollably.

"Fire again colonel Halim," I ordered. "Sam Pitts, use the Berettas with explosive rounds and aim at the Arch. Reduce it to rubble!"

There was a crackle of rifle fire as my humans opened fire and the whoosh of rockets, followed by explosions. Large pieces of the Arch began to rip apart and shower the surrounding stony ground with debris. The command chair came apart and reverted to ancient fragments. Pieces of the Dark Lord were scattered over the terrain and lay amongst the machine-gunned Dokka'lfar.

Darkness crossed the skies. I fell out of the chair and knew no more, collapsing at the feet of my Ameela.

CHAPTER TWENTY

More than a week passed while I slipped in and out of consciousness. I was fed soup when I awoke and cleaned when I became dirty. A vast mopping up campaign took place throughout the lands beyond the gorge. The mindless Dokka'lfar were slaughtered and the intelligent ones were hunted down until the last of our terrible mutation was dead. We could not afford to be merciful. To try to escape from the effects of the virus some of the overseers had slipped through the portal before I had sent the T Rex's through. They had of course developed the infection after fleeing back to the home world. The sickness had to spread! Once the meat eaters had done their work they were rounded up by the velociraptors and put to death by the dwarves and my elves.

Alaric cleared away the poisoned brier with a virus that he had brought with him and soon the scent of burning foliage filled the air. Once Prime and her clans were sure that they were not needed any more they returned to the Plains of Scion, through the gorge now empty of the stinging brier. They left carrying their mallets and sacks of smoked Dokka'lfar. The great delta began once again to flow through the gorge unimpeded and already life was returning to the swampy waters, as fish and those that lived upon them filtered downstream.

The dwarves returned to their cities, each side of the delta and started on the construction of a bridge to span the gap. Hildegard kept her relationship going with Althalos Hammer-thief and I guessed that she would bear him many children in the future. The twin cities of Skaldargate and Stormgalt planned to open up a trading facility so that tools could be bartered for meat by trading with the velociraptors. The legend of the wingless High King, 'Peterkin Long-shadow' and the defeat of the Dark Lord would be told over and over again.

A less vicious infection ranged through all the Ljo'sa'lfar, countered by the anti-virus that Alaric had cultured from the surviving captured Dokka'lfar we had imprisoned at the compound. I had subjected myself to an awesome 'mind-strain' in the destruction of the Dream-shifter and even now I needed the calming influence of the other minds that I shared my existence with.

It was during the times that I moved through delirium, that I wandered through the memories of the long dead, High Kings. The mind and memories of the ancient Freyr were mine to see in all his futile fight against the Dark Elves. I looked upon a different world as I struggled to understand the wellspring of the Dokka'lfar. The original mutation was known as Moloch and his mental powers were formidable even as a child. Even though he was so different to his mother and father it was unthinkable that he should come to harm. The child grew far larger than his parents and was nearly twice as tall when fully grown. Unlike his parents' light skin colour, he was flame red and wingless. It was not until he passed puberty that his true nature surfaced. He was the first of his kind and unlike the Ljo'sa'lfar; he became cruel and impossible to manage. When his father had tried to mentally control him, Moloch had sunk his teeth into his father's arm and bitten it off. The taste of blood filled him with ecstasy and he drained his father's mind in a reflex action. Once he had eaten his fill, he turned his attention to his terrified mother.

What had happened to produce this mutation was not known, but his insatiable sex drive and mental domination of those female elves that became his breeding creatures, had brought into being the Dark Elves. It was the second generation that had produced the throwbacks as his children mated with each other. They were unable to speak, but they could take orders and unlike the nearly immortal Ljo'sa'lfar every coupling produced young. Occasionally these retarded elves would throw up a sentient elf with a fully functional mind. They carried the same longevity as their pureblooded ancestors, but remained either coal black or bright red and they were not winged. Very, very few were born winged as were the Ljo'sa'lfar. My people shunned them as their practises filled them with disgust. They did the one thing possible, they moved away from them, putting as many miles as they could between themselves and the mutations.

All of them were fundamentally different from the Light Elves in that they desired to own what was not theirs to possess. They wished to dominate their world and take what they wanted without any thought of conservation. As their numbers rose over the centuries, food began to get scarce and attempts to grow more sucked the life from out of the soil. A practise of cannibalism began to take hold amongst the Dokka'lfar as the intelligent fed upon the retarded. Soon Ljo'sa'lfar began to disappear and confrontation between the two now distinct races of elf began to increase.

Still the numbers of the Dark Ones increased until it became obvious that the original race of elves were hopelessly outnumbered. Freyr secretly began to draw up plans for an exodus from the home world. His friend and scientific genius, Deedlit had postulated that it might be possible to travel between realities. He reasoned that there were maybe, an infinite number of parallel universes, coexisting with the one that they lived in. He began the work that eventually produced the Spellbinder.

He took the experimental ship through the Rifts and into a different reality. Here he worked with loyal goblins for centuries until the ship was perfected. Deedlit brought it back to the High King Freyr and keyed it to his genetic line, before he gave up his life to become part of the Spellbinder's mind. By now the Light Elves had retreated from the hoards of Dokka'lfar to an isolated island as far as they could get from the mainland. The intelligentsia amongst the 'Dark Ones' built an armada of galleys and the dull-witted elves were set to work to row them across the open sea. Their promise was that there would be fresh meat for all of them, once they were there.

Freyr linked his son, Auberon to the Spellbinder's mind and connected him to Deedlit. He ordered him to go, taking every Ljo'sa'lfar, gnome and goblin inside the Spellbinder's bubble. He would defy the hoards by energising the 'Star of Light' and holding them back until the Spellbinder navigated through the Rift. He made him swear an oath, that elves do not harm elves and the Ljo'sa'lfar would hold to this maxim no matter what. I was not bound by that covenant.

Abaddon led the throng against them, but could not pass the High King's mental amplifier. Every nerve ending burned like fire as the light spread over the ravening multitude. Freyr stood in front of the Spellbinder with the 'Star' held aloft and carried the agony of the hellish energy within himself, feeding his life force into the device. Behind him the Spellbinder became transparent, becoming a soap bubble, exiting this reality. As the last of Freyr's life began to ebb and the starving Dokka'lfar closed in, the Spellbinder reached out and captured his soul.

Aifheimr, home world of the Ljo'sa'lfar now belonged to the Dokka'lfar. I had the address of this hell in the memory banks of the Spellbinder, taken from the Dream-weaver. Auberon had removed it, as he had no intention of ever going back there. I on the other hand realised that more needed to be done against the Dokka'lfar than this skirmish. The one thought that tormented me was that Moloch might be able to build another Dream-weaver and seek us out again. When I was properly recovered I would need the help of my human friends again, but in a far more dangerous situation.

It was later in the day that a good reason to approach them for that help appeared. Eduardo had found someone looking like a Dokka'lfar hiding from the genocide being carried out by my people. The amazing thing was, he wasn't an elf, he was a human. He had brought him straight to me.

By now I had sufficiently recovered and was able to stand unaided. I walked around the terrified human and examined him. He was naked to the waist and his back carried the marks of the lash. One leg was considerably shorter than the other. What little clothes he wore were mainly rags. His age I estimated at no more than thirty and his skin was as black as any Dokka'lfar. He was of the same race as Spencer, but emaciated.

"Can you understand me?" I asked in elvish.

"Yes, great King," he answered and knelt in front of me, pressing his forehead to the ground at my feet.

His accent was slurred, but understandable. The speech of the Dokka'lfar had altered from the basic elvish that we all spoke as Ljo'sa'lfar. I felt his fear and his thirst wash over my senses.

"Eduardo, give this creature water to drink," I asked. "Well done on finding this person. There are things that I must know that are in this man's mind."

My loyal guard pulled him back to his knees and put a large mug of water in his hands. The creature gratefully drank. With that act of unexpected kindness, I felt his fear began to diminish.

"What is your name?" I asked and sat myself down.

"You there!" He answered and handed the mug back to

268

Eduardo.

For a few moments I just sat there as the implications of his name hit home and I shuddered.

"Are you hungry?" I asked and saw his eyes widen with shock.

"Yes, great King. I have not eaten for several days and that was upon a nearly fresh corpse that I found and hid from the others," he replied and began to drool.

"Give him some dwarf bread, Eduardo and some smoked meat. Let him eat for a while, while I think."

Eduardo vanished for a few moments and reappeared with a bowl. Inside it was several rolls of bread and a number of pieces of smoked Hadrosaur along with some dried fruit. He had also refilled the water mug and set it down by the side of the human. The crippled man began to stuff the food into his mouth and swallow it in chunks.

"Stop! Take your time! No-one will take the food away from you," I cried out. "Slow yourself up and please be assured that you are not going to die and you will not be harmed in any way. Sit down upon the floor and eat slowly. There is plenty of food to be had when you have finished what you have."

The pitiful wretch got off his knees and sat cuddling the bowl while he did slow down his swallowing, to actually chew most of the food before it went down his throat. He drank again from the mug, put it down and began to cry. The human then took hold of Eduardo's legs and hugged them with his scrawny arms, sobbing uncontrollably. What few rags he had wrapped around himself fell away, leaving him naked. He kissed my loyal protector's feet and continued to push some of the dried fruit into his continuing chewing mouth. I watched as an embarrassed Eduardo disentangled himself from the human's grasp and filled his mug with more water. As 'You there' turned his back upon me I saw quite clearly that one of his buttocks had been cleanly sliced off. It had perfectly healed and was slowly fattening up, showing no sign of infection.

"Listen to me," I insisted and took his hand in mine. "I need to look into your mind. There will be things that you have seen that I need to see to make decisions. There are other humans with me who will want to meet you. They are my friends and they will treat you well."

"Great king, I have never been asked before. I have lived with the 'Great Ones' and done their bidding. My body has been their plaything and my mind theirs to do with as they wish!"

I shuddered at the implications of what this poor creature meant. Using the contact of holding his hand in mine I sank quickly into his mind. What I saw there made me want to vomit. There had been humans taken to the home world well over a thousand years ago and they had been bred to satisfy the appetites of the ruling classes. Moloch had enjoyed the terror that the humans exhibited when he called for their company. He limited the number of boys kept to breed and ate the ones he did not keep, before they entered puberty. He only kept the girls into adulthood until he or his inner circle tired of them. They were then taken to the kitchens to be roasted or smoked and eaten as delicacies. The babies that they produced with the teenage boys were culled from time to time. Moloch developed a taste for milk fed, human babies, but rationed himself to make sure that the breeding stock was kept viable. 'You there' had managed to escape from the kitchens one night and had hidden amongst the retarded Dokka'lfar just before they had been driven through the portal.

The depredations of the home world filled me with disgust. I realised that not all the humans were killed and eaten at once. Some had been fed a certain spice to give

270

their flesh some addictive flavour. They were kept alive and pieces removed to be served up to Moloch and his inner circle of sons and daughters. Once the piece of flesh or limb had been removed the bleeding stump was dipped in 'dust' and the human healed. Not only did they heal, but also they re-grew the limb, breast or buttock and kept it until they were harvested again and again.

The Dark Lords lived in castles that were not built for a winged people. They were not things of beauty, merely functional. Surrounding them were stands of tall trees that were managed and cut to provide fuel. Away from them I saw plantations irrigated, tended by the overseers and worked by the mindless ones. They were given minimal rations to keep them alive. Every so often they were gathered in, treated as a crop and fattened up for the table. Once culled, they were taken to the kitchens and smoked to keep from decaying. They were allowed to breed and those who showed signs of sentience were kept. The overseers mated with any of the female elves that they could subdue. Baby Dokka'lfar hung onto their mothers' backs as they toiled in the fields. Those that were old enough to work soon felt the lash to encourage them. Any that looked too weak soon found themselves roasting over a fire and feeding the overseers. The scraps were thrown to the waiting slaves.

The escape of 'You there' had taken him away from the castle and through the plantations. He had eaten some of the crops in an unripe condition and suffered great stomach-ache. As I had lived on this world and eaten of the food grown here, many of the crops were unfamiliar to me. There was one crop that was in flower however that I recognised that came from Earth. On the edges of Uzbekistan close to Afghanistan I had noticed fields of flowers tended by the herdsmen in the isolated mountain valleys. When I asked what these poor people could gain by growing flowers so far away from civilization, Sam Pitts had told me that they were opium poppies. Some humans used it refined as an addictive drug and it sold for great amounts of money on the human world.

The very idea of enslaving yourself to something as addictive as cocaine filled any elf with repugnance. There was a part of being human that was a very dark place to my kind. 'You there' was familiar with this drug in the most terrible way. He and his 'crop' were fed the drug before they were carved up and healed. The high society of the Dokka'lfar enjoyed the high that they got from eating fresh meat riddled with the drug's affects. Sometimes they drank the blood of the victims instead and sent them back the kitchen cages on point of death to recover.

Shuddering with disgust I probed further into the memories of 'You there' and found out that it was quite plain that not all of the intelligent Dokka'lfar were mentally gifted. Many of them relied on speech alone to communicate with each other. This did not surprise me, as all the Dokka'lfar were related to Moloch. His children mated with one another and some of them coupled with the Ljo'sa'lfar that were still captive and mentally dominated by Moloch. Those that had managed to break away from his domination had killed themselves rather than be taken under his spell again. I was horrified to know that there were still some elves of my own pure strain still bent by his will. He kept them alive for breeding stock and whether they were still sane or not did not matter to him. By now tears were rolling down my face as I forced myself to continue. My heart beat in my chest with an icy fist, clenched around it.

One memory that stuck out from the rest was an overseer that the cripple had seen stumbling and sneezing. It had to be one of the Dark Elves that had panicked and re-entered the portal back into Aifheimr before I transported the T

Rex's. One of my gifts to Moloch had taken root!

I had never seen the home world, so all that 'You there' had seen was new to me. The depravity and cannibalising of the Dokka'lfar and humans filled me with disgust. I had a good idea how my human friends would view the situation.

I withdrew my mind and left 'You there' cuddling his depleted bowl of food, still clutching the legs of Eduardo. I now fully understood why he was a cripple and where the extent of his scars came from. I was aware of Ameela at my side, wiping drool away from my mouth, as I retched over and over again. Her eyes were full of horror as she held me tight as she had also seen some of the terrible visions.

I opened my mind and 'called' to my human allies.

Sam Pitts and colonel Halim Djurayev were the first to arrive at the control chamber. Their eyes fixed upon the naked human at Eduardo's feet and questions filled their minds. The rest of my human friends and allies soon filled the chamber.

"Where did you find this man?" Demanded Sam.

'You there' stared back at the group of people with obvious astonishment. He picked up his rags and looked from them to the clothes that the other humans wore and gave a mournful cry. Astonishment filled his soul as he stared at human beings that had never been captive. He took a few faltering steps towards these well-dressed, healthy people and froze. Slowly he dropped to his knees, buried his head in his hands and began to shudder. Dry sobs rent the air as he curled into a foetal ball.

"He was found hiding amongst the Dokka'lfar," I said and shuddered. "What I found in his mind fills me with horror and shame that my race could sink so low as to do these practises. It is difficult to understand that these creatures are an offshoot of my people. Until this moment I had never realised just what my race were subjected to, to give up their home world. There never could be any form of compromise between the Light Elves and the Dark Ones. Our journey has not finished, gentlemen. What I am about to plant in your minds came from this pitiful wretch that you see before me. Forgive me, but there is no other way for you to see what this man has escaped from and what I am sure you will want to stop!"

I opened my mind and made a bridge from 'You there's mind to theirs and watched as their faces changed and the skin grew pale and their eyes opened far wider than was good for them. Every scrap of information I passed on to the people that had risked their lives for me transfixed the soul in acid. Some of the younger ones vomited and some burst into tears. They stared at the crippled form of the human that Eduardo had found in mounting horror at the depredations that he had undergone. Henry Spencer took off his shirt and wrapped it around the painfully thin shoulders of the crippled man and held him close. They were so similar that any other elf would have thought them brothers.

Spencer stood there with his arm around 'You there's' shoulders and said in a husky voice, "We have to go there, Peterkin. This has to stop!"

Sam Pitts clenched his fists and looked at me. I felt his rage mount up as he advanced towards my seated form.

"It's as Spencer said, High King, we have to go there! We have to release our fellow human beings from that ---," and he ran out of words.

For me, I did not need them to speak. Their minds filled mine and I suffered the anguish of their horror. The dreadfulness of what 'You there' had seen and experienced would never leave them, as it would never leave me. When I had returned from the terrible mental bruising that I had experienced, I had awakened one morning determined that Moloch had to be stopped. To do this I would need the help of my human beings and I had wondered what arguments I would need to enlist their help. Never in my wildest nightmares had I conceived of reasons like this.

"I agree, but first we must return to the castle and plan! There is much that we will have to do and transport from your world to this. Those who wish to go back to their own world must be free to do so. I insist!"

The mental assault nearly lifted my skull from off my neck! It was the wives of the Uzbekistani sons of colonel Halim Djurayev who were most insistent that they stay on this world until the job was done. Their children would be safe here while their men did whatever was necessary to free the humans trapped on Aifheimr.

Teginbek spoke to me using his mind and was joined by his wife, Fatma in asking, "The 'dust' that was put on the wounds. It enabled the amputated limbs to grow back. Whatever happens over there, we must bring some back. I have seen too many die of infection and shock due to dismemberment, as has my dear wife, working as a nurse. We really must get some of that incredible growth hormone and reproduce it here. If nothing else your race owes us its freedom here on this world. This will pay us back in spades!"

I looked at Halim and then at his other two sons, Ulugh and Yusuf. They were holding onto their wives, Shara and Nila with a grim certainty. For a moment I paused and then I passed my gaze over the original humans who had agreed to come on an adventure to free Ameela and Mia from Waldwick's mad scheme. I had come to know these people. I knew everything about them, every dark secret, every fault, every failing. I also knew all of their attributes and they knew this and accepted it. I had been inside their minds and they had peeped into mine. We had become more than friends. They were my people even though they were not elves. I loved them as if they were my own brothers and now I would be taking them into a place that was far more dangerous than the Plains of Scion.

"If you want to chance your lives on Aifheimr, the birthplace of my race, you must understand that Moloch's mental powers are much greater than Abaddon's. He could make you eat each other alive. He has enslaved Ljo'sa'lfar female elves for thousands of years, making them do his every whim. Even in their insanity, he was still able to breed from them and stop them from killing their own dark children. Very few of them have managed to overcome his will and commit suicide. You cannot imagine what that means to my people. To choose death rather than life is something so abhorrent to my kind that we would have to be insane to consider it! Until this conflict that you helped to end, not one elf has lifted his hand in anger to another, until Waldwick was driven by madness to do so. Every-one of us would need to wear an iron collar to prevent him from entering our minds and bending us to his will. You have seen what kind of life 'You there' had to endure. That kind of life would be yours if you fell to him. There would be no escape. There would be no hope and you would not be allowed to die," I told them and stared round at all the grim faces. "Also you must understand that if anything happened to me, you would be marooned there! Are you sure that this is what you want to do?"

CHAPTER TWENTY-ONE

Having asked the question of my human allies, I sat overwhelmed by the response. I had taken great pains to make them sure that they understood the situation and what perils would have to be faced on the Dark Elves' world. They had all voted to come with me and would not hear of any other move. I at least knew that the Arch of the Dream-shifter had been located in the same area that Moloch's castle had been built. The spatial address was locked into the Spellbinder's memory banks. By now the T Rex's would have wrought havoc in the area as they hunted for food. I would have imagined that the only safe place was inside the castle walls. Any large entrances into the castle would have been hastily blocked.

Every T Rex had been fitted with an iron collar, bound with greased leather, so that even Moloch would not be able to control them. We could, as they had been 'programmed' to recognise us as 'not prey' and not to hunt us. There was another marked difference between the Dark Elves and my people. The Dokka'lfar emitted a strong musky scent that the T Rex's soon identified as prey. Their ability to smell and track down living things gave them an incredible range. The fact that there were thousands of Dark Elves working around the countryside close to the castle would soon draw the T Rex's further a field, as they killed and ate their fill.

At the same time Alaric's virus would be spreading from one Dokka'lfar to another, so there would be plenty of carrion lying around. There would be two factors limiting the increase of the Dokka'lfar as the beasts spread out, laid their eggs and multiplied, sniffing out those who thought to hide. We had to remove the human beings under Moloch's control before the conditioning evaporated as the T Rex's increased, as the young would tear into anything that was living meat. In a few centuries from now I was sure that Aifheimr would be a different world once I was sure that Moloch had been defeated.

I looked at the crowd of willing faces and said, "Gather whatever you think you will need. I will take the Spellbinder back to our castle and we will rest there. Sam Pitts, John Smith and Colonel Halim Djurayev give some thought to what we will need. We will meet again and sit around the great table in the banqueting hall tomorrow. First we must go home and I will have to say my goodbyes to the dwarves who have guarded this gorge for the last two hundred years."

To my surprise, they all cheered and then quickly dispersed to pack what they felt they needed. I was aware that by my side stood Mellitus.

The dwarf lent forwards and grasped me by my left hand and growled, "Listen to me, Elf friend! Do not think, High King, that you will go there without me! My species owes their existence to the Ljo'sa'lfar. Had your ancestor not taken us with you, when you fled the Earth, we would have become extinct! The human world was not the place for dwarves to flourish. We have done well here, in the time that we have lived in this place. This is our world as much as it has become the Elvish home and we will fight for it and keep it!"

At my other side an ancient gnome laughed and said, "It has been a long time since I set my eyes upon the home world! You will need a great deal of foggy minds wrapped around this ship. Moloch will know the moment you step foot upon the soil of Aifheimr without us and the power of his mind will strike you dead."

"Ranzmut! Not you as well!" I said and turned to look into his clear brown eyes.

His skin was lined and creased, but his eyes twinkled with a surge of life. The snow-white beard he wore was plaited into a leather band and the hair at the back of his head pulled into two braids. Both wrinkled hands clasped the carved head on the top of his stick as he leaned forwards to take the weight off his back. He let go of his stick with one hand and grasped my right wrist in a surprisingly tight grip.

"You are the High King, that I have waited long centuries to be born. Where you go, I will follow. I was there when Moloch was born and I argued that the baby be put to death. I could feel the evil come slipping down from the future, but the Ljo'sa'lfar would not countenance the very idea. They welcomed the mutant into their midst and could not see what I had experienced from that awful surge from the future. I was just a young gnome then, Peterkin and they would not listen to me. They shunned me and cast me out as a foolish gnome with wild ideas.

I had to watch him grow into adulthood and the awesome strength of his mind increase, year by year. Not only his mind grew! His body became massive and he stood nearly twice the height of his father. The lack of wings made him bitter and his mind became more and more warped as time went on. For the first time in their history, the Ljo'sa'lfar knew fear and began to shun him. They did what they always did in those times; they turned their backs to him and moved away from his presence!

It was already too late when that spawn of evil killed his father and raped his mother. His mental power was beyond even the power of kings. He did whatever he wanted to and he founded the race of the Dokka'lfar by using his own mother as a breeding stock. Soon he took other Ljo'sa'lfar female elves and subjugated their minds. His children bred with one another and every coupling increased the number of his race. I believe that you know the rest, as you are a High King and have the memories of all those that went before you."

"You knew all this!" I exclaimed. "How was it that you did not warn me of what was to come."

"Peterkin, Peterkin my High King, I had to let the future unfold as it had to be. I had heard the legends of the Dream-seer dwarf and could only hope that what was foretold would happen. It did! You are the wingless elf who cast a 'Long-shadow' just as it was foretold. All I can hope is that the future will bring the downfall of Moloch and the home world will be once more a place of light."

"You have not foreseen the outcome of this struggle, then my old friend?" I asked.

"The paths into the future are twisted and many. I did not see the involvement of the humans in my dreams. They are an unknown quantity in this equation! It has become obvious to me that without them you would have found it much harder to remove the Dokka'lfar from this world. Not impossible, but far more difficult! All that I can tell you is that they will fight by your side using their weapons of steel and death. You are the High King that I foresaw in every way," Ranzmut insisted and released my hand, while I thought about what he had told me.

On Aifheimr, Moloch had left the safety of his castle for the first time since Peterkin's attack, to see for himself the damage that had been wrought. He was almost alone at the castle, as nearly all of his 'children' had deserted him, running from the sickness and the beasts. There were a few second and third generations Dokka'lfar keeping the kitchens running and the day-to-day business of the castle.

The Arch of the Dream-shifter lay in pulverised ruins. Partially in this world and also fixed into the world of the

Ljo'sa'lfar lay scattered components of the reality shifting, machine entity. Many weeks had gone by since the hated Light Elves had struck back. The death count was rising all over the countryside as the mysterious illness struck down the mindless with great rapidity. Once understanding had been reached, the gifted ones that were direct descendants of his line barricaded themselves away from the hoards of infectious Dokka'lfar. Still the sickness reached them through the water supply and the very air itself. Panic set in as they fell sick inside their homes, whilst to go outside meant that they fell prey to the dragons.

Piles of dead elves were eagerly chewed up and swallowed. What was discarded were spread around by the massive T Rex's that had suddenly appeared and left to rot. All attempts to control their minds met with a slippery resistance. Every beast was collared with a band of raw iron, making it impossible to connect with their brutal minds. They had spread throughout the lands causing havoc wherever they went. The strangest thing about them was that they were single minded in their pursuit of the Dokka'lfar. When they came upon any human they would sniff them and turn away, searching always for the Dark Elves.

Outside of his castle, Moloch had surrounded himself with a guard of human beings, so that his scent became masked by the stench of unwashed humans. It had only been a few months ago that his favourite son, Abaddon had told him that the way into the 'land of plenty' would soon be forged. The tunnel made from slabs of stone was almost through the ancient barrier. There had been no warning from Abaddon that anything untoward was happening. Moloch had laughed, as he was told the Ljo'sa'lfar king had offered Abaddon his daughter and then his granddaughter to form a truce.

The mutant stared at the carnage around the ruined Arch and scowled. The T Rex's had mopped up most of the dead, but enough had been left to rot and the stink was oppressive.

Moloch swung his ugly head towards Olivia and growled, "What do you think has happened, Mother? Are the peace lovers going to come here? Answer me! I want your opinion. What do you think they are capable of? They must have changed. Something must have happened to them. Abaddon never once thought that they were any danger to us."

Olivia winced and cowered away from her son. She was heavy with his child again and very vulnerable. How she longed for the peace of insanity, but Moloch would never permit that.

"How can I know that, my son," she replied. "What could I know of the Ljo'sa'lfar mind after so many years living the life I have, amongst the beasts that I have brought forth into this world!"

Moloch's answer was a backhanded swipe to her mouth that sent her sprawling into two of the human guards. They picked her up and waited while she collected her senses. After a while she managed to stand unaided. Today at least her son had allowed her the dignity of wearing a toga wrapped around herself, as it was cold outside. Inside the quarters that he kept her with the other surviving Ljo'sa'lfar females, he preferred her to be naked and humiliated.

Her wings were chained together from two large golden rings that were set into her flesh and hammered shut. She could flex her wings, but not fly. It had been ten thousand years or more since she had spread her wings to catch a morning thermal. Oh how she hated her son! He basked in the hatred and derived a malevolent joy from it. She had not lost count of the children that she had born him throughout the long years. Every one had the taint of the Dokka'lfar running through the veins. There were so very many! All of them had Moloch's evil touch. Even the females born from their unnatural union, whilst beautiful to look upon, were consumed with the same lusts. Her son had enthusiastically coupled with his daughters, bringing more of the cursed dark spawn into the world. The mindless ones, retarded and malformed were the result of the union of his sons and daughters. They bred together over and over again, filling the lands with hungry mouths.

Olivia wept inside, that she had been the instigator of the fount of evil that had destroyed her world. She had been forced to watch as the black and red tide swept through the civilization that was once so wonderful, into ruins. Over the centuries the Dokka'lfar had spread into every corner of this once fair world and made it their own. Famine had followed the explosive birth rate. Soon cannibalisation had followed. To stay alive she had been forced to eat her share of the Dark Elves and Moloch had made sure that she had no choice.

She stared at the half eaten piles of dead left by the dragons that had come through the arch and reflected on the sickness that was sweeping through all of the Dokka'lfar. Could it be, that her people were at last striking back? A small flicker of hope ran through her mind, which she quickly stifled. Moloch stared at the half eaten corpses littered in front of the castle and moved forward to get a better look at the carnage. Amongst the dead there was the unaccustomed stink of iron mixed with the bodies. It made him uneasy, as it had been thousands of years since he had been close to the hated metal. It was a human thing that Abaddon had brought back from their world. Moloch had the weapons buried in the ground to rot far from his castle.

A piercing scream rent the air as a dragon pushed its

way through the stand of trees, chewing on one of her daughters. Its head swung round as it scented Moloch. The tail swung through the underbrush as the beast kept its balance. Slowly it put one immense foot forward and pivoted its weight and turned to face the group. Immediately Moloch controlled the humans and gathered them in front of it, to block the way. He backed away towards the safety of the castle opening behind him. The T Rex continued to chew the Dokka'lfar into shreds before tilting its head back and swallowing the rest. It was a small mouthful. The leather clad, metal band around its neck caught the sun and reflected silver from the places that had been wore away. Olivia found that her son had taken control of her body and was forcing her to walk towards the doorway into the castle grounds. Once through that narrow door the dragon would be unable to get at her. She fought her son's mental commands with all of her might to slow herself down so that the great beast would catch her.

The T Rex ignored the human beings and nosed them out of the way and advanced towards Olivia. All she could see were the rows of serrated teeth almost as long as her arm, as it opened its mouth and snapped at the empty air, roaring its hunger.

"Death would be mercifully quick", she thought to herself.

Step by trembling step Moloch forced her towards the doorway. She fought him with all of her might, willing the beast to strike and end her misery. Now the great head filled her view as the thing opened its mouth and roared its frustration at Moloch's escape. Olivia felt the drenching sticky wetness of the creature's saliva as it dripped over her. She was not prey! The eyes of the beast were concentrated on Moloch and nothing else. She felt the hand of her son upon her arm as she was dragged inside the outer wall. He spun her around and into the courtyard, where she fell into a sobbing heap.

"Not this day, Mother," the cold, hated voice echoed in her mind. "There are many more years in front of us to enjoy. As for this beast that roars outside my castle walls, be assured that it will not get in here. Eventually it will go away. I will not be so foolish again. Let it eat its fill of the retarded ones and those who are foolish enough to be caught out in the open. The humans can work in the fields and gather what food we need it seems unscathed. They will be useful as slaves in that sense as well as feeding me fresh meat."

Olivia sobbed into the sparse grass that grew out of the cracks between the stone slabs. She wiped the sticky mess from her body as best she could with the clean parts of her toga. Once again she could feel the craving beginning to mount for the spice-saturated meat that Moloch fed her from time to time. She fought against it with all of her exhausted willpower, but she knew that when the scraps of meat were offered, she would eat to take away the pain. Raw or cooked it did not matter; the effect was just the same. A feeling of wonderful warmth would steal into every nerve-ending, giving relief and she would float upon a cloud of happiness for sometimes as long as a day. Moloch would torment her by withholding the drugged meat until she begged him for it. Sometimes he would let her go the whole course of 'cold turkey' and shake the addiction for as long as a year.

Once she had trodden that path he would gleefully force her to become an addict again and start the whole process once more. Very often her babies were born addicted to the spice and it was infused into their flesh. Moloch would eat them, fresh from the womb and feed her pieces of her own children to ease her addiction.

285

The humans left outside the castle opening, had hidden from the beast as best they could and had returned to do their master's bidding once it had wandered off. They had noticed that many of the 'Master Race' had fallen sick and the mindless ones had all died after contracting the mystery illness. Some of the overseers managed to get over the sickness and returned to make sure that the humans were kept under control. Many of them seemed now to lack the mental strength to bend them to their will and relied upon the lash.

The coming of the great meat-eating beasts through the Arch had filled them with fear at first, but it was soon noticed that these fearsome beasts hunted the Dokka'lfar and ignored anything else. Never the less, the size and ferocity of them made the humans give them a wide berth. They all had seen Moloch's mistake in approaching the area of the beast without realising that it was in the vicinity. They also seen, that the Lady Olivia had been ignored by the dragon. Many of them had been in the area when the Arch of the insane Dream-shifter had been pulverised by rocket fire. The first volley over the heads of the incoming Dokka'lfar had inflicted great damage. When the dragons arrived, scenting the blood left from the barrage, they had swept through the Arch like an unstoppable tide of killing eagerness. More and more of the great beasts hopped through and spread out over the fields in front of the castle. They soon scattered throughout the countryside running after the terrified Dokka'lfar.

Suddenly the Arch itself came under a strange fire and began to crumble into dust. More explosions echoed through the Arch and the rift in space-time disappeared. The hated overseers were too busy trying to run from the great beasts to worry too much about the human beings in their charge. It did not take long for every bit of shrapnel to be picked up from the battlefield and hidden. Over the weeks to come they were beaten into sharp blades that were fitted into wooden handles to make knives and spears. It was soon found that these metal pieces could take a sharp edge and keep it. By accident, a human woman decided to wear a strip of the metal that hated water around her head, woven into a band. A weakened overseer called her over to help him and she found that he could not get into her mind to make her to do what he wanted. She stabbed him in the chest and stopped one of his hearts with her blade. There was too much good meat to waste and she rapidly butchered him, sharing the bounty with her friends. The word soon got around that the metal stopped the Dark Ones from controlling the humans' thoughts. It did not take long for the humans to find out that grease kept the sharp metal from rusting.

For the first time in over a thousand years the yoke was lifting from the captive humans.

As the weeks turned into months I mentally healed. Many times the Spellbinder and I became one, as we slipped backwards and forwards from the human world to the Light Elves castle. I felt the siren call of the home world singing in my mind. Alaric produced more of the toxic virus, sealing the contents inside the entropy flasks. All of the Ljo'sa'lfar were put in contact with the anti-virus and were now immune to what the virus did to the Dokka'lfar, as were goblins, gnomes, dwarves and humans.

The time had come to return to the ancient home world of my kind. Ranzmut was ready to pack the Spellbinder with gnomes as well as the ones that carried the crystals upon their foreheads. Each turban was bound so that it could not be dislodged. Once again the gnomes would produce flutes and begin to play a medley of tunes once we had materialised on Aifheimr.

I had also been back to the Plains of Scion and contacted Prime for her help. This time she had rounded up families of Giganotosaurus for me and my elvish adepts had bound their minds into the same way of thinking as the T Rex's. The goblins had beaten out an iron collar for each animal and bound the metal in greased leather so that it would take years to rust through. I loaded the Spellbinder with the deadly cargo and altered the time constant to put them into storage. For them a few seconds would pass while they were aboard, but in reality many days would go by. The more I used the reality shifting entity the more I found out about its capabilities. Inside each pen the giant meat eaters stood frozen in time waiting to be released.

The first trip to Aifheimr would take us through the space-time co-ordinates close to were the insane Dream-shifter had become tethered. This would be very close to where the Demon Lord Moloch lived, but we would only be there for a few seconds. I had no intention of trying to dispose of him until I was ready. I needed to drop my cargo of combined death around the world in every densely populated place that I could find, adding the co-ordinates to the memory banks of the Spellbinder as we went. Like the ripples on a pond that eventually merged, I intended that the sickness and the meat eaters would spread all over the world. This was far more important than just destroying Moloch.

The virus would go where we could not and spread throughout the population. Those that survived the virus would more than likely be sterilised and those who were not would have the Giganotosaurus to contend with. They would have plenty to eat at first. Later on when the population withered there would be fierce competition for carrion and live Dokka'lfar.

Colonel Djurayev had been very busy with Ivan in contacting others in positions of authority, who could 'lose' AK 47 rounds in large quantities. Gold ingots changed hands and certain people got rich without them learning anything about their destination. Sam Pitts called in some favours and took delivery of several thousand explosive armour-piercing rounds for the Berretta rifles. John Smith took over the sale of the now defunct warehouse and pensioned off the security staff. The money raised went towards paying the bribes and costs of what was required.

Ivan Koshensky argued that the 'factory' remained open for business as it was still a good import\export business and the engineering part might still be needed in the future.

Although Ameela did her best, the scars upon my back had hardened into calluses. There was no sign that my wings would ever grow back and that I would ever fly again unaided. Halim's son Teginbek disagreed however.

"Great King," he said, "I am sure that once I remove the calluses from over the wing-stubs and expose the raw flesh and bone, I will be able to administer the healing compound that was used on 'You there's' amputated leg. After that it is just a matter of time and we will have to wait and see."

It was a faint hope that I nurtured, deep inside my mind, but it was there, none-the-less. Could it be that one-day I might catch a morning thermal and rise into the sky as of old? I would have to wait and see, as there were far more important things to do!

CHAPTER TWENTY-TWO

The time had come to return to the world of my kind. I had seen only what the poor human, 'You there' had shown me. I reached out to the composite mind of the Spellbinder and merged my mind with that of the entity. My mind filled with the co-ordinates of where the doomed Dream-shifter had anchored itself to Aifheimr. I had rehearsed this manoeuvre many times and would climb into the sky above Moloch's castle and head west at great speed. 'You there' had shown me that a great mountain range lay in that direction. I planned that we would get well beyond the peaks and out of his mental influence, as soon as possible.

Ranzmut and his orchestra were in full spirit and the sound of flutes filled the part of the Spellbinder that they had prepared. The realities tore apart and we sailed through the Rift. I concentrated my mind upwards and to the west, taking the Spellbinder with me. Space-time warped to my will and within minutes we were swiftly moving through the rarefied air above the peaks. We heard the sonic bang of displaced air as we left the area and dropped down to the plains below. We had arrived at nighttime and we would be chasing the sunset. Darkness would hide our presence and the Dokka'lfar would awaken to a new and different dawn.

Moloch was dripping with sweat and his head was aching when it briefly filled with gnomish music. His eyes bulged as he tried to wrap his mind around the mental interference and pierce through. There was nothing! Whatever it was, was gone and could not be reached. The fever that racked his giant frame for several weeks had started to abate. His Ljo'sa'lfar females he had locked into cages where they could be fed, but not touched. He had conditioned their minds against suicide and made it so that they could not escape him into insanity. While the illness had struck him down, he had not lost his cunning and had retreated to an easily defended tower. Some of his children had survived the sickness, but many had died. Moloch trusted no one.

He had noticed the speculative looks from the human beings that now seemed to inhabit his castle in greater numbers. Moloch could taste their hatred in his mind. He would exact a terrible reckoning for their insolence once he was back in control of himself.

Human corpses hung on bronze meat hooks, cured so that they would not spoil, in an antechamber. He lost himself from the problems of tomorrow by hacking off pieces and chewing on the smoked flesh, imbued with plenty of spice. Moloch swallowed the well-chewed meat and drank fresh water to help it down his sore throat. Instantly he was filled with the warmth of the drug as it 'kicked in' and lay upon his bed. He wondered if the child that his mother carried would soon come into the world. For a few moments he wondered how she was faring with the illness that racked his body.

Olivia had heard the sound of gnomic music in her mind just for a few moments. Her heart soared with hope as her imagination went into overdrive. Could it be that her people were here on the home world? She felt the restless movement of the evil spawn within her womb and wished the child dead. The fever had been brief and she was soon back to normal. Moloch's offspring fed her and saw that she had fresh water to drink. Many times it was the humans who looked after her and gave her fresh straw to lie on. They were never cruel to her and expressed sympathy at her plight. They had such short lives measured against hers and she envied their release from servitude. She was sickened by Moloch's use of them over the thousands of years he had bred them. Olivia was ashamed that she had eaten the drug-soaked flesh of these people when she was under Moloch's control. Under the force of her addiction she had been a willing participant in her son's orgies.

Strangely, the humans seemed to understand that she was dominated by her son and used by him. Sometimes they had secretly given her treats from the kitchens, like fresh fruit when it had been available, knowing that Moloch would have punished them, had he known. His addiction to the spice soaked flesh had dulled his wits over the centuries from the razor sharp intellect that he once had. Olivia clung to her hope.

There were settlements scattered over the plains, following the rivers that flowed from the mountains behind us. Everywhere we looked the land was at the edge of famine. Fields were planted and harvests were gathered, but the land had been overused. What plants were growing were stunted and poor in yield. Some richer fields showed bones scattered across the landscape where the Dokka'lfar had been ploughed into the soil after the harvest. No birds sang and the lands were silent.

I grounded the Spellbinder and the gnomes took it in turns to pass round the turbans that carried the crystals along with the flutes. We were not observed as Mellitus took a scouting party into a remote farmhouse. The overseers were sleeping in comfort while the mindless ones buried themselves into the straw inside the empty barns. Those barns that had food stored were securely locked. There was a bone pit at one end of the farmyard and it had enough skulls and other recognisable parts to show us what filled it. By the side of the pit was a mill wheel for grinding up the bones into smaller pieces to plough into the exhausted soil.

Alaric opened a flask no bigger than a thimble and left it inside the window where the overseers were sleeping. We withdrew and I took the Spellbinder further along the river to where a town had sprung up. This time we made very sure of our deadly cargo by dropping it amongst the sleeping Dokka'lfar gathered in a work pen. The sun had set by an hour or so and darkness hid our actions. Again we were not seen. No guards were set as all the Dark Elves that commanded the multitude, had never feared attack in thousands of years. I decided to leave the busy town to wake up to a brave new dawn and discover that they would soon be terminally ill!

As the sun began to sink below the horizon we dropped off several families of Giganotosaurus outside of a large town. With the scent of Dokka'lfar in their nostrils they needed no urging towards the settlement. Tied around the necks of some of them was a flask with an ice stopper that would melt through eventually and would spread air-born spores wherever he went. I knew that they would home into the nearest group of fresh living meat. This became our new mode of attack as we dropped out of the sky, invisible to anyone looking up, sometimes right into the heart of a town. Nowhere did we find a trace of a human being. It was beginning to look as the only humans on this world lived at Moloch's castle. At the time of darkness everyone slept without any thought of danger. This was about to change!

When we reached the sea, I unhesitatingly took us across, still chasing the setting sun and landed on the shore of another continent. We released the beasts, with their garlands of death at a large fishing port under cover of darkness and continued inland. Again and again we did the same until our hold was empty of the meat-eating dinosaurs. Every flask that was left was dropped into any large town that we found in our journey across the home world. We continually followed the edge of sunset until we found ourselves approaching the lands that supported Moloch's castle.

The Spellbinder had orbited Aifheimr, staying inside the night zone as the world spun beneath us. I was very tired and needed to sleep before I could co-ordinate the next part of the plan, so I took the Spellbinder home. Alaric had salted from the thousands of the thimble sized, filled flasks of his virus, wherever we had stopped. Many of the Giganotosaurus that were loosed from the hold carried the virus straight into the populated areas. I insisted that we wait for at least a month before we returned with the Spellbinder and deal with Moloch. Before that time we needed to know what the effects of the 'seeding' had produced.

During that time Acme Engineering had been busy modifying the AK 47's by reducing the iron content and replacing it with stainless steel and bronze. The storerooms of the Spellbinder were stacked with these modified weapons and explosives in readiness for our return visit. The rescued human, 'You there' had grown back his amputated leg to the same size as the other one. Halim's son Teginbek had monitored the growth and had taken blood samples from the replacement leg. He had also done DNA tests to see whether the leg was really his and not someone else's, grafted on. It did not take long for the human to learn how to fire an AK 47 and he was certain that he was coming with us when we returned.

Alaric had refined the capsules containing the virus and had the goblins fit them to crossbow bolts so that they could be delivered from a safe distance. The entropy flasks had been miniaturised into thimble-sized containers for the first visit so it had not taken the goblins very long to adapt them to be attached to the arrows. It was agreed that the

Quetzalcoatlus would be stored inside the hold frozen in time and each one would carry an elf supplied with the modified Klashnikovs. Seated in front was a gnome, armed with the virus carrying crossbows. I would 'home in' to fixed places on Aifheimr and drop them off to spread the virus far and wide. They could also monitor the progress of the damage inflicted by our previous visit.

We had followed a northerly equatorial band around the home world dropping off the meat-eating dinosaurs along with the virus. There were plenty of lands to the south that would need to be infected. I had already taken on board another cargo of Giganotosaurus along with more T Rex's that Prime had rounded up for me. Again they all wore collars of pure iron swathed in greased leather. All of them were programmed to treat the light elves and the rest of my allies as 'not prey' and were sat inside the hold of the Spellbinder, frozen in time. I was quietly confidant that as the years went by, more and more of the Dark Elves would meet their end one way or another. Sometime in the future my people would have a massive 'mopping up' exercise. The one creature that we had to be sure of was Moloch and he could wait until I was ready to take him on. I no longer had nightmares about him.

Once again I found myself stood in front of the mural that hung on the wall of the royal chambers. Freyr stood fast holding the star of light against the onslaught of the Dark Elves. I felt him surface into my mind.

"What was ours will be ours again," his voice whispered into my ears. "You must follow the path that has been laid out for you. Destroy these aberrant creatures without pity. I should have listened to Ranzmut when he told me of his visions of the future. Keep his council! "

Auberon's voice swelled up and filled my mind as he insisted, "Peterkin, descendant of my line, you must be without mercy. To take back our world and to restore it, you must see the Dokka'lfar for what they are. They are the dark side of our race, the very embodiment of evil. Every one of them must die; there can be no survivors! We should have fought back, instead we hid."

Welling up from beneath them the murdered king, Elweard, cried out, "Grandson, do this thing. What you have done, no other of the line of Kings could ever have even thought of doing. Feel no remorse at what you have put into action. Destroy Moloch and the curse has ended. What ever brought that spawn of evil into our world, we must be sure that it does not ever happen again."

The minds of the long dead kings filled my mind with suggestions and alternatives. Each one was insistent that I listen to him. My head rang!

My mother's mind cut into the voices like an icy knife and stilled the tumult.

"My son will do what he has to. Be still ghosts of the past. He has been foretold and the visions are true. He is the 'Long-shadow' that was seen centuries ago. He will prevail. He has prevailed. This High King has allies the like of which you could not understand or know! Be still, I say! Be still! Peterkin my beloved son you should go to sleep now," my mother insisted. "You are loved by more than your race. You are the Great High King and I am proud of you, my son."

I was aware of a delicate touch on my shoulder as Ameela placed her hand upon my cheek and said, "I too am proud of what you have done, my love. And your son will be proud of his father as well."

"My son!" I whispered.

"I decided some time ago that I would bring forth a new elf into this world. Many of the other elves have decided that this world could do with some new life upon it and there are too many empty rooms in this castle. Children need to grow up together and when you are successful, the 'Home World' will be there, waiting for those who want to go back."

"That's an awful amount of belief that you all have in my abilities," I exclaimed and kissed her gently.

During the weeks that had gone by, the human population had soon learnt that the blades that had been made out of the shrapnel had better uses. Since the woman who had worn the metal in her hair had killed her overseer the word had gone out. Now the metal had been heated and beaten into strips that could be worn around the neck and fixed so that they did not come off easily. Obsidian knives replaced the metal ones as overseer after overseer fell to the disease and in that weakened condition died by the knife. They were butchered and eaten by the growing band of human rebels. As the humans got stronger, the Dokka'lfar grew weaker due to the virus that jumped from elf to elf. It killed every one of the mindless ones and many of the rulers were rendered so weak that they fell easy prey. Those that recovered found that they could no longer mentally control many of the humans. They found this out by a swift slashing blow to the throat, delivered by a human, who then watched them die.

Olivia awoke to see that human men and women had entered the room of cages. She found that she could not read their minds! She watched as they slit the throat of the overseer who Moloch had left in charge of them. They overpowered him as he rose to his feet. She could feel the weakened power of his mind battering against a shield that each human carried without result and in her mind she felt the salty taste of iron! Olivia remembered how the ground in front of the castle had been riddled with pieces of the hated metal. Moloch had dragged her inside before the beast could kill him. He had not managed to go back and rid himself of the metal. The humans had found every bit and found out what it could do! Now hope rose within her breast.

A woman picked off the ring of keys and began to open the cages that the last of the Ljo'sa'lfar females were kept. At that moment the first labour pains racked Olivia. She hung onto the bars of the cage and gripped them hard. She gritted her teeth and rode the pains. The woman noticed her plight and entered the cage.

"Can you move?" she asked. "We must get you away from here and away from Moloch's mental influence."

"The only thing that will stop him would be to collar me with iron," Olivia replied. "Do you have any spares?"

"We brought a few with us in case they were needed. The others have gone to hunt Moloch down and are making their way towards the tower that he blockaded himself inside. Do you know if he has survived the sickness, Lady Olivia?"

"Oh yes, he has survived! Even now his mind is reaching out to his children for assistance. For pities sake, collar me before he gets into my head!"

The woman smiled as she looped a collar around Olivia's neck and clicked it home.

"Dear Lady Olivia, he will need to travel a great distance to find any of his children alive. We have been very busy! Come lean on me and let us find ourselves better surroundings for this baby to come into a new world."

Olivia stood and rode another thrust from her womb. She managed to put one foot in front of the other and gripping onto the human woman, made her way out of the room of cages.

Moloch awoke that morning and reached out with his

mind. The Castle was empty of life. Not one of his children seemed to be able to talk with him.

"Where is everyone?" He thought. "Surely the virus had spared some of the Dokka'lfar?"

He reached out for the mind of his mother and felt nothing. There was an empty place in his mind that had been filled for ten thousand years. The other Ljo'sa'lfar females that he had caged up securely were also missing from his mind.

"Could they be dead?"

Moloch began to panic and reached for some more drug soaked meat to calm himself. As he chewed, the drug hit the spot and filled him with warmth. He began to drag the furniture away that he had piled in front of the door. It was time that he vacated the tower now that the sickness had run its course. He pissed into the receptacle that voided outside with relief that he could at last empty his bladder under his own control.

It was at that moment that he realised that he had no interest in sex. Everything in that area had become numb! He ran his hands over his flaccid member and could not feel any sensations of pleasure at all. Now he pulled the tables away from the doorway in frantic haste. He needed to find others of his kind.

Deep inside the castle a band of humans were preparing a trap. They had found the tower that Moloch had barricaded himself into. There was a large hall that the tower served and long tables had been used here. They pushed two together to make an arch, using a third table as a bridge. On top of this bridge, four men held a net woven from a strong fibre and waited for the entrance of Moloch. The noises from the upper part of the tower showed that the ruler of Hell was on his way down, as he removed the barricades. Tapestries had been torn from their wall coverings and draped in front of the windows, putting the hall in semi-darkness.

Moloch entered the hall and stood for a few moments staring at the smothered windows with suspicion. He filled the doorway with his huge form and shuffled forwards, his shoulders almost touching the walls. The Dokka'lfar ruler adjusted his eyes to the gloom and was suddenly shocked to be aware of humans waiting for him at the other end of the room. He clenched his huge hands, capable of crushing a skull and started forwards, reaching out with his mind to take control of them. With a sensation of amazement he realised that the minds of the humans were shielded! He could not control them!

The four men launched themselves from off the makeshift bridge with the net. They had made sure that it was plenty big enough and Moloch found that he was swathed in netting. Ropes attached to the ends were rapidly encircled around his legs, tying them securely together. While he stood there roaring with anger a hand carrying obsidian knife entered the net and hamstrung his left leg just above his heel. He went down with a crashing thud, bleeding profusely. While he tried to regain his footing another swipe with a knife cut through the other ligament on his right, effectively crippling him. He got to his knees and tried to cast off the net, only to lose the fingers of his right hand as it came into view through the mesh. He pulled the bleeding stumps back into the folds of the net in disbelief. Moloch rolled around the floor trying to get onto his knees again, screaming his rage. As he struggled to his knees a crashing blow to the head with a table leg sent him crashing forward. His forehead smacked into the table end opening up the skin over his eyes and blinding him in his own blood. Again the improvised club came down and this time split his ear. Rope was passed quickly around his

300

neck and knotted so that the two long ends were securely held, by being fastened around the wrists of two big men. He found that the constraints of the net were suddenly released, but he was securely roped and bound around his ankles and wrists. The humans pulled the ropes taut around the legs of a table until he was trussed in a sitting position onto the hard wooden boards. Each limb was tethered to a corner leg and he was helpless. The ropes from his wrists looped under the table and where tied to each other. More ropes bound him around the upper legs to the top of the table. The women pulled the tapestries away from the windows letting in the light.

Now the greatest prize of all was pulled into sight. A smaller T Rex had fought another of its species and lost, becoming a meal for the victor. The humans had found the collar and had taken it back to the castle. This was now looped around Moloch's neck, under his arms and round his back. Once in position and tight, it was riveted shut. All mental power shut down with it.

One of the men came forward and stared him in his bloody face and quietly spoke to Moloch.

"My name is Michel. I lead these human beings into a new life. Your reign of terror is finished. Pull the ropes back so that this piece of shit lies flat upon the table. The Ljo'sa'lfar are coming for you. They have destroyed your grip on power and depravity. We will wait for them, but before they come let us go to the kitchens, where you can give all of us a good meal," the human leader said. "Take off his legs and cauterise the stumps with the healing compound. He will be easier to carry in pieces."

Moloch began to scream.

Half a world away I had brought the Spellbinder to the vicinity of a delta. Here there were many ports and fishing villages and inland there were towns that were supplied by the fish that were taken by the coast dwellers. The mindless Dokka'lfar were penned, enslaved when needed and the surplus was eaten. Again the fields showed always the edge of famine and the lands were barren. I felt no remorse as I let my flyers free and spread the virus. There were times that we were seen and our weapons were used. The fact that we were killing unarmed people was balanced by the way of life that they led. My people showed not one shred of remorse as they removed the Dark Elves from my old home world. The dwarves felt that they were ridding this world of a vicious vermin. My human friends had a similar attitude and showed no mercy to any of the mutant elves. Goblins and gnomes had once had their own kind of civilisation here on this world. It pained them to see such suffering inflicted upon Alfheimr and they wished to re-seed this world with many creatures and plants.

There would come a day when the last of the Dokka'lfar had been sniffed out by the meat eaters when they would have to be hunted down or left to starve. Once we began to re-settle our home world as many would, the T Rex's and Giganotosaurus are not the kind of animals that co-exist with other creatures.

I waited until the last of the flyers had returned and pointed the Spellbinder towards Moloch's castle. The day of reckoning was finally here.

CHAPTER TWENTY-THREE

Olivia gave a final gasp and pushed with all of her might. The baby girl screamed out and curled her fingers into tiny balls of rage. It was so cold outside. Moloch's daughter was bright red in colour and as healthy as all the others that she had born. All of the long months that she had carried the child she had hated it. Now that she was born, the instinctive love that any mother would have for her child took over. She hated the father with every fibre of her soul, but this helpless baby, she could not bring herself to hate.

The human woman tied string around the umbilical cord and cut it cleanly. Olivia gave another long push and the afterbirth came away with a gush. She felt the milk rushing into her breasts and the familiar maternal feelings flood her body as the baby cried.

"Give her to me," she begged and held out her hands to her companion.

"She should die," the woman replied, but gave the little girl up to Olivia. "She is Dokka'lfar, the last of her kind. I have had children and have seen them fed to your son. By now he should be captive and restrained by my people. My man, Michel will have taken him to the kitchens by now. Can you walk?"

Olivia held the girl to her breast and felt her suckle greedily. She wrapped her arms around her and nodded.

"Give me a moment or two and I shall be able to make my own way," she answered.

She shifted the baby round to the other breast with a practised hand and gave her a few moments on that one.

"What is your name? I would like to know. You have been so kind to me, that I wish to know who you are," she asked.

The woman stared at Olivia and came to a decision.

"My name is Janet," she said. "I have been part of your son's evil practises ever since he saw that I was entering women-hood. Thankfully I lost my virginity to Michel before he noticed me. Now I shall feast upon him!"

"What do you mean?" She asked.

"The kitchens are where he is going to be kept until your people come. Michel swore that once Moloch was captured he would lose his legs and watch them be eaten by us. Just as he made us watch so many times when he kept my people alive and ate them bit-by-bit, constantly feeding them the spice that robs the will. The one thing we can be sure of is that Moloch will not run away," and she laughed until she coughed.

Olivia wrapped the baby in some of her toga and made her way towards the kitchen with her new friend, Janet. She to could hardly wait to see what had become of Moloch. Already she could feel the heat from the cooking fires and the underlying smell of wood-smoke and roasting meat began to fill the air. Olivia could hear the voices of the humans as they busied themselves in the kitchen. It was a relaxed attitude that made her feel safer than she had been for thousands of years. As she turned the corner she saw that the kitchen had been swept clean and sunshine was pouring through the open windows. The tables had been moved away from the fires and roasting spits and pushed against the walls. Inside a cage, securely fixed to a table was what was left of Moloch.

On a spit, skewered in place where two huge, well-muscled legs. They dripped fat into the flames that licked around them. Several pieces had already been sliced off leaving the raw meat beneath. Inside the cage a bloody creature glowered at his captors, pulling ineffectually at the iron band looped around his neck and back with the one hand that still had its fingers. The face was cut and bruised, showing clearly where the table leg had caught him. One ear had been mashed into his head and one eye was nearly closed. He radiated fear and hatred at his captors.

Michel had cut through both legs a few inches below the hips after applying tourniquets and snapped the thighbones with an axe. The stumps had been dipped into the healing compound and sealed. Already the skin was growing back over the raw area as Moloch's body began the process of regenerating his legs. This would take some considerable time and the Lord of Hell would not be able to move very far until this happened.

Olivia walked towards the cage and spat into his face.

"At long last you have been punished for the terrible things that you have done. It has taken thousands of years to put you in your rightful place and the sight of you caged, fills me with joy! I look forward to meeting the new High King of the Ljo'sa'lfar when he comes here. He will deal with you as he wishes. The one thing that I regret is that he will be far more merciful than I would be. Here is your accursed daughter, born this very day and the last of your abominations. I will abide with what he will decide to do with her."

Moloch wiped the spittle from his face with his one good hand and turned towards the back of the cage. He pulled himself into the corner and covered himself with what straw he could reach.

Olivia turned to Michel who was chewing on a piece of Moloch's leg and asked, "May I remove this iron collar from around my neck? If the High King is here, I can then lift my mind from this evil place and contact him? I owe you much. Please believe me, when I say that I would never betray you or seek to control you, as that evil creature that I brought into the world has in the past. I have been his plaything for ten thousand years and you have made me free at last."

Michel smiled at her and reached around the crying baby in her arms to undo the buckle holding the band of iron around her neck.

He pulled it away from her neck and said, "We start our new association with trust, Lady Olivia. Send your mind out into the world and make him welcome. Moloch is caged and neutered and there need be no more loss of life. Besides I would like to thank him personally for sending the shielding metal through the Arch and for the two other weapons he loosed upon this terrible world."

This was a desolate world! The soil had been exhausted by over-cropping and little had been put back. What wild life survived did so far up the mountains where the Dokka'lfar could not reach them. Little remained of any of the great forests, except those that were so remote that cutting the trees for fuel and transporting the logs was not possible. Here also small pockets of Alfheimr's own native life still eked out a perilous existence. It broke the hearts of all my people to see such ruin. Never the less, elves goblins and gnomes had plans to return and re-seed this world and let it replenish itself. Once the teeming millions of the Dark Elves had been exterminated from this world, a natural order would develop. After the vegetable life had been given a chance, we had our own animals brought from Earth long ago and settled into the haven we had established, to bring here.

I was carefully edging the Spellbinder across the lands separating Moloch's castle from the plains, when I heard Olivia's mental call. I stopped the gnomes from spinning their mental web and told them to put their flutes away. Olivia had summoned all of her strength to put out a broad-spectrum call, not knowing how far away we might be. Every elf on board the ship heard her mental shout. We replied with joy that she was still alive and Ljo'sa'lfar.

The news that she gave us was that Moloch was imprisoned and wrapped in iron, his mind fettered.

As we came into sight of the grim looking castle, I merged my mind with the Spellbinder and using the augmented senses I searched for the T Rex's that had been let loose. They had scattered across the countryside, seeking out the Dokka'lfar and feasting as they went. Many clutches of eggs had been laid and the mothering instincts of the dinosaurs had ensured that all had survived. As a precaution, I had my people make camp on the first terraced layer where I landed the Spellbinder, next to the field of opium poppies. I gave the order to destroy them and lay the emerging crop to waste. From here I would travel by Quetzalcoatlus upwards to the higher levels. Ameela stayed with me and my group of allies flew with us, each reptile being controlled by an elf. Hoatzin of course flew alone and my mother travelled with Spencer.

I could see several humans waving to us as we banked over the terraces and we headed towards them. 'You there' was waving back to a women who was crying and he slid off his mount, running towards her. My humans tightened their grips on their weapons as the pterodactyls dropped onto the ground. The victors in the fight against Moloch were the most ragged, dirty and fearsome men and women that I had ever seen. Their effect on my well-clothed, clean skinned people was electrifying. We had seen by 'You there's' appearance, that humans on this world lived on the edge of existence. This was the reality of that vision.

Then I saw an elf with a baby, stood with a human man. It had to be Olivia and Michel.

A brief mind touch confirmed that and I dropped off my flyer with Ameela and walked towards them. To my embarrassment they fell to their knees and bowed to me.

We must have been an imposing sight, stood there in the sun's morning glare. All of my people were dressed in black or brown leather edged with furs. They all carried weapons that the people of Alfheimr had never seen, but they could see the metal. My humans were tall against 'You there' and his kind, well nourished and clean. The goblins and gnomes were totally different in appearance to elves, as were the dwarves with their long beards. Add to that our flying dragons and the shock to the system must have been tremendous.

I held out my hands to Michel and Olivia drawing them to their feet. I smiled at the mother of Moloch and hugged her, passing her to Ameela.

To the human's amazement the next thing I did was to drape my coat around his shoulders and said, "Well done, elf-friend. All that I know is that Moloch is imprisoned and wrapped in iron. May I enter your mind and know all that I need to find out?"

Michel's eyes filled with tears and he answered, "Great High King to hear you ask, makes me feel honoured. I have had my mind desecrated so many times by any Dokka'lfar that chose to use me. Enter my mind and see whatever you wish. To be asked!"

Keeping hold of his hand, I entered his mind and saw everything. I marvelled, at what this man had done with what he had at his disposal. His bravery and that of the other human beings in taking advantage of the ruler of Hell in his one moment of weakness amazed me. I was astounded by their use of the shrapnel that was the result of the rocket attack. My eyes also filled with tears as I peeked into the lives of these people. My entrance into 'You there's' mind had prepared me and limited the shock, but I still felt such shame, that my race could have done such things to them.

I became aware of more filthy-looking female elves staring at me and falling to their knees. These were all that were left of Moloch's breeding harem, after ten thousand years of torment. They had their wings shackled so that they could not fly. Some were clothed in rags and some were naked. Every one of them had years of filth and grime scabbed all over their bodies. There were a few amongst them that had retreated into insanity and to see them made my heart ache.

"They were the lucky ones," Olivia said. "Mad or sane he could use them to breed more of his kind. I gave birth to this creature, this very day. She is his daughter and mine. She could even be said that she is also my granddaughter too. The child is an abomination and I hated her from the moment that I conceived her, but now that she is here ----. Oh Great High King how can I not love her, defenceless as she is! It must be your decision as to what her fate must be."

I stood by the side of this tormented elfin woman, shaken to the core and I just did not know what to say or do.

Her thoughts became fogged and difficult to receive and I heard Ranzmut say into my ear, "I feel no evil slipping down from the future at this moment. Stay your hand at this time. Deal with Moloch and take these people home. Give the women into your mother's care for the time being."

I smiled at the ancient gnome and said, "Ranzmut Boddywinkle your advice is listened to and your council given. I will deal with Moloch. Mellitus and Sam Pitts I want you to come with me to the kitchens. Oh and Sam, bring John Smith with you and as much C4 as you can carry. If it needs more hands, bring them. When we leave, I want this castle levelled so that nothing stands."

Using Michel's mental map I made my way through the architecture of Moloch's castle towards the kitchens.

Colonel Halim's son Teginbek and his wife Fatma guided by 'You there' entered the forbidding labyrinth of Moloch's castle. Having lost a leg to Moloch's appetite and had the re-growth hormone smeared upon the stump, the human knew where it was kept. The smell from the lower rooms was foul with the odour of rotting Dokka'lfar and the air was thick with flies. Fortunately the amputation rooms were above the kitchen floors so that fresh, drug-soaked meat could be easily transported down to the fires.

Teginbek and his wife retched at the sight of the blood-soaked wooden tables and the parts left to rot. Bronze and obsidian knives hung from the walls, along with bone cracking axes to sever the thighs. On the shelves of a cupboard was a row of sealed ceramic pots.

"That's what you need," 'You there' pointed out and opened the haversack that Fatma had strapped to her back.

Teginbek stacked them neatly into the carrier, making sure that they were not likely to get smashed, pushing straw in between them. They made sure that there were no more jars left inside the cupboard. Once satisfied they hurriedly left, making for the outside and the Spellbinder, beating their way through clouds of flies.

Underneath the dismembering room I entered the kitchen. The remains of two large legs were thrown into the ashes of the fire. They were bigger than any human being's and had been reduced to the bones. I shuddered with revulsion. This was one habit I was determined to finish. There was a snarling noise from the corner of the room and there on a table was the cage that Michel had shown me in his mind.

Inside the cage was the legless torso of Moloch. He was holding onto the bars of the cage with his one good hand. The hatred shone out of his one good eye and he tried to spit at me. His hair was matted with blood and one of his ears had been mashed to his head. Deep gashes had been inflicted across his forehead where a club had caught him. The fingers were missing from his right hand, leaving just the thumb. Wrapped around him was one of the iron bands that we had fitted to a T Rex. It circled his neck and wound around his back. Inside it was a cauldron of contained mental power, struggling to get out. I could see that the humans had made sure that this would not happen. They had hammered sharp pieces of metal into the harness, pointing inwards so that every time he struggled the points dug deeper into his flesh. He was the colour of blood underneath the stains and reeked of evil.

I felt the minds of the long dead kings reach out to me trying to tell me what I should do. Their fear rose up and I choked it off and silenced them. Mellitus took one look, handed me his cherished AK 47 and flicked the safety off.

"I am the High King," I said to the drooling creature hanging onto the bars of the cage. "I am judgment. I am the bringer of death and the destroyer of your world."

"Tell me your name," hissed Moloch.

"It is said that there are powers that can be used, if you know the name of the High King," I replied. "I shall be nameless to you. You will die here and this abomination will fall around you, burying your remains deep under the stones. Your bones will never be seen again, the sun will not shine in this place. One thing I promise you and that is, that no Dokka'lfar will ever walk this world again. What was ours is returned to us. What was taken will be restored."

I turned to my human friends and said to them, "Sam Pitts and John Smith set the detonators so that the explosives will cave in the walls and bury this thing far beneath a mantle of stone. Now I am going to be sure that you die here in front of me and by my own hand."

Moloch stared with uncomprehending hatred as I lined up the Kalashnikov with his head. I found it quite easy to pull back the trigger and reduce his head to a bloody mess. I kept the trigger closed and took the line of bullets down through his chest. Eventually the kitchen became silent and the gun ceased to shake.

Mellitus said, "I think you can give me back the rifle now High King. I do believe that he is dead."

The voices inside me were still.

I turned to the dwarf beside me and said, "Thank you Mellitus old friend. Come, it is time we left this place and made our way home. I leave the demolition of this terrible place to you, my good friends. Bury it! Leave nothing standing. Let this place be reclaimed by nature and if possible, be forgotten."

Without a backward glance at the heap of bloody flesh that was all that was left of Moloch, I turned away and led the way out. I left my human allies to arrange the explosives inside the castle and made my way towards the Spellbinder. Inside the sentient craft, Teginbek had begun to remove the shackles that had been inserted through the wings of the captive Ljo'sa'lfar and he smeared a small quantity of the growth hormone inside the bleeding holes. It would still be some time before they would fly again, but the heavy weight of the chains had gone. My mother and Ameela were supervising the bathing of these incredibly old elfin women. Those that had escaped Moloch into insanity were being set at peace and their underlying fear soothed away. Deep beneath their deranged personalities were the original psyches that my mother was certain could be saved.

The fact that they were amongst their own kind would

help them to heal. Some of these ladies were not young when Moloch had taken them and 'bound' their minds. Some of them had been maintained by him and refused the ability to die. Released from his domination they were determined to travel to the haven that we had made our own and then to die amongst Light Elves.

The poppy fields had been scorched from the land and all my people were returning to the Spellbinder. I stood outside and waited for Sam and John to emerge from the grim, grey stonework of Moloch's castle. The whole building reflected the ugliness of the person who lived in it. Sam had tossed a large bundle of C4 plus a detonator inside the cage on top of the bloody heap that was all that was left of Moloch. Colonel Halim's other two sons were also setting explosives as deep inside the castle as was possible to go avoiding the corpses. Just as I began to worry where they had all got to, I saw them re-appear.

Sam made his way towards me and stood by my side, looking back at the forbidding structure of towers, halls, captive pens and the kitchen that inside the remains of Moloch lay.

He handed me the radio-controlled detonator and said, "Its all yours, High King. Twist the key and press the button."

I took the little box from his hand and twisted the key. A red light came on to indicate that it was active. For a moment I paused and stared at ten thousand years of evil and shuddered. I pressed the key.

There was an instantaneous 'crump' and the castle seemed to implode. The towers came down, along with the roofs and every outer wall fell inwards. A cloud of dirty smoke curled up into the sky and the masses of stonework continued to fall inwards and down, as the dungeons filled. My human allies had done well, as by the time that the smoke had settled there was just a hill of grey stone. My eyes had been set on the windows of the kitchen as the tower crumbled into Moloch's tomb. There had been a small delay in the timing as the bomb inside the cage went off after the tower had collapsed, pulverising the remains of the ruler of Hell. There would be nothing under that pile of stone but scattered fragments.

I gave the box back to Sam and said, "Time to go back. I was going to say home, but I feel that this world will become home to us again sometime in the future."

We walked back into the Spellbinder and I sat once more into the control chair and grasped the staff of power. Instantly I merged my mind with the Spellbinder and warped reality to open the Rift. I set the Spellbinder alongside the terrace beside the throne room and blended into the stonework. There were a crowd of elves, gnomes and goblins waiting for us and they swarmed on board as soon as I opened the side of the craft. Amongst them was my daughter, Mia.

She hugged me and said, "Father I am so glad to see that you and mother are safe. I hear that I am to have a brother! Am I old enough to ride a dragon on my own?"

My mind reeled at the onslaught and I just hugged her back and said, "We'll see! We'll see."

Several weeks later Teginbek came to see me carrying a jar.

"Great High King," he said, "I have brought the healing compound to sort out the re-growth of your wings. I have brought painkilling injections so that I can remove all of the iron-damaged flesh from the stubs. All you need to do is to lay upon your front and let me do my work."

Ameela helped me off with my shirt and I lay down as I was instructed on a table. I felt the prick of a needle several times and then my back became numb. There was a great deal of tugging and scraping from behind me before I felt the balm being spread over the area where Waldwick had seared my flesh. Eventually the operation was declared finished and I was allowed to sit up.

"Have you analysed the compound, Teginbek? Is it possible to make more?" I asked.

"There lies a great problem, High King. Part of the compound comes from stem cells harvested from baby Dokka'lfar whose mothers have been filled with cocaine! This is mixed with human blood that has also been drained from an addict. There are other compounds that keep the mixture from going off too quickly, but the fact remains that we cannot morally produce any more. I used the last of the compound on yourself without you knowing this, as I knew that if you knew, you would have refused to use it."

He must have seen the anger well up in my face and took a step back. Ameela grabbed me by the hair and yanked my head back, so that I sat down abruptly.

"Just this once, let others do for you what you would do for others. You deserve to feel the air under your wings once more and catch a morning thermal. I want you to fly with me again. Do not rob me of that, Peterkin."

"Thank you Teginbek," I replied. "It would be wonderful to feel air beneath me one day again. Now please go back to your family, as I have something that I must do and it is all to do with elves."

I watched him as the grinning human beat a hasty retreat and walked over to the throne-room. I stood and gripped the back of the chair and sent my mind out amongst my people, 'calling' two people.

It did not take long before Olivia arrived with Ranzmut. She cradled the bright red baby in her arms. The voices in my mind became a tumult as I looked at this helpless infant. I silenced them.

"Olivia, we have not been able to have any time to give judgement upon this abomination. Ranzmut I know that you have been busy trying to cast your mind into the future," I said. "Can you 'see' the evil slipping down as you saw when you first viewed Moloch?"

"No great High King," the ancient gnome replied. "As far as I can see, this infant will not cause trouble in the future, but I am not sure."

"Has she caught the virus?"

"Yes High King," Olivia stated, "and Alaric gave her the antidote to stop her from dying. He declared that it was your decision and not his."

I swung round and stared at the little girl and thought for a moment.

I sent my mind down to the laboratories below my floor and contacted Alaric's mind and asked, "Is she sterile?"

"Oh yes Great High King. She will never have children of her own!"

I withdrew my mind and studied Olivia's face and could see the longing in her eyes.

"Give her to me," I ordered and held out my hands.

I made contact with the baby's warm flesh and felt the possible futures cascade into my mind. I saw the disruptive influence that she would cause in the years ahead. I saw an object of hatred unleashed amongst my people. As I probed into the unformed mind I felt the presence of Moloch lurking deep inside the tiny frame.

"You cannot keep her," I said. "Just remember who her father was. I am sorry, but the time of the Dokka'lfar is ended with this infant."

Olivia bowed her head and nodded, tears rolling down her cheeks.

I entered the child's mind for one last duty and turned

her life-springs off. The tiny heart bumped twice and was quiet.

The voices in my mind were silent, but inwardly I wept. I am the ruler of two worlds and the High King of my people, all of my people. It is my duty to care for them and I will, over the centuries to come.

End

Epilogue

The centuries have passed and once more Aifheimr feels the tread of the Ljo'sa'lfar. It is a fair and beautiful world. We have made it so, with the help of the humans who have settled on both worlds. I did not go back to the human world and changed the minds of those who had been my friends from that violent place, to see the benefits of living with elves. What are riches anyway, but a means to an end? The last of the great meat eaters have long been hunted down, now that the home world has been cleansed of Dokka'lfar and violence need never be raised again.

In a high place, I had built a tomb, in which I placed the bones of the six who decided to aid me. By their side are the Uzbekistanis who also gave me their allegiance. Ivan I sent back to take charge of Acme Engineering and to live his life amongst his own kind. I have a special place for Mellitus, who placed himself by my side for the rest of his life. My mother still mourns Spencer and comes here with me to think. We catch the morning thermals together and fly to the very top of the mountain above my castle where my friends wait for me. The tomb is filled with sunshine and memories.

A new generation of Light Elves have been born and are filling the empty spaces. Prime's people are now learning to farm on the Plains of Scion as well as being herders. There are human and dwarves working with them as well as elves. It should be interesting as time goes by. There is a whole world out there that needs to be discovered. In a thousand years time I will still be here watching over all my people. I have very little faith that the human world will endure. There are an infinite number of worlds that can be reached by the Spellbinder and plenty of time to do so!

About the author

Barry Woodham was born in 1943 and has lived in Swindon, Wiltshire in England all of his life.

He spent his working life as a design engineer/draughtsman and worked on the nuclear fusion project for thirteen years. Finding himself with nothing to read one lunchtime, he began to write the saga of the Gnathe and the Genesis Project. The thought occurred to him that any life form evolved to live in this world would not be able to cope with the micro-organisms of another eco-system on an alien planet. After many of his colleagues began to read the chapters as quickly as he could finish them he continued on and finished the first book. The alien Gnathe are instinctive genetic engineers and alter living creatures to be their tools by the use of their brooding pouches controlled by the third sex. This first book is set millions of years after the sun has entered its red giant stage and is set on a vastly altered Jupiter. Humanity and intelligent Pan-chimpanzees are recreated by four Guardians made of nano-technology sent towards the stars from the dying Earth, to bring back mankind. One ship is stuck in the Kuiper Belt until it begins to fall towards the new sun and the crew are activated.

He was able to take early retirement through a legacy and continued to write the next book following on from Genesis 2, called Genesis Debt. These have both been self-published on Amazon.

He has now put the final touches to Genesis Weapon, the third book in the series that has been self edited and printed in a spiral bound condition.

While writing Genesis Weapon he decided to link all the

books together as 'The Genesis Project' and write all the books into a series.

'Genesis Search' is set hundreds of thousands of years after the events that occurred in Weapon. This part of the saga concerns the deliberate collision of the Andromeda Galaxy with ours in the distant future. What kind of entity could cause this to happen and why? This book attempts to settle those questions and concerns building a hunter/killer group from the ones who defeated the 'Goss' in Book Three by going back in time to remove their DNA and clone them, restoring their stored minds into young healthy bodies. At the same time whole solar systems are being rebuilt and moved by wormhole technology to the other side of our galaxy to be launched as a globular cluster towards the Greater Magellanic Clouds and safety.

Whilst writing this forth book the idea came to be, that my group of mixed human and aliens would find themselves having to deal with the abandoned machine intelligence of Von-Neumann probes left behind by the events produced by the 'Harvester' and this would be worth considering as the fifth Book;– Genesis 3, A New Beginning.

An idea took root and he diverted his imagination into a new venture and The Elf-war was the result. This is a stand-alone book and is not part of the Genesis Project series. He is now spending his time finishing off book five – Genesis 3.

There are also 11 of The Tales of The Ferryman written as short stories (Fantasy-horror) and some ghost stories. There will be more, e-mail the author at barry.e.woodham@ btinternet.com to find out more.

The complete range of 'Genesis Project' books by Barry E Woodham are available in hard copy and eBook file formats and include:-

Book 1. 'Genesis 2'
Hard copy   ISBN 978-1-909020-79-5
eBook for Kindle   ISBN 978-1-909020-81-8
eBook for all other readers ISBN 978-1-909020-80-1

Book 2. 'Genesis Debt'
Hard copy   ISBN 978-1-909020-82-5
eBook for Kindle   ISBN 978-1-909020-84-9
eBook for all other readers ISBN 978-1-909020-83-2

Book 3. 'Genesis Weapon'
Hard copy   ISBN 978-1-909020-85-6
eBook for Kindle   ISBN 978-1-909020-87-0
eBook for all other readers ISBN 978-1-909020-86-3

Book 4. 'Genesis Search'
Hard copy   ISBN 978-1-909020-88-7
eBook for Kindle   ISBN 978-1-909020-90-0
eBook for all other readers ISBN 978-1-909020-89-4

Book 5. 'Genesis 3 A New Beginning'
Hard copy   ISBN 978-1-909020-91-7
eBook for Kindle   ISBN 978-1-909020-93-1
eBook for all other readers ISBN 978-1-909020-92-4

Also a new fantasy book 'The Elf-War'
Hard copy   ISBN 978-1-909020-94-8
eBook for Kindle   ISBN 978-1-909020-96-2
eBook for all other readers ISBN 978-1-909020-95-5

ND - #0457 - 270225 - C0 - 229/152/28 - PB - 9781909020948 - Matt Lamination